ALSO BY TATE JAMES

CLUB 22

TATE JAMES

Bloom books

Copyright © 2021, 2024 by Tate James
Cover and internal design © 2024 by Sourcebooks
Cover design by Antoaneta Georgieva/Sourcebooks
Cover images © Alisa/Adobe Stock, Youandigraphics/Adobe Stock, Carther/
Getty Images, imagedepotpro/Getty Images, Roman Studio/Getty Images,
Icd2020/Freepik, Swet/Adobe Stock, Matt LaVigne/Getty Images

Published by Bloom Books, an imprint of Sourcebooks
P.O. Box 4410, Naperville, Illinois 60567-4410
(630) 961-3900
sourcebooks.com

Originally self-published in 2021 by Tate James.

Cataloging-in-Publication data is on file with Library of Congress.

Printed and bound in the United States of America.
LSC 10 9 8 7 6 5 4 3 2 1

To the haters, who lit a fire under my ass.
Thank you, you miserable bastards, you did me a favor.

CHAPTER 1
CASS

Two Months Ago…

Irritation rippled through me as I glanced down at my watch. I'd been lurking around the bar for way too long already, yet she still hadn't emerged from her office. *Was she okay in there?*

As soon as the thought crossed my mind, I shook it away. Of course she was okay. She was *Hades*, more than fucking capable of handling herself if a bunch of mouthy upstarts wanted to test her dominance.

I glanced at my watch again. Shit. Not even a minute since the last time I checked it.

"Can I get you another drink, Cass?" the pretty young bartender, Sara, asked me with a heavy bat of her false lashes. She knew she wasn't my type, but that didn't stop her flirting.

I shook my head, declining, then finished the last mouthful of my beer. I'd hung around long enough that I was starting to draw attention, and that sure as fuck wasn't going to do me any favors. And for what? To feed my sick obsession with seeing a woman too guarded, too beautiful, and too damn untouchable to ever be mine.

With a self-disgusted grunt, I slid off my barstool with every intention of leaving the club. Yet, as if on autopilot, my feet carried me toward the narrow staircase that would lead up to the mezzanine level where I knew Hades kept her office. Where I'd caught a flash of her blazing red hair disappear hours ago with a handful of Timberwolf enforcers trailing behind like naughty puppies.

"Boss is in a meeting," the stern-faced, muscle-bound Timberwolf bouncer announced as he moved in front of me before I reached the first step. "Doesn't wanna be disturbed."

I narrowed my eyes, picturing my fist slamming into this steroid-pumped fucker's face. Vividly imagining the way his cartilage would crunch under my knuckles and the hot, wet spray of blood from his nose. But shit, he was just doing his job. So I rubbed a hand over my jaw, thinking, then gave a small nod of understanding.

"I'll swing back later, then." Even though I really shouldn't. I had no good reason to request a face-to-face with Hades. None. Except that I just wanted to *see* her. It felt like I hadn't seen her in weeks, even though we'd interacted in a professional capacity plenty. It was different under the eyes of rivals, though. I couldn't just *watch* her like I'd grown so addicted to doing—not with that punk-ass bitch Skate watching my every move.

Reluctantly, I forced myself to turn away, but the bouncer called out again.

"Hold up, Reaper." His gruff voice made me pause and tilt my head back toward him. His finger was to his ear, holding his radio earpiece in place as he listened to something. Then he raised the microphone attached to the wire and muttered a few words into it before flicking his gaze up to mine. "Boss said to send you up. She just finished her meeting."

This was undoubtedly a bad idea, but I just brushed past him and started up the stairs, nonetheless. Fuck me, I needed to turn around, walk out of the damn club, and call up a sure thing to fuck away all this godforsaken tension. But no. No, I just had to torture myself further.

The Timberwolf enforcers passed me in the short corridor that housed the administration offices, and none of their gazes were friendly. Hell, they were downright hostile, but it didn't faze me in the least. There was only one person in the state who intimidated me, and it was none of these testosterone-soaked bastards.

A second after I passed them, they were gone from my mind as I spotted the door to Hades's office slightly ajar. Goddamn if my pulse didn't kick up a gear.

Still, I kept my expression neutral and my posture relaxed. No matter how badly I wanted to do filthy things to the woman in that office, she was still a threat. I'd seen what she was capable of when pushed and knew better than to underestimate her. So I paused and tapped politely at her door to announce myself.

Her eyes swept up slowly, clearly having already known I was there before I knocked, and her gaze was as unreadable as ever when it met mine.

"Cass," she said in that hard-edged voice of hers. I ached to hear her speak to me without the carefully built fortress guarding her every fucking thought. "I didn't know we had a meeting planned."

Neither did I, and yet here I am.

I just gave a casual shrug and took a few more steps into the office, glancing around for her shadow. "Where's Zed?"

Her brow twitched with something faintly resembling irritation. "Did you come here to see me or him? My time is money, Cassiel, and you're wasting it."

Not exactly the response I'd quietly been hoping for, given I'd just sat at the fucking bar amidst a crowd of Gatsby-styled drinkers, desperate to get my fix of my worst obsession. But also not unexpected. I folded my arms over my chest, wishing like hell she'd check me out like her bartender had been a few minutes ago.

"I was in the area taking care of business," I lied. "Figured I'd

3

stop by and tell you the boys at Rex's are expecting Seph's car tomorrow. They'll get it fixed up and dropped back to you before school on Monday morning."

Yes, I could have told her this by text message. But then I wouldn't have a fresh image of her in my mind while cramming my dick down some random gang whore's throat later. I knew how fucked up that was, but so what? I never claimed to be a fucking choirboy.

"Is that all?" she asked, her eyes narrowing with suspicion. I liked to lie to myself and pretend she was too young for me, but it was the weakest of lies. It only took one look into her eyes to see she'd dealt with more in her twenty-three years than most seasoned mob bosses would see in their entire lives. She'd dived headfirst into the gauntlet of fire and come out harder than titanium.

I searched my brain for another excuse for why I was there, *any* excuse, but came up blank. *Fuck.* Now she was staring at me even harder, and it was making sweat form on my spine. How? How could she have that effect on me?

"Yeah," I muttered, still with nothing to fucking say but bluffing like a poker champ, "some prick tried to slash the tires on Zed's Ferrari on my way in. I scared him off, but he had that Wraith look about him." I gave a shrug. "Maybe look into it. Skate's been acting shadier than usual."

Hades continued to stare at me for a long moment, her eyes still totally unreadable as her fingernails tapped a rhythm on the side of her crystal tumbler. I hadn't even noticed when I'd walked in, but there was barely a mouthful left in her glass and the bottle sitting on her desk was less than half-full. Was she drunk?

"Cass, why do I get the feeling those *aren't* the reasons you came in here tonight?" she asked, tilting her head to the side. A faint smile touched her scarlet lips, and my chest tightened. She wasn't drunk—her gaze was far too steady and clear—but shit, she was probably on her way.

4

Desperate not to let my thoughts play out over my expression, I swiped a hand over my face and broke eye contact with her. This had been a bad fucking idea. But she almost always had Zed lurking somewhere nearby, unknowingly keeping me in check and reminding me that she already *had* someone. Someone with a hell of a lot less damage than me. I hadn't realized how fucking *tempting* it would be to make a move when we were alone.

"I should head out," I muttered, not answering her question. But I didn't leave.

She pushed her chair back from the desk and stood, making me freeze to the spot. Fucking hell, she was gorgeous. Her tight jeans hugged her legs in a way that made me envious of the goddamn denim. I was jealous of *fabric*. Christ, I needed an intervention.

A couple of steps carried her around the desk, and I needed to swallow heavily at the picture she painted in those sexy-as-fuck heels and the huge gun strapped under her arm right beside her breast.

"What are you doing tonight, Cass?" she asked, stepping right into my personal space so I needed to look down to meet her eyes. Fuck, she was short, even in those heels. My hands *itched* to grab her by the waist and shove her against the wall while I impaled her sweet cunt on my dick. If I thought for a second she wouldn't put a bullet in me for that, I'd have done it by now.

I gave a small frown in response. "Uh, Reaper shit," I grunted. "Why?"

Her left shoulder rose and fell in a slight shrug. "I've had a crappy day and could use some company tonight."

What...the fuck? Is she hitting on me?

Dumbstruck, I just blinked at her in confusion. Then she bit her lower lip and her usually hard gaze heated and I was a fucking dead man. My dick strained against my jeans, and my pulse raced like I was a prepubescent boy about to be kissed for the first time.

"Hades..." I murmured, trying and failing to keep the ache of longing out of my voice. But *shit*. Was I on a trip? Nah, not possible. I hadn't even smoked tonight, and unless someone had drugged my beer, there was no way I was imagining this. Was there?

She drew a noticeable breath, then reached up to place a hand on the back of my neck. The shock of her fingers against my skin was like a lightning strike, and I could barely breathe when she leaned in closer.

Fate was never so kind to me, though. The second I made the decision to kiss her, the false wall panel behind her slid silently open, and Zed met my eyes with a threatening glare, his hand resting casually on the butt of his rifle. A split second before Hades's lips met mine, I turned away, and her kiss seared a hot brand against my cheek instead.

"Sorry," I grunted as my stained soul screamed in agony. "I've got shit to do."

Anger and embarrassment flashed across her beautiful face as she stepped back, but it was gone in an instant as her signature hardness returned. "I guess I misread the way you were just eye-fucking my mouth then, huh?"

I swallowed heavily, hating myself already. But Zed's presence was the last nail in this coffin. She deserved better than my broken bullshit. Better to squash the spark now before it burned either of us.

"Yeah," I muttered. "You did. I don't fuck children."

It was a phrase I used so damn often when Shadow Grove's college girls came sniffing around, searching for a taste of the dark side, so it just fell from my lips before I could even consider the consequences. But I *instantly* regretted it when her eyes widened and her body flinched like I'd physically struck her.

Fuck. *Fuck.* What had I just done?

Too late now, though. So I jerked my head to Zed in acknowledgment and stomped my moody shit out of the office, out of the bar, and straight across to my bike. I needed to get the fuck out of there before I finally broke and begged for forgiveness at her feet. What a fucking mess.

I didn't look back once as I kicked my engine over and roared out of the parking lot, but I had to stop at a traffic light two blocks away. A sleek black Ferrari pulled up beside me as I waited for the light to change, and fury rippled through my whole damn body.

"Fuck off, De Rosa," I snarled, barely even glancing over at the driver, who'd rolled his window down.

Still, I could see enough of him to know he was smirking at me in *victory*. Son of a motherfucking whore. If I wasn't afraid of the backlash from Hades, I'd have kicked his head in by now.

"She's out of your league, Saint," he replied, but his voice lacked the mockery I was expecting. It made me turn to inspect him closer, and I found nothing but bitter regret on his face.

I huffed. "No shit. Yours too."

Zed didn't argue. He just jerked a nod. "I know."

The light changed to green, and we both peeled out in opposite directions without another word. Zed seemed to be heading toward 7th Circle, and I was on a mission to get fucked up and fucked. Anything to make me forget the monumental mistake I'd just made with the one woman who haunted my dreams day and night.

Shit. I really was a fuckup.

CHAPTER 2
HADES

Present

It was impossible to miss the venomous looks I was catching from the huge turnout of Reapers and former Wraiths gathered in the chapel. None of them were ballsy enough to outright confront me, but I could sense what they were all thinking. The mix of animosity and fear was so thick it coated my skin like sludge, but none of it affected me. None of it shook my stoic, professional expression and posture. None of them scared me in the least, so their hatred was inconsequential.

Cass had been loved by his gang; there was no question about that. He'd been the best thing that'd happened to the Reapers since they'd been formed by the D'Ath brothers three generations ago and had made more of a positive impact in just a year and a half as their leader than Zane D'Ath had over his entire reign.

So it was no great surprise that Cass's death was being honored with a full funeral service, while other fallen gang leaders barely even earned a death certificate.

I shouldn't have allowed it. He'd openly disobeyed one of my strictest rules and had paid the price. Traitors shouldn't be honored.

But when Roach, the Reapers' new leader, had asked my permission to hold a funeral, I hadn't been able to refuse. How could I? Cass was... *Fuck.*

"We shouldn't be here," Zed muttered under his breath from my right side. He was heavily armed—like almost everyone else in the chapel—and his sharp gaze continuously scanned the hostile crowd around us.

"Fuck that," Lucas hissed on my other side. "Hades can go wherever the fuck she wants. And she *wants* to be here. So shut the fuck up."

Both Zed and I turned to look at Lucas, but he just tipped his chin up and refocused on the weeping woman at the front of the chapel telling a story about some abusive ex that Cass had saved her from.

Lucas had changed *so* much since Chase had taken him a month ago. He'd always been mature for his age, but the torture he'd suffered at my ex's hands had hardened him, brought him deeper into *my* world. As much as I should have regretted it, I didn't. Every new facet of Lucas's personality that emerged was just hooking me harder.

I didn't say a damn word for the entire service, sitting on the hard wooden pew with my spine as straight as a board and my black dress immaculate. But inside, I was a mess. Every accusing side-eye from the Reapers had me reliving that moment when I'd shot one of the men I was so dangerously in love with.

Over and over throughout his funeral service I saw myself pulling the trigger of Zed's gun. I saw the bullets hit their target. I saw the blood spray, the shattered wine bottles spilling cabernet sauvignon all over the stone floor as Cass's broad frame hit the racks behind where he'd sat.

My fingernails cut bloody marks in my palms as I pretended to listen to the sermon from the Reaper-bonded priest who droned on about God's will, when all I could see in my mind was the

9

bloody mess my bullets had torn through Cass's body. I swallowed deeply as I remembered the pain of accusation in Zed's and Lucas's eyes when Chase had finally left the cellar. That had hurt almost as much as shooting Cass in the first place.

I needed to blink a couple of times when people started standing around me, and refocused on the present. Six tattoo-covered Reapers approached the front of the chapel and lifted Cass's casket between them, their faces stricken with grief as they hoisted it to their shoulders.

Most of the congregation filed out of the chapel after the pallbearers, women wailing and sobbing and more than a few tough gangster men sporting red-rimmed eyes. It'd been a good service, from what I'd paid attention to.

"Hades, sir." The newly appointed leader of the Reapers approached awkwardly, dipping his head with a nod of respect. "Thank you for allowing this."

I didn't trust my voice, so I just gave him a tight, cold smile, which only seemed to make him more uncomfortable. Poor guy had been thrown straight in the deep end, having been appointed Cass's second barely a few weeks ago. He could handle it, though. He was smart.

"Uh, I will, of course, make an official meeting request with you this week, sir," Roach continued, running a hand over the back of his tattooed neck. "But I just wanted to assure you that the…that I'm taking care of things. The Reapers are loyal to you, sir."

I knew what he was saying. He wanted me to know that he was ensuring Chase's access to the Shadow Grove drug distribution network was well and truly cut off. Whatever connections he'd made through Cass were dead, and Roach would do everything possible to ensure not a single crumb of PCP was being sold in Shadow Grove.

"See that it stays that way, Roach," I told him in a voice like ice.

"You've seen how I deal with betrayal, and I actually liked Cass." *Understatement of the century.*

Roach nodded his understanding, and that's all that mattered. "I'm handling it," he assured me. "Thank you again." He indicated to the almost empty chapel. "This meant a lot to the Reapers. Will you be joining us for the wake?"

I shook my head, already desperate to get the fuck away from the morbid, depressing atmosphere that was doing nothing but make me feel like the god of death I'd named myself for.

"No," I replied. "I don't believe I would be a welcome guest. We can discuss business next week in my office. Please call and schedule an appointment."

"Understood, sir," Roach replied quickly, smart enough not to want to hang around chatting any longer. He gave polite nods to both Zed and Lucas, then made his way out of the chapel with the last of the mourners.

I released a small breath, feeling the weight of responsibility resting heavier than ever across my shoulders. Some days, *lots* of days, I fucking hated who I was. I hated my position, my power, my carefully crafted reputation that was so firmly built on fear and violence. I hated me.

Lucas took my hand in his, but I jerked away from his touch. My hands still felt sticky and wet with Cass's blood, no matter how many times I'd washed them since that night. I could still feel the heat of his bloody flesh under my bare hands as I'd desperately tried to stop the bleeding after Chase had gone... I could still feel the burning path of my own tears down my cheeks as I'd used my own shirt as a compress.

"Let's go," Zed murmured softly. His touch to my lower back was featherlight, just enough to bring me back to the present and get me moving. He understood where my head was without me needing to tell him.

Silently, the three of us left the chapel and climbed into Zed's

Audi. Roach gave us a small wave as we left the parking lot, but I could imagine he was glad to see us gone. The Reapers blamed me for their leader's death—and rightly so. I'd been the one to fire the gun, even if he'd had it coming. They knew the consequences of crossing me, and Cass was far from the first gang leader I'd disposed of.

My phone rang in my handbag, the sound startling me. Swallowing hard, I fished it out. I needed to pull my shit together, or I was likely to end up getting caught off guard by Chase.

I gave a small frown at the caller ID and accepted the call.

"Rodney, what's going on?" My bar manager had been in the bathroom when Chase gatecrashed our meeting below Club 22. Thanks to Rodney's sudden urge to shit, he'd avoided Chase's bullet to the head. Fang hadn't been so lucky.

"Sir, I apologize for the interruption. I know today isn't…" His voice trailed off with an awkward sound, like he was clearing his throat. "Anyway. Figured you'd wanna know there's a snake in the hen house."

My spine stiffened, and my fingers tightened on my phone. "Right now?"

"Yes, sir," Rodney replied. "Doesn't seem in any hurry to go anywhere either."

I seethed with anger. "I'll be there in fifteen minutes." Ending the call, I took a hot second to scream internally, then turned to Zed. "We need to stop by Club 22. Chase is there."

Zed jerked in surprise, his jaw tightening, but he increased his speed and turned us in the direction of Club 22 without arguing.

"What the fuck is he doing there?" Lucas muttered from the back seat.

I grimaced. "Hopefully not killing any more of our employees." It sounded flippant as hell, but it was the truth. I really hoped he *wasn't* killing any more of my employees, or I was about to find myself very short of staff. As it was, we'd lost three of our girls from

Club 22 who'd quit after the incident with Jessie killing herself while high on PCP.

"You armed, Gumdrop?" Zed glanced in the rearview mirror, raising his brows.

"Of course I am," Lucas replied. "I'm not an idiot."

That night at Club 22 I'd asked Lucas to start carrying a weapon on him at all times. Now that we knew he could handle a gun and shoot with decent accuracy, I didn't want him walking around unarmed. Not after the way Chase had declared he was gunning for my guys.

One down, two to go.

I shuddered, remembering the smug satisfaction on his face as he stood over Cass's blood-soaked body.

Zed gave a small nod, then tightened his hands on the steering wheel like he was imagining wrapping them around Chase's neck. "We should just kill him and deal with the consequences later."

I gave him a sharp look. "No."

"I'm with Zed on this one," Lucas offered. "Chase can't have covered *all* his bases. You guys make people disappear all the fuck-ing time. What's one more?"

My teeth clenched as I tried to get a leash on my frustration. These arguments didn't help ease the brittle tension that had existed between the three of us since I'd shot Cass, but what the fuck was I supposed to do? I couldn't change the past, and I wasn't going to make a stupid, reckless move to try to make it up to them.

"We've been over this, Lucas," I snapped, "too many times already. We're not making any direct moves against Chase yet. Not until I *know* it's safe for everyone."

Because my ex was far from stupid and his moral compass was so far from north it was laughable. We had proof of that already. After the incident at Club 22, my aunt, Demi, had found a series of explosive devices planted around her home in Italy. If I'd shot

Chase the second he'd shown his face in my meeting, Seph would be dead. Along with everyone else in that house.

"I spoke with Steele this morning," Zed told me, clearly on the same train of thought. "They've moved Seph to a new safe house, and I've submitted a request to the Guild for assistance."

My brows rose. He hadn't mentioned he was going to speak to the Guild. "What did they say?"

"No reply yet." He gave a one-shouldered shrug. "You know what their waiting list is like."

I stifled an irritated sigh at the edge in his voice. He was still mad as hell at me, and it was bleeding into every word we exchanged. But he was still here. He was still on my side and hadn't turned his back on me yet. Neither had Lucas. They'd forgive me eventually. I hoped.

In fairness, the mercenary guild *did* have an insane waiting list, but the fact that Zed had a prior relationship with them usually gave us some kind of priority.

"Well, they need to come and collect all their guns, anyway," Lucas commented. "I don't want my mom going home until they're gone."

Running a hand through my hair, I stared out the window. These problems just kept piling up, and it was becoming daunting to imagine how the hell we'd solve them all. Lucas's connection to the Guild, his mother's shady past, Chase waging war on my business and personal life, Zed...being *Zed*. And Cass. Fuck. Cass.

My chest ached, and I rubbed the heel of my hand down my sternum. We were almost at Club 22, and I needed to get my Hades face on. My plan for dealing with Chase was paper thin, but it was better than no plan at all.

"Maybe you two should wait in the car," I suggested as Zed pulled into the Club 22 parking lot. The glares I got in response said exactly what they thought of that idea, but I just shrugged.

I climbed out of the car and smoothed my hands down the

front of my dress. Poker face firmly in place, I strode into my club with Lucas and Zed at my back.

Chase wasn't hard to find, considering the bar had only opened half an hour earlier and was all but empty. He sat dead center in front of the main stage, sipping on a tumbler of scotch and eyeing up the terrified dancer who was unlucky enough to have the first set.

His one-eyed gaze slid over to me, and he stood from his seat in a smooth, liquid movement. A wide smile split his face, and if I'd been any weaker, I would have vomited right there on the carpet. He made my skin crawl.

"Darling!" he exclaimed, coming toward me with his arms outstretched. "What an unexpected surprise."

Bullshit. Straight-up *bullshit.*

CHAPTER 3

My jaw tightened and my sweat turned to ice as Chase *fucking* Lockhart leaned in like an old friend and kissed my cheek. Shivers of revulsion crawled all over my flesh from where he'd touched me, but I didn't pull away.

"Well, isn't this a welcome change," he murmured without retreating even an inch from my face. Instead, he reached up and tucked my hair behind my ear; then his fingers trailed down my neck in a longing touch. "If I'd known you'd be so easily broken, I'd have killed someone you loved so much sooner."

I swallowed hard, choking back the angry, disgusted retort on my tongue. "What are you doing here, Chase?"

He hummed an amused sound and shifted his gaze past me. "Zayden, old friend. We're so long overdue for a catch-up, don't you think? Why don't you come join me for a drink?" Chase stepped back, indicated the bottle of scotch on the small table beside where he'd been sitting, and shot Zed a sly grin. "We can chat about all the things we have in common now."

The leer he gave me as he said that and the way he ran his tongue over his lower lip left nothing to the imagination on what he *thought* they had in common.

"How about I take you for a nice scenic drive out to Mortuary Forest and finish that last discussion we had?" Zed offered, his tone hard-edged. He stepped closer to me, his hand resting on the small of my back as his chest brushed my arm. It probably wasn't intended as a possessive gesture, but fuck if I didn't have to bite my cheek to keep from leaning back toward him.

Chase had us all kinds of messed up. Which was his intention, no doubt.

"You look surprisingly healthy, pretty boy," Chase commented to Lucas, ignoring Zed's thinly veiled threat. Their last discussion had ended in Chase repeatedly stabbing Zed with his own blade. The same blade Chase had left buried in Lucas's chest.

"Fuck you, psychopath," Lucas spat back at him.

Chase grinned wider. "I take it you found the little care packages I left around dear Aunt Demi's winery, then? Good. At least you know not to test my patience."

"Fuck your patience," I told him in a flat, cold voice. "Those precautions are keeping you alive, for now, but that won't last forever. I'll ask you one more time. What are you doing here?"

Chase's one-eyed stare shifted back to me, and he cocked his head like I was amusing him. "I thought that would be obvious, Darling. I came to offer my deepest condolences on your loss. It's so hard when you lose a loved one, isn't it?" His smirk deepened. "Even harder when you kill them yourself. Then again, it's not the first time for you, is it, Darling? You barely even look like you're grieving."

I didn't blink. I didn't flinch. I gave him *nothing*.

"If you're wondering whether I attended your funeral, Chase, the answer is no. You were dead to me a long time before I put that bullet in your face." Reaching out, I hooked a finger under the elastic of his eye patch and snapped it back against his face.

He flinched, his hand coming up to bat me away, but I was already moving, heading for the bar.

"Get the fuck out of my club, Chase," I told him over my shoulder. "In case this wasn't clear enough, you're officially banned from all Copper Wolf properties. My legal counsel should be sending the paperwork over today."

There was a long pause, but I didn't turn to look. That's what he wanted, to see any hesitation from me. Any cracks in my armor. Well, he was shit out of luck. I might as well be encased in adamantium for how hard he'd made me.

No, fuck that. He hadn't hardened me like this; I'd done that all on my own. It was just coming in more useful now than I'd ever thought it would be.

"Very well," he finally said in a slightly irritated voice. "But believe me, Darling, you'll still be seeing me around. Shadow Grove is such a *nice* city, don't you think?"

On that weird remark, he strolled out of the club like he hadn't a care in the damn world. Maybe he didn't. Maybe this was all just…entertainment to him. Chase Lockhart hadn't been in his right mind even before I shot him in the face. Fuck knows what *further* damage had been done to his brain in the last five years.

Rodney came over to me at the bar, poured three glasses of Red Head whiskey for us, and exhaled heavily. "What can I do to help, Boss?"

I picked up one of the glasses and gave him a small salute with it. "This is perfect." One swallow and the liquor was gone. "Go chat with the girls, let them know he won't be back. Zed, get his image off the cameras and distribute it to the whole Copper Wolf security team so they know he's blacklisted. Lucas—"

"Already on it." He cut me off, flashing me a smile with his phone at his ear. "Hey, Gen, it's Lucas." With a reassuring nod to me, he wandered away to talk to my lawyer about getting those papers filed to ban Chase, or *Wenton*, from all our venues. Despite how strained our relationship had been since I shot Cass in cold blood, Lucas was quietly stepping up and showing me every damn day that he was more than just a pretty face.

Zed disappeared to do what I'd asked, and Rodney refilled my drink before heading over to the backstage door. For a couple of minutes, I was relatively alone. Lucas was taking care of legal with Gen, Zed was sorting out the security teams, and Rodney was reassuring the dancers that my murderous ex would not be returning. Not that the girls knew he was really *Chase Lockhart*, but he oozed creepy. I didn't blame them for being anxious.

I slid my butt onto a barstool and took another huge mouthful of whiskey. It wasn't even close to what I really wanted, though. No amount of liquor was going to erase my sins.

"All sorted," Lucas said, sliding onto the stool beside me and grabbing one of the glasses. "Gen asked if you wanted to file a proper restraining order against him, but I figured that would be counterintuitive to what you're planning." He raised one brow at me in question, and guilt burned through me.

"I don't know what I'm planning," I admitted in a quiet voice. "But thank you."

Zed returned, his jaw tight with anger.

"Done," he announced. "Shall we go?"

I nodded, then downed his glass of whiskey, seeing as he was driving, before sliding off my stool. "Let's go."

The three of us strode back out of the club, and I wrinkled my nose when I saw it had started raining—almost like the weather could sense my crappy mood and wanted to set the scene.

"Mother*fucker*," Zed snarled, ignoring the pouring rain as he strode over to his Audi. All the way along the side, from headlamp to taillight, someone had keyed his paint. "What the fuck? Is he *twelve*? Who keys someone's car?"

Lucas grimaced. "I'm starting to get the idea that nothing is beneath Chase when it comes to getting under your skin."

I sighed and slicked a hand over my rain-wet hair as I climbed into the passenger seat. "I have a feeling you're right. Chase isn't going to make this quick *or* easy, but I think that can work in our favor."

"Care to share your ideas?" Zed demanded, slamming his own door shut and stabbing at the ignition button.

His attitude, while understandable, was pissing me right the fuck off. So I just glared back at him. "Not right now, no."

Lucas let out a small groan from the back seat. "Come on, guys, give it a break. All this bickering is giving me a hell of a headache."

Zed shot Lucas a scowl over his shoulder but said nothing more as he drove us out of the Club 22 parking lot. I knew full well that wasn't the end of it from him. We hadn't had a proper *discussion* in almost a week. There had been some bitter, hurtful words exchanged that night as I frantically tried to save Cass from the gunshot wounds I'd inflicted, but that was it. Now it was all just bitter swipes at each other.

Lucas, despite his age, was handling it all a hell of a lot better than either Zed or me. While I admired that about him, I was also envious. I'd somehow totally lost my coldhearted, levelheaded nature in the past few months. Loving these men was making me soft. Weak. I hated it.

I also didn't think I could live without it. If I didn't fix things with Zed and Lucas soon, I was likely to lose them. Fuck. I needed to sort my shit out.

"Are you okay, Hayden?" Lucas asked after several minutes of silence in the car. I'd been staring out the window, looking out at the rain and dwelling on Chase's weird visit to Club 22, but Lucas's question dragged my attention back to him. It was a loaded question and not one I could even remotely start to unpack.

Was I okay? After having just attended Cass's *funeral*, then been paid a visit from my dead ex-fiancé who was determined to break me in every possible way? No. Not even close to okay.

"She's fine," Zed answered for me, giving me a quick glance

from the side of his eye as he drove. As mad as he still was, he cared. He understood. I was far from fine. Lucas knew it too. But it was sweet of him to ask anyway, just in case I felt like talking about it all.

"I'm fine," I agreed with a heavy sigh. I shook my head, trying to clear the gut-wrenching images of shooting Cass that had just resurfaced, and scrubbed a hand through my hair. Fucking hell, I was one step away from a mental breakdown.

Lucas was silent a moment, then undid his seat belt and leaned over to pop open the glove box in front of me. "Here," he said, grabbing out Zed's flask of whiskey and handing it to me.

"Hey," Zed protested, shooting Lucas a scowl as the grinning stripper sat back into his seat. "How the fuck did you know that was there?"

I turned my face slightly so I could see Lucas roll his eyes.

"You guys seriously underestimate how observant I am, huh?" He gave me a soft smile, showing he wasn't actually offended.

I unscrewed the cap of the flask and took a long drink of the liquor. It barely even burned as it joined the whiskey already in my stomach and did nothing to shake my melancholy mood. Not that I was surprised. There really was only one thing—one *person*—who had any hope of improving my mood, and we'd just left his funeral.

"I'm just tired," I admitted in a whisper. "I need a vacation."

Zed snorted a bitter laugh. "You can say that again."

I took another gulp of the whiskey, then passed it back to Lucas. It wasn't a long drive back to Zed's house, but the relief I felt on passing through his heavily secured main gates was palpable. It was weird how rapidly I'd adjusted to thinking of Zed's house as my home, but it was. More, even, than my apartment had ever been.

"Have you spoken to Seph?" Zed asked as he waited for the garage door to open.

I gave a small nod. "Briefly. She sent me a message yesterday to let me know she was still safe at Demi's and to tell me I was dead to her."

Zed grimaced. "She needs a solid dose of truth to pull her head out of her ass." It was an old argument where Zed felt like Seph needed to be told the whole sordid story of the *real* Timberwolves and why I'd eventually murdered our father and his whole loyal inner circle.

I snapped a sharp glare at him. "She needs nothing of the sort," I growled. "Let her be. Ignorance *is* bliss, so leave her that much."

Zed just grunted, and I knew he was far from in agreement with me. But he wouldn't directly disobey. Not over this.

Irritated, I climbed out of the car without waiting for him to turn it off and started into the house without another word, but Zed called out after me, nonetheless.

"Dinner will be ready at seven, Dare."

I just flipped him off over my shoulder and continued inside ahead of him and Lucas both. My shoulders ached, my head was throbbing, and my heart hurt. I wanted nothing more than to get back to my room, so I increased my pace until I was just a step off running and all but crashed through my door.

Only after I closed it and turned the lock did I feel like I could really *breathe* again. Like the tense, depressing day was all worth it.

CHAPTER 4

A strong arm banded around my waist, lifting me slightly off the floor and making me gasp.

"You couldn't have cried even a little bit?"

I melted into the broad, hard frame at my back and gave a soft laugh. "Hell no. I've given you enough of my tears to last a lifetime."

His teeth scraped my neck in a teasing bite. "Damn, Angel. Not even crying at my funeral. Tough crowd."

I twisted in his one-armed grip and smiled up at his ruggedly handsome face. "Because you're not really dead, you asshole. You can only get me to cry when I think maybe you are, and I'd really, *really* prefer we didn't play that game again. Okay?"

Cass's lips pulled up in a lopsided grin. "I think we can agree on that one."

I blew out my breath in a sigh as I smoothed my fingers over the dressing that covered the side of his head and part of his ear. Then I stroked my palm ever so gently over his shoulder where his left arm was held suspended in a sling.

"I'm so sorry," I whispered for the thousandth time since shooting him.

He gripped my chin with his free hand, bringing my mouth to his for a long, lingering kiss. "Stop apologizing, Red," he murmured against my lips. "You did what you had to do."

It still didn't make me feel like any less of an asshole. Our *plan* had been to shoot him in the chest where he wore a slim Kevlar vest. But when I'd seen where Chase had been positioned and the way the shadows were falling across the room, I'd known he wouldn't have been fooled. Not unless I made it as real as possible. So I'd done exactly what Chase had expected. Two bullets to the chest—one on the vest as planned and one through his shoulder to cause a believable bleeder. Then the headshot. That was the one that still made me feel sick when I thought about it. My hand had already been shaking from shooting Cass twice, and my bullet that was intended for the wine behind him had actually connected.

"I can't believe you watched your own funeral," I told him with a short laugh, changing the subject as I pulled away from his embrace and headed over to the huge flat-screen that now showed an empty chapel.

Cass followed me and picked up the remote to turn the screen off. "Why not? It's half the fun of being dead."

I bit my lip and shook my head. "The Reapers are going to be beyond pissed if they find out you're still alive."

Cass shrugged and threaded his fingers into my hair, twisting the strands and tugging my face back to meet my eyes. "Fuck them," he growled. "You're the only person on this whole damn planet I care about, Red. If that means playing dead for the rest of my damn life, then I'll do it."

My heart thumped against my ribs, and warmth rushed through my veins. "You're crazy, Saint," I whispered.

He gave me a faint smirk. "Crazy in love with you, Angel," he replied, then kissed me until I forgot how cheesy that line had been. Hell, he kissed me until I barely even remembered my name. But the point remained the same. He might be crazy in love with me, but the feeling was mutual. There wasn't anything I wouldn't do for him, including help fake his death.

My only regret was hiding our plan from Zed and Lucas. That was an oversight I was still trying to mend, but I simply had no good excuse. There was *no* plausible reason why Cass and I would keep that plan between the two of us...except that we hadn't known we were going through with it until it happened. It'd been a backup plan at best.

"Is Roach doing what he needs to do?" Cass asked, pulling away to meet my eyes with a concerned frown. This was the part he hated, where he had to lie low at Zed's house and let everyone else continue like he truly was dead.

I nodded. "He is. The small amount of PCP you let through has all been recovered, and the Reapers who'd flipped to Chase's side are already dissolving in a vat of acid up in Canada. He'll do well, I think."

Cass gave a small nod. "And if he doesn't"—he shrugged—"I'll take care of it."

He tugged lightly on my hair, tilting my head back up again. "You look exhausted."

My answering smile was weak. "No shit. You have no idea how hard that was to sit there at your *funeral* and remember how close I'd come to losing you. Fuck, Saint, if my bullet had landed an inch to the left—"

"It didn't, though." He was firm in cutting me off. "So what do I have to do to make you forget about it?"

Warmth blossomed in my belly, and a sly grin curved my lips. "You're injured and supposed to be on bed rest."

"Fuck that," he grunted. "I don't need bed rest for a shoulder injury." His fingers released my hair and tugged the zipper of my dress down. The fabric slipped easily down my body, pooled at my feet, and left me in a strapless bra and thong set.

"Cass..." I started to say, but he cut off my flimsy protest with

25

a searing-hot kiss, stealing the breath from my lungs and filling me with burning desire.

I moaned against his mouth, curving my body against him as he deftly flicked open my bra clasp one-handed, then tugged at the side of my thong. The message was clear as day, but after the day I'd had, I'd earned a bit of fun. So I slapped his hand away and danced out of his reach.

"Cassiel Saint, you're recovering from two bullet wounds and a hell of a bruise from the one that hit your vest. You're in no shape to be—" My teasing was cut short with a small shriek as he damn near tackled me onto the bed and flipped me over onto my stomach, and I dissolved into laughter.

"What was that, Angel?" he retorted, slipping his fingers under my thong and straight into my cunt. My laugh quickly shifted to a moan as I arched my back and pushed against his hand. Fucking hell, for only having one hand, he was far from awkward.

When I didn't reply, he stroked a finger over my clit, making me shiver. "That's what I thought. Now take this off before I tear it off with my teeth." He flicked the elastic of my thong, and I gave a small growl of protest. But I was also intuitive enough to recognize the shift in his tone, so I quickly scrambled to do as instructed.

"Cass," I warned, looking at him over my shoulder as he coaxed me onto my knees in the middle of the bed. "If you—"

"I'm fine," he growled back at me, undoing his belt and jeans with deft movements. "Trust me, Red. I'm a big boy."

The timing of that statement as he released his cock from his pants couldn't have been more perfect, and I licked my lips. "Hell yeah, you are."

He chuckled at my lame joke, his fingers wrapped around his inked dick as he met my eyes. "Face against the mattress, Angel. Don't move unless you're told."

Hot arousal filled my veins, and I did as he said, leaving my ass up in the air and on full display for his hungry gaze. "Happy?" I asked, an edge of teasing sass in my voice.

His gaze darkened, and his palm cracked against my ass cheek. "Not yet," he muttered, smoothing his hand over the sting in my flesh as I groaned and tried *really* hard not to move, per his direction. "But I can't think of a better way to celebrate my own death than this."

He thrust into me, his thick cock filling me up and making me gasp. He gripped one of my hips, pulling me back onto him as he pushed deeper. Then he smacked my ass again, and I yelped.

"Holy shit, Red," he hissed, his fingers kneading the hot skin of my ass cheek. "Fuck, you're tight."

I almost laughed at that comment. He'd literally just smacked my ass so hard I yelped; *of fucking course* my pussy had reacted like a vise. But he started moving in me before I could get my sassy comment out, and within moments I'd totally forgotten what I was going to say.

Cass's one-armed grip on me was possessive and desperate, but I was finding it hard not to writhe. I wanted his other hand in play *so* damn badly. I wanted him to play with my clit or finger my ass or pull my fucking hair. Shit. I wanted all of that…all at once.

"Saint," I moaned, "let me ride you."

His rhythm faltered, and his breathing spiked. I thought for a second he would refuse, but then he pulled out and moved to sit on the edge of the mattress.

Grinning my victory, I scrambled into his lap and sank down onto his slick shaft. My knees met the bed on either side of his hips. His jeans were barely even pulled down to midthigh, and my arms looped around his neck.

"Say it," he demanded, his fingers tangling in the back of my hair. I loved how he did that. It was one of his favorite things to do when we kissed, and it never failed to soak my panties, no matter what situation we were in.

27

I grinned again, running my tongue over my lower lip as I clenched my pelvic floor and rocked my hips. "You first," I replied.

His dark eyes glittered at my defiance, but I knew I was getting my way. This time. His teeth scraped over my jaw, then nipped at my earlobe before he uttered some of the sweetest words on earth.

"I fucking love you, Red."

A shiver ran through me at the rumble of his confession in my ear, and I damn near came right then and there. He wasn't letting me off the hook so easily, though. Apparently, his trusting me to kill him without *actually* killing him meant that I wasn't allowed to gatekeep my own feelings anymore.

"Red…" he growled, his fingers releasing my hair and wrapping around my throat instead. "Anything you want to say?"

I tilted my head back, meeting his eyes as I rocked against him, feeling the sweet ache of his thickness buried deep within me. "I love you too, Saint," I whispered, then crashed my lips into his for one of those soul-deep kisses he was so damn good at giving.

It was only a couple of moments before I got restless and started fucking him properly, rising and falling with my fingers gripping his shoulders and his teeth nipping the flesh of my throat. His hand grasped my bare breast, his fingers playing rough with my aching nipple until I thought I was about to explode.

The bedroom door crashed open, and I flinched slightly in shock.

"Are you fucking serious, Dare?" Zed roared, meeting my eyes with blazing fury.

I couldn't help myself. I smirked back at him. "I'm seriously fucking, yeah."

Cass kissed the side of my neck, his choppy breath the only hint that he was all kinds of amused. "Tease," he whispered against my damp skin.

"Dare—" Zed exclaimed, but his anger was drastically undermined by the heated way his eyes ran down my naked body and the way his breath hitched.

"Zed," I replied, sarcastic as hell, "can this conversation wait until *after* I come? I was *right* there when you interrupted."

His jaw dropped. I could only assume it was at my audacity, but what the fuck did he expect? No way in hell was I letting him bust in here and ruin my orgasm. I'd had a *rough* day, and I deserved to get my rocks off, dammit.

With a shrug, I dismissed him from my mind and sealed my lips back against Cass's as I started riding him once more. I wasn't joking either. I'd been within sight of my climax when Zed had busted in, and now I needed to chase it down all over again.

Surprisingly, it hadn't gone far. Zed's presence wasn't even slightly cooling the bonfire of arousal inside me. Hell, if anything, he was just stoking the flames hotter.

"Fuck this," my friend muttered, and I assumed he was leaving. So imagine my shock when he grabbed a handful of my hair and wrenched my lips away from Cass. I barely had enough time to gasp before Zed crashed his mouth against mine, his tongue sweeping into my mouth and stealing the kiss.

A small squeak of shock and protest escaped when he released my lips for a moment. But then he was kissing me again, and this time I was helpless to do anything but kiss him back.

Cass gripped my hip, shifting his position and taking over the work, thrusting up into my soaking pussy as Zed kissed me dizzy with one hand in my hair and the other cupping my face.

But then Zed released my face and put that hand to much, *much* better use.

"Oh fuck," I gasped against his mouth when his fingers found my throbbing clit. My whole body was coiled so fucking tight I was positive I was going to snap any second. Zed was playing with me, though, circling around my clit, teasing me, and driving me wild. It wasn't until I was trembling and my breath coming in short, sharp gasps that he finally gave me what I so desperately craved.

His index and middle fingers pinched my clit, and I shattered.

Zed continued kissing me, swallowing my screams, and Cass fucked me even harder as my cunt tightened and spasmed around his cock. A second later, Cass joined me in climax, his hot seed pumping into me with a few hard strokes as I shuddered and moaned, my lips still against Zed's.

He kissed me once more, then straightened up and held my gaze unblinking as he brought his fingers to his mouth and sucked them.

"Dinner's ready," he announced in a rough voice, his cheeks flushed and his pants tight. "I think we're all overdue for an honest conversation, don't you?"

I swallowed hard, words failing me. But he didn't need my response. He just gave me a knowing look and exited the room.

What the fuck just happened?

"That," Cass murmured, kissing my throat, "was hotter than I'd anticipated. Looks like Zed is done with sitting on the sidelines."

I gave him a startled look, then quickly realized he was dead right. Zed was done waiting for me to come to him, and that could only spell disaster for our friendship. Groaning in frustration, I rested my forehead on Cass's shoulder. He still wore his T-shirt, it being too difficult to undress with a sling on, but I was stark naked.

"Fucking hell," I cursed, then raised my head to meet his eyes. "It was hot, though. Jesus, I'm screwed."

Cass huffed a short laugh. "Literally. I reckon Zed could wait a couple of minutes if you want help in the shower." The tiny curve to his lips was pure mischief, and I could practically see his intention painted across his ruggedly handsome face.

Rolling my eyes, I climbed off his lap and snatched my robe from the back of the door. "And I thought Lucas had stamina," I muttered, then threw him a look over my shoulder. "Coming?"

He couldn't fuck me in the shower, not with his arm incapacitated. But we were nothing if not imaginative, and Cass *did* love to show off his tongue skills.

CHAPTER 5

Zed and Lucas were both waiting for us at the dining table when
we eventually came downstairs, and the look Zed gave me almost
made me trip. It was pure, unfiltered desire, and I needed to swallow hard to shake away the so-recent sensations of his lips against
mine and his fingers between my legs.

"Shit, you look rough, grandpa," Lucas told Cass with a grin.
"Aren't you supposed to be resting or some shit?"

Cass scowled over at Lucas. "You're one to fucking talk,
Gumdrop. I took a bullet to the shoulder. You got stabbed in the
chest, beaten, and branded. I don't recall you *resting* for long either."

Lucas smirked. "Touché."

"Sit the fuck down," Zed grumbled. "Food is already getting
cold."

Cass took the seat beside Lucas, which left me to sit beside Zed.
I took my seat gingerly, my butt cheek still burning from Cass's
handprint. But if I was being totally truthful, I was also feeling
all kinds of awkward. Yes, Zed had made his intentions clear and
we'd kissed before, but this...this felt different. Way more intimate.
Which I guess made sense seeing as he'd just made me come on
another guy's dick.

Wow. Yep, now I understood where Madison Kate was coming from. There had to be some kind of medical term for the intoxicating addiction I was in the throes of. Dick drunk. That's what I was.

Lucas and Cass traded a couple of good-natured barbs while dishing up their food, passing the plates back and forth like we'd all lived together for years. Zed had cooked, and it smelled incredible. Slow-roasted lamb shoulder with pommes dauphine, green beans, honeyed carrots…fucking heaven.

After a few minutes of dead silence between Zed and me, he reached under the table and dragged my seat closer to him.

"What?" I asked, giving him a frown.

His raised brow in return said he wasn't buying my shit. "You know what."

"Fuck you." I stabbed a carrot with my fork and took a bite.

Zed continued staring at me with a slight smirk. "Please do."

I choked on my carrot—just a little—but enough that my cheeks flamed and I earned curious looks from across the table.

Unable to form the appropriately sassy comeback needed, I simply ignored Zed and glared at Cass and Lucas as if to say *Shut the fuck up, both of you.*

Lucas was the first to take pity on me and change the subject. "So, now that you're officially dead and buried," he said to Cass, "will you fill us in on the plan? I'm assuming there was a plan in play."

Cass gave a nonchalant shrug, his mouth full of food. Zed placed a hand on my knee under the table, his fingers stroking the inside of my thigh.

"Dare's been avoiding that question for a full week, Gumdrop." His tone was salty, even though his hand still gripped my leg. "What makes you think she's going to crack now?"

"I'm right here, asshole," I snarled. "Don't fucking talk *about* me."

"Well, then speak up," he snapped back, his grip on my leg

tightening. I didn't hate it, either. What the fuck did *that* say about me?

"Chill, De Rosa," Cass drawled, then sipped his beer. "It was my plan." Then he grunted. "Sort of."

Lucas gave me a considering look, then hopped up from his chair and went to the kitchen to grab me a wineglass and a bottle of Sangiovese. I winced when he held it up and shook my head.

"White," I told him, wrinkling my nose. "I don't think I can drink red wine again for a while." Not after having the smell of rich, earthy cabernet sauvignon mixed with Cass's fresh blood imprinted permanently in my memory.

Lucas returned with a chilled bottle of pinot grigio and poured me a glass while Zed and Cass just watched him with curious gazes.

"You two have something to say?" I asked, bringing the glass to my lips and taking a sip. "Thank you, Lucas."

"Anytime," he replied with a grin. "So, I sort of figure the whole fake death has something to do with freeing you from your gang?" The question was directed to Cass, but his gaze flicked back to me like I was magnetic.

Cass grunted again, putting his beer down. "Reapers are old school."

"No such thing as retirement." Zed gave a small nod of understanding.

I took another sip of my wine and explained those statements better for Lucas's benefit. "Reapers don't let members just quit. Once you're in, you're in for life. There have only ever been a couple of exceptions and never for a gang leader."

Zed blew out a long breath, his hand still warm on my knee. "I suppose orchestrating another massacre like we did for Arch would have been a crapload more work than this."

"No shit," Cass agreed.

"But…why did Chase think you were dealing his drugs?" Lucas

pressed, his brow creased in confusion. "Why was he so confident you'd betrayed Hayden?"

Cass met my eyes across the table, his gaze steady as he replied, "Because I did."

Lucas's eyes widened, and Zed jerked like he'd been slapped. I rolled my eyes and stabbed at a piece of meat on my plate.

"Calm your tits," I drawled. "He did not *betray* me. Grumpy Cat is getting dramatic in his afterlife."

Cass huffed a short laugh, and Zed glowered. "Explain."

"Chase had been working on flipping the Wraiths for a hell of a lot longer than we realized. His original agreement was with Ferryman, and Skate just inherited the bullshit. Instead of wiping out the Wraiths entirely, Cass thought it might be useful to simply... let them continue and watch what they did." I paused to eat some of my dinner because I was hungry and it was delicious.

"So you knew Chase was using the Reapers to distribute angel dust?" Lucas asked, a frown of disbelief creasing his brow. "But... why would you ever be okay with that? Your history with drugs and Chase and—"

"Because you can't make an omelet without breaking a few eggs," Zed answered for me. "But what I want to know is why the fuck *I* didn't know about it."

"We," Lucas corrected, and Zed shot him a withering glare.

I bit the inside of my cheek. Zed's hand was still on my leg, but the tension in his grip told me how pissed off he was, despite his relatively calm voice. The truth was that I'd had no *good* reason to keep it from him. I just...had. Cass had already committed to the plan prior to informing me, and while I'd been mad as hell at the time, I agreed with his reasoning. But Zed would only have seen it as a betrayal.

Fuck. Nothing I could say in response to that was going to make things better. It was why I'd been avoiding the whole fucking thing all week since shooting Cass and making Zed and Lucas think I'd really gone and killed him.

One silver lining to that scenario, though, was the three of them seemed to be rocking a stronger bromance than ever. It was just me that two-thirds of them were pissed at—and rightly so.

"Mm," I mumbled, then took another bite of my dinner. "These potatoes are really good."

Zed's grip on my leg tightened, and Lucas shot me a frustrated—yet amused—glare.

Right as I started to sweat my weak-ass reasoning, Zed's phone rang loudly on the kitchen counter. I arched a brow and tilted my head in the direction of his phone.

"You should probably get that," I suggested. "Could be important."

He glowered. "It's not."

I shrugged. "You don't know. Maybe it's the most important call of your whole life."

Zed just continued glaring, but his grip on my leg softened somewhat. I still hadn't slapped his hand away, and I couldn't explain why.

Lucas pushed back from the table and headed over to grab Zed's phone. "It's from, uh, 3982? How is that a complete number?"

Zed jerked upright, startled, and held his hand out for the phone. "It's not," he replied. "It's a code name."

Lucas tossed the phone to him, and Zed answered the call in one smooth motion as he brought it to his ear.

"Danny," he said to the caller.

My brows raised, and I indicated for him to put the call on speakerphone. If the mercenary guild was calling, then maybe they would help keep Seph safe in Italy.

"Zed, hey," the woman on the other end replied. Her voice was husky and low, like I remembered. I'd only met her once, briefly, but goddamn, she scared even me. "This is a friendly heads-up," she said, sounding hushed. "You've pissed someone off in the Guild.

35

They've assigned someone to Shadow Grove, and I *don't* think it's to help you out."

A ripple of apprehension ran through me at that, and I licked my lips. "Danny, it's Hades," I said. "Have you heard anything about Chase Lockhart?"

"Speakerphone. Cool," she replied. "Lockhart... Wasn't he one of the scumbag traffickers you offed in the Timberwolf massacre?"

"Yeah, he was. Except he didn't stay dead." I didn't think there was anything to be lost in revealing that information. Chase wasn't going to any great lengths to maintain his Wenton Dibbs identity now that the curtain had been pulled back.

"Shit," Danny muttered, sounding distracted. "Sounds like you're in a world of trouble down there."

Zed huffed an annoyed sound. "Yeah, you could say that. I submitted a job request to the Guild this morning—"

"Don't hold your breath," she replied in a dry voice. "Like I said, someone is not happy with you guys." There were some voices in the background, then the line went dead.

A tense silence filled the air before Cass broke it with a long exhale. "Well, that can't be good."

"No shit," Zed snapped and threw a carrot at Cass's head. For a dead man, Cass had impressive reflexes. He caught the vegetable before it smacked him in the face and took a bite of it instead.

"This is about me, isn't it?" Lucas asked in a quiet, thoughtful voice. "Whatever my uncle was doing with the Guild...or whatever he had planned for me?"

I wanted to reassure him, to tell him this likely had more to do with Zed and me or with Chase and the war he was waging on the Timberwolves. But...the Guild had never involved themselves in gang politics before; why would they start now? At that thought, it was unsurprising we hadn't heard back on help to protect Seph. They might have viewed Chase and his sham company Locked Heart as a gang dispute and declined on that basis.

"Probably," Zed admitted before I could think of a nicer way to say it. "The arsenal under your house raises a whole heap of red flags. Hell, I'm still not one hundred percent convinced you're who you seem."

I groaned. "Don't fucking start with that shit again."

"He's got a point," Cass rumbled, side-eyeing Lucas. "What if Gumdrop is some kind of sleeper agent and one day a duck will quack and he'll murder us all?" This time all three of us looked to him in bafflement, and Cass just shrugged. "It's been a long week being fake dead," he admitted. "I watched a lot of Netflix."

A slightly hysterical laugh was bubbling up in my throat, so I swallowed a couple of times to hold it back before turning my attention to Lucas. "There's a good possibility it has to do with you, yes. But whatever it is, we can work it out. Obviously, your uncle *tried* to train you up as a kid, but I think your mom took you out of town to keep you safe."

"It'd be useful if she could give us some more information," Zed said, drumming his fingers on the tabletop.

Lucas screwed his nose up and shook his head. "Yeah, I don't think that's happening any time soon. Every time I see her she seems to have lost more of her lucidity. It's weird, like there's some-thing else going on, but her doctors haven't found anything outside of her MS."

"I'll look into it," Cass muttered, turning his attention back to his food and ignoring the way Lucas stared at him.

"Look into what?" Zed snapped. "In case you forgot, you're officially dead. You can't freaking leave the house, or we'll have the entire Shadow Grove Reapers breathing down our necks."

Cass's tiny smirk was way too fucking smug. "Who better to fly under the radar than a ghost? Don't worry, Zeddy Bear, I won't get caught."

Zed spluttered, choking on the sip of beer he'd just taken and turning red in the face. Lucas just grinned so wide I thought he might burst out into laughter. And as for me? I didn't know what to fucking do with that. Cass had just given Zed the most ridiculous nickname in gangster history, worse than Gumdrop, and I had a psychic hint it was going to stick.

"I'll come with you to see her tomorrow," I told Lucas, deliberately sidestepping Zed's new nickname. "Maybe she'll be having a better day."

Lucas shrugged, looking dejected. "Yeah, maybe." Then he flashed me an appreciative smile. "Thank you."

Warm bubbles of emotion fizzed through my belly as our gazes connected, and I smiled back at him. It was impossible *not* to.

Zed's phone rang again, and he showed me the caller ID displaying Alexi's name on the screen.

"Take it," I told him, pushing back from the table.

Zed gave me a nod and answered the call as he moved away from the dining table to find out what Alexi was calling for. Cass tried to help me stack the dishes up, but I gave him a stern look and eyed his sling.

"You've done enough tonight," I scolded. "Go watch a movie or something. Just chill and let that shoulder heal." His eyes narrowed and his lips parted as if to argue back, but I hardened my glare. "That's an order, Cassiel. Don't test me."

"Better do what she says," Lucas offered, stacking up dirty plates and carrying them into the kitchen. "You wouldn't want to get shot again."

Cass scowled in Lucas's direction but reluctantly did as he was told. I picked up more of the dishes from the table and took them through to where Lucas was already rinsing and stacking plates in the dishwasher.

"I've got this," he told me when I tried to help. "Zed will probably have business shit to discuss when he gets off the phone anyway."

I wrinkled my nose, not really even wanting to know why Alexi

38

had called. When Cass had proposed the idea of faking his death to free himself from the Reapers, I hadn't even given it a second thought. I got it. Sometimes I wished I could kill off Hades, too.

"Hey." I tucked my arms around Lucas's waist and rested my cheek against his back. "I'm sorry I didn't trust you with the details."

Lucas didn't respond immediately, his shoulders bunching as he gripped the side of the counter. Then he exhaled heavily and turned around to hug me back.

"I get it," he said against my hair. "I don't *like* it, but I get it. You've got no real reason to trust me, not with something as serious as all of that."

I pulled back, wanting to disagree, but he silenced me with a gentle kiss.

"Not *yet*, anyway," he amended. "But one day you will. In the meantime, I'm not going anywhere." Then his gaze turned sheepish. "If that's okay?"

Flashing him a reassuring smile, I reached up and pulled his face to mine for a lingering kiss that filled me with those effervescent bubbles of happiness that he always created. "More than okay," I told him in a whisper as we broke apart, breathing heavily. "Want to leave this mess for later?" My intent was clear as I pressed my body into his and nipped his lower lip with my teeth.

Lucas groaned, then shook his head. "So fucking tempting, Hayden. But I actually have a stack of assignments to do for school. I'm, uh, I'm a bit behind. If I don't catch up soon..." He let his voice trail off with a grimace.

A flash of guilt stabbed through me. Lucas should be completing his senior year at Shadow Prep and preparing to go to university, not learning how to fight and surviving a nearly fatal stabbing at the hands of his older lover's ex-fiancé.

"Maybe I could get your help on my economics paper tomorrow, though?" he asked with a hopeful tilt to his voice. His arms were still banded tight around my waist, and I never wanted him to let go. "Zed told me you're a little bit amazing when it comes to business subjects, and that's majorly my weak point."

I huffed a short laugh. "Zed was the one who tutored *me*," I informed him, "but I'd love to help. I'll make sure I save some time in my schedule tomorrow."

He responded by kissing me again, which quickly turned heated, and the next thing I knew, he was lifting me up onto the counter and stripping my shirt over my head.

"Gumdrop," Zed barked, stomping his grumpy ass back into the kitchen. "Don't you have shit to do?"

Lucas dragged his full lower lip through his teeth, his heated gaze locked on my face as his hands caressed my breasts through the thin lace bra I wore. "Hell yeah, I do," he murmured, and I didn't suspect for even a second he was referring to his schoolwork.

Zed gave an irritated sound. "Dare—"

"Dial it down, Zed," I told him in a cool voice that only slightly implied violence. "Don't forget your place."

His mouth snapped shut, but his glare intensified until I huffed and slid out of Lucas's embrace.

"Rain check," I murmured before rising up to kiss Lucas quickly. Then I stalked toward Zed with my shirt in hand. "I take it Alexi wasn't calling for a friendly chat?"

He gave a tight headshake, but his eyes were glued to my chest. Fuck's sake. In an attempt to redirect the energy, I tugged my shirt back over my head.

"Right," he muttered, shaking his head. "Let's talk in the office."

He led the way, and I didn't argue. I got the feeling he was only relocating to the office to help his head shift gears into work mode, not because he didn't trust Lucas and Cass overhearing what we spoke about. So I took his cue and gave myself a quick mental slap before we got to the office. Compartmentalizing was my sharpest weapon.

CHAPTER 6

Zed didn't sit down at his desk, which was a smart choice. My patience was running thin with his attempts at bigger dick energy than mine. It was a competition I had no interest in coming in second place for, so he was wise not to fucking test me.

Instead, he stopped in the middle of the room and spun around to glare at me with blazing eyes as I closed the office door.

"We need to talk," he snapped, "about what happened upstairs."

I shook my head, the denial strong. "Nah, I'd rather not. What was Alexi calling for?"

Disbelief flashed across his handsome features, and a frustrated frown creased his brow. "That's childish."

"Is it?" I retorted, my face carefully expressionless and cold. "Luckily, I don't give a shit. What was Alexi calling for?"

Zed glared at me a moment longer, then swiped his hand over his face. "He got a tip about a situation down in Arizona, some botched smuggling job that got busted by the feds."

"Okay, so what does that have to do with us?" I folded my arms over my chest and stiffened my stance so I wouldn't be tempted to pace nervously. As it was, I could barely focus on keeping my game face on so Zed couldn't catch me checking him out.

Zed grimaced. "The shipment was *girls*. When the job got botched, someone must have tipped the smugglers off because every single girl was dead when the feds got there."

I stiffened, ice forming in my gut. "Dead *how*?"

"Alexi's guy didn't have the specifics but said it looked like they'd been poisoned." His gaze was hard, and I knew exactly what he was thinking.

Closing my eyes, I swallowed back the furious scream that threatened to rise in my throat. "Chase."

Poisoning the human cargo with lethal gas was an initiative Chase's uncle had come up with. No witnesses meant no one could link them to the trafficking. In case any of their "shipments" were ever threatened, there was a remotely triggered gas canister stored in every container.

"That was my thought," Zed agreed. "This was out of state, so it could be a copycat. Plenty of scum have stepped into the void left by the Lockharts and your father's Timberwolves."

I sighed. "Could be, yeah. But you know what I think of coincidences."

Zed jerked a nod. "I told Alexi to keep his ear to the ground and report back if he hears anything more."

"Good," I muttered, biting the edge of my thumbnail. "We need to start getting proactive with Chase. My plan with Cass is long-term, but we need to start cutting Chase off at the knees *now*. Otherwise, none of us will be alive to play the long game."

His eyes narrowed. "Why haven't you filled me in on this plan?"

I bit my nail harder, accidentally nipping skin and tasting blood. No response was needed, though.

Zed just gave a short, bitter laugh and shook his head. "You don't trust me."

I cringed. "I do trust you," I whispered. "But—"

"I get it." He cut me off, giving a bitter smile. "Believe me, Dare. Of anyone, I *get* it. I know how it feels to have him inside your brain, making you second-guess everyone. But you can't let him do that to you. Don't let him get between us again."

Zed reached out and grasped my wrist, pulling my thumbnail away from my teeth. He didn't let go, though. Instead, he used my wrist to pull me closer as he stepped into my breathing space.

"Between *us*?" I repeated, feeling like my brain had just turned to mush.

The corners of his lips tugged up in a half smile, and his free hand cupped the back of my neck. "Yes. *Us.* When are you going to quit playing dumb and admit there's a hell of a lot more to *us* than mere friendship? There always has been."

Words totally failed me as I stared back into his eyes and found his gaze overflowing with desire and *pain*. Fuck. What was I doing to us? My stubborn refusal to see what was right under my nose was going to destroy our bond much faster than any failed romance.

"Zed…" I breathed his name like a plea, but I had no idea what it was that I really wanted. For him to drop this whole thing and go back to the way things used to be? Back when I refused to admit I'd never fully gotten over my crush on him and couldn't seem to look away when he was making out with random women in our clubs? Yeah, fat load of use that would do me. Despite my stubborn level of denial, I couldn't even lie to myself that I would take that situation well. Not now. And no one needed me going off and killing innocent girls for hooking up with him.

I never claimed to be rational when it came to Zayden De Rosa. But previously, I'd kept those feelings on lockdown, never to see the light of day.

"Dare," he replied, his own voice a husky whisper as his eyes searched my face. "You can't act like you don't feel the same way for me. I know you too well."

I sucked in a short breath, preparing to deny his accusation. But…no words came. The next thing I knew, I was leaning in, closing the gap between us, and kissing him softly. Zed stiffened like that had been the last thing he'd expected, but before I could pull away in embarrassment, he kissed me back.

His hand tightened on the back of my neck, pulling me closer as he released my wrist and grabbed my waist. Our mouths moved together like we were sharing one brain, one soul, and knew precisely what the other wanted…*needed.*

Then the door slammed open like someone had deliberately shoved it, and I all but leapt away from Zed like he was electrified.

"Oh, whoops," Lucas said in the most sarcastic voice I'd heard in my life. "Was I interrupting something? My bad. Nothing worse than being cockblocked, huh, Zeddy Bear?"

A laugh bubbled up in my throat before I could clap a hand over my mouth, and Zed speared me with a pained glare.

"Sorry," I muttered. "It's pretty funny."

Zed swung his glare back to Lucas. "Call me that again, and I'll shove my foot so far up your ass you'll be licking my toes. Now *fuck off*, we were in the middle of something."

Lucas's grin was pure evil. "Aw, snookums, no need for that level of animosity. Hayden, Cass is asking for you. He says his shoulder is aching and he can't find the pain pills."

Zed threw his hands up in exasperation, stalking away a couple of paces. "It was barely a fucking scratch. He's being a baby."

I shook my head at their antics and decided it was probably for the best. Zed and I had been rocking the friend zone for twelve years. What was a little longer?

Biting back a smile, I met Zed's heated gaze and instantly shivered. "Rain check," I muttered before I could filter that promise. His brows hitched and a small smile tugged at his lips as he nodded.

"I'll hold you to that," he replied, and I quickly made my exit before I came up with an insane plan like inviting Lucas to stay and join us while we destroyed the friend zone once and for all.

As I headed back in the direction of the living room, I caught Lucas's voice again. "Payback's a bitch, huh?" Then he groaned. "Ow, not cool, Zeddy Bear. Don't solve problems with violence."

I rolled my eyes, guessing what had just happened but not stopping to go back and break it up. They were both big boys; they could sort their own shit out. Besides, for the most part and despite their differences, I was getting the impression they actually *liked* each other.

Cass was on the living room sofa, looking kicked back and relaxed with a movie on the big-screen TV. When I walked toward him, his eyes followed me in that darkly sexual way that never failed to raise my pulse rate.

"You okay?" I asked, propping my hands on my hips. "Lucas said you need painkillers."

Cass arched one brow. "Huh?"

I smiled and shook my head. "That's what I thought." Lucas hadn't even spoken to Cass; he was just getting Zed back for interrupting us in the kitchen. Fucking men and their jealousy…equal parts amusing and infuriating. Then again, I supposed that was something I needed to get used to, given that I had zero intention of choosing between my current lovers.

Ugh. I hated that word. *Lovers.* Made me feel like a damsel with a French-speaking, long-haired pirate sweeping me off my feet. But it fit a hell of a lot better than *fuck buddies*, so that's where we were at.

Cass reached out his hand to me, coaxing me closer, then pulled me into his lap when I tried to sit beside him. "Hey," he murmured, wrapping his arm around my waist as I cuddled into him without bumping his shoulder. "We've got this, Red."

I released a long breath, consciously forcing myself to let go of some tension that I seemed to carry with me day and night. "I know," I replied. "But it's still scaring the crap out of me. When I realized we were actually going through with that plan…when I had to shoot you…" A lump formed in my throat, and I swallowed hard.

Cass pressed a kiss to my forehead. "I had total faith in you. You knew what you were doing, and it worked."

I grimaced. "As far as we know. Chase was at Club 22 after your funeral, just being a fucking nuisance."

Cass grunted. "Good. Shows he thinks he won that round. He couldn't resist rubbing it in a bit."

He was right, but I was still anxious as hell. What if Chase *wasn't* fooled. I'd gambled—and won—on the idea he would be so smug about his "victory" that he wouldn't stay and check Cass for signs of life. He hadn't, but those few minutes waiting for him to leave so I could call for discreet medical assistance were etched onto my memory in harsh, vivid detail.

"Don't ever ask me to shoot you again, Saint," I told him in a quiet voice, not even trying to hide the pain I was still feeling over that moment.

He didn't offer me empty promises, just nudged my face to his and kissed me long and slow. His kiss washed away the anxiety and fear and filled me with the warm glow of confidence once more. Filled me with *love*. And that made me feel damn near invincible. I wasn't fighting this war with Chase alone. I never had been, with Zed at my back. But this time I also had Cass and Lucas, and goddamn if we weren't a force to be fucking reckoned with.

"I'll have to leave in a couple of days," Cass murmured when our kisses slowed. "All the details are almost worked out."

Sadness stabbed through me. "I changed my mind. I don't want you to go."

The corners of his lips curled up, and he combed his fingers through my hair. "Cute."

I frowned. "I'm not saying that to be cute. I'm serious. We can think of something else that doesn't involve you leaving me."

His fingers tangled in the back of my hair, and he slammed his lips against mine, this time kissing me hard and aggressively, stealing the protests from my lips along with the breath from my lungs.

"I will *never* leave you, Red," he told me in a harsh whisper when he was done kissing me stupid. "Nothing on this entire fucking planet can make me leave *you*."

I swallowed heavily but nodded. I knew what he was saying because I felt exactly the same way. But still, I couldn't shake the steadily building sense of dread every time I thought about what was to come, about what we all needed to do to deal with Chase once and for all.

CHAPTER 7

I fell asleep wrapped up in Cass's embrace after he spent half the night making goddamn sure I wouldn't forget his touch while he was gone, but when I woke up, it was to Lucas softly kissing my cheek.

"Hey, you," I mumbled, rubbing at my eyes.

"You slept in," he told me with a smile. "I left you as long as I could, but visiting hours—"

"Oh fuck," I cursed, sitting up with a gasp and swiping a hand through my hair. "It's *that* late? How? Shit, I'm sorry. Give me five minutes. I'll—"

"Hayden, it's fine." He cut me off as he grasped my face between his hands. "Take a breath. It's not a big deal, but I spoke with my mom's nurse and he said she was really clearheaded today. Maybe it'll be a good chance to speak with her properly."

I blinked away the last of my sleep fog and pressed a quick kiss against his lips. "I'll be quick. Where's Cass?"

Lucas wrinkled his nose. "You don't want to know." He didn't look *worried*, so I just gave him a suspicious look until he kissed me, then released my face. "I'll wait downstairs?"

Giving him a vague nod, I watched him leave the bedroom,

then hurried to grab some fresh clothes and shower away the evidence of my night with Cass. I was ready in a little over five minutes, dressing casually since we were heading to Sunshine Estate and my intention wasn't to intimidate the answers out of Sandra.

After I raced downstairs, the sound of voices coming from the gym pulled my attention, and I changed direction to investigate. When I pushed the door open, I had to do a double take with what I found in front of me.

"Are you two fucking serious?" I demanded, blinking twice in case my mind was playing tricks on me. But nope, the image didn't change. Zed and Cass were *actually* sparring. Cass's left arm was still strapped in the black sling, but his other hand was covered with a boxing wrap and his upper body was bare and gleaming with sweat.

Zed was also shirtless, both of his hands in wraps as he danced around Cass and taunted him with quick jabs to the body.

They didn't fucking stop when they saw me, either. Not that I blamed them; I'd bet they were both cautious of the other taking a dirty shot while they were distracted. It's what I'd have done.

"Cassiel *Idiot* Saint!" I barked, striding across the gym to stop them by any means necessary, even if that meant decking both of them. "You've got to be fucking with me. In what world did you think this was a good idea? Either of you?" My accusing glare swung between Zed and Cass, but neither of them had the grace to look ashamed.

"Don't give me that look," Zed responded, then flicked out a lightning-fast jab at Cass's face, which Cass dodged and answered with a sharp right hook that caught Zed across the cheekbone. "Ouch." He winced and shook his head with a rueful grin. "Besides, Grumpy Cat started it."

"Fuck off, Zeddy Bear," Cass sneered back. "You started this because your balls are so blue they're basically fossilized."

"That doesn't even make sense," Lucas drawled from the doorway. He gave me a shrug when I turned to look at him. "They've

49

been at this for ages. Better just leave them to get it out of their systems."

I hesitated, but Cass just gave me a one-shoulder shrug before swinging his leg up in a hard kick that caught Zed in the side. I winced but then shook my head and followed Lucas's advice. Fuck it, they didn't need me refereeing whatever the hell they were dealing with. So I just threw my hands up in exasperation and exited the gym with Lucas by my side.

"If it's any comfort, Cass is winning," he murmured with an edge of laughter as we headed through to the garage. "Even with one arm in a sling, he's a fucking weapon."

The admiration in his tone was unmistakable, and I gave him a curious side-eye. "Did you research Cass before or after you knew who he was to me?"

Lucas shot me a smirk. "I can't give away *all* my secrets, Hayden. He hardly needs the ego boost of knowing I used to watch his old fights online."

Something about that was way too adorable, so I grinned and headed over toward Zed's Shelby Mustang, as the Audi was nowhere to be seen. No doubt he'd already taken it in to get the paint touched up.

"Hey, um…" Lucas paused before we got to the car, his hands toying with the brim of the ball cap he held. "Any chance I could drive?"

My brows shot up, and I considered his question as I grabbed the keys off the hook near the car. "Sure," I said, tossing the keys to him and giving him a stern look, "but don't fucking tell Zed, okay? He's a total diva about his cars."

The smile that split Lucas's face was worth Zed's wrath, and I couldn't stop myself from smiling back as he put his cap on backward and popped the driver's door open. It had been a good decision. Lucas looked like he was straight out of a sex dream behind the wheel of the Shelby in his hoodie, backward cap, and sexy fucking grin.

"Stop staring at me," he teased as we started driving. "You're making me want to blow off this visit to my mom and dirty up the back seat of Zed's car."

Dammit if my pussy didn't tighten just at the idea of that. "Maybe on the way home," I replied with a sly smirk. "But we really *should* talk to her if she's having a good day. At least see if she can tell you whether you do have any older siblings."

Lucas grimaced. Zed and I had told him about the redacted file we'd found, and we'd theorized on what it all could mean. But ultimately, there was no conclusive evidence that Sandra had ever had another baby before Lucas, only that she'd had some form of IVF treatment as a teenage girl. Which in itself seemed suspect as hell, but it didn't mean that it'd ever resulted in a pregnancy.

Then again, maybe it had. Maybe multiple pregnancies. Only Sandra could tell us, as our attempts to dig further into her medical records had gone nowhere. One thing was for sure, though, and that was the Guild was *heavily* involved in the Wildeboer family.

"Is it bad that I sort of don't want to know?" Lucas asked after a few moments of silence.

I reached out and threaded my fingers through his where his hand rested on his knee. "Not even a little bit. But I do think you *need* to know. Something sketchy is going on with the Guild, and more than anything, I need to know how to keep *you* safe. So…I need to know what the whole story is so I can see where the threats might be hiding."

His hand squeezed mine, but he didn't look reassured. "This is the last thing you should be stressing about, Hayden. You've got enough going on with Chase."

I shook my head. "And that situation will become so much easier to deal with when we can cross the fucking mercenary guild off our list of concerns. Besides"—I drew a breath and licked my lips—"I love you, so, you know…I'd do anything to keep you safe."

Lucas didn't respond immediately, and even as fast as my heart raced, I wondered if maybe he hadn't heard me. But then he pulled over onto the side of the road and turned to stare at me.

"What did you just say?" he demanded, his lips twitching with a smile.

I wrinkled my nose. "You fucking know what I said, don't pretend you don't." My cheeks were hot and my palms sweaty, even though our hands were still joined. Shit. Why was I suddenly turning into such a...*human*?

Lucas gave a soft laugh and leaned over to kiss me softly, his lips moving against mine and his tongue exploring my mouth in a relaxed, confident way that was totally at odds with the panic I was experiencing at telling him I *loved* him for the first time.

"I've loved you from the moment you kissed me that night at 7th Circle," he whispered against my lips as his hand cupped my face like I was his most treasured possession. "So I'm glad you're finally on board."

His teasing made it easy to quit panicking. He knew exactly how to handle my shit, and I loved that about him. Or about us. So my heart was ten tons lighter as I pushed him away gently and rolled my eyes.

"Okay then, Captain Emotionally Stable. Can you keep driving, please? We're going to miss visiting hours, and then I'll have to threaten the poor nurses to let us in against the rules."

He just grinned and leaned in to kiss me again, then pulled back out onto the road to continue toward the medical center his mother was being treated at. We drove in silence for a few minutes, then he raised our linked hands and kissed my knuckles.

That gesture, more than any words, struck me right in the heart. Lucas never hid his feelings, but I'd just never truly recognized them. But now I had, and it was a feeling I wanted to hold on to forever.

CHAPTER 8

More often than not when I brought Lucas to visit his mom, I would wait outside simply because my presence and my resemblance to my dead mother, who'd been Sandra's friend, caused her undue stress. But today Lucas kept my hand in his as we made our way through the facility to his mom's room.

"Luca," Sandra greeted her son as we entered her room, "how lovely to see you. Oh, you brought your friend." Her smile slipped clean off her pretty face when she saw me enter behind Lucas.

Lucas's grip on my hand tightened. "My girlfriend, Hayden," he corrected her. "Yes, I did. I hope that's okay."

Sandra Wildeboer arched a brow at her son, then gave me a flat look. "Doesn't sound like I have much choice, does it?"

Lucas gave an irritated sigh as he sat down in the window seat and pulled me to sit beside him. "Not really, Mom. Not today, anyway. Hayden's been super respectful the last few weeks and waited outside while I've visited you, but it's about time we got some answers. Okay?"

Sandra looked like she'd just bitten into a lemon, and I caught the quick dart of her eyes toward the nurse call button as though she was really considering using her illness to escape this conversation.

Then she huffed a short sigh and fixed her gaze on the wall to the side of Lucas. She was already preparing to lie and couldn't look him in the eye.

"What do you want to know, Luca? I've never kept secrets from you." Her voice was hollow and resigned like she knew he'd long since stopped believing that line.

I leaned in to Lucas's side slightly, offering him some silent support. I was more than prepared to ask Sandra everything I wanted to know myself. But at the same time, I had to offer Lucas the opportunity to handle this his own way. She was his mother, and for most of his life, she'd been the only family he'd ever had.

"Okay," he murmured, running a hand over his face. "Am I your only child?"

Sandra jerked like she'd been slapped, her face draining of color.

Lucas shook his head and gave a bitter laugh. "I take that as a no. Who? When? How—"

"Stop it," she hissed, cutting him off. "Of course you're my only child. I think you'd remember if there had been any older siblings running around the house, don't you? What a ridiculous question."

"I never said *older*," Lucas muttered. "But whatever. What do you know about Uncle Jack being in the mercenary guild?"

Sandra swallowed visibly. "Gosh, you're just... Where is all of this coming from, Luca?" Her eyes darted to me and narrowed in an accusing way. "Has this woman already dragged you neck-deep into her world? I knew it would only be a matter of time. Like father, like daughter."

"I wasn't aware my father had any ties to the Guild," I replied in a cool voice, ignoring the insult. "But your brother had an entire guild arsenal stashed underneath *your* house. And now there's a mercenary sniffing around Shadow Grove, which seems far too coincidental not to be linked to your family. To Lucas. So do me a favor, Sandra, and cut the bullshit. I'm trying to keep your son safe."

She gaped at me like she was having a hard time formulating a response, then her gaze darted to Lucas and her face creased with pain. Slowly, she shook her head, then she reached out and pressed the nurse call button.

"I'm sorry, Luca," she whispered, her voice choked with unshed tears. "I'm sorry, but you need to let this *go*. Stop digging, stop asking, just *stop*. The mercenary guild *doesn't exist*. Drop it!"

Her volume had raised enough by the end that the nurse who'd just walked through the door gave us a startled look. "Sandy, we okay in here?" the nurse asked, giving Lucas a small frown and me a wary glance.

"I think I've overdone it today, Bryce." Sandra's voice was suddenly frail and weak, and I fought an eye roll at the theatrics. "Would you mind showing my son and his friend out?"

Nurse Bryce gave Lucas and me a hard, accusing look like we'd deliberately stressed his patient out. Lucas just gave his mom a frustrated glare, then stalked to the door with angry steps.

"I asked you to look after him," Sandra muttered as I slowly got to my feet. "I *told* you to keep him safe. And this is what you do? Don't think I didn't notice he was carrying."

I paused, arching a brow at her. "For once, this has nothing to do with me. Your brother was housing a Guild arsenal below your house, and Lucas somehow knows how to shoot with impressive accuracy. Either you spill some secrets, or we will uncover them ourselves."

Sandra all but hissed at me. "Drop it. If you care about my boy *at all* you won't keep digging." Her face was ashen and her hands trembling, but her gaze was hard and focused.

"Okay, I think Sandra needs to rest now," Nurse Bryce prompted, indicating that I should leave. We definitely shouldn't have been discussing the Guild in front of him, that was for sure. Not that he gave any flicker of understanding.

I continued staring down at Lucas's mom, but she just flicked her eyes away from me, pausing briefly on a framed photograph of a military man, then stared out the window in clear dismissal. Ballsy bitch. I could see where Lucas got his sass from, that was for sure.

With an internal sigh, I continued out of the room and caught up to Lucas near the foyer, where he was pacing with anger and frustration.

"What is her fucking problem?" he spat out when I joined him. "It's not her mind, not today. That was a deliberate, barefaced lie. She knows *so* much more, and she's not telling us. Why? I'm her son! If she can't tell *me*—"

"Then the threat for her silence has to be pretty severe." I cut him off, giving him a pointed look. "Come on, let's go. She gave us enough."

Lucas hurried to catch up with me as I headed out to the parking lot. "Wait, what? She didn't give us anything!"

I flashed a quick smile at him as we reached the car, and Lucas headed straight for the driver's seat once more. Zed was going to kill us if he checked the garage security feed…and yet somehow that got me all tingly.

"Yes, she did," I replied, sliding into the passenger seat. "Let's head to your house."

Lucas buckled his seat belt but didn't start the car just yet. "I don't get it. Did she say something after I left?"

"Just told me off for not looking after you," I answered in a slightly dry voice. She wasn't totally off base with that accusation; my whole presence was putting Lucas in danger. Chase had him in his sights, and I wasn't stupid enough to think my deranged ex was satisfied with the damage he'd already inflicted. Nope, Lucas would be next for Chase to try to "cross off" because I just *knew* he was keeping Zed for last.

"She's wrong," Lucas growled, starting the car and rolling us out of the Sunshine Estate parking lot.

I just gave a shrug as I pushed guilt aside to focus on more pressing issues. "Well, anyway. Before I left, she gave me a clue, and I'm pretty sure it was intentional. On her dresser there's a framed picture of a guy in military uniform. Do you know who it is?"

Lucas shot me a confused frown. "Huh? Yeah, of course. That's my dad. Allegedly. I'm starting to question if that was all made up, though. The whole 'army man who died in combat before you were born' just seems a bit convenient now, doesn't it?"

I ruffled my fingers through my hair, then gave him a soft smile. "A bit, yeah. But I think she was deliberately giving me a starting point. What do you know about him?"

He grimaced. "Fuck-all. His name, Nicholas Porter. That's about it."

"That's a start," I assured him, reaching out to weave our fingers together. "Don't worry, Gumdrop, we've got this."

He shot me a sharp look, then grinned. "I used to think that was the worst nickname possible, but I'll take Gumdrop over Zeddy Bear any day." He raised our linked hands and kissed my knuckles. "All right, so we're heading to my house?"

I nodded. "We sure are. I want to have another look around. Last time we were there, we were so focused on your uncle's secrets that none of us stopped to wonder what your mom might have been hiding."

"You think she would have hidden any physical evidence at the house? She seems pretty hell-bent on taking whatever she knows to the grave." He winced at his own choice of words, then shook his head.

"She strikes me as the kind of woman who would have insurance policies. Backup. Whether that's at the house or not is anyone's guess. But I think *somewhere* out there Sandra is keeping some hard-copy information about the Guild. And whatever she's got, it's important enough for someone to threaten her."

Lucas pondered that for a few moments. "I don't know if I agree, but there's no harm in looking."

I squeezed his fingers. "But we should be quick. I've got something for you at home." Or rather, it'd been Cass's idea, but Zed and I were also claiming credit, seeing as we'd missed Lucas's birthday a week earlier and Cass had needed our help to sort it out.

Lucas gave me a curious look, but when I mimed zipping my mouth shut, he just gave a laugh and continued driving. Goddamn, he looked hot with his cap backward, a shadow of stubble dusting his jaw, and his strong hand wrapped around the Shelby's steering wheel. I needed to let him drive more often so I could admire that image.

The ride to Lucas's house was only about half an hour from Sunshine Estate, and when we pulled into the driveway, I scanned the house with a fresh perspective.

It was perfectly nondescript, looking exactly like every other house in the neighborhood. There was no excessive security—other than what I'd had my guys install—and nothing to ever suggest this was anything more than a middle-class suburban home. Lucas's uncle had been posing as an accountant, and that's exactly what his house presented as. A flawless cover identity.

"I don't have my keys," Lucas said, hesitating after we got out of the car.

I continued up the steps of the front porch. "Rio changed the locks over, so there should be a passcode entry." Taking an informed guess, I gave the whole handle plate a firm push to the side, revealing a digital number display. "See?"

Lucas's brows hitched as he inspected the new lock. "That's cool."

I keyed in the generic code that worked on all the locks I got Rio to install so I always had access to Timberwolf properties, and the lock clicked open audibly. With a smile to Lucas, I closed the panel and turned the handle to open the door.

"It's practical, more than anything," I told him, standing aside to let him enter first. "For one thing, no one can steal your keys.

For another, there is a digital record of anyone who enters, and it takes a picture of anyone activating the keypad."

Lucas nodded his understanding. "Makes sense. Thank you." He paused in the foyer, looking around at the subtle improvements my team had made to his house. Doorways had been widened to allow his mom's wheelchair through easier, ramps placed over any uneven floor joins, and of course the elevator installed that had led to us discovering the basement in the first place.

"You really didn't have to do all this, Hayden." He shifted his weight from foot to foot as he pulled his cap off and fluffed his hair. "This had to have cost a fortune."

I snorted a short laugh, closed the front door, then moved over to where he stood. "I owed you," I said softly, rising up on my toes to kiss him gently. "Come on, let's get searching."

Before I could spin away, he caught me with his arms around my waist, pulling me back against him as his lips found mine once more. This time it was no quick peck; it was a soul-deep *promise*. I kissed him back with equal intensity and moaned as he spun us around to press me into the door and slipped his hands under my shirt.

"Let's get something straight," he murmured against my lips, his palms sliding up my rib cage, pushing my shirt up as he went. "You owe me *nothing*. I'm with you because I'm completely, irrevocably in *love*, so there is absolutely nothing I regret. I'll wear these scars proudly to the end of my days because they're a part of my new life. With *you*."

A rush of affection surged through me so hard my knees weakened, and I sagged against his grip. "Lucas," I whispered, "that's not healthy. You almost died because of me."

"Almost," he replied, kissing my neck, "but I didn't. And what doesn't kill you makes you stronger. Right?" He pulled back to meet my eyes, bringing a hand up to cup my face. "You know that better than anyone."

The truth of that statement hit me like an electric shock, and I sucked in a sharp breath. I hated the thought that I was changing Lucas, but I was too selfish to give him up. I was too invested already. He was too deeply lodged in my heart.

He didn't pressure me to reply, instead just bringing his mouth back to mine and kissing me deeply. His hands moved down to my ass, lifting me up and making me instinctively wrap my legs around his waist as he walked us through to the sitting room. As he laid me down on the couch, he flashed me a cocky grin, then tugged his hoodie and shirt over his head in one smooth movement.

"Fucking hell," I breathed, running my gaze and hands down his perfect body. Not even the raised, dark-red lines of his scars could detract from his sexiness. Hell, they just added to it. "It should be illegal to be so gorgeous."

He huffed a short laugh in response, bending over with a delicious flex of his back muscles as he kissed my stomach and pushed my shirt over my bra. "You're one to talk, babe. You're pure perfection."

His mouth moved over my stomach, making my skin tingle and my muscles contract, and I tugged my shirt over my head. Fuck getting home quickly for Lucas's late birthday surprise. This was a much better use of our time.

Lucas made fast work of my jeans, stripping them—and my panties—down my legs and tossing them aside with my shoes. Then he took his time exploring every inch of my skin with his lips, removing my bra in the process, until I was a needy, panting mess on the couch beneath him.

Only when my cheeks were flushed with heat and my fingernails clawing at him in desperation did he give in to what I wanted. His own jeans hit the floor, and a second later I screamed my relief as his huge cock entered my aching cunt.

For a moment, I wasn't even capable of real words, just incoherent mumbling and gasps as he lined his hips up to mine, pushing deeper inside and making me see stars. We didn't need words, though. Lucas kissed me as he moved between my legs, fucking me brainless and making me totally forget all the shit going on in my life. Lucas had the most incredible way of taking my mind to another place where only the two of us existed. Where nothing mattered except the touch of our bodies, the movement between us, and the shared sighs and moans.

I didn't try to fight it when my orgasm crept up in a matter of minutes. I just cried out against his mouth. He swallowed my screams as my pussy tightened and pulsed around his length. His movements slowed to a gentle grind as I rode out the waves of my climax, my breathing rough and sweat running down my neck. Then he pulled me up off the couch in a fluid movement, spun me around, and sat me down in his lap, his front to my back, as he thrust back up into me from underneath.

"Fuck!" I cried out as he filled me up from a whole different angle. "Shit, Lucas…"

His response was just a dark laugh as I shifted my balance and started riding him like…uh…like a cowgirl in reverse. His strong hands gripped my body, searing my skin everywhere he touched. It wasn't long before his fingers found my swollen clit and reignited that flame once more.

A long string of curses fell from my lips as I dropped my head back, resting against his shoulder as he fucked me from below and rubbed my clit between two fingers like he was playing a miniature violin. Needless to say, I came again harder than fucking ever—so hard that my vision went spotty and my ears started ringing while my whole body turned weightless and heavy at the same time.

This time, though, he came with me. His hips jerked beneath me and he grunted his release as he filled me up and bit my neck.

For a minute, we just stayed like that with me in a boneless slouch in his lap, his cock still buried deep inside me. Then I groaned and peeled myself up off the couch. Dizziness hit me as I stood, and I gave a shaky laugh when I looked down at Lucas.

"That…" I shook my head with a groan, then licked my lips as I took in the sight of him sprawled out naked with his massive dick still half erect. "That was fucking incredible." I held a hand out to him. "Shower with me?"

A broad grin curved his lips, and he snatched my hand eagerly. "Hell yes," he enthused, basically leaping to his feet and tossing me over his shoulder.

I let out a small shriek of surprise but didn't protest even the slightest bit as he raced up the stairs to the bathroom. Screw it. We could search the house for clues after a few more rounds. After all, my Gumdrop had *stamina*.

CHAPTER 9

Our search of Lucas's house, when we eventually got around to it, turned up a whole lot of nothing. Fucking *nothing*. Which wasn't really so shocking considering Lucas and his mom had only moved in there a couple of weeks before we moved her to Sunshine Estate.

As a last resort, we thought to check the basement level to see if his uncle had anything other than guns stashed down there. I led the way, heading down the secret stairs in the guest room closet, and flipped on the industrial lights as we stepped into the basement room. Then I jerked to a stop.

"Uh…" Lucas hovered behind me like a huge shadow. "Did you guys—"

"Nope," I replied, running my eyes around the very *empty* basement. "Not us."

I took a couple of steps forward, peering around and shaking my head. Every single wall, every single rack that had been stocked with weaponry was empty. Not a single bullet or blade was left—so far as I could tell.

"The Guild," Lucas muttered, rubbing the back of his neck. "Nice of them to tell us they were stopping by."

I grimaced. "Typical mercenary-guild bullshit."

Lucas arched a brow at me. His full lips were puffy from kissing me—and other things—and it was all kinds of distracting. But goddamn, that man could eat pussy like nobody's business.

"Have you had a lot of interaction with them?" His tone was curious, not accusing, and I shook my head in reply.

"Not really. But Zed briefly entertained the idea of working for them when they tried to recruit him. He even tried out a consultant role, but after a couple of months told them he wasn't interested." I smiled at the memory, the warmth of amusement filling my gut as we headed back upstairs.

Lucas was naturally curious. "Why'd he do that? He seems like the perfect mercenary type."

I grinned wider. "Apparently he questioned why they'd recruited him and not me. He didn't like their answer and told the recruiter to go fuck a cactus."

Lucas followed me out of the house, his hand resting gently and comfortably on the small of my back as I activated the front-door lock once more. The fact that the guild had cracked my code wasn't a surprise at all. They were that dangerous; no locks would keep them out.

"Well, shit, now I'm curious," he said with a laugh. "What did the recruiter say for him to respond like that?"

I snickered. "He said that they recruited and trained *mercenaries*. Or rather, that's their adopted term for *assassins and spies*. But he wanted highly skilled killers who could be controlled, not psychopaths or serial killers."

Lucas gaped at me in horror as he popped the Shelby door open and slid inside. "He called you a psychopath? To Zed?"

I nodded. "Sure did. It was luckily over the phone, or the Guild would have been looking for a new recruitment agent that day."

Lucas gave an easy laugh as he turned his cap backward again—groan—and started the car up. "Man, I'd love to have seen that interaction. Zed would have burst a blood vessel."

We drove for a few minutes in comfortable silence, the radio playing some '90s rock station that Zed always listened to, but I could tell Lucas had something on his mind.

"What's up?" I asked after some time. "I feel like you've got something to say."

He flicked a quick glance over at me and gave a small smile. "You're good at reading people."

I shrugged. "It comes in useful with my line of work. So?"

He drummed his finger against the steering wheel a couple of times, clearly thinking about his phrasing before speaking.

"You're good at reading people," he repeated, giving me a pointed look, "so why are you being so hard on Zed? It's clear to anyone with eyes how painfully in love with you he is. I don't believe for a second you haven't noticed."

Words failed me as I tried to formulate a reply to that. My eyes widened in surprise at his candidness, and my first instinct was to slam my walls up and retreat into Hades mode. But just one gentle look from Lucas had those same walls crumbling and leaving me open and vulnerable. *Fuck.*

"Look, don't get me wrong," he continued, throwing me a bone by giving me a hot second to gather my thoughts, "I love reaping the benefits of all that sexual tension, and I know Cass does too. But…I dunno. You guys love each other so much it hurts just watching you sometimes. And it's not even a question of *picking* someone. Cass and I have already proven we're happy to share. I think there's probably not much Zed wouldn't do for you too."

A hard lump of guilt formed in my throat, and I had to swallow before I could reply. "It's not that easy, Lucas."

He glanced over at me, his gaze calm and totally free of judgment. "I know. But that's why I'm asking, because I care about you, I *love* you, and Zed…" He let his voice trail off and blew out a long breath. "Zed's not the worst, I guess. He's an okay dude. And he totally worships you, so I have to give some credit for good taste."

65

I bit the edge of my lip as a smile crossed my face. Lucas was so damn skilled at putting me at ease. Right at the point where a conversation turned way too personal, way too real, he somehow managed to relax me. It made the heavy subject feel like a casual chat. I loved that about him.

"It's not that easy," I repeated with a sigh, running my hand through my hair and staring out the window, "because I'm scared."

Oh fuck, did I seriously just admit that out loud?

"That's understandable," Lucas murmured. "But the best chances are always scary. If you could have seen how fast my heart was racing when I approached you at 7th Circle that night..." He flashed me a blinding smile when I glanced over at him, and I melted.

I didn't reply for a few minutes, and he placed his hand on my leg as he drove, silently reminding me that he was there for me, physically *and* emotionally.

"I'm scared," I whispered eventually, "that I'll lose my best friend. Zed's my safe place. He's the *only* person who has always had my back, no matter what. Even Demi questioned me when I came to her with the evidence of what my father was doing with the Lockharts, and Seph... Well, Seph doesn't know any of it. But Zed *never* questioned me. Never made me second-guess myself. Never made me feel alone in my fight. He's my best friend, and I can't—" My voice cracked, and I drew a shaky breath. "I can't lose that. I'm terrified that without Zed, I'll lose myself. Even in my darkest days, he held on to my sanity—my humanity—for me, safeguarding it until I'd done what needed doing, then put it back where it belonged. What the fuck would I be today without him?"

Lucas didn't respond immediately, instead taking the time to really think about what I'd just confessed. He gave my opinion, my feelings the respect of really listening to them and considering them before he formulated a thoughtful response.

"Why would that ever change?" he finally asked.

I blinked at him in confusion, my lips parting. "Because…" I had no quick reply. Why would that change? Because that's what happened when friends fucked. Everything changed.

"I'm only saying Zed's already in love with you. He's probably been in love with you this *whole* time. And you with him. Finally admitting those feelings, finally *accepting* them… That's not going to change things. Not in the way you're afraid of, I don't think." Lucas drummed his fingers on the steering wheel as he drove, his eyes on the road ahead. "In fact, I'd bet it would only strengthen what you've got. If you're worried he only wants to hit it and quit it, you're so, so wrong."

I spluttered a sound of shock at that statement, and Lucas shot me a wolfish grin.

"What?" he teased. "I know firsthand there's no man alive that would only want one night with you."

I gave a short laugh, shaking my head. "You're only saying that because you're madly in love with me." I was teasing, trying to lighten the intense mood in the car, but Lucas's gaze was dead serious when he turned his face to meet my eyes.

"Hell yeah, I am," he murmured. Then he licked his lips, and my nipples hardened. Shit's sake. "Anyway, just my perspective."

We drove in silence for a while, and his words rolled over and over in my mind, making me experience a whole roller coaster of emotions. Eventually, I sighed and rubbed my eyes.

"You'd probably make a good psychologist one day," I told him. "You've got an impressive way of opening my—"

"Legs?" he guessed, grinning wide and shooting me a wink.

I rolled my eyes. "I was going to say my *mind*. But yeah, that too."

"It'd be an interesting area to study, for sure," he agreed. "I never really had a *career* plan before."

I smiled. "Well, you're almost finished with senior year… Do you want to go to SGU? I can get you enrolled."

Lucas arched a brow at me and gave a short laugh. "Nice subject change, babe. Subtle. So, so smooth."

We'd reached Zed's front gate and paused briefly to wait for the gates to open before continuing up to the house. Surely the guys'd had enough time to set up our little surprise for Lucas because I'd already kept him away several hours longer than planned. I sent a quick text to Zed letting him know we were back, just in case.

"Why do you look so mischievous?" Lucas asked suspiciously as we got out of the car.

"Hmm?" I batted my lashes up at him. "I'm not."

He clearly didn't believe me but didn't push the issue as we headed into the house. When we got to the courtyard, I pushed the doors open with dramatic flair.

"Happy birthday!" I announced with a wide smile. The courtyard was all decorated as I'd instructed Cass and Zed, with balloons everywhere and a huge cake from Nadia's on the table. No one else yelled *Happy birthday* with me, though, and I glared death at Zed and Cass, who sat on the lounge with drinks in hand and unamused expressions on their faces.

"Seriously?" I glowered. "That's all the enthusiasm you could muster up?"

Zed and Cass exchanged a look, then Zed sighed. He sat forward and snagged a pair of pointed party hats from the table and placed one on Cass's head and one on his own. Meanwhile, Cass pulled a party blower from the seat beside him and gave it a loud honk as the sparkly streamer unfurled. All the while maintaining a dead straight face.

I glared at him, then shifted my attention to Zed, who was now waving a little flag that read "Happy Tenth Birthday" with colorful gumdrops all over it.

"You suck."

An amused smile cracked his straight face. "You love it."

With a groan, I spun around to face Lucas and looped my

arms around his neck. "They both suck. Happy late birthday, Lucas."

The grin on his face damn near lit up the night sky, and he kissed me hard. "This is incredible. You guys are amazing. I've never had a birthday party before."

Cass honked his blower again, the streamer smacking Zed in the cheek. "Well, you're in luck then. Red even sorted out presents." He held the blower between his teeth as he spoke, and it was ridiculously attractive. Actually ridiculous, with his party hat still on his head.

Lucas wrapped his arms around me, tucked his face into my neck, and kissed my skin. "Thank you, Hayden. You're the best thing that's ever happened to me. No one can ever say otherwise."

I knew he was thinking about his mom, and it tightened my chest. But I couldn't even feel bad. I loved that he thought that about me. I loved *Lucas*. And I'd go to the ends of the earth to make him smile like that every damn day.

CHAPTER 10

Sitting around the courtyard fire eating birthday cake and drinking scotch, I could almost convince myself we were just normal people. Normal polyamorous people, not killers, gang leaders, teenage strippers, or ghosts.

"Okay," Cass announced after some time, placing his empty cake plate down on the table. He grimaced as he stood up. "Let's get this shit done before I'm too wasted to see straight lines."

He pulled a joint from his sling as he said that, bringing it to his lips, then indicated for Zed to toss him a lighter.

Lucas gave me a confused look. "Get what shit done?"

I just grinned back at him. "Your present from Cass. He has to leave tomorrow, so we figured tonight was perfect timing."

"C'mon, *sport*," Cass drawled, indicating with his head. "Time to sort out that scarring." He didn't wait to check if Lucas was following, just swaggered his sexy frame inside the house, and I gave Lucas a jab in the ribs to tell him to go.

Lucas still looked confused as hell, but he trusted us enough—or maybe he was just drunk enough—to follow Cass inside without asking any more questions.

All of a sudden that left Zed and me alone, and the sexual

tension, which had started at a pleasant, warm thirty, ramped straight up to one hundred in a matter of seconds. He met my gaze over the fire, and my mouth went as dry as the fucking Sahara. Lucas's wise words were still echoing through my head, but...it was one thing to know a fact. It was a whole other thing to accept it and act on it.

I wasn't there yet. Nope. Not yet. So I took the coward's path and rose to head inside as well. Except I needed to pass Zed to get around the fire, and he wasn't backing down so easily. He grabbed my wrist as I moved closer, holding me totally immobile with just his fingers.

"Dare, why are you being so fucking stubborn?" he asked in a rough whisper. It was a fair fucking question to any outsider, anyone who didn't know *us* or everything we'd been through together. But Zed knew. He *knew* so much more than I'd ever wanted him to know...and I couldn't get that out of my head.

Everything I'd told Lucas in that car had been the truth, but there was more to it. There was so much pain and desperation tangled up in my history with Zed, and I couldn't shake it. I hadn't made peace with my own past enough to take Zed out of the friend zone completely. It was all so much worse now that I knew he'd *seen* what Chase had done to me on those recordings.

My whole body shuddered as the memory slammed into the front of my mind, and I stifled a gasp. I wasn't... Nope, no way. I wasn't remotely ready to deal with those memories yet, and I couldn't take things further with Zed *without* addressing those issues.

"Hey," he murmured, standing up but not releasing my wrist. He wasn't holding tight, and his thumb stroked gently over my pulse point as he tilted my face up with his other hand. "I'm sorry. I didn't mean to make you feel—"

"It's fine," I croaked, cutting him off before he could elaborate on what emotion he'd just recognized in my eyes. "I'm just..." I let my words trail off with a small shrug and a bitter laugh. "Really fucking damaged."

Zed gave a small shake of his head, his gaze holding mine as his fingers brushed over my cheek. "That's where you're wrong." His voice was so soft, his lips barely moving as he spoke. "You're a diamond, Dare. All the shit you've gone through, all the damage Chase *tried* to make stick? It's just revealing more of your shine."

My breath caught as he leaned in, but this time it was just a gentle kiss to my cheek. This time he was the one to walk away. Frozen, I could do nothing but stare after him. Then with a long exhale, I sank my ass back down to the seat Zed had so recently vacated.

I took a couple of minutes to pull my shit together, pouring another glass of scotch and downing it in one huge gulp. Shaking off the intense need to scream or cry or…fuck, run after Zed and climb him like a scared cat on a tree, I headed inside to check on Cass and Lucas.

They were already set up in the living room with Cass's professional tattoo gear that Zed had picked up from his apartment a few days earlier. Lucas was shirtless on the padded table, his arms linked behind his head and an easy, excited smile on his face as he chatted with Cass.

My one-armed Grumpy Cat was hunched over the table sketching out a rough outline of the design he'd put together for Lucas. He'd started drawing it weeks ago, and I'd spotted it on his desk when I was at his apartment. There was no mistaking who it'd been for because it was made up of all things that screamed *Lucas*.

"I'll fill in the details while I work," Cass told him, handing over the rough sketch. For some reason, he wasn't showing Lucas the whole design he'd already completed in his sketch pad, but I wasn't going to call him on it.

Lucas cast his eyes over the paper, then shrugged. "I trust you, bro. You clearly know what you're doing." He referred to the fact that Cass was pretty much head to toe covered in tattoos, and Cass huffed a sound that was close to a laugh.

"It might hurt a bit over the scar tissue," Cass continued, preparing all his work tools one-handed. "Or shit, maybe it won't hurt at all. Depends how your nerves are healing."

Lucas just grinned. "Can't hurt more than getting the scars in the first place, huh?"

Cass snorted. "Too fucking right, Gumdrop."

I hesitated a moment, unsure whether Cass was cool with me staying to watch him work. But damn, I wanted to.

He raised his head to peer at me when he was finished prepping everything and tipped his head to the vacant seat beside him. "Sit down, Red. I might need your hands."

Biting back a smile, I did as instructed, pulling my seat closer so I could get a good view as he worked. There was no way he actually needed my hands; he was too damn stubborn not to do it all himself. But I was happy to take the excuse.

"I'll do you next," Cass murmured, shooting me a wink as he started his tattoo gun.

I just licked my lips and grinned. I already had a few tattoos, so I sure as fuck wasn't going to refuse that offer. But chances were he was going to wreck himself on the *hours* of work he had ahead on Lucas.

"We'll see," I replied.

Cass worked in silence for a few minutes, the only sound in the room from the buzz of his tattoo gun as he began inking Lucas's chest. But when Zed joined us, he flicked the sound system on, and Cass grunted his approval at the rock music that poured from the hidden speakers dotted around the room.

I quickly became mesmerized, watching Cass create a work of art on Lucas's flesh, and propped my head up on my hands to watch without being a distraction. Lucas gave a heavy yawn about half an hour into the session and closed his eyes.

73

When he didn't open them again, I grinned and peered closer.

"Is he seriously sleeping through a tattoo?" I asked quietly, and Cass paused to glance up at Lucas's face.

"Huh," he grunted. "That's a first. Gumdrop's a bigger psychopath than I gave him credit for."

"High pain and low boredom tolerance," Zed murmured from the other side of the dining table where he'd been drawing idly in Cass's sketchbook. Zed had never been an artist to the level of Cass's tattoo creations, but he'd gone through a graffiti phase as a preteen and still had a tendency to doodle little patterns or create logos in the margins of documents or on my newspapers.

I smiled at Lucas's peaceful face. He really did look like he was properly asleep and totally unbothered by the work Cass was doing on his chest.

"Did you get anything useful from Lucas's mom today?" Zed asked, closing the sketch pad and tossing it back onto the table.

I shook my head slightly. "Not...exactly. She was vehemently against us digging around about the Guild."

Zed nodded. "So she's been threatened."

"Seems that way," I agreed. "But she gave me a small clue. She has a framed picture of Lucas's dad on her dresser. Nicolas Porter. She seemed to look at his picture very deliberately as I was leaving."

"You're thinking her room might be bugged? That's why she was unwilling to talk about the Guild?" Zed leaned forward, clasping his hands together on the table as he stared into space, thinking. "Or at least that's what she believes, whether true or not."

I gave a one-shouldered shrug. "That was my guess. We searched her room at Lucas's house, but there was nothing there."

"They moved around a lot, didn't they?" Cass murmured without raising his head from his work. He was doing it all one-handed, so he had to frequently stop and reposition himself to get the angles right.

"Yeah, ever since they left Shadow Grove when Lucas was

four." I sat up a bit straighter. "That's a good point. It would make more sense if she had a safety deposit box or something, right?"

Cass flicked a quick look at me, then dropped his eyes back to the tattoo. "Suppose so. Isn't that what people do with valuable things they want to keep hidden?"

Zed and I locked eyes, and he tilted his head to the side, silently telling me he'd look into it.

"What about the whole redacted-IVF-files situation?" Zed asked, glancing at Lucas quickly, then back to me. "Any leads on a potential sibling for the Gumdrop?"

"Could be you," Cass grunted. "How fucking coincidental would that shit be?"

"Funny guy," Lucas muttered, sounding sleepy but not opening his eyes. "I'm not asleep, dickhead, just chilling."

Cass flashed a lightning-fast grin. "Just saying, you joke about being brothers. What if you are?"

Lucas cracked one eye and gave Cass a long glare.

"Aside from the fact that Zed is basically a male carbon copy of his mom," I commented, trying really hard not to laugh at Cass's teasing, "the age gap is wrong."

"Unless those IVF cycles didn't work for a few years," Zed commented, looking thoughtful. I gave him a startled look, and he shook his head. "Not *me*, but if there were any babies born from whatever the fuck Sandra was involved in, they could be any age between nineteen and, what? Twenty-nine?"

Both of Lucas's eyes snapped open, and he jerked enough that Cass muttered a curse at him.

"Sorry," Lucas replied, then looked to me in alarm. "How old is Chase?"

"Twenty-six," I replied, "same as Zed. They're a week apart."

Zed snickered a laugh, then swiped his hand over his face. "Oh man. Wouldn't that be a mindfuck."

I shook my head, firmly in denial on that one. "Nope. No

way. That's..." I grimaced, my stomach roiling. "Nope. Just hell no."

Zed, still laughing, got up and went to the kitchen for a moment, then returned with a bunch of sterile cheek swabs in sealed tubes. "Better safe than sorry." He popped one open and indicated to Lucas to open his mouth.

"Why do you have cheek swabs in the kitchen?" Cass muttered, raising one eyebrow at Zed like he was questioning Zed's sanity.

Zed shrugged. "Why not? Useful now, isn't it? Open wide." He waved a second swab at Cass's face.

Cass just scowled back. "The fuck you need my DNA for? I'm five years too old for this hypothetical."

Zed smirked. "You're, what, fifteen years older than Gumdrop? Or sixteen? Sure sounds old enough to father a baby you never knew about."

I hadn't known Cass could glare harder than he'd already been, but hey, what do you know? He could. And did. I actually shifted in my seat. The tension ramped up so high, but Zed wasn't backing down.

"Come on, Grumpy Cat, it's just a cheek swab. If you're confident you didn't have any random one-night stands with an older woman when you were fifteen, there's nothing to worry about." Then Zed did something that had me seriously questioning how much he'd *actually* had to drink. Because only alcohol or drugs could explain where he found the audacity to *boop* Cass on the nose with the swab.

I choked on my own tongue for a second, and all three of them turned to look at me. Fair, I was coughing like I was drowning, but I quickly got ahold of myself and wrinkled my nose at Cass. "Just do the swab. He's in a mood to make a thing out of this."

Holding my gaze with a clear this-is-fucking-ridiculous expression, Cass opened his mouth and let Zed take the sample with a quick swipe.

Cass returned to Lucas's tattoo with a few muttered insults in *Zeddy Bear's* direction, and Zed swabbed his own cheek before sealing the tubes up.

"Can't hurt to double-check," he told Lucas, who was staring at him with an incredulous expression.

I gave a soft laugh. "Better tell our lab tech not to test for anything else. How shit-faced are you right now?"

Zed uncapped another swab and held it out to me. "Not very. Here."

I frowned in confusion. "Why do *I* need one?"

"Why not? Better safe than sorry. Imagine if you and Lucas were blood-related." He arched a brow at me, and I snatched the swab from his hand, quickly rubbing it inside my cheek. The thought that Lucas and I could be related? Hell no. My moral compass didn't come anywhere close to pointing north, yet incest was too far even for me. Like Zed said, better safe than sorry.

Zed smirked and sealed up my sample in its tube. Then he presented me with another fresh swab. "We need a sample from one-eyed dickface."

I grimaced but took the tube from him. "I'll work it out."

Lucas gave me a small smile of reassurance. "I think I'd know if you were my sister, babe. Don't stress. Zed's just being a prick."

Still, my stomach twisted uncomfortably. "Thanks for killing the mood, asshole," I muttered to Zed. "I'm grabbing drinks. You guys want something?"

They gave me their preferences, and I made my way into the kitchen to grab them. My mind was a million miles away, though, ticking over a plan for how I might get a DNA sample from Chase. My flimsy long-term plan for dealing with him depended on getting a bit closer anyway, but…how close could I handle without totally losing myself?

For the next few hours while Cass continued Lucas's tattoo, Zed and I hung out in the living room playing some *Call of Duty* and then starting a movie that we'd both seen enough times to recite the dialogue word for word.

"Done," Cass announced eventually, sitting back and stretching his neck.

Lucas looked down at his inked chest and grinned wide. "Holy shit, Cass. That is incredible."

I hopped up from the couch where Zed and I were trading off on Keanu's lines and went to see the finished product. Cass had almost perfectly replicated the sketch I'd found, turning the Darling brand on Lucas's chest into a star constellation over a stormy sea. A highly detailed lighthouse cast light over the waves, and on the rocks there was a small, silhouetted woman looking up at the lighthouse. Her shadow cast across the ground in the shape of a wolf, but the best part of the whole thing—in my opinion—were the rocks.

The rocks at the base of the lighthouse, where the ocean crashed with startling realism. The rocks that looked a whole lot like gumdrops dusted with sugar.

"You said you didn't wanna get rid of the brand," Cass muttered with a shrug as he applied antibacterial cream and a plastic film over the new tattoo. "Figured you needed some ink to look a bit more badass. Keep it covered till morning, then just keep it clean while it heals."

Lucas was still smiling so hard I thought he might try to hug Cass, but he contained himself to a bro fist-bump instead. "Thank you, man. This means a lot."

Cass just grunted, then jerked his chin at me. "Get on the table, Red."

Lucas slid off, heading over to show Zed his new design, and I arched a brow at Cass in question.

He just gave me a flat look in response. "Come on, it's not your first. Don't you trust me? Take your shirt off."

Rolling my eyes, I tugged my shirt over my head and sat my

ass up on the tattoo table. Cass gave my flesh a critical look, then swiped a hand over his face.

"Bra too," he murmured, his voice deep and rough, "and lie back."

I shot a quick glance over at Zed, who was watching us closely, then flicked my bra clasp open and tossed it aside. Lying back on the table, I draped my arm over my breasts, and Cass released a long breath.

"I'll be quick," he told me, moving my arm slightly so he could access the area he wanted, right below my left breast, where he stroked his thumb across my skin and made me shiver. The buzz of his tattoo gun started a moment later, and I forced myself to stay dead still.

He was done in just a couple of minutes, looking a bit fucking smug as he wiped the excess ink away and applied a swipe of ointment to the lines. Then he placed a featherlight kiss against the side of my breast, right above my new ink, and I almost died. At the very least, I drenched my panties. Fucking hell, Cass was going to kill me with those tender moments.

Wordlessly, he handed me a little mirror out of his kit and let me inspect the finished design. When I saw what it was, I couldn't wipe the smile away.

"Is it okay?" he muttered after a minute, and my gaze jerked up to his.

I blinked a couple of times, then sat up and looped my arms around his neck. My lips met his, and I kissed him with all the overwhelming emotion he was causing inside me. The tattoo was small and simple, but it was perfect: a little skull with cat ears and a scowl. He'd given me a dead grumpy cat.

"I fucking love it," I told him, my arms still locked around his neck and my breasts smooshed into his shirt.

He kissed me again quickly, then pulled away. "Good," he murmured. "So you don't forget me while I'm gone."

I snorted a laugh, taking my shirt from Lucas as he offered it to me, and tugged it back over my head without my bra. "Like that could ever happen."

Cass shot me a heated look, then swatted my ass as I climbed off the table. "It's late. Get your fine ass to bed, or you'll be a fucking grouch tomorrow."

I scowled at him but couldn't really deny that fact. "Fair point," I mumbled, rubbing my eyes.

"Zeddy Bear," Cass rumbled. "Help me pack up."

Zed scoffed. "Screw you, Grumpy Cat."

"Don't be like that," Lucas teased. "Cass is injured. Help him out. I'll take care of Hayden."

Seeing a dick-measuring competition coming, I threw my hands up and exited the room. They could sort their own shit out, and really, I wasn't interested in being forced to pick favorites at this time of night.

Lucas hurried to catch up with me, but as we started up the stairs, I could have sworn I heard the tattoo gun start up again. Or maybe that was just exhaustion and liquor buzzing in my brain.

CHAPTER 11

I woke up in the best possible way, with Cass's face buried between my legs. The fog of sleep held me firm as I stirred, my legs tightening under his grip and my fingers tangling in his hair while he tongue fucked me into the sweetest of orgasms. Then, while I lay there all boneless and gasping for breath, he kissed his way up my body and found my lips.

"I've got to go," he rumbled in a low whisper. "My ride is here."

The last residue of sleep faded in an instant as I wrapped my body around him and clung on tight. "I changed my mind," I whispered back. "Don't go."

Cass just gave a low laugh, knowing as well as I did that wasn't really an option. Not when we'd gone to such lengths to turn him into a ghost.

"I'll check in when I land. Stay safe, Angel." He kissed me again, and then he was gone.

I lay there for a long time staring up at the ceiling in the darkness and feeling like a piece of my soul had just walked away. But then the slight burn of my new tattoo reminded me that Cass was only gone *physically*. And for a damn good reason.

With a groan, I hauled my ass out of bed and checked the

time on my phone. Four o'clock. Worst fucking time to be awake. Ruffling my hand through my hair, I stood up and stretched, then hunted out some exercise clothes. If I couldn't sleep, I might as well get a workout in. There was so much to be said for working out my feelings on a punching bag.

I didn't make it that far, though. On the way down the hall, I paused outside Zed's room, where the door was partly open and the flickering of his TV lit up the darkness. Thinking he was awake, I pushed his door open further and stepped inside.

But even though the TV on his wall still played reruns of *Supernatural* with the volume turned way down low, Zed was fast asleep. I should have backed out quietly, but I've never claimed to be perfect. How boring the world would be if we always did what we *should* do.

Zed didn't flinch as I tiptoed closer, seeking out the TV remote to turn his screen off. When I'd plunged the room into darkness, I crossed around to the other side of the bed and, as carefully as possible, slid under the covers. I knew he rarely slept all *that* heavily, so it was unsurprising when he stirred and rolled toward me. His eyes cracked a millimeter open, and he exhaled as though in relief.

"Cass gone?" he asked in a sleep-thick mumble. I gave a small nod, and Zed just reached out to pull me into his embrace. I cuddled into his warmth, drawing comfort from his familiar touch, and my heart ached when he kissed my hair. "He'll be fine," Zed whispered, reassuring my unspoken fears for Cass's safety. "Still got eight lives left, remember?"

I smiled and laid a soft kiss on his shoulder where I'd snuggled my face. Maybe I could get back to sleep after all.

When I next opened my eyes, the sun was well up in the sky and I was all alone in Zed's bed. The blankets were all tangled up around my legs, and my sports bra, which I'd put on for my workout that never happened, was digging uncomfortably into my ribs just below my new tattoo. Damn it.

Scrubbing my hand over my face, I crawled out and headed for the shower. Even if Chase wasn't being a mega-creep and clearly planning something, I still had an empire to run, and I couldn't keep leaning on Zed to do the heavy lifting while I stayed home and rode Lucas like my own personal pony.

I took my time getting ready, making sure my hair was blow-dried and curled perfectly and my makeup precise. My outfit was all business, with a tight, black velvet pencil skirt and a slate-gray silk blouse. I carried my shoes and gun downstairs in my hands, though, because those felt like a bit much to be wearing indoors.

Lucas was already at the dining table, eating his breakfast with his laptop open in front of his plate and a stack of textbooks beside him.

"Good morning, babe," he greeted me with a smile. He was shirtless, in just a pair of sweatpants, and his new tattoo looked even better in the light of day—red and sore, of course, but the artistry was incredible. "How'd you sleep?"

I wrinkled my nose. "Um, good. Sort of. Working on assignments?"

He nodded back with a grimace. "Sure am. This is probably my whole day. Unless you need me for something else?"

Shaking my head, I bit back my desire to look more into his father's history. That was research I could get done without him, anyway. It was much more important for him to catch up on schoolwork.

"Nope, you're all good. I have to head in to work, though." I hesitated, not wanting to make him feel like a child by asking if he was okay to stay home alone but also not wanting to leave him vulnerable.

Lucas read my mind, though. "I'll be fine on my own, Hayden. I don't know if you noticed, but Zed's house is legitimately Fort Knox." He shot me a sly smile. "Besides, he already gave me a whole fucking big-brother lecture about not opening the door to anyone and showed me where all the guns are stashed around the house."

I scoffed a laugh. "Of course he did. Is he down here somewhere?"

Lucas nodded toward the courtyard doors. "Out there on the phone. Has Cass gone already?"

"Yeah, before dawn." I wrinkled my nose and shook my head before I could start worrying about the big grump again. "I'm going to make coffee. You want one?"

He grinned wide and nodded. "Please. You're the best."

I smiled back and kissed him before heading into the kitchen in search of liquid energy. The machine was still warm, so it didn't take long at all to make lattes for both Lucas and me. I delivered his, then took mine with me out to the courtyard where Zed was pacing with his phone to his ear.

He looked up when I approached, his eyes meeting mine with a flash of hot, raw desire, making my stomach tighten and my pulse race.

"I don't fucking care what it takes, D'Ath," Zed barked down the phone. "Just sort it out. You're more than capable." He paused while Archer responded to him, and whatever was said made Zed scrub a hand over his face in frustration. He hadn't shaved, and the shadow of stubble on his face was all kinds of sexy.

I arched a brow in question, perching my ass on the outdoor lounge and sipping my coffee.

"Believe me," Zed snarled in reply to whatever Archer had said, "you do *not* want to end up on Hades's bad side. Or did you fucking forget what she's capable of when Seph's in danger?"

Both my brows shot up, but Zed ignored me, continuing to threaten one of our closest allies.

"What happened to Cass was business. Nothing more. You know the rules with Timberwolves, just like he did. Don't like the consequences? Don't play the fucking game." His voice was hard and low, all business. It shouldn't have been such a damn turn-on... yet here we were.

Taking another sip of my coffee, I folded my legs and tightened my thighs in an effort to stop thinking about fucking my best friend. I needed my head firmly screwed on my shoulders for work today, not fantasizing about group sex.

Zed stalked closer to where I sat, listening to Archer speak again. Then he grunted and gave me a pained look. "Just keep Seph safe, D'Ath. That's it. Pull your head in and stay out of shit that doesn't concern you."

Without waiting for a reply, he ended the call and tossed his phone onto the table. With a long groan, he sat heavily on the seat beside me and held his hand out for my coffee.

I handed it to him and waited for him to fill me in on his phone call. He took his sweet-ass time, though, holding my gaze as he brought the mug to his lips and took a long sip. Prick. He was deliberately playing up the sexual tension now.

"Everything okay in Italy?" I finally asked, cracking under his pressure like no one else could make me do.

His lips curled in victory. "Yeah, all good. D'Ath is being a little bitch about you shooting Cass. Apparently, Madison Kate was pretty fond of the grumpy shit and is taking it hard."

I wrinkled my nose. "She'll get over it."

Zed gave me a skeptical look. "Sure, when she finds out he's not dead. But will Seph get over the many, many secrets we've kept from her?"

I drew a long breath, hearing the vague accusation in his voice. Zed still wasn't over the fact that I hadn't included him in my plan with Cass.

"She will hopefully understand that in situations like this, the fewer people who know, the better. If she's mature, she'll realize it had nothing to do with *her* ego and let it fucking drop. What's done is done, after all." I gave him a hard glare as I said that, letting him read between those wide-open lines.

He just glared back at me and took another sip of my coffee. "Whatever," he muttered. "We should get over to Copper Wolf. Hannah called your phone this morning and said there's FBI sniffing around. Gen's on her way, but no one invokes the fear of Hades like Hades herself."

Grimacing, I stood up from my seat and reached for the last of my coffee in Zed's hand. "Wait, why the fuck were you answering my phone?"

He stood as well, ending up so close that my breath caught involuntarily. "Because you were passed out cold and drooling on my pillow, *Boss*. Figured you needed the sleep."

He had a point. Evidently, I *did* need the sleep if I was so deep in it I didn't hear my phone ring or notice him get up. But I sure as fuck wasn't thanking him for blurring the lines of our professional relationship, so I just scowled and stalked back inside to drop my coffee cup in the sink.

"Have a good day, you guys!" Lucas called out as I paused to strap on my gun and slide my feet into my Louboutin pumps.

Zed tossed his jacket over his own weaponry and jerked his head in acknowledgment to Lucas. "Remember what I fucking told you, Gumdrop."

"Yeah, yeah," Lucas replied, waving his hand dismissively as he turned his attention back to the laptop screen.

Zed gave me an exasperated look, and we made our way through to the garage. He went straight for the Shelby that Lucas and I had borrowed the day before and slid into the driver's seat. Then he glowered at me when I got in.

"Did you let Gumdrop drive my car?"

My brows hitched. "What? Uh…why would you even ask that?" Because apparently I wasn't capable of lying this morning. Dammit. I needed more coffee.

Zed's glare flattened. "I can tell. Does he even have a driver's license?"

I covered my smirk with a fake cough and looked out the window as Zed drove us out of his fortress. "Of course he does. He's nineteen, not nine." Then, before Zed could diss Lucas for his age any more, I changed the subject. "Any chance we can grab more coffee on the way?"

He gave a slight nod. "Yes, sir."

I gave him a sidelong look, letting amusement play over my lips. "And a bagel. I'm starved."

He shot me a quick look back. "Anything you want, Boss. Literally. Anything." As if we needed *more* sexual tension in a small, confined space. Thanks a lot, Zeddy Bear.

CHAPTER 12

En route to the Copper Wolf office, we stopped for coffee and bagels, then made another stop to drop off our DNA samples at the pathology lab that the Timberwolves funded. So by the time we got into Cloudcroft to the Copper Wolf headquarters, it was midmorning.

That hadn't deterred my pet FBI agent, though. Dorothy Hanson was seated on one of the lobby couches, waiting, and popped to her feet when Zed and I entered the building.

"Ms. Timber," she snapped as we approached.

I raised a cool brow at her and tilted my head. "I'm sure you're mistaken, Dorothy. It's Ms. *Wolff.*"

Her jaw tightened with anger, but she jerked a nod. "My mistake, Ms. Wolff. I've been trying to get an appointment to meet with you, but your secretary has been more than difficult on the matter of your schedule."

Amusement rippled through me. Hannah needed a promotion. My company accountant was going to have to forgive me for stealing her assistant, but she was just too good at this.

"Well, I'm a busy woman, Dorothy. I'm sure Hannah did her best." I made as though to walk past the enraged agent, but she grabbed my arm to stop me and I stiffened.

Agent Hanson snatched her hand back off my arm again before I could say anything, and her cheeks reddened. "I'm sorry," she apologized. "Sorry, I shouldn't have... Look, I need to speak with you, and this won't wait for an appointment next April."

Next April? Damn, Hannah was creative.

"Is Daria a suspect in a case, Agent Hanson?" Zed asked, intervening with a no-nonsense tone.

The FBI agent shot Zed a quick look, then shook her head. "Not on this case, no. Which is why I'm politely asking her to spare me ten minutes out of her busy day to chat. Or would you prefer that I escalate this and find some way to name her as a person of interest?"

I held a general disdain for *most* law enforcement because I knew firsthand how easy they all were to corrupt. But something about Special Agent Hanson amused me. She was ballsy, if a bit of a confused mess.

"You know what? I think I can make some time." I indicated to the elevators. "Come up to my office, Dorothy. I'm curious to know what is so important."

Zed eyeballed me like I'd just started speaking in Korean, but I simply strode across to the elevators and pressed the call button without acknowledging their looks.

Several other people got into the car with us, eliminating the need for conversation on our way up to Copper Wolf's floor. We stepped off, and I led the way through to my office, where I found Hannah at her usual desk opposite Macy. Gen, my legal counsel, was perched on the edge of Hannah's desk with a coffee in her hand, but she jerked to her feet when she saw me.

"Ms. Wolff," she greeted properly with raised brows. "Zed didn't mention you were coming in today."

I turned my head slightly to arch a brow at him, but he just gave a small shrug. "You were fast asleep, Darling. I didn't want to wake you." He placed a possessive arm around my waist as he said that and dropped a light kiss to my shoulder, making me shiver.

Somehow, miraculously, I didn't hate the way he used my middle name. Because Chase almost *always* called me Darling, it gave me full-body creeps when anyone else used it. But from Zed...I didn't hate it. Surely that was progress?

Or maybe not, seeing as I'd just immediately thought of Chase. As shitty as it was, Zed and Chase were still majorly twisted together in my mind.

Gen's sharp gaze took in Zed's hand on my waist, and her smile slipped at his suggestive response. It sounded and looked a whole lot like Zed and I were fucking. And I did nothing to correct that assumption.

"Agent Hanson," Gen snapped, straightening up more as she spotted the FBI agent behind Zed. "This is turning into harassment."

"We're fine, Gen," I assured her. "I told Dorothy I could spare a couple of minutes." I indicated for the agent to accompany me into my office, and Zed closed the door behind us.

Circling my desk, I gestured to a vacant chair before slipping my jacket off and sitting down. Agent Hanson gave my gun a long look before sitting down herself and clearing her throat.

"Thank you, Ms. Wolff," she started, shooting Zed a cautious look. He'd taken up his usual spot behind me, leaning against the wall in a casual yet vaguely threatening pose. "This isn't, in fact, regarding any of my official cases."

I pursed my lips thoughtfully. "Explains why you weren't throwing your authority around to secure an interview. What *is* it regarding, then?"

With a short sigh, she pulled out her phone and brought up a photo. "This," she said, sliding the phone across my desk to show me the image, "is agent Harold Laurens."

I glanced down at the serious-faced young man in the

photograph but kept my expression neutral as I looked back up at Agent Hanson. "And?"

She gave a small, frustrated frown. "Agent Harold Laurens was assigned an undercover mission just one week after graduating from Quantico."

I shrugged. "Is that uncommon? I'll admit I don't pay a huge amount of attention to the inner workings of your bureau. I was under the impression that sort of work was fairly normal."

She shook her head. "He wasn't remotely ready for that sort of mission. Hell, he never should have passed basic training."

Zed shifted slightly in the corner of my vision, and I resisted the urge to look over at him for his opinion. I was leaning too heavily on him these days as it was; I needed to reassert myself as the boss.

"What does this have to do with me, Dorothy?" I kept using her first name because I liked to push people's buttons. She wasn't rising to the bait like most of her male counterparts did, though.

Agent Hanson gave a short, sharp exhale, her eyes flicking between Zed and me. "Because his placement was within Shadow Grove and he's since disappeared completely." She paused, but I said nothing. If she had a specific question, she needed to spit it out. "Look, everyone in the entire bureau knows you own Shadow Grove, and Cloudcroft too. Hell, you run most of the damn state. So if anyone knows what happened to Agent Laurens...it's you."

I tapped my fingernail on the desk, carefully studying her face, her posture, her pleading eyes. She wasn't here on official business; this was personal. "Who is he to you, Dorothy?"

She drew a breath, her shoulders tightening. "My nephew."

I gave a small nod. I could understand where she was coming from, wanting to know what had happened to her family. But she was barking up the wrong tree, thinking I could help her out. I hadn't held my position of power as long as I had by incriminating myself to FBI agents. No matter what the circumstances.

"I'm sorry, I can't help you." I folded my arms, sitting back in my chair. Call me paranoid, but I wasn't keen on leaving my fingerprints on her phone by pushing it back across to her.

Zed shifted his weight again, and this time I gave him a curious glance.

"Agent Hanson, why'd you say he shouldn't have graduated?" His frown was drawn tight, and he looked like he had something on his mind.

She sighed, patting at her hair. "I don't have evidence. But I know my nephew and all his shortcomings. His handwriting is appalling, to the point of being almost illegible. But I happened to see one of his written assessments, and the penmanship was immaculate."

Zed's brows twitched. "He cheated? Why didn't you report that?"

She grimaced. "I did." With a shake of her head, she tightened her lips. "Never mind. It was a long shot. I just had to try." She stood from her chair and offered me a nod. "Thank you for your time. I can see myself out."

Neither Zed nor I made any move to follow her as she retreated out of my office once more, and when the door closed, I swiveled my chair to look up at my second with a curious gaze.

"That was unprofessional of her," I commented.

He rubbed a hand over his stubbled cheek, nodding his agreement. "Very. But also very interesting. That kid in the picture looked familiar."

"He should," I murmured with a grimace. After all, that was the undercover agent I'd shot in the knee weeks ago underneath Anarchy. "Cyanide pills for a brand-new FBI agent during his first week on the job? Doesn't add up."

Zed frowned. "Not even slightly. Chase, on the other hand…"

"Makes sense that Harold was on Chase's payroll. The poison pill is much more his brand." I leaned back in my chair, keeping eye contact with Zed as I analyzed the thought on the tip of my tongue.

Zed narrowed his eyes. "What's that look for?"

I almost shrugged it off but then inhaled deeply and found my big-dick energy once more. "Why do I feel like you're keeping something from me, Zed?"

A lightning-fast flash of shock crossed his face, gone as fast as it appeared, and he pretended like it'd never happened as he gave me a confused look. "Like what?"

I shook my head slowly. "I'm not sure. You just…" I let my voice trail off, not actually having the words to describe how his whole energy had changed since we'd arrived at the office. "Never mind," I finally murmured. "Maybe I'm overthinking things."

Maybe it was the way Gen had fluttered her lashes at Zed when we walked in that had set me on edge. I wanted to say I wasn't used to feeling jealous of the female—and male—attention my best friend drew, but that was a lie. I'd been jealous of his revolving door of women for a *long* time, I just hadn't identified that's what it was. Now, though? Now I could see it for what it was. Primal, irrational jealousy.

Zed leaned down, bracing his hands on the arms of my chair as he smirked at me. "I already confessed my deepest secret to you, Dare. There's nothing else to hide."

He leaned in closer but stopped when our lips were just an inch apart, and I stopped breathing.

"I want to kiss you so fucking bad," he confessed, his voice a rough whisper. "But I can't stand that conflicted look in your eyes."

My soul screamed in frustration, but no sound exited my mouth. I just sat there frozen as he straightened back up and quietly left my office. But what the fuck could I have even said back to that? He was right. Every damn time we kissed, those dark memories flashed across my mind. No matter how briefly, no matter whether I even consciously acknowledged those memories, they left a mark. It tainted the emotions of Zed's kiss and left me… conflicted. Uneasy. Vulnerable. And I *hated* that.

I sat there at my desk for a long time, mentally berating myself for being such a damaged, broken bitch. Screaming at myself internally for pushing Zed away when he was one of the best things to ever happen to me. And yet I didn't get to my feet and rush after him. I just...I wasn't there yet. Maybe I never would be.

The sound of Zed's low voice and Gen's laughter outside my office made my teeth grind together, but I just pushed it all out of my mind. Turning my stereo on to drown out the distractions, I went to work on my digital to-do list that Hannah had kindly compiled for me.

Putting my mind into work mode, I flew through all my outstanding tasks, then put together an email to Hannah offering her a promotion to my full-time assistant. Before sending it, I sent Macy a quick message to inform her that I was poaching her assistant.

My accountant emailed back almost instantly, telling me she'd already been training Hannah's replacement for the past week.

I snorted a laugh at that and hit Send on the job offer to Hannah. Then I shut down my computer and grabbed my shit to leave.

"Yes!" Hannah squealed as I opened my office door. "Yes, I accept!" She popped out of her office chair and launched at me like she was going to hug me, then caught herself halfway and ended up on her ass at my feet.

I peered down at her with one brow raised. "Are you okay?"

Cringing, she nodded. Her thick black hair was up in two high buns like an anime character, and they bobbed with her head in a slightly comical way.

"Um, yep. Sorry, sir," she replied, scrambling to her feet and smoothing her hands down the front of her skirt. "Got carried away."

I didn't prolong her obvious embarrassment, just gave her a nod and continued out of the office. Zed and Gen were nowhere to be seen, so I was going to assume they were downstairs. Even if Zed wanted to piss me off, he still had business on his mind, and we were due for a meeting with Alexi over at Anarchy in the afternoon.

Still, I breathed a long sigh of relief when I found him leaning against the door of his car. Alone. Waiting for me.

CHAPTER 13

Our meeting with Alexi only produced more headaches. According to him, several of the staff from 7th Circle, who we'd been trying to place in other clubs so they wouldn't be out of work, had gone missing or, at the very least, weren't responding when my team tried to reach out to them about shifts.

An uneasy, anxious feeling twisted my stomach as Zed and I left Anarchy sometime later. We'd done everything we needed to do work-wise, but the issue of 7th Circle staff not responding was plaguing my mind.

"Do you think Chase has a hand in this?" I asked Zed after we were back on the road. "Or am I just being paranoid?"

"I don't think there's such a thing as being *too paranoid* when it comes to him right now," Zed replied with a heavy sigh. "We thought he was bad before... He seems a hundred times worse now. What has me curious, though, is why now? It's been five years. Why is he coming for you *now* and not years ago?"

I nodded slowly. "You think something triggered him? Or... he was waiting for something?"

Zed shrugged. "No fucking clue. It's just bugging me. I wish I could work out what the connection was."

"Same here." I groaned and ran a hand through my hair. "Can we stop and grab pie from Nadia's on the way? I feel like I need the sugar hit."

He arched a brow at me. "You wanna go to a Reaper business right now? We're not exactly their favorite people."

I wrinkled my nose. "Yeah, I know. But we also have to remind them who is in change. And Cass isn't *actually* dead."

"All right. But maybe let's keep it quick. I don't fancy needing to clean up bodies and bullet holes tonight." He grimaced. "'Cause you know Cass would shit a damn brick if we left that mess at his grandmother's café."

I jerked in my seat. "*What?*"

Zed blinked at me. "What?"

"Nadia is Cass's grandmother?" I gaped in shock. "Since *when?*"

He gave me an amused chuckle. "Uh, I imagine since her daughter gave birth to his grumpy ass. That's usually how someone becomes a grandparent. Isn't it?"

"Oh, ha-fucking-ha. Smart ass. Why didn't I know this already? And how'd *you* know?"

He gave an easy shrug. "I pay attention."

I scowled at the side of his face, knowing full damn well he was winding me up. "You're insufferable, Zeddy Bear."

He shot me a quick look, a relaxed smile playing over his lips. "You love it."

I bit my tongue before I could lie and tell him I didn't. Ugh, maybe I needed to find a good therapist to help me work through all my unresolved trauma. Maybe then I could let go of all my nasty, icky hang-ups and let myself love Zed the way I already knew I did.

But then again, what kind of therapist could work with a mind as messed up as mine?

"Have you thought any more on what to do about Chase?" Zed asked after a long silence. "I know we can't just kill him, but we should at least get his DNA sample to rule him out as Gumdrop's mysterious big brother."

I blew out a long breath, fluffing my fingers through my hair. "Fuck me, I wish we could just kill him once and for all. How easy that would be."

But Chase wasn't that stupid, and he knew I knew he wasn't that stupid. Like he'd proven with the explosives placed around Demi's Italian home, he had his bases covered. I knew it was no coincidence that he'd mentioned my FBI tail, too. He had someone in the feds firmly in his pocket, and I'd put money on it that if he went "missing," I would find myself in a jail cell faster than you could say *evidence*. Or worse, someone I loved might take the blame.

I couldn't risk it. Not until I was sure it was safe. Then... Well, they do say revenge is a dish best served cold. I'd bide my time. For now.

"What if Chase really is related to Lucas?" I murmured, putting voice to the fear that had kept me out of Lucas's bed last night.

Zed gave me an understanding look. "Or if one of us is?" He shrugged. "Doesn't make a difference, does it? I mean, sure, if *you're* related, then that's something that will probably need a whole lot of therapy because you guys used to fuck like rabbits. Ow!" He rubbed his arm where I'd just whacked him with the back of my hand.

"You're a prick," I muttered, "but you're right. Blood doesn't mean shit, even if he is related to that sick fuck. I do *sort of* have a plan for getting Chase's sample. It'll just depend on getting close enough."

Zed's glance was sharp at that comment. "Dare, you can't... Just no. I'll get the sample. It's as easy as grabbing a glass he's been drinking out of."

I shook my head, having already thought through all the options. "I don't trust it. If we're taking a DNA sample from Chase should-be-dead Lockhart, then I want a clean, unquestionably *his* sample. Straight from his mouth." Or better yet, from his veins.

The tension basically vibrated from Zed as he gripped the steering wheel tighter, and I understood completely.

"I'll do it," he growled, stubborn as hell.

I just rolled my eyes. "We'll deal with it when an opportunity arises. But if Chase is even a tiny bit like the guy we both knew, we also know he has a major blind spot that can be used against him."

Zed exhaled a muttered string of curses. "You."

I nodded, and neither of us said anything else for a long time. Zed silently reached out and placed his hand on my knee, though, and I didn't push him away.

We arrived at Nadia's Cakes a few minutes later, scoring a parking spot right in front of the café. It was late afternoon on a weekday, and she didn't look too busy, which was a small relief.

Even so, my spine was tight with tension as we stepped out of the car and made our way inside. Lots of eyes were on us. Reapers mostly, people who knew who we were and what I'd done. But there were also plenty of normal customers who had no clue about the gangs who really ran the city they lived in.

"I admit I didn't think I'd see you around here," Nadia commented in a terse, clipped tone as she came around the counter. She wore an apron branded with her company logo and wiped her hands on it as she approached Zed and me. As she got closer, though, I noted the lack of real heat in her eyes. The lack of authentic anger in her posture. For a woman whose grandson I'd supposedly shot a week and a half ago, she was awfully calm.

"We couldn't resist your cakes, Nadia," Zed smoothly answered for us, leaning down to kiss the old woman's cheek and making her smile tightly.

She arched a knowing brow at me. "I hope your pretty one enjoyed his birthday cake."

The penny dropped. Fucking Cass had been in touch with his

grandmother. I hadn't even questioned it when they'd had a beautifully decorated cake set up for Lucas the night before.

I gave her a small smile back. "He did, thank you. Zed and I just wanted to pick up an apple-and-blackberry pie, if you have any?" For some reason I was seriously craving that.

She pursed her lips, then indicated to some vacant seats near the counter. "Sit down. I'll sort you out."

Zed and I followed her instruction, sitting down at the small table, and a minute later one of the waitresses came over with a couple of coffees for us.

"Nadia said it'll be twenty minutes, so have a coffee while you wait." The woman gave a shrug, raking her eyes over me like I was a rare animal in the zoo or something. Then she met my eyes, blanched, and retreated away from our table quickly.

I gave a small sigh, picking up my coffee as Zed covered a laugh with his hand.

"What's so funny?" I muttered, narrowing my eyes at him.

"You are," he replied, just as quietly. "She was checking you out. Then she spotted that monster lurking in your glare and changed her mind so fast it gave her whiplash."

I frowned. "What? No, she was gawking at the woman who murdered the beloved Reapers' leader then had the audacity to show her face in Reaper territory."

Zed snorted. "Okay then."

Scowling, I locked my gaze on the table and sipped my coffee, ignoring the eyes on me from all around the room. If this had been any other gang's territory, I wouldn't be giving it a second thought. But this wasn't *any* other gang. It was the Reapers. And Cassiel fucking Saint had left a hell of an impression behind.

Zed leaned in close, brushing my hair over my shoulder. "For what it's worth, I like the monster behind your eyes. She's sexy as hell."

I caught a sharp breath at that, my gaze jerking up from the table, but it locked on someone about to walk through the door instead. "Get fucked," I breathed.

"Uh...what?" Zed replied, recoiling somewhat.

"No, not you," I snapped, "*that.*"

The front door chimed as it opened, and I locked eyes with my nemesis. He didn't even seem the slightest bit surprised, like he'd known I was here. Was he tailing me? Or had someone in the Reapers tipped him off?

Not that it mattered. He sauntered over to us as Zed stiffened beside me, and I laid a hand on his knee to silently remind him we couldn't kill Chase yet.

He got the message but wasn't remotely happy about it, shooting me an angry glare before flicking his scowl back to Chase.

"Uh-oh," Chase said with a chuckle, "do I smell trouble in paradise here? What a shame. You two are the ultimate star-crossed lovers, like something straight out of a Shakespearean tragedy." His sick smile spread wide, and his single eye bored into me.

"What do you want, Chase?" I asked in a cool, unemotional voice. "Zed and I were having a nice time until you decided to stink the place up with your foul energy."

Chase parted his lips to reply but was interrupted by Nadia storming out of the kitchen.

"You!" she barked, shaking a finger at Chase. "You get out of here. You're not welcome in my establishment."

For whatever reason, Chase genuinely seemed surprised that this old woman was scolding him and gaped at her for a moment, speechless. I smirked, leaning back in my seat and stuffing my hands into the pockets of my leather jacket.

"You heard me, *Mr. Dibbs*," Nadia continued, making a shooing motion at Chase. "You're a known enemy of Hades, so you're an enemy of the Reapers. Now get."

My fingers touched something in my pocket, and I tilted my head, trying to remember what it was. Then it struck me. This was a jacket that had survived the apartment bombing. I knew *exactly* what was in my pocket and couldn't fight the smile as a rapid plan formulated in my mind.

"Actually, Nadia," I spoke up, drawing everyone's gazes, "Mr. Dibbs here was just passing by. I don't mind handling this if that's okay with you." I gave Cass's grandmother a sly smile, letting a spark of my evil intent show through my gaze when she met my eyes.

She jerked a nod, understanding that I had things firmly in hand, and with a parting glare at Chase, she stomped back to the kitchen while muttering insults about him under her breath.

Chase's lip curled as he refocused his one eye on me. "Oh, you've got me *handled* do you, Darling? Been a really long time since I've had you handle me, but I remember it like it was yesterday." He ran his tongue over his front teeth, and I tightened my throat to hold back the bile threatening to decorate Nadia's pretty tablecloth.

Instead of telling him where to shove his memories, I stood up and gave him a small smile like I was really joining him on that little trip down memory lane. Or nightmare lane, as it may be.

With a well-practiced sleight of hand, I passed the vial of drugs to Zed as I brushed past him to approach Chase. Like Zed and I had just discussed earlier in the day, the Chase Lockhart we both knew had one huge blind spot. It was about time to test whether that was still the case or not.

"I just bet you do," I murmured, stepping right into his personal space and placing a hand lightly on his chest. His muscles twitched under my touch like he was shocked I'd willingly touched him. In fairness, I was amazed I'd done it without breaking out in hives, too.

"What...do you think you're doing, Darling?" he asked in a low voice, his eye locked on my face as I leaned in closer still. "If you think you can play me by reminding me what an excellent lay you are—" He broke off with a sharp inhale as I bit his earlobe between my teeth. It wasn't hard enough to rip the flesh from his head, no matter how badly I wanted to disfigure him further than I already had. Nope, this was one of his erogenous zones, and he loved it rough to the point of pain.

Chase moaned, and my stomach tightened with disgust. And a little bit of fear. His arm snaked around my waist, pulling me hard against his body and showing me just how turned on that one bite had gotten him. Then he released me like I was made of barbed wire and took a firm step back.

"You sneaky minx," he hissed. "You're up to something." He gave a short laugh, but I could hear unease in the way his voice shook ever so slightly. I'd unnerved the hell out of him, and it made my smile wide and wicked.

Chase shook his head, pointing between me and Zed, who was still seated at the table and sipping on his coffee like he wasn't also shaking with rage. "You two think you're so much smarter than me. You're wrong. I've had five years to plan my revenge, and you're just making it up as you go along. Pathetic."

He leaned over and swiped my coffee from the table, shooting me a smug grin before drinking it all. I hated sharing my coffee. Despised it. Chase knew it, too, and used to always steal my coffees just to enrage me.

When I gave no response to that little blast from the past, though, he slammed the mug down so hard it shattered on the tabletop. If the whole café hadn't already been watching our inter-action, they sure as shit would be now.

Chase looked around with a sneer. "What a cute little café. I understand that old bitch is your deceased lover's grandmother too. Sure would be a shame to see anything happen to this place. Or her."

One of the big, tattoo-covered Reapers at a nearby table over-heard that comment and made a move to come at Chase, but I gave him a short headshake.

"I think you've overstayed your welcome, Chase," I told my ex with a smile as I returned to my seat beside Zed. He draped his arm around my shoulders, and Chase's scowl flickered with violence and fury.

He was smart enough to recognize when Zed was deliberately trying to get a rise out of him, though, so with another sneer at us, he spun on his heel and started toward the door.

As badly as I wanted to wash my mouth out with bleach after willingly touching Chase, appearances were everything. I couldn't let him see anything but confidence and strength, and washing my mouth out with harsh chemicals would only tell him just how badly he made my skin crawl. Instead, Zed calmly handed me his own coffee and I took a sip as we watched our nemesis leave. Or... he tried to.

He made it to within a few steps of the main entrance to Nadia's Cakes, then staggered, swayed, and dropped like a sack of bricks.

No one in the cafe spoke. They all just stared in shock at the motionless man on the floor or at me and Zed sitting there with the smuggest of smiles.

"Oh good," Nadia commented, coming out of the kitchen with a pie box. "You killed him. 'Bout damn time."

I snorted a laugh, standing up from my chair once more. "I wish. Nadia, do you have any cotton swabs or Q-tips or something?"

The old woman just frowned at me in confusion. "No, why would I?"

"I do!" the waitress from earlier announced, diving under the counter. She popped back up with her makeup bag in hand, dug around inside, then pulled out a fresh box of Q-tips, still unopened. "I use them for makeup," she explained, handing them over.

I gave a small smile that was probably pure evil and plucked two from the box. "Perfect. Do you also happen to have a permanent marker and a ziplock bag?"

The waitress bobbed her head and rushed away again, and I

headed over to where Chase was unconscious on the floor. Just because I couldn't help myself, I delivered a hard kick to his ribs, and one of the Reaper guys watching hissed a sharp breath.

My gaze jerked up to meet his, and I shrugged. "He deserves worse."

The guy gave a grim smile. "What'd you drug him with?"

Crouching down beside my fallen enemy, I allowed myself the luxury of this small win. "A lady never reveals her secrets," I murmured, rolling Chase over and opening his mouth so I could swab the inside of his cheek thoroughly with the Q-tips.

The helpful waitress hurried back to me, holding a plastic sandwich bag open for me to drop the saliva-wet Q-tips into.

Zed took the sealed bag from her and tucked it into his jacket pocket, looking down at me with an arched brow. "Now what? He's going to know we drugged him for a reason."

I shrugged and took the permanent marker from the waitress. "So what? Not much he can do about it now." I uncapped the pen with my teeth, then went to work drawing a massive dick on the side of Chase's face, complete with hairy balls.

When I was done, I capped the pen and pushed to my feet to admire my handiwork. "Not bad," I commented to myself.

Zed looked like he was on the verge of full-blown laughter as he snapped a photo on his phone. "Some skills never fade, no matter how long it's been."

"You sure you don't wanna put a bullet in his brain right now?" Nadia asked, her hands on her wide hips as she scowled down at the unconscious man. "Save yourself a hell of a headache."

I grimaced. "You have no idea how tempting that is, Nadia." I kicked Chase again, just letting out a little pent-up frustration, then took the pie box from her. "Drop him out into the alleyway or something. He *should* focus blame on me, but—"

"If he burns my café down, you'll be paying for it," she finished for me with a stern look.

My lips twitched with a smile, equally shocked and impressed that she gave zero shits who she was speaking to with that attitude. No wonder Cass had such respect for women with a role model like her.

"Absolutely," I confirmed. "Best keep some of these boys around for personal safety too." I nodded to the Reapers, who weren't even pretending not to be listening in.

Nadia pursed her lips and gave a tight nod. "I've stayed alive this long. I'm no idiot. You just take care of"—she drifted her eyes to Zed, then back to me with a meaningful look—"of your family. Understood?"

The message was loud and clear. Keep Cass safe and alive, or I'd have Nadia to deal with.

I jerked a nod. "Thank you for the pie."

She huffed. "Thank you for the entertainment."

Zed and I exited the café as several of the big Reapers moved to haul Chase up roughly. Our car was right there outside, so we didn't speak until we were back on the road again, the fresh pie sitting warm in my lap. Yum.

"What did we just dose him with, and why was it in your pocket, Dare?" Zed asked as he drove, shooting me an amused look.

I smirked. "Chloral hydrate. Demi gave me that little vial months ago when I was having trouble sleeping. She puts just one drop of it in her chamomile tea when she can't switch her brain off from work."

Zed gave an amused huff. "Lucky break."

I shrugged. "I'll take it. And now we know that Chase hasn't changed all that much. Better the devil we know, right?"

"Too true," he murmured, then cranked the music up loud as we drove in the direction of our paid pathology lab. No time like the present to get Chase's sample analyzed.

CHAPTER 14

Zed wanted to sit at the lab and watch our tech run the DNA samples through so there could be no possibility of contamination or corruption in the results. But I was bored as hell and itching to see Lucas, so I left Zed there and took his car home.

After I parked and headed into the house, I followed the sound of thumping music through to the gym, where I found Lucas, shirtless and sweaty, pounding the crap out of one of the punching bags.

His music was up loud enough that he didn't hear me enter, so I stood there for a while, watching him like a giant creep. Okay, in fairness I was a little bit checking his form and taking mental notes of things he could tweak to tighten his guard or add force to his hooks. Mostly I was drooling over the way his muscles bunched and shifted, his sweat gleaming on every slope and angle as he ran through one of Zed's training combinations.

When the song on the stereo ended, he stepped back from the bag with his freshly tattooed chest heaving and his gloved hands hanging loose at his sides.

"Not bad," I commented, startling him. "You're a quick learner."

His smile spread wide, then he used his teeth to loosen the

Velcro on one of his gloves. He pulled them off, tossing them aside as he crossed the room toward me.

"How long were you watching me, Hayden?" His eyes were heated and his expression predatory as he stalked closer.

I grinned, unable to help myself, and tipped my head back to hold his gaze when he got close enough to touch. "Not long," I admitted. "You've got good form. Keep training with Zed and you'll be asking to fight at Anarchy soon."

Lucas scoffed a laugh. "And risk messing up this face? Hell no." He braced his hand on the wall behind me, then leaned down and caught my mouth in a gentle, unhurried kiss.

I leaned in to his touch, parting my lips and weaving my arms around his sweaty neck as he deepened the kiss. Fucking hell, Lucas was like something straight out of my dirtiest dreams. I never wanted to let him go.

"I should shower," he muttered eventually, releasing my lips but keeping his arms tight around me like he was echoing my thoughts.

I grinned, kissing his jaw. "Can I join you?"

A low groan dragged from him as I ran my tongue down his neck, tasting the saltiness of his sweat, and scraped my teeth over his skin. "Fuck yes," he breathed. "I don't think I'll ever say no to sharing my shower with you, Hayden."

In a dramatic move, he swept me up into his arms and kissed me again as he strode out of the gym. He raced up the stairs with me still carried in his arms like I weighed nothing and all but kicked open the door to his room while I tried not to laugh.

"You probably shouldn't be carrying me," I scolded gently as he crossed the room to the attached bathroom.

He just shot me a cocky smile. "I probably shouldn't be under-age drinking or working in a strip club either. But I have no intention of doing what I *should* do." He set me down gently, his hands already finding the hem of my blouse to lift it up over my head.

I was loving his attention enough that I let him strip me down, then waited while he got the shower running warm. But just as he indicated for me to step in, his words sank through the thick haze of arousal.

"Uh, you don't work in a strip club anymore, hot stuff. Or did you forget the whole gas-leak-explosion situation?" I tied my hair up in a high bun to keep it dry, then took his extended hand. He pulled me into the shower and into his warm, naked embrace. Delicious.

He guided me carefully into the water, letting me get warm and running his hands over my skin like he was committing my curves to memory. "How could I forget?" he murmured in response. "But Zed said he's got me on the schedule at Club 22 instead."

I jerked backward, placing a hand on Lucas's chest just beside his fresh ink. "Zed said what?"

Lucas quirked a brow at me. "Uh, he said that all the 7th Circle staff were being spread out between the other Copper Wolf venues so no one loses their job. I asked if I could go to Club 22 because it's my favorite one. It's so classy with everyone dressed in theme."

I gaped at him a moment; then a simmering anger built within me. "I'm gonna have to kill him," I muttered.

"Um, can I ask why?" Lucas reached for the bodywash and squeezed a healthy handful out into his palm.

I scowled. "Because he fucking well knew he wasn't supposed to put you on the dance schedule. He's constantly pushing my fucking buttons these days."

Lucas hummed a sound, gliding soapy hands over me and making my breath catch. It was really damn hard to stay mad at Zed while Lucas was playing with my nipples like that...

"Why not?" Lucas asked, pressing me into the cool shower wall with his body, his hot, hard length teasing at my belly. "I asked him to." His hands moved from my breasts and slipped down my sides, curving around to cup my ass.

I gasped as his hips pinned me and he caught my lips in a quick, open-mouthed kiss.

"Yeah, but you're not… I mean, you and I are…" I was having a difficult time chasing my train of thought as his hands tightened under my thighs, lifting me and coaxing my legs around his waist. His thick shaft crushed against my aching pussy, and I almost forgot everything I was trying to say.

"You mean you're still hung up on not dating employees?" he murmured against my neck before kissing my pulse point and making me sigh in ecstasy. "Don't you think it'd be kinda hot to sneak around and fuck in your office? Don't you wanna watch me dance, knowing all I can think about is what I wanna do to *you*?"

Oh fuck. That did sound hot. But…ugh, there was something not sitting right with me.

"Lucas," I moaned, arching my hips as he ground against me. "I just… Wouldn't it feel a whole lot like I was taking advantage? Besides, I'm *never* letting you pay me back for your mom's medical, so—"

"Hayden." He cut me off, his voice sharp and firm as he met my eyes. "Maybe I wasn't clear on this. I'm not dancing at Club 22 because I'm desperate for money. I'm doing it because I *enjoy* stripping. I *enjoy* dancing and showing off my athletic skill on the pole. I'll do it for free, if that makes you feel more comfortable, but it's something I want to do."

My lips rounded into a silent *Oh*. Because that actually hadn't occurred to me. And now I felt like a bigger asshole for not considering the fact that it was something he *liked* doing.

"I get it," he said with a laugh, kissing my stunned lips. "You don't want to feel like a sleazy boss. But if it makes you feel better, Zed has that crown permanently affixed to his head. The stories the girls at 7th Circle used to tell…" He shook his head, grinning.

I winced, not wanting to think about how many of the girls, both dancers and sex workers, that Zed had made his way through. It was only going to make me more likely to dump hand sanitizer on his dick before it came anywhere near me.

"Don't worry, babe," Lucas whispered, kissing my neck as he shifted my weight, pressing me back into the tiled wall again. "I don't have eyes for anyone but you. You're my first and my last."

Oh *fuck*. What's a girl to say to that?

I couldn't have spoken coherently even if I had something perfect to say because his shower-slick cock pushed into my cunt, stretching my walls and making me cry out in pleasure.

My fingernails dug into the flesh of his back as I tightened my legs, pulling him deeper and groaning at the slide of our flesh. "Lucas…"

"Hayden," he replied, my name like a prayer on his husky voice. "You're exquisite." His hips rolled, pulling his length out of me partly before slamming back in. I grunted at the impact, shivering with the electric waves of arousal chasing across my skin.

Clinging to him tighter, I reclaimed his lips with a fierce, demanding kiss. Our breath became one as Lucas pounded me into the wall, his hips pistoning faster with every stroke until my entire being seemed to be filled with liquid fire.

"Oh fuck," I hissed as my pussy walls tightened around his enormous dick. That appendage really was a gift from some generous god. "Lucas, I'm going to come."

"Good," he groaned back, "'cause holding out is killing me."

I gave a short, shaking laugh, but after two more thrusts from him, I shattered. He swallowed my screams with kisses, fucking my mouth as thoroughly as he was fucking my pussy, and joined me in climax just moments later with his cock buried deep inside me.

We were both breathing heavily when he gently lowered my feet back to the floor, but I was pure jelly, incapable of anything but propping myself up on the wall. Lucas knew it, too, grinning with satisfaction as he washed me, cleaning up the slick, hot spill of his cum between my legs, then soaping me all over again.

When we were clean, he carried me out to the bedroom and laid me ever so gently down on the bed. He barely gave me a minute to rest, though, before tugging me up onto my knees and sliding back into my pussy from behind.

As my sensitive, throbbing core lit up once more, I groaned long and hard and grinned into the bedding. Lucas had—no joke—a supernatural-level refractory period. Maybe he was making up for lost time after not losing his virginity until two months ago with me.

This time, since we'd both come so recently, we took our time with long, drawn-out, lazy fucking in a handful of different positions until eventually we both gave in to soul-shaking climaxes.

Neither of us made any move to get under the blankets or even turn off the lights, and I quietly loved being able to see all of him. So we just lay there with our limbs intertwined, staring into each other's eyes while our breathing slowed and our sweat cooled. If anyone had told me a few months ago that's what I'd be doing with my nineteen-year-old dancer, I'd have laughed in their face.

But there was nothing awkward or uncomfortable about it because he was a part of me now. He owned a piece of my heart, like I owned a piece of his.

Eventually, he shivered and reached for the crumpled blankets to pull over both of us, then propped his head up on his hand to peer at me thoughtfully.

"Did you and Zed have a good day? I noticed he didn't come home with you. Are things…" As his voice trailed off, he raised his brows to imply the rest.

I rolled my eyes, shifting my position to rest my cheek on my folded arms. "It was a business day," I muttered, even though my mind automatically went to that moment in my office when Zed had come so close to kissing me…then walked away. "He stayed to oversee the DNA testing, make sure no one tampered with the samples or results."

Lucas nodded his understanding. "I see. So you didn't…"

I gave him a slow smile. "Are you asking if I fucked Zed in my office, Lucas?"

He didn't even look slightly embarrassed, just gave a one-shouldered shrug.

I rolled my eyes. "No. We're not... We didn't. I'm just not there yet. We've got shit to work through, and then there's Chase..." My excuses sounded lame even to me. Lucas just arched a brow, so I flipped the tables on him. "Why? Would you have been upset if we *had* screwed?" Because I could have sworn there'd been a touch of relief in his eyes when I said no.

Lucas grinned. "Upset? No. No way. Not with how I *know* you feel for him. But jealous? Oh my god, yes. Every time you go to Cass, it takes everything I've got not to march in there and steal you back. Drives me fucking insane."

His cheeks pinked as he admitted this, and I raised my head to peer at him in surprise. Of all of them, Lucas had taken the whole *sharing* idea the most comfortably, maybe because he considered himself the newcomer, despite being the first one between my thighs.

"So why don't you?" I murmured, already feeling the warmth of arousal as my imagination wandered.

His brows raised. "Why don't I...what? Bust into your room while you're with Cass? Well shit, for one thing, that would be rude as hell and totally contradictory to everything I said I was okay with in this relationship." He swiped a hand over his face, giving me a rueful smile. "For another, I don't fancy Cass bashing my head into a wall for cockblocking him. Grumpy Cat is in a foul mood on the best of days. I badly don't want to see him if he got interrupted midfuck."

I couldn't help laughing at that imagery. But I knew something Lucas didn't: Cass had been perfectly content to let Zed join us that night by the fire.

"What if he didn't get angry?" I suggested in a low, seductive whisper. "What if he let you join us?"

Lucas's brows rose even higher, and his cheeks flushed with

deeper color. "Like...like a threesome?" His voice was tight with surprise, his eyes locked on mine like he was trying to gauge what the "right" response to that would be. I knew full well that I was his first, but goddamn, I was curious if that would ever be a possibility.

I nodded, biting the edge of my lip.

He cleared his throat, looking to the ceiling for a moment before returning his gaze to mine. "Have you...um...have you ever had a threesome before?"

My body stiffened, my spine crackling with ice. I should have thought this through before suggesting it. Still, I owed Lucas my honesty, and he'd more than proven he could handle anything I said.

Swallowing heavily, I nodded. "Not..." My voice was rough, and I tried again. "Not willingly." Because I didn't consider that little show for Zed a three-way. Nor did I count the other day when he played with my clit while Cass fucked me. No...the *real* threesomes—and more—that I'd been involved in were deeply entangled in Chase's abuse.

Lucas didn't respond for a long moment; then he leaned down and kissed me softly. "I understand," he whispered, even though he really, truly didn't. No one did. Except maybe Zed...because he'd seen the tapes.

A deep shudder ran through me, the memories creeping through my mind like wet tar as I fought against curling into a fetal position and crying.

"I would give anything in this world to chase those demons out of your eyes, Hayden," Lucas told me in a soft, deeply sincere voice as he kissed my cheek. "Literally anything. A threesome would be the *least* of what I'd do."

I tilted my head, bringing my lips to his for a soft kiss, desperately trying to show him how much he meant to me with just my kiss alone. But it wasn't enough. It'd never be enough because being with Lucas gave me hope that I wasn't irreparably damaged. That those horrific, nauseating memories *could* be erased and replaced with good ones. And he was making it his mission to help me do that.

"I love you, Lucas," I whispered, the unshed tears thick in my voice.

His lips parted mine, and he kissed me with all the intensity and passion of a storm, making my emotions build to the point of painful inside my chest. Then he soothed it all away with gentle strokes of his tongue that reminded me of his promise so fucking early in our relationship.

He was the lighthouse in the storm. He was my safe place. My saving grace.

CHAPTER 15

I had no idea what time it was when Zed woke us up by slamming the door open and barking that he had the test results. But the second his words registered, I sat bolt upright, all residue of sleep fleeing my brain in an instant.

"What happened?" I demanded, alarmed enough that I forgot I was naked. Until Zed's eyes rounded and his gaze seemed to become laser-targeted to my nipples. I drew a sharp breath, grabbing for the sheet as Zed gave a pained grimace.

"Test results?" Lucas prompted with a heavy yawn. He had barely even moved, his cheek still pressed into the pillow with his face toward me. His bare back showed a multitude of red marks from my fingernails, and I caught the way Zed's eyes narrowed as he took that all in.

Then Zed's attention jerked back to me, and his expression shuttered. "Yeah, genetic results all came back, and they found a positive familial link."

That...was *not* what I'd been expecting. My heart thumped hard against my chest wall, and even Lucas sat up slightly to squint at Zed.

"Who?" The one-word question left Lucas's lips with dread.

Zed held my gaze steadily, then shifted his eyes to Lucas and back to me again. Then he gave a small, apologetic shrug.

My gut twisted, and a cold sweat broke out all over my body. "No fucking way," I said in a choked whisper. "No."

Lucas, confused, frowned at me with his lips parted in question. Then my panicked expression must have clicked the thoughts together for him, and he gasped in horror and damn near leapt out of the bed.

"Zayden De Rosa," I barked, giving my best friend a hard glare. There was something off about his posture...or maybe that was just wishful thinking because I badly, *desperately* didn't want to find out I'd been fucking my biological brother. Oh fuck. I was going to throw up.

"What?" Zed replied, tilting his head to the side.

Lucas was already in his pants and stalking across to Zed. He snatched the paperwork out of Zed's hand—I hadn't even seen that there—and ran his eyes over the page.

His shoulders sagged as he let out a long sigh of relief, then his fist snapped out and clocked Zed in the face.

"Not *fucking* funny!" Lucas snarled as Zed recoiled.

I sprang out of bed, abandoning my sheet and modesty in favor of saving Lucas if Zed chose to strike back, but the *shithead* was just laughing as he cupped his eye.

"Oh, come on," Zed groaned, a devilish grin plastered over his lips. "That was *hilarious*."

Lucas wasn't laughing. He was enraged, and I was pretty sure he wanted to hit Zed again, so I got in front of him and gave him a solid push toward the door. "Take a minute, Lucas," I told him in a calm, firm voice. "I'll deal with this."

Fury held his jaw tight and his eyes narrow, but he jerked his head in understanding and left the room as instructed. Which left me alone with a grinning idiot.

"You're a bastard, Zayden De Rosa," I whispered on a long

exhale. The adrenaline that had hit me so suddenly when I thought Lucas and I were truly siblings had drained away, leaving me trembling and cold.

He didn't even *try* to wipe the smile off his face as he stepped closer to me. "Aw, come on, you'd have done the same thing if you saw the opportunity."

My jaw dropped at the accusation. "Fuck no, I wouldn't have! Zed, you made us think we'd been…" I shook my head, a deep shudder running through me. "You're a bastard," I reiterated.

He reached out a hand, grasping my waist and pulled me a step closer to him. Fuck. I was still totally naked, and his gaze was suddenly so hot it was like looking into the sun.

"That's not exactly news, Dare." His face dipped, his nose brushing a teasing line down the side of my neck that made my nipples tighten painfully and my body sway into his.

I swallowed, fighting for some brain power. "I thought you didn't like the look in my eyes when we're together." Oh wow. If there was any question whether I was attracted to Zed, the raw sex and longing in my voice would have sealed the deal.

He straightened up enough to meet my eyes as one of his hands cupped the back of my neck and his thumb tilted my chin up. "I don't," he agreed. "But you know what I hate more?"

I had a fair idea, yes. But for the sake of flirty banter, I played the game. "What?"

"I hate not being able to touch you." The pain in his eyes was almost enough to make me crumple. But it wasn't as simple as just my own stubborn bullheadedness holding me back. It was all my shitty, toxic baggage.

So I forced a lighter tone as I replied, "You're touching me right now, Zed."

My attempt at a joke fell flat as his gaze hardened. "Not the way I *want* to touch you, Dare. Not the way I've been… *Fuck*. Not the way I've been literally dreaming about for goddamn years."

I bit the inside of my cheek, totally at war with myself on what to do next. But even as strictly disciplined as I kept my emotions, my tongue was one thing I couldn't seem to control around Zed. Not when he looked at me the way he was.

"So show me," I told him in a low whisper. "Show me how you really want to touch me, Zed."

He drew a shuddering breath, his eyes flashing with uncertainty like he was questioning whether he'd imagined that request.

So I said it again, despite the fear gnawing at my stomach. "Show me, Zed, or quit your fucking moping."

That snapped something in him. One second we were standing in the middle of the room, and the next I was against the wall with the light switch digging into my bare back. Zed kissed me with savage intensity, his thrusting tongue parting my lips and destroying my soul. I melted under his touch, my body curving into his like we were magnetized, and heat flushed through my lips as his hands explored my body.

He paused when his fingers brushed over my inner thigh, though, like he was second-guessing how far my challenge really extended.

In a desperate effort to run from the nightmares in my mind, I tilted my hips, encouraging him, as I bit his lower lip a fraction harder than playful.

Zed groaned, and his fingers slid inside me with startling ease. Really, though, I shouldn't have been so surprised. Zed had been getting my panties wet a long damn time before I'd even admitted I was crushing on him.

"Holy fuck," he breathed against my kisses. "Dare..." He pumped his hand, fucking me with his thick fingers as I quivered and squirmed, my arms banded around his neck.

I kept kissing him, trying with *all* my strength to keep myself here, in the moment. With *Zed* and no one else. But the sound of something breaking downstairs made me flinch a hundred times harder than I *ever* would have normally, and Zed froze.

Then he peeled my hands away from his neck and gripped my face between his palms, forcing me to meet his eyes.

I swallowed back the frustration and fear, knowing and hating the fact that he could see it all. He could see how *not* okay I was… how fucked up I still was. And how deeply intertwined *he* was with those awful memories and emotions.

After a long, tense moment, he kissed me ever so gently on the lips, then stepped away.

"I'll go see what Lucas broke," he said in a rough, pained voice. Then he left the room without another glance, and I slid down the wall until my butt hit the carpet.

I'd fucked up. Again. This time I might have even pushed things too damn far to recover from, and I had no one to blame but myself. So I only allowed myself a hot second to wallow in self-pity before pulling my shield back around me.

When I pushed back to my feet and went in search of clothes, I wore my Hades identity like a force field. Nothing and no one could penetrate it. Not unless I let them. So the solution seemed simple: Just *don't*.

I dressed quickly, making a snap decision to skip showering right now. The small, vulnerable part of my mind that was still sobbing over hurting Zed was desperate to keep the phantom touch of his hands on my skin a little while longer.

Before heading downstairs, I grabbed my phone and checked the messages there. Most were work-related, but the one that I'd been waiting for all day had finally arrived.

GC: Successful first day.

That was it. Three words from a burner phone that shifted a thousand tons of worry and stress off my shoulders.

I replied truthfully, not allowing myself a moment to second-guess my message until *after* I'd sent it.

The second it delivered, a wash of panic swept through me, and I tried to unsend. But he'd already seen it. Crap.

The bubble popped up to show him typing. Then disappeared. No message came through, the bubble didn't reappear, and I groaned out loud. Why'd I have to go all needy like that? Fucking hell, he'd barely been gone a day, and I was acting like a clingy, codependent weakling.

Irritated at myself, I tossed my phone back onto the bed and headed downstairs. I was burning with curiosity to know what the *actual* DNA results were, and more than that, I was anxious to see Zed and assess how badly I'd fucked up.

I found Zed and Lucas in the kitchen, where Lucas sat cross-legged on the kitchen counter while Zed swept up broken glass from the floor.

"What happened?" I asked in a carefully neutral voice, tensing my entire body to keep from flinching when Zed raised his eyes to mine. His expression was tightly guarded, giving away nothing, and that almost hurt worse than if he'd shown me anger or disappointment.

Lucas looked up at me from the paper in his hand, but there was no panic or concern on his face. "Oh, nothing. I was distracted reading this and dropped the wineglasses I'd pulled out for us."

I frowned, looking at the pile of glass Zed was tipping into the trash. That answer seemed almost too normal. Anticlimactic. Then again, Lucas didn't strike me as the kind of guy who broke shit when he couldn't deal with his big emotions, so it actually made a lot of sense. He was way too well adjusted for that macho shit, and he'd already gotten it out of his system by punching Zed.

Speaking of which, Zed's left eye was coming up red and puffy, and the stubborn fool hadn't iced it at all.

Marching over to the freezer, I pulled it open and retrieved an ice pack. "So, what are the *real* results?" I asked Lucas. Zed had just put the dustpan and brush away, so I handed him the ice pack and gave a stern nod toward his bruised face. "Ice it. Idiot."

Zed's lips twitched with a tiny smile. "Yes, sir."

I grabbed the cordless vacuum from the butler's pantry and gave the kitchen floor a quick once-over because I sure as fuck didn't want any shards of glass in my bare feet.

"So, good news," Lucas announced when I was done. "Or, I dunno. Good, I guess? None of the samples, *including* Chase's, were a familial match to mine."

My brows rose, and I nudged Zed out of the way so I could retrieve some fresh wineglasses. "That's a relief," I commented, then gave Zed a curious look.

He just shrugged back at me. "I never said it was you. You *assumed*, and you know what they say about assuming." He'd only moved a couple of inches out of my way, so his arm was close enough to brush mine as I poured us all a glass of chilled Riesling.

"I hate you," I muttered, not even remotely meaning it. He knew it, too, smirking as he took the glass I offered, his fingers deliberately brushing mine.

Instantly I released a bit of the breath I was holding. That small touch was the reassurance I needed that he wasn't pissed off at me or disgusted. He was just giving me space and time.

"Lies," he whispered, bringing the glass to his lips and shooting me a wink.

"Whatever," Lucas growled, glaring daggers at Zed. "Still not funny. But Zed also wasn't lying. The lab tech found a familial match in one of their other databases but had a hard time uncovering *who* the match was for."

I handed Lucas his glass of wine, then leaned my ass against the counter beside Zed to sip my own. "Why would they not know who the match was for?"

Lucas grimaced. "Because it was assigned a number, not a name."

My brows shot up. "They matched it to a military database." I was genuinely surprised at their initiative. "When did our lab techs get access to those servers?" This question was directed at Zed, who glanced at me from the side of his eye as he sipped his wine.

"Dallas," he said by way of explanation. "He's been getting increasingly more badass with his hacker skills. He stopped by the labs a couple of weeks ago to format their computers and loaded a little back door into some classified servers for situations just like this."

"Useful guy," I murmured, mentally patting myself on the back for extracting him out of the Wraiths a year and a half earlier.

Zed grimaced as he flipped his ice pack over, pressing the colder side to his eye. "I spoke to him on my way back here. He's going to work on decoding the system to get a name for the number. Said it shouldn't take more than a day or two."

"That answers the question of whether my mom was lying, I guess," Lucas said with a hard sigh. "Why would she do that? If she had other kids…where were they my whole life? And why lie about it?"

Zed and I exchanged a knowing look. "The Guild," I replied. "Didn't she say something about your uncle hurting her babies?"

Lucas gave a jerking nod, his brow furrowed. "Yeah, when she thought I was him."

"I wonder if the Guild took her other baby—or babies—away from her. It would explain why you never knew…and why she was determined to get you away from Shadow Grove at such a young age." I leaned an elbow on the counter behind me, and Zed seemed to shift closer. A quick glance at his face betrayed nothing, though, and I wondered if I was imagining things, hypersensitive to his every movement and reading way too much into them.

Lucas ran a hand through his floppy hair and gave a small groan. "That's what I was thinking too. With my uncle giving me that shooter software and shit… It sure seems like they were in the business of training recruits young, right?"

"Speaking of," Zed rumbled, "any word from Grumpy Cat?"

I jerked a nod. "He checked in. Said it was a successful first day."

Lucas grinned wide. "Super informative. Typical fucking Cass."

I smiled back because he was right. Cass had his orders and was just getting the job done. I doubted we would hear much in the way of progress reports until he was done, and that was fine. I trusted him.

I gulped down the rest of my wine, then rinsed my glass in the sink. "I'm going to bed." I didn't elaborate on that any further with excuses, just leaned in to kiss Lucas softly on the lips. Then, before I could lose my damn nerve, I dropped a quick kiss on Zed's lips too.

That move shocked him immobile, and I took the opportunity to get the hell out of the room. Our damage could sleep and be dealt with in the light of day. Maybe.

CHAPTER 16

A gloved hand covering my mouth woke me up, and I bucked my body violently, thrashing to free myself from my assailant.

"Red, it's me," a familiar throaty voice muttered in my ear right as my fingers closed around a dagger tucked into the side of the bed, and my whole body relaxed.

"Saint," I breathed as he pulled his hand away from my lips. My eyes blinked a couple of times, finding his in the darkness. "What the fuck were you thinking? I could have killed you!"

"Again?" he teased. "Come on, get dressed. I don't have long."

Wrapping his arm around my waist, he all but lifted me out of bed and placed me on my feet. His gloved hands raised the hem of the oversized T-shirt I'd worn to bed, and I caught a flash of teeth as he grinned.

"Are you sleeping in my shirt, Red?" He sounded way too damn pleased about that fact, and I groaned, tossing it aside, and snatched my bra from the pile of clothes he'd prepared on my bedside table.

"It's comfy," I snapped back. "What are you doing here? You're supposed to be in—"

He cut me off with a harsh kiss, his gloved hands cupping my breasts through the lace bra as I hooked it on. "You needed me," he rumbled when he released my lips once more.

I cringed, remembering my needy message that he hadn't replied to. "Moment of weakness," I muttered in reply, hurrying to finish dressing. He'd chosen dark jeans and a long-sleeved black top for me, along with my leather jacket and boots. "I shouldn't have gone all girlie like that on you."

He huffed a sound of disagreement. "Bullshit, Red. For one thing, I love when you go girlie on me. For another, you wouldn't have done it unless you were in a vulnerable place. So, I'm here. But we don't have long, so hurry up."

Curiosity radiated through me, and I yanked my boots on quickly. The display on my phone told me I'd only been asleep for a few hours, but I was more than awake and excited to see what Cass had up his sneaky sleeve.

He wrapped his hand around mine to pull me out of the bedroom and laid a finger across his lips to tell me to be silent. We hurried downstairs, and I checked out his ass in the black leather pants he wore—sexy-as-hell motorcycle pants, but unlike anything I'd seen on Cassiel Saint before.

It wasn't until we reached the garage that it clicked why they seemed familiar. "Cass," I whispered, squeezing his gloved hand. "Did you borrow Zed's motorcycle leathers?"

He just tossed a sly smile over his shoulder at me and continued through the dark garage to where my cherry-red Ducati was parked. "Damn right I did," he replied, grabbing my red helmet and passing it to me. "They're a bit snug around the crotch, though. Zed must have a pencil dick to fit these comfortably." He grabbed his junk in demonstration, and I bit my lip to hide my grin. It sure looked like he filled them out perfectly.

Cass headed over to one of Zed's street bikes, an all-black Kawasaki Ninja, and pulled one of Zed's black helmets on before straddling the bike. Decked out in Zed's leathers and helmet and riding his bike…no one would suspect this was Cassiel Saint and not Zayden De Rosa.

"I see you, Saint," I said with a laugh, pulling my own helmet on and swinging my leg over the sexy red Ducati that Cass had given me. "Smart man," I murmured inside my helmet.

He gave me a silent nod, then started his engine and led the way out of the garage. We took it easy down the driveway and out the front gate. Then by some unspoken agreement, we hit the gas.

It didn't take long to work out what Cass's objective was. Within minutes my heart was racing with exhilaration and my smile was achingly wide under my helmet. He'd seen my message for exactly what it was: a cry for help. So he was helping by reminding me how strong I was. How in control. A high-speed bike race through the early hours of the morning was the perfect way to do that, too.

Not to mention the fact that he showed up just to do this for me reminded me that he would quite literally drop everything for me. All I needed to do was ask, and he would be there. Because he *loved* me—something I'd never thought would apply to Cass and me, yet here we were.

We both slowed to a stop at a red light on the outskirts of Shadow Grove's downtown, and I looked over at him. Fucking hell, if I didn't know any better, I'd have been totally fooled into thinking it was Zed beside me. Cass was an inch or two taller and slightly broader across the chest, but when he was head to toe in leather to hide all identifying features, it was a solid disguise.

He revved his engine, tilting his head up at me in challenge. I snorted a laugh and settled myself, ready to take off the second the light changed. Cass wanted a race? He'd damn well get one.

I watched the lights for the road perpendicular to ours, waiting for their light to change, which gave me a split-second head start when ours turned green.

My Ducati took off like a shot out of a gun, roaring down the street fast enough to turn the streetlights into colorful streaks in my vision. Cass was right on my tail, though, keeping the pressure turned up and making me laugh out loud as we slowed down for the next red light we hit.

We waited in comfortable silence, the empty streets of Shadow Grove feeling a whole lot like our personal playground at this eerie time of night. Then the light changed, and this time Cass got the jump on me, pulling ahead from the get-go. He didn't hold the lead for long, though. My Ducati was just a better bike than Zed's Ninja, and I closed the gap before we even sailed through the next green light.

Laughing, I overtook him and thanked the gods of traffic lights that the next several sets were all green. It allowed me the space to leave Cass well behind, extending my win in the unspoken race we were both engaging in.

The road ahead ended in a parking lot, so I took the next left, counting on Cass being close enough behind that he'd see me turn. I'd barely rounded the corner, though, when I had to screech to a halt that almost had me flying over the handlebars. As it was, my back wheel lifted off the ground, and only my riding experience and light weight saved me from becoming mincemeat on the concrete.

"What the *fuck*?" I cursed, glaring in outrage at the two SUVs that had just pulled up from the other direction and stopped, blocking the road entirely.

I barely got a second to process the oddity of the situation before Cass's bike skidded around mine in a perfect arc as he pulled a gun from inside his jacket and fired a round of bullets at the SUVs.

On reflex, I reached for my own gun before realizing I hadn't put it on. I'd been in such a hurry to get out of the house with Cass that I hadn't grabbed it from the nightstand where Cass had laid it out with my clothes. *Shit.*

"Go!" Cass boomed at me, and I didn't hesitate. I jammed my

foot down on the ignition and jerked my handlebars to turn in a tight circle. More shots rang out behind me as I fled, but I didn't stop. I was severely underdressed for *that* sort of party and had no desire to sign my own death certificate so soon. So I did the only sensible thing possible and tore through the night.

Only when I felt sure the SUVs weren't following did I risk a glance over my shoulder and let out a long sigh of relief when I spotted Cass only a half block behind me. His gun was still out as he drove one-handed, but from what I could see, he was still in one piece. Shit, the last thing he needed was more bullet holes less than two weeks after I'd shot him myself.

Dammit, that stubborn fool wasn't wearing his sling anymore. I should have known he'd ditch it the second he was out of my sight. But I could also understand why. Never let enemies see you're hurt.

I kept glancing back at him, though, worried that he'd done some damage. So I almost didn't notice when someone casually strolled out into the street ahead. Luckily, my reflexes were sharper than Japanese steel after the SUV attack, and I slowed to a stop just a couple of feet away from the man.

His face remained neutral, totally unconcerned that I could have run him over. He just stood there with his feet shoulder-width apart, looking casual as all hell.

I tugged off my helmet and glared daggers. "I suppose that ambush was your doing?"

The model-handsome man met my gaze with his ice-blue eyes, tilting his head to the side like my question was too stupid to warrant a response.

"The Guild appreciates you having returned their property, Hades," he said in a low, calm voice. Cass had pulled up a few yards behind me, hanging back and keeping his disguise in place but there as backup if I needed him.

I grunted, assuming he meant the gun stash. "Nice of the Guild to let us know they'd be stopping by." Sarcasm edged my voice, and

I mentally slapped myself for losing my cool. "What's this charade for, Leon?"

The Guild mercenary ran his eyes over me. It wasn't a sexual gaze; it was a calculating one. He was one of the mercs who'd come to Shadow Grove to assist Archer when his girl was being stalked, but I'd crossed paths with him before that. He mostly played the role of tech-geek, but I knew better. We monsters recognized one another.

"No charade, Hades. Just delivering a message from the Circle." His sharp, intelligent gaze shifted past me to Cass, his eyes narrowing slightly as he visually inspected my backup.

I swallowed, steeling my spine. "The fuck does the Circle want in Shadow Grove?"

The Circle...the governing body of the Guild, made up of nine scary-ass motherfuckers. The Guild said they didn't recruit psychopaths or serial killers, but that was only because they were *owned* by the worst kind of nightmares in the world. It took a real sick fuck to run an organization like the mercenary guild, after all.

"Nothing," Leon replied, clasping his tattooed hands in front of him. For all appearances, he looked totally unarmed. I knew better. "That's what I came to tell you. The Circle has investigated Jack Wildeboer's death and declared it from natural causes. We have no further interest in Shadow Grove...*unless* you keep trying to hack our servers. Then? Well, then we have a problem, Hades."

Shit. They knew we'd been digging. Did they know why?

"Tell Lucas to stop fucking looking," Leon continued, his jaw twitching with anger. "Take this as a professional courtesy warning. Stop drawing attention, or my next visit will be considerably less polite."

I jerked a nod, quietly horrified that Leon even knew Lucas's name. The casual way he used it, too, sent a chill of understanding through me. He'd been watching us longer than I'd known.

Leon stared at me for an extended, tense moment like he was

weighing whether I was taking his warning seriously or not. Then he inclined his head in a small nod and shifted his eyes back over my shoulder.

"De Rosa. I'm going to assume I have some bodies to clean up." Leon didn't look even slightly upset by this prospect, like it was just a normal Tuesday night. Like I'd said, Leon was far from the chilled-out hacker he liked to play on jobs.

Cass said nothing, not betraying his disguise, and Leon didn't seem to require an answer. The mercenary just touched his fingers to his forehead in a mocking salute to me, then strolled back into the shadows at the side of the street.

I didn't go after him, knowing full damn well he'd have disappeared already. Those upper-level Guild bastards were slippery as shit.

Taking a second to calm my racing pulse, I glanced over my shoulder to Cass. Then I pulled my helmet back on and started my bike once more. Suddenly, I wasn't so interested in being out on the streets. I just wanted to get home…to debrief with Cass, Zed, and Lucas.

Cass followed close as we returned to Zed's fortress at almost double the speed limit the entire way, but no words were exchanged until we got safely back into the garage.

I pulled my helmet off, hooked it over the handlebars of the Ducati, then strode over to Cass. He'd just taken his own helmet off and knew exactly what I was doing when I unzipped his borrowed jacket and pushed it off his shoulders.

"I'm fine, Red," he told me in a gruff voice. "Not even a scratch on me."

I released my breath. "Good. How's your shoulder?"

"Stiff, but fine." His response was clipped, his fingers dragging my own zipper open. "What did that bastard mean about the Circle?"

I wrinkled my nose. "The Circle. They run the Guild, and I'd seriously rather not be on their radar. The fact that he ambushed us so easily—"

"I swear to you, Red, that wasn't a setup." Cass's growl was low and threaded with concern, his eyes blazing as he met my gaze.

I frowned. "That never even crossed my mind, Saint. I trust you. Those fuckers are good enough that he could have had my bike chipped or had eyes on the gate or anything." I rose up on my toes and pressed a kiss to his lips. "We're in this together, Grumpy Cat. You're way past the point of suspicion."

His strong arms banded around my waist, pulling me in to his body as his lips closed over mine in a hard, domineering kiss that left me shaking and flushed with heat.

"Good," he muttered when he released me. "I have to get back."

I let my lips tug down in a small pout, and my hands went to the waistband of his borrowed pants. "Right now?"

He let out a small groan as I flipped his button fly open and slipped my hand inside, cupping his dick. "I could spare a couple more minutes."

I grinned at my victory. "Good choice, Saint."

He gave a throaty laugh as I sank to my knees and tugged his pants down enough to free his rapidly thickening erection. "Like there was ever a choice, Angel." His fingers tangled in my hair, controlling my head in a way that flooded my panties. "Now show me that pretty tongue."

CHAPTER 17

Lucas handed me a coffee the moment I walked into the kitchen the next morning. He kissed me long and hard as I took the coffee from his hand, and I melted into his touch. Fucking hell, he knew how to kiss.

"Good morning, babe," he murmured after taking his time with my lips. "You still look half-asleep." He combed his fingers through my messy hair and peered into my eyes with a small, concerned frown.

I gave him a smile back. "I am. Thank you for the coffee." I rose up on my toes and smacked another kiss on his lips, then followed my nose over to the stove where Zed was cooking.

He was wearing nothing but a pair of sweatpants under his apron, the flimsy strings tied around his bare waist like a tease, and I bit the inside of my cheek to keep myself from drooling.

"Hey, you," he murmured when I stopped beside him. On a whim, I wrapped my arm around his waist in a half hug and leaned in to his side. He didn't even hesitate a second in swapping his spatula to the other hand and hugging me back. "Did you have a good night?"

Clearly he knew what I'd been up to all night, so I just gave a small nod, inhaling the delicious aromas of parmesan and chives from the scrambled eggs he was cooking. "Interesting night, that's for sure."

I reluctantly peeled myself away from him as he moved the frying pan off the heat and scraped the cooked eggs out onto the three waiting plates.

"How's Grumpy Cat doing with his mission?" Zed arched a brow at me, and I couldn't fight my answering smile. Of fucking course he knew Cass had snuck into his house last night. Nothing got past Zayden De Rosa.

I gave a small shrug. "We didn't discuss it, but I'm sure he'd tell me if it wasn't going well."

Lucas placed some freshly buttered Turkish toast on the plates with our eggs, like he and Zed had been working together in harmony to get our breakfast ready. *I wonder what else they could work together on…*

Clearing my throat, I pushed thoughts of threesomes aside and took my coffee over to the dining table, which was already set with cutlery and orange juice. I could definitely get used to living with these two, that was for sure.

"Something else happened last night, though," I told them both. Sitting, I took a sip of my coffee.

Zed grimaced. "I don't think we need the details."

I shot him a hard glare, quietly making a mental note that Zed was more than likely never going to be okay sharing. He was too jealous and possessive. It was something I'd need to seriously think about if we ever did take things further.

"Not what I meant," I replied with an edge of irritation. "Cass and I had a run-in with Leon."

Zed's brows shot up, his forkful of food frozen halfway to his mouth. "Leon from the mercenary guild?"

I nodded. "The same. He came to tell us to quit trying to access the Guild servers. Specifically mentioned that Lucas needs to stop searching for answers." I gave my Gumdrop a soft look, and he let out a frustrated groan.

"Shit, guys," he muttered. "I'm sorry. I wanted to educate myself, so I did some Googling…" He let his voice trail off with a wince. "I didn't think it would be that bad. I didn't hack anything."

I gave him a small headshake and a smile. "The hacking was probably us. Or Dallas. But maybe just lay off on the Google searches for the time being. They definitely track those things, and the last thing we need is for them to show up and try to recruit you."

Lucas just gave an easy laugh and shook his head. "They wouldn't have much luck with me. I'd just tell them no."

Zed and I exchanged a look, knowing full well the Guild wasn't always polite or professional when recruiting new members. I had to hope that Leon had been telling the truth when he said they were done in Shadow Grove.

"Well, anyway," I continued, smoothing past the subject of Lucas being recruited, "whatever database we touched gained the attention of the Circle."

Zed almost choked on his food. "Um, what?"

I nodded, agreeing with that sentiment. "Yeah. So just tell Dallas to be a shitload more careful. He's good, but Leon's better. Dallas needs to cover his ass, or he'll catch a bullet to the brain."

Zed grimaced. "Understood. I'll speak with him this morning."

We ate our breakfast in silence for a few moments, and Zed stretched out his legs under the table, letting his ankle rest against mine. I looked up at him from my food, and he met my gaze with an unreadable expression. Fucker just had to stay inside my head constantly. The message was clear, though. He was backing off, not giving up.

"Hey, I know we've got a bunch of other shit going on," Lucas said after a while, "but I wondered if it would be okay to move my mom home. Now that the guns are all gone…" He gave a shrug.

"I just think she might be more willing to talk when she's not in Sunshine Estate. Like, maybe she's worried there's someone listening or something."

I placed my almost empty coffee mug down and yawned heavily. "I agree. I spoke with Rio yesterday, and he's doing a thorough sweep of the house today to check if the Guild left anything behind. But if it's all clear, there's no reason why she can't go home." I paused then, looking to Zed for solidarity on the next point I needed to raise. He gave me a slight nod, holding his coffee mug to his lips.

Lucas didn't miss the exchange, either. He narrowed his eyes at both of us and frowned. "Why do I feel like there's something more?"

I sighed and raked my fingers through my hair. "I've organized a live-in nurse to stay with Sandra when she gets home. Considering how much she's deteriorated in the last few weeks and the unknown element with her memory and confusion, her doctor at Sunshine recommended there be someone around-the-clock for assistance."

Lucas looked slightly taken aback and gave me a confused look. "Oh. I mean, yeah, that makes sense. I just figured…"

"You figured it'd be you," I murmured when his voice trailed off. "I think…" I let my own voice trail off myself because, shit, how did I tell him what needed to be said without sounding like a controlling bitch?

"We think it's best for you to stay here a while longer," Zed finished for me, his tone clipped and unemotional. No arguments. "You're still on Chase's radar, and if you get hurt again, Hades will scorch the earth in retaliation."

I snorted a laugh and rolled my eyes. "Drama queen. But, uh, yeah. Pretty much. Is that okay, Lucas?"

He frowned at me, not appreciating Zed's weak attempt at humor. "I understand where you're coming from, but don't you think we could have discussed this?"

I parted my lips to respond, but I had no excuses. He was right. It *should* have been a conversation, and yet I'd just gone ahead and done it all without ever asking what he wanted to do.

Zed cleared his throat and pushed back from the table. "I'm just going to..." He picked up the empty plates and carried them back to the kitchen as he muttered, "Not be here for this part."

"Shit," I breathed, giving Lucas a sheepish look. "I'm sorry. You're entirely right. I should have asked what you wanted to do."

His frown softened slightly. "Come here, Hayden." He indicated for me to come around the table to where he sat, and I did as instructed. When I got within reach, he pulled me into his lap and cupped my face between his hands. "I get it. You do shit without asking anyone's permission because that's what you've always done."

I bit the edge of my lip, embarrassed. The fact that he was right didn't make me any less of an asshole for totally ignoring his opinion or permission.

"It's fine," he told me, holding my gaze with a hard look. "But next time you go making decisions that directly impact *me*, I expect you to at least *mention* it. Clear?"

I nodded as much as possible with his hands on my face. "I *am* sorry. This whole...caring-for-other-people thing is new to me. It's always just been me and Zed. And Seph."

Lucas arched a brow. "I bet you do shit without consulting her too, huh?"

I groaned because he knew he was right. I never *once* asked Seph if she was okay with all the safety measures I put in place around her. But how could I? She had no idea *where* the danger lay, so how could she effectively protect herself? Again, that was on me for not informing her, but it was a choice I was sticking firm on.

Lucas pulled my face to his, kissing me softly. "I love you, Hayden," he whispered, "but I'm not one of your Wolves. Treat me like an equal, or we're going to have problems."

This time when he kissed me, it was forceful and dominating, his fingers digging into my skin a whole lot harder than usual—like my Gumdrop was finding his alpha-ness. Shit. Just what I needed, another big-dicked, alpha asshole.

His hands left my face, shifting my position in his lap to straddle his waist, and his cock swelled underneath me. I quickly amended that mental commentary to *huge*-dicked alpha asshole. Apparently, I had a type.

My hips rolled, grinding into him with need, and he bit my lip as if warning me that he was in control this time, not me. Shit, that was hot.

He slipped a hand under the waistband of my sweatpants and found my slick cunt in an instant. A small cry left my lips as he slid his fingers inside, fucking me with his hand as I writhed in his lap. His mouth held mine captive, though, his tongue controlling our kiss in a way that set my whole body alight.

His skillful fingers worked me into a frenzy until I was shaking and panting, and then he withdrew. I groaned in protest—I was *so fucking close*—but he just grasped my waist and lifted me out of his lap.

"Sorry, babe," he told me with a heated stare. "Consider that your punishment for treating me as anything less than your equal." He stood up, not even remotely trying to hide how hard he was. Then he brought his fingers to his lips and licked them, one at a time, while holding my gaze.

"Lucas—" I breathed, shocked and *beyond* turned on by him testing limits with me.

He ran his tongue over his kiss-swollen lower lip and gave me a solid eye-fucking. "I'll finish you off later." And with that, he left the room.

I stared after him, my lips ajar in stunned disbelief and my pussy throbbing in protest. Then I became aware of Zed watching, and my gaze flicked across to him as I wondered how much he'd seen.

He gave nothing away, though, just looked me over in a hungry way before snapping back to business Zed. "We should probably head over to Anarchy," he told me, his voice touched with a rough edge. "The marketing team wants to discuss the next main-event fight."

I swallowed heavily and nodded. It was all I was capable of. Silently, I made my way back upstairs to the bedroom I'd claimed as my own and transformed myself into Hades, boss bitch. But internally, I was a mass of butterflies. How in the *hell* had all three of my love interests suddenly grown balls big enough to rival my own?

CHAPTER 18

The meetings at Anarchy ran smoothly, which was a nice change. The marketing team had put together their top choices for the next matchups, based not only on the contestants' fighting abilities but also their marketability. They, like my Timberwolves, had sensed there was trouble brewing and had stepped up to work on Copper Wolf's success. I appreciated the hell out of that, so gave them full approval to run with their matchups.

Lucas was at Sunshine Estate getting his mom ready to move home, and we'd left one of our trusted Timberwolves with him for security while Zed and I handled work. So no one was around to buffer the conversation when the marketing team left and Zed pinned me with a hot stare.

"So, little Gumdrop wants to be an equal, huh?" Zed all but purred that question with an amused smile pulling at his lips. We were on the low velvet couches of the Fun Zone VIP bar, where we always held Anarchy meetings, but we were all alone.

I rolled my eyes. "Of course you were eavesdropping."

He shrugged, unapologetic. "It's my house."

I blew out a long breath, propping the ball of my high-heeled shoe on the edge of the low table as I glared at him. "He's not wrong. I'm so used to just *doing* things without asking anyone's permission."

Zed was directly opposite me, his arm draped along the back of the couch and his expression guarded. "Because that's your job. That's what gets shit done and keeps people alive. Lucas needs to understand that... And as much as he might *want* to be an equal—"

"I know." I cut him off. "But he's learning. It won't be long before he's giving you a run for your money." I meant it as a casual taunt over Zed's marksmanship and Lucas's seemingly natural talent with guns. But the second it left my lips, my mouth went dry.

Zed just snorted a laugh and shook his head, seeming to let me off the hook. This time. He stood up and extended a hand to me, which I took. Then he pulled me a whole hell of a lot closer than I'd anticipated, his face dipping down until his lips brushed my ear.

"No matter how ballsy the Gumdrop gets, he'll never be a real threat. Nothing can ever match what we have, Dare. You damn well know it." He punctuated that statement with a scorching kiss to my neck. Then he stepped away again as Alexi came striding up the stairs with a deep furrow on his brow.

"Boss," my head of security greeted, then gave a nod to Zed as well. "I've got Gen downstairs to see you, but you didn't mention having another meeting?" He asked it like a question, his expression worried. Then his gaze flicked down to where Zed still held my hand captive, and Alexi's brow tightened.

"Gen's fine," I told him, ignoring the testosterone rolling off them both all of a sudden. "Send her up. And can you also get us some water?"

Alexi jerked a nod and stalked back downstairs to do as I'd asked. Zed just turned to me with a small smirk on his lips and a knowing look in his eyes.

"Feeling thirsty all of a sudden, huh?"

I rolled my eyes and tugged my hand free of his. "Shut up,

asshole." But I said it with a smile and didn't protest when he sat down beside me as Gen joined us.

"Hey, guys," she greeted with a tight smile. Alexi followed not far behind her and placed a tray of glasses and a pitcher of water down on the table for us. Gen sat on the couch opposite Zed and me and gave Alexi a shy smile when he poured her water.

"What's happened, Gen?" I asked when Alexi was gone. There was no *good* reason why my new legal counsel would stop by for an in-person meeting without calling first.

She grimaced, confirming my suspicion. "Your license applications for Timber have all been rejected by Cloudcroft City Council. Too many objections from neighbors."

Fury swept through me, but I kept it contained through years of practice. Externally, I just gave a small nod of understanding. "I see. And those neighbors?"

Gen wrinkled her nose. "All buildings owned by Locked Heart."

A small, livid breath hissed from between my teeth, and my jaw tightened to the point of painful.

"I'm working on it, though," she assured me. "But if you have any, you know, less conventional ideas? That might be quicker. I know you want to open Timber in October, but without liquor or gaming licenses…"

"Understood," I snapped. Without those licenses I'd be asking for trouble with the Cloudcroft PD, and if Chase had been buying up property, there was a solid chance he'd also been buying up law enforcement.

Zed shifted beside me, clearing his throat as he draped his arm along the back of the couch. It was the same pose he'd been sitting in earlier, except this time his arm was draped over my shoulders and his fingers brushed my exposed upper arm, thanks to the sleeveless top I wore.

"Anything else we need to know, Gen?" he asked, calm as anything.

She shook her head, her whole posture tight like she expected me to bite her head off for delivering this less-than-exciting news. "No, sir. Sirs. That's it. I was driving past and saw your Ferrari here. Figured it was quicker to tell you in person."

I simmered with something uncomfortably close to jealousy. Or possessiveness. She'd seen *Zed's* car. She'd come to tell *Zed* in person. I didn't enjoy feeling like that toward Gen because she had earned my professional respect already. And that was rare.

"We appreciate it," I told her in a carefully cool voice. "We'll get it dealt with."

Her gaze flicked between Zed and me, then she jerked a nod and made her exit. Smart woman; she knew she'd been dismissed.

When we were alone again, I breathed out a long, angry sigh. "Fucking Chase."

Zed hummed a sound of agreement, his fingers still idly stroking my arm. "Wanna go shoot some shit to blow off steam?"

I snorted a laugh. "Yes. I'd rather shoot some*one*, but sadly, no one has challenged my authority lately."

Zed arched a lopsided smile. "I think you scared them all straight when you killed Cass."

Speaking of my Grumpy Cat, I pulled my phone from my bag and checked to see if he'd messaged me. He hadn't, but I did have a series of missed calls from Special Agent Dorothy Hanson.

I showed Zed, then hit redial on her latest missed call if for no other reason than to satisfy my own curiosity. I'd made it pretty damn clear that I wouldn't help her find her nephew's body, so what was she calling about now?

"Ms. Wolff," the FBI agent answered, sounding all business. "We need to speak in a professional capacity. Would you like me to come to you?"

Surprise and intrigue rippled through me. "That depends, Dorothy. Will another of my venues explode if I agree to meet you again?"

There was a strained silence, broken only by the echoing click of her shoes on a floor. Then she grunted an irritated sound. "I guess I can't make any guarantees. You've got a lot of enemies, Ms. Wolff."

Surprised, I felt a small laugh escape my throat. "Fair call, Dorothy. I have to head over to Club 22 for an appointment. I can meet you there in two hours when I'm done."

I ended the call, then turned to look at Zed.

He just stared back at me like he was thinking, then tilted his head to the side. "What appointment do you have at 22?"

I couldn't stop the smirk creeping over my lips. "Maxine is meeting me to go over her dance routine again." His brows shot right up, and I gave a laugh as I pushed up from the couch. "I don't renege on my deals, Zeddy Bear. A bet's a bet."

He scrubbed a hand over his face and gave a pained groan before standing up as well. "I'll drive you."

I swallowed my smug laughter, not even slightly surprised at the offer. But if he thought he was going to sit in and watch me fumble through Club 22's sexiest *and* most athletic striptease, he was sorely mistaken. My rehearsals with Maxine were behind closed doors.

Hannah called me as we climbed into Zed's car, and I put her on speakerphone as she ran through my schedule for the rest of the week and gave me quick but detailed updates on the other initiatives she'd taken. I'd never had my own assistant before, so she'd identified jobs I didn't even know needed doing. All in all, I was impressed.

"I like her," Zed commented after I ended the call.

I clucked my tongue in irritation before I could catch myself, and Zed let out a low laugh. "Not like that, Dare. Fuck, you're quick to think the worst of me."

I rolled my eyes, shifting my gaze to look out the window. "Can you blame me?" After all, he was notorious for sleeping his way around our female employees. Not that I'd been a freaking nun, but I didn't bang our staff and make a whole thing about it.

Zed didn't respond to that comment for an extended moment, then let out a long breath. "Fair call. But that's not what I meant about Hannah. I just think she's a good addition to Team Hades, you know? Her background fully checks out too. No skeletons, other than her shitty ex-boyfriend, but Cass handled that one pretty well already."

I gave a grim smile, remembering how Cass had beat the ever-loving snot out of Johnny Rock and then broken his arm as a message from Hannah. Served him fucking right for laying hands on a sweet girl like her.

CHAPTER 19

My rehearsal with Maxine was grueling at best. I'd never felt as uncoordinated and unsexy as I did while attempting to emulate her lithe grace and seductiveness. There was a reason I owned the clubs and didn't dance in them.

Maxine, to her credit, had managed not to make fun of me too hard. There was more than a healthy dose of amusement in her eyes every time I fell off the pole, though.

"This is a disaster," I groaned, rubbing my head after falling out of an inverted spin and smacking my forehead on the stage. I'd kicked Zed and Rodney out when Maxine had arrived, so thankfully, we didn't have an audience. The same couldn't be said for Friday night when I'd be fulfilling my end of the stupid shooting bet I'd made with Zed.

Maxine bit back a smile as she offered me a hand up. She wore staggeringly tall heels and didn't even wobble in the slightest as she pulled me up. I had to hand it to her, she was impressively strong.

"It's not as bad as you think," she told me as I stretched my aching limbs out. "You're actually picking it up really fast. But... if it's okay, Boss, I might make some tweaks to remove those few moves that you're stuck on."

A small wave of relief rushed over me, and I nodded. "More than okay. The last thing I need is to publicly humiliate myself right now." I winced, touching that sore spot on my head again.

Maxine grinned. "I'll get you some ice. I should probably go now anyway. I have class in half an hour." She sashayed across to the bar like those seven-inch stripper heels were nothing but an extension of her long legs and filled a cloth with ice for me.

"What class have you got?" I asked when she returned and handed over the ice. I sat on the edge of the stage and unstrapped the acrylic heels she'd loaned me to dance in. She insisted shoes changed the way a stripper moved, for the better, and I had to admit she was right. They added an extra sway to each movement. Sexy as hell, on her.

She sat down beside me, taking her own shoes off. "I'm doing online classes with SGU, working toward my doctorate in phys-iotherapy," she told me with a proud smile. "I'm fascinated with muscle structure and how to ease pain for athletes and dancers."

A loud knock on the front door interrupted us before I could ask her anything else—or even question why I was suddenly feeling compelled to get to know my staff on a personal level.

"You done in here?" Zed called out through the cracked door. "Agent Hanson just pulled into the parking lot."

I stifled a groan. "Yes, we're done, you can come in."

He pushed the door open further and sauntered in with a curious expression on his face. His sharp eyes ran down my body, taking his damn time checking out the skimpy outfit Maxine had me wearing for practice. She said I needed skin to grip the pole properly, and she wasn't wrong.

"Hey, Zed," my tutor greeted him, and his gaze shifted to her briefly before coming back to me.

"Max," he replied, with an edge of…something. Warning? Oh, for *fuck's* sake.

She cleared her throat and quickly gathered up her things,

stuffing them all into her bag as she moved. "I should run. See you on Thursday, sir?"

I nodded. "Yep, Thursday. Thanks, Maxine."

She all but ran out of the bar, and I glared daggers at Zed. "You fucked Maxine, didn't you?"

His lips curled in a lopsided smile as he came closer to where I still sat on the edge of the stage. "Ages ago," he replied with a shrug. "You jealous?"

I narrowed my gaze. "Just surprised. You never really hide your conquests, and I had no idea about—" I cut myself off, understanding clicking in my brain. "You didn't fuck. You *dated*." Because the only time Zed was ever circumspect about his love life was when it was more than just fucking.

He cocked a brow, laying his hands on my bare thighs and standing in the gap between them. "Again, are you *jealous*, Hades? Max and I were over a long time ago."

"Don't call me that," I whispered before I could catch the thought and keep it inside.

Zed tilted his head, the warmth of his hands on my thighs all kinds of distracting. "Hades?"

I gave a short nod as I licked my lips, not trusting my voice. But shit, it just hit differently now. Now that he'd reverted to calling me Dare, I didn't want to backslide. No one close to me actually used the name *Hades* anymore.

Zed didn't push the issue or make a big deal out of it. He just brushed his knuckle over my cheek in the softest of gestures. "Go shower and change, Dare," he told me in a gentle voice. "I'll entertain Agent Hanson until you're done."

I bit the inside of my cheek hard enough to make it bleed, but instead of kissing him like I wanted to, I climbed to my feet and headed out to the dancers' showers. Zed had made his position clear, and I needed to respect that. He wanted me to kiss him and be fully present in the moment *with him*, and I just wasn't sure I could do that yet. I'd a thousand times over rather torture myself than hurt him again.

Still, all throughout my shower I kept hoping, *wishing* his control would snap and he'd join me. Vivid fantasies of Zed nailing me against the shower wall played out across my mind, and I had to finish my shower on ice-cold.

It took me a whole lot longer to get dressed than was polite, but at the end of the day, I still held the upper hand. Whatever Agent Hanson wanted to discuss, *she* needed *my* help, or this wouldn't be a polite meeting on my turf.

Lucas had called earlier to tell me he wanted to stay with his mom tonight, and while I wasn't *thrilled* about him being in danger, I also had to respect his wishes. So I took an extra couple of minutes to check in with Alexi and ensure Lucas's house was under heavy protection in case Chase tried to take another swipe at my Gumdrop. When I received confirmation back that the team was in place, I let a small bit of tension ease and headed back out to the main club.

"Dorothy," I called out as I strode across the dance floor to where Zed had seated her in a small booth. "Nice to see you again so soon."

She gave me a tight smile but didn't offer her hand for me to shake.

"Agent Hanson, now that Hades is present, why don't you tell us what this is about," Zed suggested smoothly, informing me that she'd been unwilling to fill him in without me. Curious.

The fed cleared her throat and linked her hands on the table in front of her. "Yes, I'll make this quick. I'm here to make inquiries about a young woman named Maryanne Green."

The name meant nothing to me, but I could tell Zed knew something, based on the way his spine straightened slightly.

"I don't believe I know Maryanne Green," I replied to the agent honestly. "I'm not sure how I can be of any help."

149

Agent Hanson gave a short sigh. "She also used the alias Mercedes Glitter. I understand she was an employee at your club 7th Circle."

That name seemed a whole lot more familiar. Mercedes was one of our back-of-house employees—a high-class prostitute. Officially, she was employed as a cocktail waitress, though.

"Yes, I know Mercedes," I confirmed, "but I haven't seen her since 7th Circle blew up." I looked to Zed in question, knowing he had been working on reassigning all our staff to other clubs so none of them were left unemployed. Sex workers or not, they still had bills to pay like any other working adult in society. It wasn't their fault my psychotic ex had blown up their place of business.

Agent Hanson grimaced. "No, I suspect not. Her body was found in her apartment this morning by a neighbor who was investigating the smell. Looks like she was killed at least a week ago."

I flicked a quick glance at Zed and registered the confusion in his eyes before refocusing on Agent Hanson. "That's awful," I said with sincerity. "I'm going to assume it's foul play or you wouldn't be here. Actually, why *are* you here? Shouldn't this be SGPD's jurisdiction?"

Dorothy gave a slight nod. "It would be, if the manner of death didn't echo the way some girls were recently killed in three other states. And there's the fact that she was an employee of a known gang organization."

I met her accusing glare without even the slightest hesitation. If she honestly thought I couldn't look her dead in the eye as I lied, she'd severely underestimated me.

"I think you're mistaken, Agent Hanson," I said in a cool tone. "Copper Wolf Enterprises is a legal business, paying taxes and adhering to all industry standards for hospitality venues. If you're thinking of the Tri-State Timberwolves, I think you'll find they were wiped out some five years ago."

Her eyes narrowed. "Sure they were, *Ms. Wolff.*" The sarcasm was heavy, and I almost laughed. Almost. "Look, I just came to ask if you know of any altercations she might have had while she was under your employment. Any overly aggressive customers or maybe a lover?"

"Nothing I can think of right now," I replied truthfully, "but I can have Alexi, my head of security, look back through our logbook and check for any incidents involving Mercedes."

Agent Hanson gave a small nod. "I'd appreciate that. You have my number if you find anything."

She got up to leave, but I clucked my tongue thoughtfully. "I get the feeling you didn't expect to actually get anything from this conversation, Dorothy. Care to tell me why you really came here today?"

The sneaky bitch just shot me a knowing smile. "Not really. You have a nice day, Ms. Wolff. Mr. De Rosa."

She exited the club, and I swiveled my gaze to pin Zed to his seat. "Start talking, Zayden. What do you know?"

He groaned and scrubbed a hand over his face. "Mercedes and I were...friendly."

My stomach twisted with anger and jealousy *again*, and I had to swallow the curses that threatened to spew out at him. "Of course you were," I muttered instead.

He let out a frustrated growl. "It wasn't recent. But she was a nice girl. She definitely didn't deserve to get murdered."

I gave a short, humorless laugh. Any normal person might have questioned if *anyone* deserved to be murdered. Zed and I knew better, though. Plenty of people deserved it, every damn day. It was just a shame those people weren't the ones dying.

My phone vibrated in my pocket, and I pulled it out to check who was calling. A slice of red-hot fear hit my chest when I saw the caller ID, and I hurried to answer.

"What's wrong?" I asked, biting the edge of my thumbnail.

"I'm fine," Cass replied, reassuring me, "just wanted to hear your voice, Red."

My breath rushed out, taking the panic along with it and leaving me with a slight tremble in my limbs. "You fucker," I whispered. "I thought something had gone wrong."

Zed knew who I was talking to and remained silent. He shifted his position to let his thigh rest against mine, though, offering support as always.

"Nah," Cass replied with a yawn. "I was just thinking about last night, about the way you looked on your knees with my dick in your mouth... Made me wanna call you."

Warmth rushed to my face, and other places, and I became acutely aware of Zed's leg against mine.

"I'm just at Club 22 with Zed," I told Cass, silently begging him not to push this further. Not right now.

He gave a low, husky laugh on the other end of the phone line, catching the warning in my voice. "Fair enough, I should have waited to call later. But I was wondering if you could help me out on something."

"Anything," I murmured.

Zed shifted in his seat, his hand finding my knee. Goddamn it, he had some kind of sixth sense for knowing when I was turned on. It didn't help that Lucas had left me high and dry earlier, too.

"Can I get you to stop by Scruffy's tonight? I heard whispers that Roach is having some teething pains with his leadership. Might be good to remind the rats that he has Hades backing him." Cass sounded like he resented even having to ask, but he was right. What better way to pull the Reapers back in line than to remind them their leader had my approval?

"Of course," I replied. "Lucas is staying with his mom tonight, but Zed and I can go. Anyone in particular that needs to learn a lesson?"

Cass grunted an angry noise. "Yeah, little bitch calling himself Mad Dog. He's been stirring shit up about why they're locked out of the PCP market. Got a couple of the other young ones on his side too."

Anger simmered in my belly. Loads of Reapers—just like Timberwolves—were decent human beings making the best of a bad life. Some, like this *Mad Dog*, were not. "I'll take care of it," I promised him.

"You're an angel," he rumbled back, and that sound went straight to my pussy. Goddamn, I needed to relieve that pressure soon. *Fucking Lucas* was officially on my shit list.

Zed's fingers stroked the inside of my knee, and I shot him a warning glance. "Anything for *you*, Saint," I replied, holding Zed's gaze like a challenge. Fucking hell, what was wrong with me? I couldn't seem to stop taunting Zed, even though it was *my* damage and *my* hang-ups standing between us.

Cass gave another one of those husky laughs. "Text me when you get home tonight," he ordered.

Agreeing, I ended the call and arched a brow at Zed. "Looks like we're heading to Scruffy Murphy's tonight to pull some Reapers into line."

A wicked grin curled Zed's lips. "Sounds like fun. It's a date."

It definitely wasn't a date. It was *business*. So why didn't I correct him? Because I was a goddamn mess, that's why. I was a goddamn *head over heels in love with my best friend* mess. And ultimately, the idea of going on a *date* with Zed had my stomach all aflutter with excitement.

CHAPTER 20

"It's not a fucking date, you stupid twit," I muttered at myself in the mirror as I touched up my winged eyeliner. "It's fucking business. Not a date."

And yet that message seemed impossible to get through to the brainless butterflies causing havoc in my belly. Maybe just because I'd grown so used to having either Lucas or Cass around as a buffer between Zed and me? The times we were alone were clearly defined business situations, but checking in on the Reapers was blurring the lines. Scruffy Murphy's wasn't one of our clubs, and I had no real obligation to insert myself in Reaper politics. It was a favor to Cass, and now that Zed had put it in my head that it could be a *date*, I couldn't seem to shake it off.

I was so fucking pathetic. Whispering a few more curses at myself, I swiped on a coat of my favorite smudge-proof red lipstick, then called it done. I wore a tiny black dress that just barely covered my ass and showed off a whole lot of leg. Over the dress I wore my black leather gun holster and knife harness. They crisscrossed my chest and wrapped around my waist in a sexy-as-hell BDSM sort of way. Except functional, for holding my weapons.

My red-soled heels were tall—of course—and a thin strap wrapped around each of my ankles like little ankle cuffs.

I'd tied my hair up in a high ponytail, the softly curled length brushing my bare back, and I paused briefly before leaving my room to carefully slide a stiletto blade into my hair. One could never be too heavily armed when strolling into a potentially hostile environment. Not to mention Chase was still out there somewhere, and he'd undoubtedly be looking for revenge for those knockout drugs.

"Fuck me dead," Zed groaned when I left my room and found him leaning against the wall opposite, waiting for me. "You're actually trying to kill me now, aren't you? This isn't fair."

I couldn't help the wide smile that lit up my face at his reaction. I'd be lying if I claimed I hadn't dressed with Zed on my mind the whole time.

"I don't know what you're talking about," I lied. "This is my usual business attire."

Zed scoffed a laugh, his heated gaze running down the exposed length of my legs as he shook his head. "Bullshit," he accused in a whisper. "This is definitely a date now."

"Have you heard anything from Archer?" I asked, changing the subject as we headed downstairs. "Seph is still not responding to me. She currently hates me for murdering Cass."

Zed's hand rested on the small of my back as we made our way through to the garage, and it took all my strength not to spin around and pounce on him. I should have flicked my own bean in the shower to relieve some tension, but apparently I loved the torture.

"Maybe it's time you told Seph the truth," Zed suggested, not for the first time. "She's eighteen now, surely she's old enough to hear the whole story."

I snorted a bitter laugh. "You think Seph can keep a secret as important as Cass being alive? No. Sorry, just no. I'd rather have her hating me for something I didn't do than pander to her sense of importance and potentially get Cass killed for real."

Zed sighed, opening the passenger door to his Ferrari for me. His Audi was back in the garage, too, having come back from the body shop a day earlier. The scratch Chase had left was totally gone. "Yeah, fair point," he admitted. He closed my door for me, then circled around to his own side. "I still think she needs to know the rest, though. About Chase, certainly. Maybe if she understands the danger, she'll quit being a pain about all the protection."

I grimaced. He was right, and I knew it. But selfishly, I didn't *want* my little sister to know the truth. I hated the idea of admitting everything I'd gone through with Chase when I was a teenager. Telling her my whole sordid tale would mean admitting just how much I *let* him get away with, how much abuse I *let* him dish out, and all because I stupidly believed I loved him. Or, in the later days, because I was just too weak, too broken to resist. My own sense of self-preservation had been so low that I'd done nothing to save myself. It'd taken a threat to Seph's safety to finally make me act… and that was one of my deepest regrets.

I should have valued my own life higher. I *should* have done any number of things that might have meant Seph was never placed so close to danger. But I couldn't change the past. And reliving it for the sake of informing Seph? It gained us nothing.

"I know," Zed said with a sigh when I didn't reply. "Agree to disagree. Again." He shot me a quick look as he drove, and I mustered up a tight smile to show him I wasn't actually pissed at his persistence.

"You want me to fill you in on the Reaper bullshit?" I offered, getting comfortable in my seat. "Or leave it as a surprise?"

He gave a short laugh, shaking his head. "I love when you get ruthless, Dare. But you'd better fill me in so I don't shoot the wrong person in a misguided attempt to impress you."

I rolled my eyes, but a stupid grin creased my lips. Only Zed would think killing someone was the way into my heart—and my panties. Thing was, he was already well into my heart, and

I was starting to think my panties may not prove such a barrier after all.

Nonetheless, I gave him all the vague information Cass had offered over the phone and added my own thoughts around this Reaper rat talking smack about PCP. At some point while I was talking, Zed's hand found my knee, and my breath hitched. He fucking heard it, too, because a smug smile crossed his lips, and he kept his hand there for the rest of the drive to Scruffy Murphy's.

The security on the door recognized us instantly and hurried to usher us past the crowd lined up outside. It wasn't even the weekend, but Scruffy's often had popular bands playing and could be busy any night.

"Hades, sir," one of the tattoo-covered security guards inside the club greeted me. "Zed." He nodded to my second.

I gave him a cool look, trying to place his name and coming up blank. "Where's Roach?" I asked, giving up on trying to remember his name. It was something to do with snakes, I thought. But then maybe I was just guessing that because he had a huge snake tattoo around his neck and up his bald head.

"He's out back," the snake guy replied. "I'll show you the way."

"Unnecessary," Zed told him. "We know where it is."

The dude gulped and nodded, stepping out of the way. Zed followed me closely as I made my way through the packed bar, his hand on my back *again* in a touch that I was growing way too comfortable with. We knew that "out back" was the private room in the back of the bar where Reapers hung out, like a clubhouse. When Zane had been running the club, the whole place had been a shitty dive bar, not a fraction of the success it was now. The back room then had been full of gangsters sitting around drinking and doing drugs or fucking gang whores in full view of their friends. Typical male-run gang shit.

We passed down the corridor where the restrooms were located, and Zed leaned in close to murmur in my ear, "Oh look, a supply closet."

I snorted a laugh and shot him a clear shut-the-fuck-up look. Still, it was a supply closet that would forever hold fond memories for me. It was where I'd unknowingly taken Lucas's virginity.

When we reached the door at the end of the corridor, I didn't hesitate before pushing through it and strolling in like I owned the damn place. A quick glance around told me it had only marginally cleaned up since the last time I'd seen it. Then again, no one ever expected the Shadow Grove Reapers to be sitting around studying the Bible in their free time.

"Roach," I called out, spotting the new Reapers' leader at the pool table in the corner. He sank a ball, then glanced over to see who was calling him. When he spotted Zed and me, his eyes widened, and he slowly straightened back up.

Before he could say anything, though, a clearly intoxicated guy stumbled closer and gave my cleavage a long leer.

"Who's the new whore?" he slurred, licking his lips as he looked me up and down. The entire room went silent, but the drunk fuck didn't even notice. "She's *so* fucking hot. Tight little waist and shit. I bet I know what else is tight." He lurched forward, his hand extended toward my crotch.

He never made contact, though, as I grabbed his wrist with one hand and drove one of my daggers into his throat with the other. I didn't tolerate sexual assault, and I *sure as fuck* didn't tolerate disrespect in an environment like this one.

The stupid Reaper remained frozen, my knife in his throat right up to the hilt and blood beginning to pool around the entry point. I held him like that for a moment, then raised my foot and kicked him backward. My knife slid free with a sickening, wet pop, and blood spray arced across the dirty floor as the Reaper collapsed in a heap, choking and gurgling as he died.

Still, the whole room remained silent like no one wanted to draw my attention by moving or making a noise.

Zed handed me a dark-gray handkerchief from his pocket, and

I used it to calmly clean off my knife as best I could before sliding it back into its sheath.

"Roach, I understand you're new to this position, but I think you can guess my feelings toward disrespect in any form. No?" I tilted my head to the side as I eyed the new Reapers' leader. Fuck, he was young. I hoped to hell Cass knew what he was doing on this one.

He jerked a sharp nod, meeting my eyes in return and not flinching at the unrestrained violence he must have seen there. Good.

"My deepest apologies, Hades," he replied, casting a disgusted look at the dead man. "Mad Dog has been letting his addiction to our supply get out of hand. This was inevitable."

I arched a brow. "Mad Dog, huh?" That was convenient. I'd planned on killing him tonight anyway. "I imagine that concludes my reason for visiting you this evening."

Understanding flashed across Roach's face, and he gave a short nod. "Yes, sir. I imagine it does." Then he raised his voice as he addressed the still dead-silent room. "Does anyone *else* want to challenge my authority over the Shadow Grove Reapers? Maybe you need a reminder that I have the support of Hades and the Timberwolves."

Not a single one of the Reapers spoke. Smart little gangsters.

Zed gave a cold chuckle. "I think they got the message." He clapped Roach on the shoulder like they were old friends. "Don't hesitate to call if you need a hand with anything."

The violence in his eyes said exactly what kind of help he was offering, and I doubted anyone missed the implication.

Roach jerked a nod. "Understood. It was nice of you both to stop by."

I inclined my head in acknowledgment. "Macy will be in touch tomorrow." Because my help didn't come for free. Macy, my lovely, mild-mannered bookkeeper, would issue Roach an invoice. After all, we weren't friends, and all businesses needed to remain profitable. Even the illegal ones.

"I look forward to it," Roach responded without hesitation. His gaze was steady and confident, and he earned a small amount of my respect for not flinching. He was already doing a hell of a lot better than the previous Wraiths' leader. Fucking Skate had been like a skittish weasel.

Zed and I turned and left the clubhouse area like we were goddamn royalty, feeling the hostile eyes of the Reapers on us the whole damn way. I didn't blame them for hating me; it was understandable. But they also *feared* me, and that was the important part.

"Well, that went a whole lot quicker than anticipated," Zed murmured as we headed back toward the main club. "Feel like staying for a drink?"

I wrinkled my nose at the sweaty death-metal crowd. "Not here. We could go check out that new club over in Shadow Heights."

Zed peered at me with a brow raised in surprise. "Meow Lounge?"

I gave a casual shrug. "Sure, why not? Always good to check out the competition, right?" Because as rapidly as Copper Wolf was expanding, I still couldn't own *every* bar and club in the state. There would always be competition; it was up to us to keep up-to-date with what they were doing and where the customers were favoring. Right now, the Meow Lounge was getting a lot of hype for being so newly opened, and I was curious to see what they were doing differently.

Zed gave me a bemused smile, then brushed his hand over my back. "Seems like as good a reason as any," he murmured, "and you're definitely dressed for it."

I gave him a puzzled look as we made our way out of Scruffy Murphy's and headed back to his car. "Is there a dress code?" Not that it mattered; I'd go wherever the fuck I wanted and wear whatever the fuck I wanted. But I did like a good dress code. It was what I enforced at Club 22—with Gatsby-era costumes—so I was interested to know what Meow Lounge was asking of its patrons.

"Oh…" Zed chuckled. "You'll see."

CHAPTER 21

If the lineup of scantily dressed patrons decked out in leather and PVC wasn't a clear sign of what kind of "club" the Meow Lounge was, then the woman strapped down and being spit-roasted by two masked men on the main stage would clue me in.

My face must have registered a hell of a lot more shock than I intended because Zed smirked at me like a smug fuck and guided me toward the bar.

"Everything okay, Boss?" he asked in a teasing voice, leaning his elbow on the bar like he was right at home. He'd ditched his suit jacket in the car, and his black shirt was rolled up to the elbows, showing off his strong, tanned forearms. With his own guns still holstered, he fit right in. Shit, he was gorgeous.

Clearing my throat, I schooled my face calm before meeting his gaze. "Fine. Why?"

His smug-fuck grin said he knew *damn* well I'd had no clue the Meow Lounge was a sex club, but he was happy to play along. "No reason. Just thought I saw a hint of a blush here." He brushed a knuckle across my cheek, and I almost growled my irritation.

Zed just gave another throaty chuckle and turned his attention to the bartender. There were plenty of patrons, both singles and couples and more, who were just drinking and people-watching, so I doubted there was any requirement to *participate*. Not that I would, even if that was their rule. I had a reputation to uphold.

I let my gaze drift around the room as we waited for our drinks, taking in the various stations where enthusiastic patrons were "performing" for anyone who wanted to watch. It was hot as hell; I wasn't even going to pretend otherwise.

"See something you like, Boss?" Zed murmured in my ear, and I gave a sharp inhale. I hadn't even realized I'd fixated on watching one particular grouping until he said that, and I instantly looked away.

"You're enjoying this way too much, Zed," I muttered back, accepting the sugar-rimmed cocktail from his hand.

He just grinned and indicated I should walk with him over to a free table. Here in Shadow Heights, outside of the usual gang territory, we had a certain level of anonymity. The security knew who we were, so they'd quite deliberately ignored the amount of weaponry on full display for both of us. But the patrons largely had no clue. I quite liked not having so many people watching my every damn move. It was refreshing.

"So, I'm going to assume you've been here before?" I asked Zed with an arched brow as we sat down. The table was tiny, barely large enough for our two coupette glasses to sit side by side, and the seat was just one miniature velvet sofa. To avoid landing on the floor, I practically had to sit in Zed's lap. Oh, the hardships.

Zed was way too fucking amused for his own good; he was likely to catch my fist in his nuts soon. "Nah, I haven't actually. They only opened a month or so ago."

I gave a shrug. "So? This seems like your kind of place." I watched him from under my lashes as I sipped my cocktail, a sidecar.

"Because I'm such a deviant," he replied, his tone dry but still entertained as hell. "I've been a bit busy lately. Besides…there's only one woman I want to fuck, and *she* wasn't here."

Oh. Yeah, fair enough. That made sense.

Zed draped his arm around my waist, ever so casual, and took a sip of his own cocktail. "They make good drinks, I have to admit."

"Mm-hmm," I agreed. My attention had somehow returned to the same grouping that I'd been watching earlier, despite my attempts *not* to stare. When I caught myself, I huffed a frustrated sigh.

"It's okay to watch," Zed commented. His fingers were teasing the back of my bare arm, and that was only adding to my sexually frustrated state. This was, of course, a *terrible* idea, considering the tension radiating between us. But I was too stubborn to bail out of the club so quickly. That would be far too close to running scared, and that was something I would never do. Especially from Zed.

So instead, I relaxed my shoulders and leaned in to his side to get comfortable. "I know," I replied, sassy as fuck. "I was just taking notes."

That comment made Zed stiffen, and his eyes followed to where I'd been looking. It was a small area near the side of the room where a woman wearing nothing but some leather straps was being worshipped by three extremely well-hung men. At the same time. I wasn't even joking about taking notes; whether I wanted to or not, my mind was already jotting down ideas. Never say never.

Zed didn't respond to that comment; he just hummed a sound that could have been approval or disagreement and calmly sipped his drink before placing it back down on the table. I put mine down too, not totally sure I wouldn't spill it from how hyperalert I was to his touch.

Curious, and somewhat emboldened by our anonymity, I shifted to peer up at him. "You like to be watched, don't you?"

His brows lifted and he looked down at me with an edge of surprise. "I do." His tongue swiped across his lower lip, and I swallowed heavily. Damn, I wanted to kiss him. Did he know how turned-on I was?

"So," I continued, chasing my thought train, "do you also like to watch?"

A bemused smile touched his lips, and he shifted his grip to pull me closer as he dipped his face. His mouth was so close to my ear when he replied that his breath tickled my skin, making me shiver.

"Are you asking whether I *liked* watching you and Cass fucking in my garage before the fight," he murmured, "or watching you riding his dick after his funeral the other day?"

I gave a throaty laugh. "You didn't *just* watch that time." He didn't respond, clearly waiting for me to answer his question. "Yes, that's what I'm asking." My breath rushed out at that admission.

Zed's nose teased a line along my neck, and I needed to stifle a moan as his lips brushed a kiss across my skin. "Well then, yes. I watched it, loved it, replayed it again later with my dick in my hand and came harder than I have in fucking years."

Oh *fuck*. My pussy throbbed at that mental image, and I found myself clenching my thighs on reflex. I couldn't hide how my breathing had spiked, though, not with Zed still placing hot, open-mouth kisses against my neck.

"Zed," I whispered, hoarse with need. He heard me, though, and heard a hell of a lot more than just his name. He raised his face from my neck and caught my lips with his in a kiss that shattered my reservations like a hammer against fragile glass. I leaned into him as his tongue traced the line of my lips, coaxing them apart so his mouth could devour me in the sweetest way.

His hand moved to my thigh, sliding up the bare length from my knee and teasing at the short hem of my dress. I wasn't even worried about the fact that we were in public where anyone could see us. I just *so* badly wanted his hand under my skirt for him to finish what he'd started in my bedroom when I'd challenged him.

"Well, I have to say I didn't expect *this* kind of show tonight," a sickeningly familiar voice said, and a deep shudder of revulsion ran through me as I pulled out of Zed's embrace.

Outrage, disgust, and fury vied for dominance within me as I glared absolute, violent death at my ex-fiancé, who'd just dragged a chair over from another table and sat his ass down.

"Chase," I hissed. "What the *fuck* are you doing here?"

Zed radiated tension beside me, his fingers on my waist tight enough to leave bruises, but I wasn't complaining. "Oh, damn," he growled. "Looks like this club has a roach infestation."

Chase, smarmy fuck, just clucked his tongue and grinned. "Now, now, no need to be hostile. It's so rare to find you two alone these days, I couldn't resist the opportunity to catch up. Just like old times, eh Darling?" He shot me a lascivious wink that made me want to gag.

Then again... "Was that a wink or a blink?" I pondered aloud. "So hard to tell." There was no mistaking the venomous glare he responded with, though, and I snorted a laugh.

"Fuck off, Chase," Zed drawled, deliberately forcing a slouch into his posture, like Chase was beneath our concern. Like he was nothing more than an annoyance. "Dare and I were in the middle of something."

Chase ran his tongue over his teeth. "So I saw. Please, don't let me stop you. Continue." He waved a hand and sat back in his seat like he was settling in for a show. Deluded fucker.

Simmering with anger that he'd ruined what was turning out to be a pretty great night with Zed, I sat forward and picked up my cocktail to take a sip. It gave me a moment to gather my thoughts and formulate a quick plan.

"Fuck this," Zed spat out. "Let's go somewhere with a more discerning guest list, babe." He punctuated that suggestion with a slow and deliberate kiss to my shoulder, marking his territory as surely as if he'd pissed all over me. Luckily, this was one situation I didn't even remotely mind it. It infuriated Chase, and that made me smug as fuck.

"Actually," I replied, humming thoughtfully, "maybe Chase

has a point. We could just have a drink and talk out our differences like adults. After all, the three of us used to be closer than blood. Remember that, Chase?" I tipped my head to the side, forcing softness and sincerity into my eyes.

His single eye narrowed at me suspiciously, and his gaze darted to Zed, then back to me. A brittle smile creased his lips. "How could I forget? We were going to rule the world together." He snapped his fingers in the air, calling for one of the waitresses in a latex bodysuit. "Three Sazeracs, gorgeous," he demanded when the woman stopped to take his order.

She nodded and murmured acknowledgment, then leaned down to gather our almost empty glasses. As she bent over the table, though, Chase grabbed a rough handful of her breast, squeezing and twisting until she cried out in pain.

It took *every* inch of my willpower not to pull a gun and shoot him right then and there. The fury made my hands shake, and I needed to disguise the tremor by pulling my phone from my purse. Forcing myself to ignore the way Chase assaulted the waitress right in front of us, I swiped through my phone and checked messages.

He was taunting me, testing me. As badly as I abhorred sexual assault, it'd take more than that for me to show my hand. Not when I'd invested so damn much in my long game. My plan to deal with Chase wouldn't be so simple as splattering his brains all over the pretty floor of Meow Lounge. Nor would it be so quick and painless.

So I swallowed my disgust and kept my calm as he released her and left her to retrieve our drinks from the bar.

"I see some things haven't changed," Zed drawled. "You still can't get women willingly."

Chase barked a sharp laugh. "It's always more fun when they scream and fight back. Isn't that right, Darling? I can hear your sweet, terror-filled screams like it was just yesterday. Tell me, gorgeous, are you still afraid of the dark?"

I locked down my emotions tight, not allowing even a hint of my true reaction to crack through my expression. Chase wanted me to play his game, and he was shit out of luck.

"Nothing scares me anymore, Chase," I replied in a cool voice, meeting his hungry eye unflinchingly. "Nothing and no one."

He held my gaze for a long moment, a sick smile playing across his lips. "I don't think I believe that, Darling girl. You thought you were so untouchable once before, too. Remember? When really all you needed was the right motivation to *scream* for me. A bigger monster and blacker darkness." He gave a sexual groan, biting his lip as he reminisced.

I drew a steady breath, desperately clinging to my inner calm and drawing strength from Zed's solid warmth glued to my side. He was keeping quiet, letting me handle Chase, but he also made it abundantly clear that he was more than ready to jump in if I needed him to.

"Is that what you did to Maryanne Green?" I asked, taking a guess. "Made her scream while you got your rocks off, then killed her?"

Chase tilted his head to the side. "I don't believe I know anyone by that name. Then again, I don't tend to exchange names with my prey. None of them really matter, they're just warm-ups. Appetizers. Only the main course can really sate my hunger."

It wasn't hard to guess what the main course was. Or who.

I bit the inside of my lip, thinking. But my phone vibrated in my purse, breaking my concentration. I pulled it out and saw Lucas's name on the caller ID, so I shot Chase a tight smile. "Excuse me a moment," I murmured, sarcastically polite.

Without waiting for his response, I slipped out of Zed's embrace and took a couple of steps away from the table before answering the call.

"Hey, Lucas," I said, bringing the phone to my ear. I kept one eye on Zed and Chase, making sure they didn't kill each other, but otherwise I was focused on why Lucas was calling. "Is everything okay?"

"Hey, you," he replied, sounding relaxed. "Yes, totally fine. I just wanted to check in and let you know that your security team is doing exactly as instructed and guarding the place like we're holding the Hope Diamond here."

I wrinkled my nose at the accusation in his voice. "Better safe than sorry, right?"

He gave a sigh. "Hayden, you told me you were assigning *a* security guard. Not seven."

"Eight." I quickly moved on. "Look, I said I was assigning a security *team*. Or…that's what I meant. But better to be overprotected than under, right? No harm done?"

He huffed, but I could tell he wasn't *that* mad. Over at my table the waitress had returned with our drinks and Chase was manhandling her again. Poor girl. I needed to leave her a hell of a tip when we left.

"Haven't had anything suspicious happen here," Lucas was saying in my ear. "Chase is probably still trying to scrub that permanent marker off his face."

I snorted a laugh because of course Zed had shown Lucas the picture he'd taken. "Yeah, I wish," I replied. "He's here being a slimy creeper."

"Wait, *what?*" Lucas exclaimed. "Hayden—"

A burst of movement caught my attention, and I missed whatever Lucas was saying. Zed had just grabbed Chase by the throat and thrown him to the floor, making several people scream in fright.

"I've gotta go." I ended the call as Zed put the barrel of his gun against Chase's forehead.

As calmly as possible, I strode over and planted my hands on my hips as I peered down at Zed and Chase.

"Zed," I snapped, my voice like a whipcrack.

He didn't look up at me, but he also didn't pull the trigger. "This demented fuck just tried to drug your drink, Boss." He bit the words off like they were dipped in poison, and my blood ran cold. "Check his hand."

Giving Chase a cold glare, I put the ball of my shoe on his wrist and applied pressure until his fingers opened, revealing a roughly crushed pill in the middle of his palm.

He didn't look like he felt even slightly guilty, just grinned up at me. "Can't blame a guy for trying," he said, seeming unconcerned by Zed's knee on his chest, hand around his throat, or gun to his head. "Little payback for that stunt at the café yesterday. Besides, you used to *beg* me for a little angel dust in your cocktail."

Zed drew a deep breath, his grip tensing on the gun. He was a microsecond away from pulling that trigger.

"Careful, Zayden," Chase taunted. "You wouldn't want to test my insurance policies, would you? There're so very many people that you both care about these days. So very many lives that could be ruined with the right series of events."

My stomach knotted tightly, and cold sweat ran down my spine. As badly as I wanted to crush Chase under my heel, he was *still* three steps ahead of me. He wouldn't be forever, though. I just had to be patient.

"Zed," I barked again. "Put the gun away."

Several of the Meow Lounge security guards were hovering on the fringes of our little scene but clearly reluctant to become involved. They knew damn well I could handle it without their intervention, and I appreciated the restraint.

The same couldn't be said for my second. He didn't shoot Chase, but he did pistol-whip him with the butt of his gun.

"Let's go," I snapped to him, with my anger at his lack of self-control warring with my satisfaction at seeing Chase get smacked in the face.

Zed grunted an angry sound and climbed to his feet as he

put his gun away. Chase was out cold but wouldn't stay that way forever.

"Please accept my apologies for the disruption," I told the closest security guard.

He just nodded, clearly not knowing what the fuck to say back to that. Zed grabbed my hand and just barely restrained himself when he clearly wanted to drag me out of the club behind him. But I was no damsel in distress, and I sure as shit wasn't his arm candy.

I paused near the bar to pull a wad of cash from my purse and hand it to the girl Chase had assaulted. She was trembling near one of the other waitresses, tears rolling down her cheeks, and just gaped at the money in confusion. No amount of money could erase an unwanted touch from her skin, but fuck, at least she could pay for some good counseling if that's what would help. Or she could blow it on shoes and handbags. Therapy came in all shapes and sizes.

Zed and I didn't exchange another word as we headed outside, striding toward where we'd parked the Ferrari in a lot across the road. Before we reached the car, though, a solid weight slammed into Zed from behind, throwing him to the gravel and wrenching his hand out of mine.

"Come on, De Rosa," Chase taunted, straddling Zed's waist and pounding a hard fist into the side of his head. "That all you've got? You can't kill me, but I didn't think you were *that* much of a little bitch." *Smack*, another hard hit to Zed's face as my second scrambled to get his guard up.

"Seriously, Chase?" I snapped, bracing my heels on the gravel to hold my balance. "You're still relying on surprise to get your hits in? Pathetic."

My insult was enough to get his attention, allowing Zed to buck up underneath him and shove him off. Chase, for all his stereotypical villain grandeur, had clearly let his fighting skills slip. Zed turned the tables in a flash, pounding the crap out of my unhinged ex with a violence that made my breath catch.

I did nothing to get between them, just stood back and enjoyed the show for a minute as blood flew and clothing tore. Chase fought back as best he could, but Zed was *lethal*. He rained blows down on Chase's body, hitting him deliberately to make it *hurt*, and I took way too much pleasure out of the sound of Chase grunting in pain.

A flash of metal caught my eye a split second before Chase slashed Zed's side, making him shout and roll out of reach in an instant.

Fear trickled down my spine as Zed pressed his hand to his side and pulled it away coated in blood. He didn't look worried, only more determined, but I'd seen enough.

"Stop this," I ordered, getting between them before they could reengage. "Zed, get in the fucking car."

Chase, back on his feet as well, sneered in Zed's direction. "Better do what Darling says, De Rosa. That's a good dog."

I whipped a small knife out of my chest strap and threw it with lightning speed. The short blade hit its intended target, sinking deep into Chase's shoulder and making him grimace.

"Shut the fuck up, Chase," I snarled, then threw another warning glare at Zed. "Get in the damn car before I leave you here."

Zed's expression was pure venom, but he reluctantly did as he was told. He slid into the driver's side, the stubborn fuck, and slammed the door shut as I swung back around to face my nemesis.

"I may not be able to kill you *yet*," I told him with cold violence in my voice, stalking closer to where he swayed slightly on his feet. "But I have *zero* qualms about hurting you. Remember that senator's son you tortured for three days over my sixteenth birthday? The one your dad told you to *use your imagination* on?" I cocked my head to the side, waiting for him to find the memory in that fucked-up brain of his.

He gave a wicked smile. "How could I forget? Kid sobbed like a baby as we cut him up. It was a shame he died so quick."

I gagged internally when he said *we*. But I'd helped, hadn't I? Back then, I'd thought Chase was my entire fucking world. No matter how much he hurt me, I still did everything he asked of me.

Forcing aside the guilt, I gave Chase a cruel smile, the same sort of smile I'd seen his mother use a hundred times before I killed her. "What was his name again? Thomas something?"

Chase inclined his head. "Thomas Sanderson III. Little turd. Father was so angry when he realized we'd accidentally killed him."

I nodded. "That's right. Well. Remember how many *creative* ways you made him hurt?" I reached out and wrapped my hand around the hilt of my knife, which still protruded from his shoulder. "I promise you, Chasey-baby, I'll make that look like child's play if you push me." I wrenched my knife out, making sure to twist it brutally on the way.

Chase barely even made a sound, just grinned at me like I'd offered him flowers.

Unnerved, I decided not to push my luck any further and beat a quick retreat back to Zed's car. Zed said nothing as I slammed the door closed behind me. He just revved the engine and squealed out of the parking lot. We barely avoided flattening Chase's sorry, bleeding ass, too. More's the pity.

CHAPTER 22

My bloody fingers shook so badly that I could barely work my phone as Zed sped through the streets of Shadow Grove, but I still managed to send the message I was trying to sort out.

"Dare," Zed said after several minutes of silence.

"Not yet," I bit back. I was still too firmly gripped by my fear and anxiety and the looming, suffocating presence of my worst nightmares.

He puffed out a short sigh, his busted knuckles oozing as he gripped the steering wheel tighter. "Don't fucking shut me out," he growled, anger and frustration threaded through his voice. "We're in this *together*. Always have been, always will be."

A bitter laugh escaped my lips. "Sure didn't feel like we were in it together when Chase punished me for kissing you by forcing a near-lethal dose of PCP down my throat. I was pretty fucking alone the nights he waited until I was terrified of my own breathing, then let his father and uncles use me for *sport*." Panic clawed at my throat, making it hard to breathe, and I desperately tried to take calming breaths. These confessions weren't news to Zed, though. He'd seen Chase's dirty little tapes showcasing all that and more. Those recordings exposed the *worst* of his abuse, which he always executed in one revolting room of horrors.

Zed was about to pull over, I could sense it, so I gave him a hard glare with the last dregs of my strength. "Just fucking drive, Zed," I snarled. "I'll be fine in a minute."

He continued driving, but he was far from ready to let it go. Not this time.

"You're so far from *fine* it's sickening," he spat out, pressing his foot harder to the floor and making the scenery outside my window blur. Despite his tone, I knew it wasn't me he was disgusted with. It was himself for not knowing what was happening to me behind closed doors.

That, of all things, helped me claw my way back out of the years-old stale fear. I took a couple more calming breaths, and then inch by inch, I forced my body to stop *fucking* shaking.

Finally, I reached out and placed my hand over Zed's where it gripped the gearshift. "Just get us home," I whispered, all traces of my anger gone. "You need patching up."

His hand twisted under mine, linking our fingers together. He shot me a quick, worried look, then jerked a nod. He didn't say anything more, but the way he raised my hand to his lips and kissed my bloody knuckles told me we weren't even close to done on this topic.

The house was silent when we pulled back in. Cass was still gone and Lucas was at his mom's and somehow I was glad for the privacy. Zed and I... Fuck. We were a mess.

"Go and wash up," I ordered him in a quiet voice as we walked through the foyer. "I'll get the medical kit."

He nodded and silently headed up the stairs toward his bedroom, where he could clean up and get clean clothes.

I made my way to the kitchen, pausing on a stool long enough to unbuckle my shoes and kick them away. Then off went my gun holster and knife sheaths. I didn't need to be armed inside Zed's home—*our* home—and if I did, there were more weapons hidden around the house than I could count.

Inside the butler's pantry I pulled out the medium-sized first aid kit and snagged a bottle of whiskey from the bar. I got the feeling we'd need both.

Upstairs, Zed had left his bedroom door ajar and the lights off. But the sound of the shower running and the light pouring from the en suite doorway pointed me in the right direction. Sucking up my shredded courage, I pushed open the bathroom door and plonked my supplies down on the marble vanity.

"Probably not an amazing idea to shower with an open wound, idiot," I commented, opening the lid of the first aid kit but grimacing when I saw the state of my hands.

Zed's blurry form shifted in the fogged-up shower behind me, the motion in the mirror too hard to resist looking. "It's barely a scratch. I've had worse," he replied. "Besides, I wanted to wash his stink off my skin."

I sighed. "Can't argue with that." Pushing the medical kit aside, I thoroughly soaped up my hands in the sink and scrubbed all the blood off them. Between Chase and Mad Dog, it took some vigorous scrubbing to get them properly clean. Next I grabbed a washcloth and wiped the splatters from my arm and forehead. What a mess.

The shower shut off, and my breath stilled in my chest.

"Hand me that towel?" Zed asked, reaching a hand out of the shower in the general direction of his towel rack.

I did as he asked, slightly disappointed that he wasn't just going to step out all naked and dripping. Then again, he was respecting my boundaries, knowing full well how hard my walls had slammed back into place, which I appreciated.

Zed stepped out with the towel wrapped low around his hips, and I almost swallowed my tongue as I met his eyes in the mirror. Maybe my walls weren't as solid as I'd thought.

The rapidly spreading red stain on the top of his towel jerked me out of my trance, and I spun around to inspect his wound.

"It's just a scratch," he said again, despite the fact that his three-inch-long "scratch" was still bleeding freely.

I rolled my eyes and patted the vanity countertop. "Sit here so I can get a better look."

He did as he was told, hopping up with the towel still tucked securely around his body, and I flicked the harsh makeup light on. The light was why I'd brought the medical kit into his bathroom instead of the bedroom. If I needed to stitch him up, the offensive brightness would give me the best light.

I bit the inside of my cheek as I worked to clean the gash, reminding myself to remain professional. He needed my medical help, not his dick sucked.

But goddamn, that was hard to remember when his abs flexed at the sting of antiseptic on his wound and he leaned back against the mirror with a small groan of pain. Yeah, I knew how fucked up that was—he was in pain. But Zed somehow made it into a sexual act, and I couldn't convince myself otherwise.

"Hmm, you got lucky," I finally announced, tossing the blood-stained cotton swabs into the bin and grabbing a packet of butterfly tapes. "I think it's just a scratch."

Zed snorted a laugh that flexed his stomach muscles and made the cut ooze more blood. "Told you, smart-ass."

I huffed and carefully applied the butterfly tape to hold the long cut closed, then I stuck an adhesive gauze patch over it to protect it from infection while it started to heal. He didn't seem to need stitches, though, so that was something.

"Hands," I ordered, and he obediently held them out to me. "You're a fucking idiot, you know that?"

His lips curled in a smile. "That's nothing new."

I gave him a hard look, then went back to work dabbing his knuckles with antiseptic cream. He'd split those fuckers so many times that there was permanent scar tissue across a few of them. It also meant we were well experienced with fixing them up.

"He's had that coming for a *long* time," he muttered after a few moments of silence. "And a hell of a lot worse. I can't wait to make him pay for real."

"Get in line," I replied, my mouth set in a grim line as I applied a couple of Band-Aids to his knuckles. They weren't busted up enough to warrant proper bandaging this time.

Zed tightened his fingers around mine where I held his hand, stopping my admittedly unnecessary fussing.

"Dare." He tugged on my hand, gently bringing me closer until my hips brushed the edge of the counter between his knees. "Look at me."

I tightened my jaw and flicked my gaze up to meet his. I'd been avoiding eye contact with him since the moment we'd left Chase in the parking lot. Apart from that one brief moment when he'd stepped out of the shower, I'd been looking *past* him. Like a coward.

"Dare," he growled in warning. "*Really* look at me. Drop those walls and *look*."

My breath escaped from behind my clenched teeth, but he knew I couldn't deny him anything. Not when he asked like that, with such raw desperation underscoring his words.

"What?" I whispered when it started to feel like the walls were closing in around us. "What do you want to see?"

He gave a sad shake of his head. "It's what I want *you* to see, you stubborn bitch." A teasing smile touched his lips, making that an endearment rather than an insult. "I want you to see that no matter what happened in the past, I'm in this with you one hundred percent. I wasn't there when you needed me then, but I'm here *now*. I'm not going anywhere, and I'll do whatever it takes to fix what he broke inside you."

He released my hand, cupping the back of my neck instead. Leaning forward, he pressed his forehead against mine, his eyes locked on mine.

"I won't push you, Dare. But I love you so fucking much it physically hurts some days. All I want to do is erase all the hurt, wipe away the nightmares. But I don't have any fucking clue how to do that when it's *me* reminding you of those dark things."

My hands went to his waist and slid tentatively around his bare skin as I leaned into his touch. "I don't know either," I admitted in a small voice. "Every time we start…*anything*…it's like I'm instantly back in my eighteen-year-old body listening to Chase rant and scream about how I'm an unfaithful whore for kissing *his* best friend." I swallowed the lump of emotion clogging my throat and pushed on, laying it all out there. "And I'm so, *so* fucking scared this will be a passing thing for you. That you'll move on to some new waitress or dancer next week, and I'll be left with a hole in my heart and no best friend."

Zed didn't respond immediately. He pulled his forehead away from mine just enough to look at me properly, his eyes searching my face. Then he gave a thoughtful frown.

"Okay. So, those are the two biggest problems?"

Confused, I jerked a short nod.

His hand still gripped the back of my neck, his fingers rubbing my sore muscles in tiny circles. "Dare…" He paused to heave a sigh. "I don't know what else I can do to show you how much you mean to me. You're not *some girl* to me. You're *the* girl. The only one. But me telling you this only goes so far because at some stage you just have to fucking trust me. Take a leap of faith and *trust* that I'll catch you. Every. Fucking. Time."

I blinked at him, speechless. He was right. He'd been telling me over and fucking over how much he *loved* me. Not that he wanted to fuck me or even that he was attracted to me. What he felt for me, what *I* felt for him was so much deeper, heavier, and more dangerous than sex. But how the fuck did I expect him to prove that to me if I never let him?

He brushed his thumb over my cheek, his eyes soft. "As for the other thing, I wish I knew how to change the past, Dare. You have no idea how badly I want to go back to that time and drastically alter how it all played out."

A small, sad smile touched my lips. "Me too."

Zed leaned in again, but his soft kiss landed on my cheek. "Do you want to get changed and watch some TV or something? Just… hang out?"

I blinked at him a couple of times, processing the way he'd just shifted himself back into the friend zone so firmly. Then I gave a tight nod and stepped back to let him down off the counter.

"Yeah, sure. Sounds good." But disappointment and regret filled me up so much I was practically choking on it. "I'll go… change."

Despite how everything had turned out with Chase and my damage and the knife wound in Zed's side, I'd still thought the night might end a little less platonically and a whole lot more naked. So I just stood there for a hot second, mentally berating myself for fucking it all up. Again.

CHAPTER 23

Zed made his way out to the bedroom ahead of me, his towel still around his waist. "Here, you can have one of my shirts." He grabbed one from the dresser and tossed it over to where I stood in the bathroom doorway. His bedroom lights were still off, making it hard to see him, but a small voice in my head whispered that he was just passing the ball back into my court. Like he'd said, he wasn't going to push me. But if I wanted to take things further…

"Can you unzip me?" I asked, a bit breathy with anticipation as I turned around to offer my back. The dress zipper was well within my own reach. I knew it, and so did he.

Zed padded back across the carpet, pausing a second before dragging the zipper of my dress down. He didn't move away when it was done, and neither did I. After a frozen moment, his hands went to my shoulders, his fingers caressing my skin as he pushed the dress fabric aside. I made no attempt to catch it, simply letting it drop to the floor, leaving me in a sexy, black push-up bra and matching thong. Like I'd said, I'd dressed with Zed on my mind.

"Fucking hell, Dare," he breathed, his fingertips skating ever so lightly down my spine. "Are you trying to kill me?"

Pushing aside my doubts and anxiousness, I turned around

to face him, meeting his eyes with confidence this time. "No," I replied, reaching up and linking my arms around his neck. "I'm trying…to take a leap." I wrinkled my nose, feeling like a total dork for reusing his metaphor.

He understood me perfectly, though. His hands gripped my bare waist, pulling me closer to him as his face dipped down to meet mine. He didn't kiss me, though. His lips stopped just an inch away, and he just fucking *waited*, wanting me to take that final step and close the gap between us.

"If we do this," I whispered, already dizzy with his nearness, "our friendship is totally fucked."

His lips curved. "It already is. Has been for months. This will only make us stronger."

I groaned, but he was right. So I closed the gap and threw myself off the metaphorical trust bridge.

Zed kissed me slowly, lingering like he was savoring every stroke of my tongue, every slide of our lips, every breathless gasp. His hands gripped my waist tight, and he started to lift me up before I stopped him with a hand to his chest.

"Do *not* try carrying me after I just patched up a knife wound in your side, Zayden De Rosa," I warned, giving him a push further into his bedroom.

It was only a few steps across to his bed, and we kissed the whole damn way before he shot me a smirk. "It's just a scratch, gorgeous." Then he winked and picked me up and dropped me onto my back in the middle of his bed with one swift movement. Somehow, magically, his towel was still wrapped around his waist. But it wouldn't be for long, if the shape of it was any solid indication.

Zed followed me onto the bed, his lips finding mine again with ease in the near darkness, the only light in the room pouring from the bathroom. I arched into him, spreading my legs in a clear invitation to get closer, and he gave a groan.

"You can still change your mind," he murmured as he kissed

down my chest, his fingers finding the fancy front clasp of my bra and snapping it open. His breath hissed between his teeth as he caressed my breast, then he closed his lips over one taut nipple.

"I'm not changing my mind," I replied, breathless as I wriggled free of my bra. "Just…I don't know. Just be patient with me?"

Zed pushed up on his forearms, giving me a dead-serious look. "How is that even a question?" He arched a brow, and I gave him a knowing smile. Of course it wasn't a question. Just because this was new territory for us didn't mean we were new people. He was still Zed. He was still the boy I'd befriended at killer camp. I couldn't believe I'd been pushing him away for so long.

Winding my arms back around his neck, I crushed my mouth to his and kissed him hot and heavy until his fingers found my nipple once more and made me gasp with ecstasy as he played.

"Zed," I groaned as his kisses moved down my neck and his towel-covered hips brushed my inner thighs. "How is that fucking towel still on? What did you do, superglue it in place?"

He chuckled a deep laugh against my throat, and his hand moved from my breast down to my thong so his fingers could hook under the waistband.

"It's a talent, gorgeous." He was amused as hell, but he still sat up and slowly, torturously slowly, removed my thong and left me totally naked on the bed beneath him.

For a moment, he just sat there and stared down at me. The light from the bathroom cast a glow on one side of his face and one side of my body, but the rest of us was in shadow. It seemed…oddly fitting for my state of mind.

"Is there a problem?" I asked when he didn't continue. The pause had gone past casually gathering his thoughts and moved right into awkward territory.

A lopsided smile curved his lips, and he shook his head. "Not even slightly," he replied, his palms smoothing up the outsides of my bare thighs. "I was just thinking about all the different ways I want to have you. All the fantasies I could make reality…" He let his voice trail off with a pained groan, biting his lip as he gripped my thighs and spread my legs wider. "*Fuck*, Dare."

Embarrassed, I hooked a leg around his back and gave him a tug closer. "Zed. Quit staring, it's fucking rude."

He laughed sharply but took the hint and leaned back down to kiss me again. This time, though, I'd grown impatient with waiting and reached down to tug his towel free myself. All it took was one yank and it was gone. So how in the *hell* had it stayed on so long? Goddamn magic.

Zed mumbled another curse against my lips as his hot, hard length ground against my core, making me shudder with longing. I didn't even want to mess around with foreplay. We'd had *months* of foreplay already, and I was more than ready for him.

"Please," I gasped, rocking my hips. "Zed…"

"Impatient," he chastised. His fingers skated down my body and found my throbbing cunt. I moaned and writhed under his body as his fingers slid inside, his thumb teasing circles around my clit until my whole body felt like a live wire.

"Zed!" I protested, more insistent this time. I pulled my knees up higher, angling my hips in a desperate need for his dick. His breath heated my neck as he gasped, and he withdrew his hand to line himself up. But just as his tip nudged at my entrance, a flash of dark terror slapped across my mind like a metal-tipped whip, and I froze.

He sensed it, too, and instantly stopped.

"Dare," he breathed, his voice low and calm. "Hey, baby, what just happened?"

I shook my head, frantic to regain the bliss of two seconds ago. What the fuck had just happened? "N-nothing," I stammered. "I don't even fucking know." I swiped my hands over my face and shook my head. "I'm fine. Sorry. I'm fine."

Zed leaned down and kissed me softly. "Don't ever fucking apologize to me. Not for this."

He started to shift away, and I jerked up, grabbing his shoulder. "Whoa, what? Where are you going?" He arched a brow at me in the darkness, and I frowned back. "Did I say to stop?"

"Uh…" He rubbed a hand over the back of his neck. "No, you did not."

"Well then, what are you waiting for?" Just to punctuate my point, I locked my lips back on his and hooked a leg around the back of his thighs, pulling him closer.

He gave a pained groan, but my movement had put him perfectly back in line. With just one thrust, he sank into my aching pussy, and I gasped against his kiss.

"Holy shit," he said in a strangled whisper, then shifted his position to drive in deeper with the next thrust. Then deeper again on the next.

I kept kissing him as he settled inside me, my pussy stretching and clenching his cock like a fucking welcoming party. But kissing him kept me grounded right here in the moment with him. It kept my mind focused on the present.

Of course, the second I acknowledged that fact, I let the shadows back in, and a deep shudder of fear ran down my spine, locking my limbs right up.

"Shit, baby," Zed breathed, stilling his movement and placing a hand on the side of my face. "Talk to me."

"I don't know what my problem is," I confessed in a pained whisper. "I don't understand why this is happening with you. It's not the sex. It's—"

"It's me," he agreed. "Do you want to stop?"

I shook my head firmly. "Fuck no." I swallowed hard. "No. It's… God, this is infuriating. It's you…but not *you*. This doesn't make any fucking sense. I'm sorry."

Zed gave a soft growl of warning and placed a gentle kiss on my jaw. "What did I tell you about apologizing? Tell me what I can do. What eased the fear just before?"

I rapidly thought it through. That first flash of fear... What had eased it off? It'd been Zed. It was always Zed. I just needed to stay *present* with *Zed* and not give Chase or my trauma any space between us. I haltingly told him as much, feeling all kinds of broken, but he just took it in with a calm nod.

"Let's try this," he murmured. He reached over past my head and flicked the bedside lamp on, filling the room with light. Then he propped his head up on his hand right beside my head. "Better?"

My lips parted, confused, but then I realized what he was doing. I needed to stay in the moment with Zed, so he'd turned the lights on and eliminated the darkness and shadows from the room. So when he leaned in to kiss me again, there was absolutely no mistaking that it was *Zed*.

"Yes," I sighed between kisses. "It's better."

"Thank fuck," he replied with a pained laugh. "Can I...?"

"*Please* do," I said, rocking my hips to give him permission to move once more. I had to commend his control for remaining balls deep inside me while talking me through the start of a fucking panic attack.

Still, he took his time kissing me as he shifted his weight once more and started out slow, moving between my legs with shallow strokes. With the lights on, I could see the tension in his brow and the worry in his eyes, and it soothed my monsters. Zed would never hurt me like Chase had, and he wasn't to blame for the outcome of our first kiss. I needed to break through that wall once and for all, and this...this was the perfect sledgehammer.

"Zed," I moaned, arching my back and tilting my hips to feel him deeper. "Fuck me properly. I won't break."

He huffed a breathless laugh, kissing my neck. "I know you won't. You're harder than diamonds and a hundred times more beautiful."

Oh shit. My heart almost leapt straight out of my chest and into the palm of his hand. "Zed..." I pleaded. My pussy was throbbing and desperate, not giving a fuck that we'd been working through some major psychological damage.

"Yes, Boss." He chuckled, picking up the pace and slamming his hips into mine with a little more force. His gaze held me as he worked, barely even blinking as he kept my attention captive. "More?"

I jerked a hasty nod, and he grinned.

"All right. Stay with me, baby." He winked, then hooked his hands under my thighs to force my legs wider apart and my knees almost up around my elbows. He changed his position subtly, and then he started fucking me *for real*. My chest heaved with labored breathing as he slammed into me, over and over. Every time my mind started to slip away—and it did, more times than I could count—he was there, meeting my eyes, reassuring me that I was safe. Fucking hell, it worked too.

When my cunt started tightening and my core filled with that rapidly building euphoria, I grabbed onto his neck, bringing his lips back to mine so I could kiss him as I came. And holy crap, did I come. Zed swallowed my screams greedily, his cock striking me deep and hitting the perfect place to prolong my orgasm like nothing I'd ever felt before.

He waited until I was done—and I wasn't even remotely quick—before he finished off himself with a couple of hard thrusts. It only sparked the need in me for more, and I found myself writhing under him as he came, panting and groaning.

"Holy shit, Dare," he said with a laugh when my hips continued moving. "Hold on, baby. I've got you."

With that sinful promise, he slid down the bed, hooked my legs over his shoulders, and dove face-first into my pulsing cunt. He didn't even flinch at the fact that his own cum was inside me, just used his tongue and his fingers to send me screaming into another otherworldly intense climax. And then another.

"What the fuck?" I gasped when my spirit returned to my body.

Zed just gave me the smuggest of smiles and climbed back up to lie beside me on his bed. Then he reached out and stroked some stray hair away from my face with a gesture so tender it made my chest ache.

"We good?" he asked, his own voice rough and husky.

I sighed, more relaxed than I could ever remember feeling. "We're beyond good, Zed, and you damn well know it."

He just smirked and kissed my sweaty shoulder.

Therapy really did come in all shapes and sizes after all. Mine just happened to be in the form of my six-foot-four, well-dressed, and well-hung best friend.

CHAPTER 24

After that first time with Zed, everything seemed to change. Not just in the freedom we'd unlocked to explore each other in ways we'd both been dreaming about for years, but inside my mind. It was like breaking through that wall had healed a festering wound in my soul, and every subsequent orgasm at Zed's hands—or mouth or cock—only soothed it further.

"Anyone who tries to tell me sex isn't therapeutic," I mumbled into the pillow when I crashed out, half-dead as the sun started rising on the horizon, "can kiss my ass."

Zed gave a husky laugh, flopping into the mattress beside me. "I'd never argue that fact, but I'd happily kiss this anytime you asked." He slapped my bare rump, making me squeak. I was too exhausted to do anything more than that, though.

"How's your scratch?" I asked, turning my face to the side so I could meet his eyes. It'd started bleeding again somewhere around the time he'd had one of my legs over my head, and I'd made him stop to patch it up before he was allowed to fuck me again.

Zed rolled slightly to the side, peering down at the new bandage. "Totally fine, basically healed already."

I just smiled, and he reached out to stroke his knuckles over my cheekbone.

"We should shower," I said with a sigh. "And sleep. Otherwise, we'll both be worse than useless at work today."

Zed arched a brow at me like he wasn't sure if I was serious or not. Then he got up, headed to the bathroom, and returned with his phone in hand. He climbed back into bed beside me, bringing his phone to his ear.

"Hannah," he said when the call connected. "Cancel all of Hades's appointments today. She's taking a sick day."

Startled, I pushed up to sitting and tried to grab his phone, but he scooted out of reach with a sly grin on his face.

"That's right," he replied to Hannah, "hold all her calls too. She needs to stay in bed all day with no distractions." He shot me a wink, and my whole body lit up with desire again. It was like the more of Zed I had, the more I wanted. "Excellent, thank you, Hannah. Oh, and I'm also unavailable." He ended the call quickly, not giving her a chance to question him further, and I groaned.

"You asshole. You basically just told my new assistant that we're fucking." I smacked him with a playful punch. He caught my hand before I could pull back, though, and kissed my knuckles one at a time.

"Good," he growled, all possessive caveman. "I want the whole fucking world to know that you're *mine*."

A ripple of unease struck me at that, and I inhaled deeply. We really should have had a clear conversation about how this would all play out with Cass and Lucas…because I wasn't giving them up, no matter how strong my feelings for Zed were.

Before I could crack open *that* uncomfortable can of worms, though, my stomach gave a loud rumble that made my gut ache.

Zed gave me an amused smile. "Hungry?"

I rolled my eyes. "Gee, what gave it away? We never got dinner last night, thanks to Chase crashing our date."

He leaned in and kissed me softly. "Stay here. I'll get snacks."

With a groan, he rolled his shoulders, then pulled some sweat-pants over his sexy ass and left me in the sweaty pile of sheets on his bed. Knowing Zed, though, when he said he was getting snacks, it wouldn't be protein bars and a piece of fruit. No, he'd cook some-thing from scratch, and my mouth watered just at the thought of it.

Deciding I needed to freshen up, I forced myself out of his bed and raced through a near-freezing shower and brushed my teeth thoroughly. I needed the cold to try to shock myself out of the sex fog I was so deeply trapped within, but if anything, it only made it worse. I got out shivering and thinking about all the ways Zed could warm me up again.

Yeah. I had issues.

I didn't bother heading to my room for clothes, opting to pull one of Zed's Dean Winchester sweatshirts on instead, then fol-lowed my nose downstairs to see what he was cooking.

"Is that chocolate?" I asked, sliding my arms around his waist and kissing his bare shoulder as he stood at the stove. I realized after speaking that he had his phone to his ear, and I started to pull away. But his free hand clapped over mine, holding me where I was.

"I've got to go," he told the person he was speaking to. "Something more important just came up." He tossed his phone onto the counter, then spun around to face me with raw hunger in his eyes. "I thought I told you to stay in bed, Dare."

I grinned up at him as his arms looped around my waist and held me tight. "I knew you'd be cooking something good," I admitted. "So what is it?"

He gave the frying pan a cursory glance, then reached back to turn the gas flame off completely. "Nutella pancakes. But they need a few minutes to cool, or the melted Nutella will burn your tongue."

My stomach rumbled again, and my mouth watered. "Well, shit, what will we do while we wait?"

The wicked smile on his lips told me *exactly* what he had in mind, and the butterflies in my stomach flapped around like they'd just snorted an ounce of coke.

"I can think of a few things," he murmured. "In fact, there's something I've wanted to do every damn morning I see you in my kitchen." His hands turned me around so that I faced the island counter, and his lips brushed over my neck. "Can I fuck you like this, baby?"

My breath caught, and I pushed my ass back into his hardness as he found the hem of his sweatshirt on me and started pushing it up.

"Can I?" he asked again when I didn't respond. He only lifted the top enough to expose my backside, leaving it on my upper body.

In answer, I leaned forward, bracing my elbows on the counter and rising up on my toes to wiggle my naked rear end. "Better be quick, those pancakes are calling my name."

Zed barked a laugh but wasted no time tugging his sweatpants down to free his sizable erection. I watched him with hooded eyes as he stroked himself once, then stepped closer. Gripping my hips, he pulled me back onto his cock, and a low groan sighed from my chest as he filled me up.

Pulling out, he gave a grunt, then thrust back in harder, pushing me up against the cold counter. "Holy shit, Dare," he moaned, "you feel so fucking good. So much better than I imagined."

Incapable of speech, I just rose up on my tiptoes, offering him a deeper angle that he happily accepted. He moved slowly, deliberately, until I was writhing and panting with need.

"Harder," I gasped. "Zed, fuck me harder."

His hand slipped on my hip like I'd surprised him. Then his next thrust slammed into me hard enough to make the counter bite into my hips. Perfect.

"Yes," I panted. "Yes, fuck, Zed...*harder*." My plea was a sexual moan, and he grunted as he did what I asked. One of his hands left my hip, reaching up under the sweatshirt to toy with my nipple and make me buck against him desperately.

"I've got you, gorgeous," he promised in a husky whisper, his own breathing labored as he fucked me senseless over his kitchen counter. He abandoned my breast and pulled me back onto his dick hard enough to make me yelp, then he reached his hand around and found my clit. In an instant, my yelp turned into a cry of pleasure, which turned into screams when my climax hit me with the force of a freight train.

Zed rode it out, not finishing himself inside me as I came, so I forced some strength into my shaking limbs and peeled myself out from between his body and the island.

"Dare, what are—" His question cut short as I sank to my knees on the kitchen floor and wrapped my fingers around his throbbing shaft. He met my eyes, his brows raised in surprise, but he didn't protest when I took his tip between my lips and rolled my tongue around his crown.

"Oh shit," he moaned as I took him deeper into my mouth, his hands coming to my head in encouragement. "Baby, *fuck*." His next words melted into a groan as I took him into my throat as far as possible, sucking him with confidence and knowing he was near climax.

I gripped his ass, pulling him closer and giving him the permission he needed to control the pace. His thrusts into my mouth were tentative for a second, then as his finale crept closer, he became rougher and more desperate.

Zed fucked my face, muttering curses and compliments about my sinful mouth as I sucked and licked, using every ounce of my exhausted energy to give him the blow job of his life. When he exploded, I swallowed, taking it all, then ran my tongue down the length of his dick as he withdrew.

Looking up at him, I couldn't help the overwhelming sense of satisfaction at the expression he wore. Because *I* had done that to him.

Gasping for breath, he gave a disbelieving shake of his head as he coaxed me back to my feet and kissed me long and hard. "You're incredible, Dare."

I smirked back at him. "You're not so bad yourself." With another quick kiss, I nudged him aside and reached for one of the Nutella pancakes in the frying pan. Surely, they were cool enough to eat by now.

Zed just watched me with hungry eyes and picked up his phone from where he'd tossed it when I came into the kitchen. Holding my gaze, he brought it back to his ear and grinned devilishly. "You still there, Gumdrop?"

I froze, the pancake halfway to my mouth.

Zed gave a throaty laugh and shook his head. "Payback's a bitch, huh? Catch a ride home with Alexi. Dare is indisposed for the day."

He *actually* ended the call this time, then leaned in and took a bite of the pancake in my hand. "Mmm," he hummed, "delicious." Yet the look in his eye told me he wasn't talking about the food. "Better eat up, baby. You'll need your strength. I want to fuck you on every damn surface of this house before Gumdrop gets home."

Goddamn if that didn't make my belly flutter in excitement, but I sure as shit wasn't telling him that after his phone stunt with Lucas. Then again, like he'd said, it *was* payback. Lucas really hadn't been as subtle as he'd thought when he'd fucked me with Zed on the phone.

So I folded the pancake in half and took a huge bite. After all, I needed my strength.

CHAPTER 25

As it turned out, Zed and I only managed to christen a handful of areas in his house before Lucas got home, and Zed reluctantly disappeared into his shower so I could talk to Lucas alone.

"So…" he drawled, flopping down on the couch beside me. Zed and I had been taking a break, napping and casually watching TV reruns when Lucas had arrived home. "You guys worked some shit out?"

His expression wasn't angry, just curious. With a small dose of jealousy, which a shitty part of me actually enjoyed.

"Um, yup," I replied in a hoarse voice. I'd done way too much screaming and moaning for one day, and it was wreaking havoc on my voice box. "We had a really good…talk." I wet my lips, unable to keep the heat from my cheeks at that evasion. But shit, Lucas knew full fucking well what I meant. Hell, he'd had the full audio of our session in the kitchen first thing in the morning.

"How's your mom doing?" I asked, changing the subject away from Zed and me. Sure, Lucas had already given his approval and had even pushed me to give in to what I so clearly wanted with Zed. But that didn't really make it any less awkward. Especially seeing as beneath the blanket I wore nothing but a T-shirt and still had the sticky residue of Zed's cum on my thighs.

Lucas stared at me a moment longer, like his mind was still firmly on the subject of Zed and me fucking. Or maybe he was remembering what he'd heard on the phone, given neither of us had been particularly quiet. Then he blinked and sighed.

"She's okay. No, she's good. I think being at home is going to be really good for her. And the nurse you hired seems really lovely. Mom likes her. They were having tea and chatting when I left." He rubbed a hand over his hair, and I noted how tired he looked.

Shifting in my seat to face him better, I reached out to link our fingers together. "You don't look like you slept much, though. Is something else wrong?"

He shot me a wry smile. "You're one to talk about lack of sleep. Did you two even stop for water? Zed's not exactly nineteen, you know. He probably needs to sleep for a week now to recover."

I snickered, not correcting him. Zed wasn't nineteen, sure. But he was more than eager to fill in his *rest* time by using his mouth and hands on me instead.

"I've just been studying late," Lucas explained. "I picked up a couple of online courses for personal growth." He looked a little awkward about admitting that, so I decided not to push for more information, despite how curious I was.

I yawned heavily and rubbed my hand over my face. "Fuck. I really am exhausted. Last night was…" I grimaced. "Did Zed tell you we had a run-in with Chase?"

Lucas's brow furrowed. "No, he didn't. But the last thing *you* said on the phone was that he was there with you. Then you hung up and didn't answer any of my messages for the rest of the night. That's why I ended up calling Zed this morning."

My lips rounded to an O, and I cringed. "Shit, I'm sorry. I totally forgot I left you hanging like that."

Lucas huffed. "Yeah, well, I would have come home sooner,

but I didn't have a car and your security team wouldn't let me leave the house. The only thing that stopped me from sneaking out and walking the whole way back was the fact that you'd told Cass you were safe." His glare was hard and accusing, making me feel like a total asshole.

"Technically, I think I intended to send that message to *you*," I offered with a sheepish smile. "I was sending Cass something else and must have sent both to him instead." Because my mind hadn't been all that focused while Zed and I were leaving the parking lot after clashing with Chase.

Lucas gave a shrug. "I figured. So did he, which is why he forwarded it to me."

That reminded me I needed to call Cass and check that my other attachment had downloaded properly. I hadn't seen my phone all day, but I vaguely remembered leaving it in the kitchen when I'd taken my shoes and weapons off when we got home.

With a groan, I stood up from the couch and let the blanket fall to the floor. Even stretching my arms over my head, Zed's T-shirt was still long enough to cover my ass. Just. But Lucas was still seated and got an eyeful as I rolled the tightness from my shoulders.

"I should get dressed and check my messages," I said with a sigh.

"Or," Lucas murmured, sitting forward to place his hands on my bare thighs, "you could come back here and let me finish what I started at breakfast yesterday."

I shuddered with raw, potent desire at the suggestion, but my core ached and not in a good way. More like an overused, under-rested sort of way.

"I think I need a break," I admitted, pouting as I turned around to place my hands on his shoulders. "Or my pussy does, anyway. Rain check?"

He sighed but accepted my consolation kisses when I leaned down to seal my lips to his. "Fine," he muttered. "But Zed needs to learn how to share, or he'll wake up to find his balls superglued to his asshole."

My lips parted in shock at that suggestion. "Lucas..." I gave a laugh, not totally sure what to say back to that.

He just shrugged. "What? Cass would do worse."

I cringed because he was totally right. Cass would be *so* unimpressed if I turned him down because Zed had already fucked me so raw it hurt to walk.

"We'll have to work on that," I agreed. "But not right now."

Lucas nodded, standing up with me. "Cool. Whenever, whatever, I'm game." He shot me a wink, and I shook my head as I headed upstairs to shower and change. Alone.

When I found my phone—after my shower—I only had a handful of messages. One very sweet one from Hannah told me she hoped I would feel better soon and not to worry about work while I rested. There were a couple from Lucas from the night before, and the rest were from Cass.

Rather than texting back, I called him as I headed over to the freezer to fetch one of the small ice packs that Zed kept on hand for injuries.

"About damn time," he rumbled when he answered my call. "I was just about to head back to Shadow Grove and teach you a lesson about ignoring my messages, Red."

I shivered at the dark desire his words conjured up, and then shivered again with cold as I wiggled the ice pack into my panties. My swollen cunt needed it, though. Ho-ly *crap*, it needed it.

"Promises, promises, Grumpy Cat," I purred back at him, a grin on my face. Fuck, I loved hearing his voice. "Did you get the file I sent?"

"Of course I did." He grunted. "Made me want to break his fucking face over and over. I sincerely hope you made him hurt."

I wiggled the ice further into my panties, getting it into the right place to soothe my raw flesh, then slightly waddled through the house to where music poured out of the gym. "Zed certainly left his mark on Chase's face," I told him.

Cass gave a husky laugh. "Good. You were smart, recording him like that. It'll come in useful, even if he did incriminate you at the same time."

My breath hissed from behind my teeth in frustration. "It's a start. How are things on your end?"

"Slow," he replied, sounding irritated. "Much slower than I want. It's killing me to be away from you, Red."

I bit my lip, my heart racing. "I feel the same." I reached the gym door and peeked inside to find Lucas and Zed in some kind of pull-up competition. They were both dressed for a workout and had their hands wrapped like they were about to work on sparring. It reminded me that I wanted to talk to Zed about tightening up Lucas's right hook.

"Hey, I should go," I told Cass regretfully. "Stay safe out there, okay? Stay out of sight." We badly didn't need whispers getting back to Chase or the Reapers that Cassiel Saint was, in fact, alive and kicking.

"Understood," he replied with an edge of amusement. "I'll see you soon."

He ended the call as I narrowed my eyes at the screen. What the fuck did he mean by *that*?

"Hey, you coming to join us or just standing there enjoying the view?" Lucas called out, swinging down from the bar he and Zed had been doing their pull-ups on.

I pushed the door the rest of the way open and placed my hands on my hips. "Why do I get the feeling you two are working through some macho bullshit that I want no part of?"

Zed scoffed a laugh. "Who are you trying to fool, Boss? You live for the macho bullshit. Come on, show us what you've got." He jerked his head to the pull-up bar in challenge, and I ground my teeth together. Fucking prick knew I couldn't resist showing him up.

Rolling my eyes, I tossed my phone down on the mat and tugged my sweatshirt off. Underneath, I just wore a sports bra and a pair of yoga pants. The tight pants held my ice pack nice and secure, but the fucker was already warming up. I'd need to go and swap it for a fresh one after I trounced both Zed and Lucas in their silly competition.

As it was, we'd barely even gotten started when my phone started ringing again on the mat. I dropped immediately, practically throwing myself across the room when I recognized the ring tone. There were only a handful of people important enough to get a specific ringtone, and the one echoing through the gym above the music was Seph's.

Considering she still thought I'd shot Cass in cold blood and had vowed never to speak to me again, whatever she was calling for had to be important.

"Seph!" I exclaimed, grabbing my phone and answering the call in one quick motion as I hit the mat on my belly. "Seph, hey, I'm here. What's happened?"

For a second she didn't reply, and I worried that I'd missed the call. But then the ragged sound of her sobs caught my heart in a vise and twisted it to the point of physical agony.

"Dare," she croaked between sobs. "I think I'm in trouble."

CHAPTER 26

Panic washed through me in dizzying waves as I scrambled to my knees, the phone clenched between my fingers tight enough I was in danger of breaking it.

"What do you mean, Seph?" I asked, keeping my voice totally calm despite fear for my sister making my limbs tremble. "What kind of trouble?"

I needed to keep some focus and perspective. Seph was dramatic as hell and thought I would be mad at her for inviting Lucas over to our apartment just a few months ago. That was her level of trouble. Besides, she was with Archer, Kody, and Steele. She was protected.

She drew another couple of shaky breaths on the other end of the phone, which did little to allay my fear, then let out a small whine. "Dare, I fucked up. I fucked up real bad and—" Her voice was becoming more panicked, more strangled with tears. Lucas crouched beside me, concern etched all over his face while Zed strode across the room to unplug his phone from the sound system.

"Seph, sweetie, calm down." I tried to soothe her. "Take a breath and tell me what happened. I promise I won't be mad." She probably crashed into someone's expensive car or something.

Yeah, that's what it was. She was just doing normal teenage bullshit. Nothing a bit of cash couldn't fix.

She was crying again, and I couldn't make out her words. It was infuriating and just added to the gnawing feeling that all was *not* okay—that this was bigger than dumb teenage shit.

"Seph," I tried again. "*Persephone*. Put one of the guys on the phone."

"I–I can't," she whispered back.

Her words shocked through me like an electric bolt, and my spine stiffened. "What do you mean? Where's Archer, Seph?" I hit the speakerphone button, knowing the guys needed to hear what was going on too.

Zed let out a loud curse, smacking his fist into the punching bag near him before striding across the mats and showing me his phone. On the screen was a text message from Archer D'Ath, sent just minutes ago. Two words turned my stomach and made me want to throw up from fear.

Archer: Code Red

"Seph, tell me where you are," I demanded, panic rising in my voice as she continued crying.

"I don't know," she admitted finally, her voice small and scared. "I don't know where I am. Dare, I thought…I was so stupid. I thought I could trust him."

"Seph," Lucas spoke up, catching my gaze with a steady, reassuring look. "It's Lucas. Hayden's freaking out a bit, hon. Can you tell us if you're okay? Are you hurt?"

I swallowed hard, trying to put a lid on my emotions. But Seph was my Achilles' heel…and Chase fucking well knew it.

"N–no," Seph replied. "No, I'm not hurt. Not yet. I'm just really scared." Her words trailed off into more soft crying that tore my heart to shreds.

"Okay," Lucas continued, his tone calm and soothing as he took the phone from my trembling hand. He didn't go anywhere with it, though. He just stayed there on the mat with me as Zed paced the room and sent furious texts on his phone.

"Seph, who are you with?" Lucas coaxed. "What's his name? Where'd you meet?"

My little sister dragged in a shaking breath, and I could almost see her trying to pull herself together. "Um, Paulo. His name's Paulo. I met him l-last w-week when we arrived in Santa Agatha. I thought he was just a normal guy. Fuck, I'm so stupid. No wonder Dare always treats me like a child."

Pain flashed through my chest, and Lucas reached out to grip my hand. He squeezed my fingers in a clear message of support.

"Okay, you're doing good, Seph," he continued, keeping that calm energy radiating through his words. "Can you tell us what happened? Where is everyone?"

"Um," she started, taking another shaky breath. "Something happened last night. We were in Sorrento for brunch, and…" Her voice trailed off and she gave a strangled sort of groan. "I don't even know what happened. One minute we were sitting there eating pastries and drinking prosecco, then…I don't fucking know. Someone threw a knife at us or something? But MK jumped in front of me, and it hit her." She started crying again, and I scrubbed my hands over my face in frustration. This was so much worse than teenage drama. So much freaking worse.

"What happened next, Seph?" Lucas prompted. "We need to know everything so we can help you."

My sister took a couple of gasping breaths, then continued her story with a shaking voice. "It was all just fucking chaos. The guys lost their shit, MK was bleeding on the ground, Demi was trying to drag me away. But I didn't want to leave MK." She paused but kept going before Lucas needed to prompt her again. "When we got back to the house, everyone was yelling and angry, and I just… I felt *so* bad that MK got hurt because of me. If they weren't babysitting me, none of that would have happened. Then Kody said something about Demi's home almost being blown up, and…I…"

My breath rushed out in a long exhale. I knew exactly what she'd done.

"You ran away, didn't you?" I asked in a deathly cold voice. Anger was starting to override my fear, and that would only make me stronger in dealing with this.

"Don't be mad, Dare," Seph whined. "I wasn't thinking. I know it was dumb, but I couldn't risk MK getting hurt for me again. Or Aunt Demi and Aunt Stacey losing their winery. You know how much they love that place." More sobbing, but this time I had a hard time keeping a leash on the caustic reprimand that sat on the tip of my tongue.

Lucas squeezed my fingers again, then spoke up before I could say something I'd regret later. "Seph, how'd you end up with Paulo? Did he help you run away?"

She sniffed hard. "Sort of. I left on my own while everyone was busy yelling at each other and Steele was trying to stitch up MK's arm. Then, when I was walking down the road with *no* idea where to go, Paulo drove past and offered to give me a ride into Sorrento."

I rolled my eyes at the sheer *stupidity* of it all. When would she fucking *learn*?

"And then what?" Lucas pushed.

"And then nothing," she replied, sounding scared all over again. "I don't remember anything past getting into his car. I woke up *here,* and I don't know how I got here or where here is or—"

"Okay, okay, take a breath," Lucas soothed when she started sounding hysterical. "Describe what you can see."

"Um." She took a few shuddering breaths. "Um, it's just a room, like a shitty motel kind of room but no windows, and the door is locked."

I glanced up, locking eyes with Zed and silently communicating my questions to him. He gave a terse nod and crouched down beside us.

"Hey, brat," Zed said, his version of calm a whole lot rougher than Lucas's. "Where'd you find your phone?" He was thinking the exact same thing I was. If she'd been kidnapped, why the hell had they left her phone out where she could call for help?

"Uh, it was still in my bag," she replied, confused. "Is that bad?"

Probably, yes. But she didn't need to know that.

"It just means someone knew you'd call your sister before anyone else," Zed told her with a sigh. "You're gonna be okay, brat. We'll get you out."

"How?" Seph squeaked.

It was a good fucking question.

"What else can you tell us, Seph?" Lucas suggested. "Maybe what time it was when Paulo picked you up or anything you can hear or smell."

"Um, it was around midday, I think. Or earlier? I don't know." The faint sound of her moving around created static, then she sighed. "I can't hear or smell *anything*. It's like I'm in the middle of a black hole."

I chewed the edge of my lip, pondering whether that was helpful or not, then Seph gasped.

"Someone's coming," she whispered.

"Seph—" I started to say, but there was a bang on her end of the phone call, like a door had just slammed open, and my sister gave a terrified scream.

"I think I'll take this now," a heavily accented male voice said, and the muffled sounds made me guess he'd just taken Seph's phone from her.

She shrieked in anger. "Paulo, give it back! What the hell are you doing? Let me *go!*" Her protest cut short with the sickening sound of a fist meeting flesh, and then the line went dead.

For a long moment I just sat there, frozen and staring at the phone in Lucas's hand, willing it to ring again. But it didn't, and I doubted a return call would even connect. Her phone had served its purpose; her captors wouldn't keep it around to be traced now.

"He's a dead man," Zed promised me, his face hard and his eyes violent. "We *will* find him, and you will make him pay for hurting her."

I gave a numb nod. "Yes. But what state will we find Seph in?"

Lucas gave a firm shake of his head, his fingers tangling tighter with mine. "She'll be fine. She's tougher than either of you two realize."

I barked a bitter laugh. "I'm not so sure about that." I'd heard the panic and desperation in her distraught voice. I knew just how easy it was to lose yourself to terror. Even if by some miracle her captors didn't hurt her physically, it would still leave a mark.

"I am," Lucas replied, stubborn as fuck. "She's *your* sister, after all."

Zed grimaced, checking his phone. "Cass is on it. I've called in a favor with an old connection close to him. They'll fly him out the second nightfall hits, and Demi will meet him on the other end. We'll find her, Dare. I promise you we *will* find her."

I tipped my head back, giving him a brittle smile. "Don't make promises you can't keep, Zed. This has Chase's fingerprints all fucking over it."

Zed's eyes blazed with determination, and he grabbed my ponytail as he crashed his lips against mine for a bruising kiss. "I swear it, Dare. He won't get away with this one."

He released me and stood up abruptly. "I'm going to call D'Ath and find out how the fuck Seph managed to slip out from under their watch." His hand curled into a fist at his side, and I suspected he was cursing the distance between us and Italy right now. He looked like he would happily take out all his fury on Archer's, Kody's, and Steele's asses. Come to think of it, so would I.

Before he could make it out of the gym, my phone rang again, this time from an unknown number. Lucas held it out to me, his head tilted in question, and Zed froze near the door.

A sickening feeling built within me, and I already knew who would be on the other end.

Wetting my lips, I took the phone from Lucas and slid my thumb over the answer-call button. "I'm going to kill you," I croaked when the call connected.

Chase's laughter filled the room, echoing out of the phone speaker. "I love when you talk dirty, Darling. Tell me, did something important recently go missing?" He laughed again, and it took all my self-control not to throw my phone at the fucking wall.

"What do you want, Chase?" I snarled back. As much as it turned my stomach, I knew that playing his game would get me Seph's location a hell of a lot faster.

"Same thing I've always wanted, Darling," he replied, sounding like he was grinning. "You."

Zed started storming back across the gym, but I put up a hand to halt him in his tracks. He'd had his turn at Chase last night.

"Be more *specific*," I spat out. "What will it take for you to let Seph go *unharmed*?"

Chase made a thoughtful hum, as if he hadn't already planned it all out in his twisted little mind. "Well, you know what? I'm feeling kind today. That little catch-up last night reminded me of the good old days. Let's say…dinner at that adorable restaurant in town. What's it called? Zanzibar? Tomorrow night."

My teeth ground together hard enough to send spikes of pain into my head. "Dinner," I repeated.

"Yes," he hissed. "Just you and me. No weapons, no pretty stripper boys, and certainly no Zayden De Rosa." Chase spat out Zed's name with thick hatred. "I'll send a car to pick you up at eight."

"I think I'll drive myself," I snapped back. "And Seph?"

"Pretty little Stephanie will be just fine where she is for another day. If you can refrain from trying to kill me for the entirety of our date, I'll give the order to release her. If not..." He clucked his tongue. "I think you can use your imagination, Darling."

Zed jerked like he wanted to snatch the phone from my hand, but I held my palm up again, stopping him.

"Fine," I growled. "Eight o'clock tomorrow at Zanzibar."

"Come alone, Darling," Chase reminded me, "and unarmed. Consider it a peace negotiation." His laughter seemed to echo through the room long after he'd ended the call, and I dropped my head between my knees to try to keep myself from passing the fuck out.

When I felt confident I wasn't going to swoon like a damsel, I raised my head to lock eyes with Zed.

"You can't go," he told me, his eyes pleading.

"Then find her," I ordered. "Before eight o'clock tomorrow night. Otherwise, I'll have no choice. I'll do whatever it takes to keep her safe, and you know it."

Zed grimaced, but it was Lucas who said what we were all thinking.

"So does Chase."

And *that* was the problem. *That* was what filled me with cold apprehension. Because how far could my strength and my sanity stretch, if pushed? How far would Chase bend me with my little sister's life in his grip?

I had a feeling I would soon find out.

CHAPTER 27

Despite the high level of anxiety coursing through me at how painfully *helpless* I was to save Seph, I eventually fell asleep. The exhaustion from not sleeping the night before, combined with the amount of physical activity I'd undertaken with Zed all damn day, finally caught up on me, and I fell into a deep, dreamless sleep.

When I woke, I was less than excited to find that it hadn't all been a nightmare. Seph was still missing, and we were no closer to finding her without playing Chase's game.

Actually, that wasn't true. Cass's transport had arrived in Italy, and he'd linked up with Demi already. Between the two of them, they'd already mapped out a radius that fit the missing time frame Seph had described. Between Paulo picking her up and her calling me, we had a solid estimate of how *far* he could have taken her.

"Waiting around like this is going to drive me insane," I muttered into my coffee. Zed had already been out to get groceries and reluctantly handed me the newspaper when I asked him for it. I placed my coffee down and started flipping through the pages, heading for my favorite section.

"Why do you like to read the obituaries, anyway?" Lucas asked, peering over at the page as he sipped his own coffee. He had a stack of textbooks already out on the island counter where we sat and had been up before any of us working on assignments for his classes.

Zed snorted a laugh in the kitchen, where he was loading the dishwasher, and I gave him a wry look. To Lucas, I just answered, "Because clearly, I have issues, Gumdrop." Then I changed the subject because it was way too early in the morning for psycho-analysis. "How is your tattoo healing? Cass will skin you alive if it gets infected."

Lucas leaned back in his chair and lifted his shirt to show the scabbed-over tattoo. "So far, so good," he reported. "Now Cass is going to need a Darling tattoo as well so he can be on Team Hades."

Zed snorted a laugh. "He already has one."

Startled, I jerked my face in Zed's direction. "What? Since when?"

He just gave me a lazy grin, continuing to load the dishwasher. "Uh, same night he did Gumdrop's. After you two went to bed, he got me to put it on his back."

I frowned, my eyes narrowed in suspicion. "Cass doesn't have any free space on his…" My voice trailed off as I took in the way Zed was focusing extra hard on the dishes. Then I snickered. "You tattooed Cass's ass?"

Zed gave an annoyed groan. "No. It wasn't his *ass*. It was just… his back. Lower back." Yet he still wouldn't meet my eyes, so I definitely needed to check that out for myself.

Lucas grinned like he'd just been given ammunition to tease Zed, but Zed spotted the look before Lucas could get even a word out.

"You'll keep your smart remarks to yourself if you know what's good for you, Gumdrop. Don't make me retaliate in the gym later."

Lucas cringed and held his hands up in surrender. "Not a word, bro." He mimed zipping his mouth shut but sent me a smirk when Zed turned away once more. I just shook my head but had to admit how natural it felt to be interacting with them both like this. It was comfortable, except for that nagging sick feeling in my stomach over Seph's safety.

Fucking hell. I was going to *kill* her when we got her back. What kind of dumb-shit move did she think she was pulling by running away from the very people keeping her safe?

Growing angrier with every thought, I almost tore the newspaper pages as I turned them. When I found the obits, I took a couple of calming breaths and started reading through them one at a time.

"Fuck's sake," I groaned before I'd even made it through half a page.

Zed braced his hands on the other side of the counter from me—in the exact spot he'd fucked me yesterday. "Let me guess."

I rubbed my eyes. "No guessing necessary. 'All actions have consequences, my Darling. It's not nice to throw knives.'" I read the not-even-slightly subtle message from the memorials and looked up to meet Zed's eyes. "In case there was any doubt, the attack on Seph was payback for me throwing a knife at him."

Zed grimaced and shook his head. "I'd bet he already had this plan up his sleeve. He just tweaks the details to make it seem like it's a direct retaliation."

I folded the newspaper up, having finally lost my desire to read the obits. "Well, whatever. Either Cass and Demi find her today, or—"

"Or *nothing*," Zed snapped. "You're not fucking going to meet Chase tonight."

Linking my fingers together in front of me, I gave Zed a cold glare and drew my Hades mask on as easily as a pair of old socks. "Don't presume to tell me what to do, Zayden. Just because we fucked a couple of times does *not* give you any power or control over me. Let me be perfectly clear: I wasn't asking your permission. If Cass doesn't find Seph by eight tonight, I *will* do whatever it fucking takes to get her freed. End of discussion."

Zed glared back at me, his eyes blazing with rage and his hand balled into a fist on the counter. But he knew me. He knew damn well when I could be pushed and when he needed to back right the hell off before shit turned nasty.

So he gave a frustrated, angry snarl and stormed out of the kitchen, slamming the dishwasher door shut on his way toward the gym.

"Shit," Lucas groaned. "He's going to take that out on me, you know." He offered me a small smile to show he was joking, but I was still too hardened to reciprocate.

Zed's voice boomed down the corridor a moment later. "Lucas! Get your ass in the gym!"

Lucas gave me an exaggerated pout with puppy eyes, and it was just enough to crack through my Hades shell.

"You're adorable," I admitted, giving him a weak smile back, "but I'm not rescuing you. Zed needs to learn that I'm not one of his cheap fucks and I won't fall in line to his manly opinion just because he's been inside my panties. Nothing changes. I'm still the boss."

Lucas nodded his understanding, then leaned in to kiss my shoulder where my sleep T-shirt had slipped off. "You sure fucking are, Hayden. Zed will work it out. In the meantime, I suppose I'll let him work out some of that rage on me."

I scoffed. "You secretly love his training. Don't think you have me fooled." Zed roared Lucas's name again, and I smacked a quick kiss on Lucas's lips. "Go. I'll come join you soon."

Lucas grinned. "Can't wait." He leaned in to kiss me back properly, then took off running toward the gym and his enraged trainer.

I took my time finishing my coffee, staring at my blank phone screen the entire time, silently praying for it to light up. But by the time I got to the bottom of my mug, I had to admit I was being pathetic. With a heavy sigh, I slid off my stool, carried my mug over to the dishwasher, and finished the task Zed had started before his temper tantrum.

Just as I was setting the wash cycle, my phone chimed, and I practically threw myself across the kitchen, my heart racing.

It wasn't Seph, though. Nor was it Cass or Demi. Hell, I'd even settle for a call from Archer and his boys if Cass hadn't put them all in the hospital for letting Seph get taken.

Pressing a hand to my chest in a useless attempt to slow my frantic pulse, I opened the message.

Dallas: Found something about NP.

I frowned a moment before I understood who NP was. Then my eyes widened, and I quickly tapped a reply.

Hades: Come over to Zed's.

Because even though Dallas had worked some impressive security on all our phones, I didn't trust Leon not to have somehow hacked our server. If he had felt inclined to keep tabs on us to make sure we had dropped our guild research, it didn't seem out of the realm of possibility.

Dallas: Yes, sir. Be there in 20.

Tucking my phone into the pocket of my sweatpants, I hurried upstairs to get dressed for business. Maybe my day wouldn't just be sitting around waiting for good news after all. It wasn't the news I'd *wanted*, but it was better than nothing. I hoped.

Dallas arrived exactly twenty minutes later, and I led him through to the gym where Zed was barking *encouragement* at Lucas while my Gumdrop ran through a familiar set of speed-punch drills.

The music was up so loud I wasn't going to try yelling to be heard, so I just picked up a yoga ball and pitched it at Zed's head.

213

It hit him perfectly, bouncing off and making him scowl in my direction while Lucas laughed.

"*Take a break,*" I mouthed at him, tipping my head to Dallas in the doorway behind me.

Zed gave a nod of understanding and muttered to Lucas that he could rest for a bit. Sweat dripped from Lucas's brow, and the smile he sent in my direction was pure relief. Zed really had worked him hard.

"Let's head out to the courtyard," I told Dallas as Lucas tugged his gloves off and accepted a cold, wet towel from Zed. As we passed through the kitchen, I deliberately placed my phone on the counter and silently indicated Dallas should do the same. I was being paranoid, no question. But considering Leon had mentioned we were on the Circle's radar, I didn't want to run the risk.

"Can I get you a drink?" I offered Dallas, feeling far too fucking comfortable in Zed's home.

Dallas noticed it too, sharp bastard, and gave me a curious look before shaking his head. "Nah, I've gotta get back to look after Maddox before Bree leaves for work."

"We won't keep you too long then," I replied, indicating one of the seats by the cold firepit. Lucas and Zed joined us a few seconds later, both still in their gym gear and Lucas breathing heavily, but neither had brought their phones with them.

Zed sat down first, taking the seat directly beside me. It was his usual position, just a whole lot closer than normal. "Dallas, I'm guessing you dug something up on the genetic match?"

Dallas shot me an uncertain look, rubbing a hand over the back of his tattooed neck. "Uh, nah. Hades told me to give that a rest. But I still had some bots running searches that I forgot to switch off."

Zed snorted a laugh. "Forgot. Sure."

"You found Nicholas Porter?" I prompted.

Lucas sat up straighter at the mention of his biological father, whom he'd never even met. But his mom had given me Nicholas Porter as a hint for something, so I hadn't been *super* firm when I told Dallas to stop searching.

Dallas nodded. "Yep, sure did." He reached into his inside jacket pocket and pulled out some folded papers, which he handed over to me. "Sergeant Nicholas Porter, born and raised in Estes Park, Colorado, enlisted with the U.S. Army at age eighteen."

"That's where my mom grew up," Lucas commented thoughtfully as I unfolded the papers and scanned them. "Maybe they knew each other as kids or something."

Dallas shrugged. "Probably. It's a small town, and they're the same age. Only one problem."

I clucked my tongue, spotting the detail he was talking about. "Nicholas Porter died during a training exercise gone wrong," I murmured, frustration simmering in my veins.

"Yeah, that's what Mom told me," Lucas confirmed.

I wrinkled my nose, looking up at him. "He died two years before you were born, Lucas. He *can't* be your bio dad."

"Unless Gumdrop's date of birth was fabricated and he's actually twenty-one, not nineteen," Zed offered with a casual shrug.

Both Lucas and I swung our heads around to stare at him over that suggestion, but Zed just blinked back at us, unapologetic.

"What?" he muttered. "Cass gets to suggest Lucas is some kind of sci-fi sleeper agent, but I can't make a rational hypothesis that he's older than we think?"

Dallas cleared his throat. "Uh, well, I mean, sure, that's *maybe* possible. But I did also locate all of Lucas's birth records and shit, so... I mean, I don't think that's the right theory." He spread his hands in an awkward gesture. "I'll look into it. I guess?"

Elbowing Zed, I refocused. "Zed's being a dick. I think the plausible explanation, and certainly why Sandra seemed to point in the direction of Nicholas Porter, was that she'd used him as a smoke screen."

Lucas sat forward in his seat, his elbows on his knees. "So… now what?"

Dallas shrugged. "Beats me. I just find the info you ask for. What dots you connect to make a picture, that's up to you guys. Way above my pay grade."

I sighed. "Fair call. Cover your ass, Dallas. I cannot impress this on you enough. *Cover your ass.* Trust me when I say you don't want the Guild paying a visit. Keep looking, but don't take risks. Clear?"

He nodded in understanding and got to his feet. "Yes, sir. I should have a name off that genetic match by the end of the week."

"I'll see you out," Zed announced, standing as well and leading the way back out of the courtyard, leaving Lucas and me alone for a minute.

He said nothing, his eyes locked on the pavers at his feet until I reached out and nudged his knee with my foot.

"Hey," I said softly when he looked up. "You okay?"

His answering nod was tight and his smile brittle. "Yeah, of course. I never knew Nicholas, so this means nothing to me. Just more lies from my mom, nothing fucking new there."

My heart ached at the sadness in his eyes, and I desperately wished I had the right words to soothe his emotional wounds.

"Lucas—" I started, but he swiped a hand through his hair and stood up.

"I'm gonna head back to the gym," he announced. "Zed was going to teach me some new grappling moves."

He stalked back into the house without waiting for me to reply or follow, his shoulders tight with tension like he carried the weight of the world on them. It might not have been the whole world, but simply carrying his mother's secrets seemed to be heavy enough.

Fucking Sandra had some shit to answer for.

CHAPTER 28

The day seemed to drag out from there. Lucas tried to speak with his mom to ask why she'd lied about who his father was, but her nurse confirmed Sandra wasn't having a good day. As frustrating as it was, we couldn't force answers out of an unwell woman.

No calls came through from Cass or Demi. No updates arrived on Seph. I entertained one very brief, very terse conversation with Archer, who confirmed they were assisting in the search, but otherwise it was just…waiting.

As seven o'clock rolled around, I reluctantly headed into my bedroom to get ready for my dinner date with Chase.

Zed and I had grown more and more irritated with each other all damn day, arguing over whether I would meet Chase on the terms stipulated. I'd ended up shutting my bedroom door on him and locking it while I put on makeup and found something to wear.

"To be clear," Lucas commented from his position seated on my bed, his back against the headboard, "I also don't think you should go."

I arched a brow at him while flipping through the clothing in my closet. It'd all been chosen by Hannah, and I had to appreciate how she had an impeccable eye for my style. "You haven't said much on the subject," I replied. "Not like Captain Opinion out there." I jerked my head toward the closed door, and somewhere down the hall another door slammed.

Lucas gave a wry smile, rubbing a hand over his cheek. "Because I'm not an idiot. You're smart as hell, Hayden. I don't think you'd make reckless choices without thinking them through. Or...I *hope* you wouldn't." He gave me a pleading look, and I sighed.

"I wouldn't," I confirmed. "Chase isn't going to kill me just for turning up at this dinner unarmed. He's playing a game, and if I want him to release Seph unharmed, then...fuck it. I'll grit my teeth and play along."

Lucas didn't respond for a moment, his worried gaze on my face. Then he sat forward with a sigh. "He's going to hurt you, babe."

I scoffed. "He wouldn't dare."

Lucas shook his head. "Maybe not physically. But he's got something planned to dent your armor again. I just know it. He's going to push just to see how much he can get away with, then—"

"I know," I snapped, cutting him off because, fucking hell, I didn't need to hear it out loud. I already *knew* what I was likely getting myself into, but nothing either Lucas or Zed could say would talk me out of it. I'd survived much, *much* worse from Chase before. This would be no more uncomfortable than a root canal.

Lucas was smart enough to shut up and just sat on my bed with his gaze locked on me as I got dressed. I opted for pants instead of a dress because I planned to take my Ducati. Also because this *wasn't* a real date and I had no desire to offer Chase any kind of easy access to my vagina. No fucking thank you.

Out of habit, I picked up my gun holster, then gritted my teeth as I put it back down. I held the Desert Eagle out to Lucas to take.

"Keep this safe for me," I said quietly. "I feel weird leaving it behind."

He took it gently from my hand, his fingers brushing mine and his gaze serious. "This was his, right?"

I grimaced, remembering the night I'd claimed it as my own, literally taking Chase's power from him and shooting him in the fucking face with it.

"Sure was." I puffed out a breath. "I have a feeling he wants it back, too." I hadn't missed the covert glances he gave my gun whenever we were in close proximity, like he couldn't help lusting for it.

Lucas nodded his understanding. "I'll guard it with my life then."

I smiled. "Maybe not that hard. It's just a gun, and you're far more important to me." I bit back the desire to pounce on him and turned back to my closet to find some shoes and a jacket. When I was ready, I only had twenty minutes to get to dinner, so I kissed Lucas quickly and made my way down to the garage.

Zed was waiting for me there. His furious gaze swept over my body, and his jaw clenched with tension.

"Save it," I snapped, grabbing my helmet and swinging a leg over the Ducati. "Just keep your fucking phone on. As soon as Chase gives up Seph's location, I'll call."

"I'm coming with you," he announced, folding his arms across his chest defiantly.

I arched a brow, my helmet still in my hands. "Like hell you are. You'll stay here and follow up with Cass for a progress report. In case there's any confusion, that's an *order*, Zed." My voice crackled with authority, and his eyes hardened.

Not hanging around to hear more of his arguments, I gave a nod to Lucas, then jammed my helmet on and kicked my bike to life. Both of them watched me go, neither of them even remotely happy about it, but...too fucking bad.

I spent the entirety of my drive into the city rebuilding the walls Zed had worked tirelessly to break down just two nights earlier. By the time I slowed to a stop directly in front of the trendy downtown restaurant Chase had chosen, I was firmly locked inside a mental iron fortress of my own making. Within those protective shields, I was prepared for anything Chase might throw my way.

Possibilities flashed across my mind in quick succession as I slowly climbed off my bike and removed my helmet. Images of ambush, restraints, torture, sexual assault… No matter what I'd told Zed and Lucas, I knew there was a whole lot Chase could do that wouldn't result in death. I was prepared for all of it just to get my sister back.

Two nondescript guards stood on either side of the main door, both eyeing me up as I strode past, but neither stopped me. Of course, they worked for Chase and he was expecting me. So long as I'd come alone, there was no need for them to be anything more than a looming threat.

Of course, the one thing I *wasn't* prepared for…was exactly what he delivered.

Striding into the empty restaurant, I looked around with a frown of confusion. The whole place was vacant except for one table right in the middle of the dining room. That table was set up for two with flickering candles and a champagne bottle on ice to the side.

I paused, not seeing Chase…or anyone. Then he stepped into view with a sly smile pasted over his lips and a single black rose in his hand. Bruises decorated his face from Zed's fists a few nights ago, and one eyebrow looked like it had a stitch in it. Served him fucking right.

"Darling," he purred, approaching me without a hint of hesitation. "You look…" His gaze raked down my body, then returned to my face with a small frown. "Well. I might have liked to see you in a dress, but I suppose this will do."

Another man stepped into view, his expression blank. Pure business.

Rolling my eyes, I slipped my jacket off and extended my arms to the sides to allow him to pat me down for weapons.

"You scared, Chasey?" I mocked as his man patted me down a bit more firmly than really necessary. "You think I'd need weapons to kill you if that's what I wanted to do?"

Chase didn't bite at my mockery, just waited for his guy to give the signal that I wasn't armed before offering me the black rose in his hand. "For you, my goddess of death."

Unamused by his theatrics, I brushed past him and made my way over to the table set for our *date*. A quick glance didn't reveal any traps or manacles or torture instruments laid out. Did he simply plan on drugging my food? Seemed like his style. I sat down carefully, laying my keys and phone on the table beside my cutlery.

Chase seemed unperturbed by my rudeness, just cleared his throat and sat opposite me at the table, smiling like we were celebrating our anniversary or some shit.

"There's no need for such hostility, Darling," he purred, totally at ease in his seat. Totally in control of the situation. Bastard.

His man who'd patted me down seemed to be the only other person in the room, and there was an edge of familiarity about him. The lighting was so low that very little was visible beyond the sphere of candlelight on our table, so I filed that away in my brain for later.

Chase reached for the champagne, poured a glass for each of us, then indicated I take mine.

"You must think I'm an idiot," I murmured, shaking my head as I sat back in my chair. "I'm not risking being drugged tonight, thank you. I agreed to come to dinner. I never agreed to eat or drink."

Chase's single eye narrowed in annoyance, and he snapped his fingers impatiently. His guard silently approached the table and picked up my champagne flute. Watching me from under low lids, the man raised my glass to his lips and took a noticeable sip before placing the glass back down.

As he swallowed and licked his lips, recognition sparked. He was the same guard who'd been outside the Locked Heart offices the night I'd first confronted Chase. He'd seemed familiar then and even more so now. How strange.

"You see?" Chase snapped. "Perfectly fine. No drugs."

The silent guard arched a brow as if confirming that he was, indeed, not drugged. But shit, call me paranoid, I still didn't trust my certifiably crazy ex.

To avoid things turning nasty so soon, though, I gave a tight smile and raised the glass to my own lips. Chase held my gaze as I took a sip, seeming satisfied, and didn't seem to notice when I simply spat the champagne back into the glass again before lowering it.

Such a douche, he let his own arrogance and ego blind him to simple deceptions. No doubt that'd work in my favor at some stage.

"What am I doing here, Chase?" I asked when he just sat there looking at me for an uncomfortably long time. To be fair, the total lack of ambush or assault had thrown me for a loop, and I was way off-balance.

He tilted his head to the side. "Enjoying a nice dinner date with your fiancé, Darling. What else?" He gave a sick, evil laugh. "Can't a man just want to spend quality time with his future wife?"

My stomach churned. "You're deluded," I muttered.

"Or determined," he shot back. "I hope you're hungry, the chef has cooked quite the masterpiece for us tonight."

That poor chef had probably done it all with a gun to his head.

Restraining the urge to fidget, I carefully avoided looking at my phone. But I'd placed it there on the table deliberately so I'd see if anyone called with an update on Seph. Not that they'd had any luck as of the last time we'd spoken to Demi, but a girl could hope.

"I see polite conversation is asking too much this evening." Chase sighed when I didn't respond to his comment about dinner.

"Would you feel more comfortable if we spoke about our shared interests?"

"Oh, we have those?" I replied, sarcastic as hell.

Chase gave a soft laugh. "Darling girl, we're so much more alike than you care to admit. We always have been, remember? You used to call me the other half of your fucked-up soul. We were *made* for each other, something you proved when you so ruthlessly shot your Reaper lover without hesitation."

His eye sparked with excitement as he said that like he was remembering the moment and slightly getting off on it. Sick fuck.

"We're nothing alike, Chase," I lied.

He just sneered. "Speaking of your dead lover...he was awfully fascinated with the Lockhart legacy, wasn't he?"

Confusion rippled through me, but I didn't let it show. "Were you always this self-important? Or is this something you've picked up since suffering a bullet to the head?" I tipped my head to the side, my fingers toying with the stem of my champagne flute. "No one gives two shits about the Lockharts anymore because they're all *dead*."

Chase gave a shrug. "If that were true, I wouldn't have found an entire hard drive of research in the Reaper's apartment. Digital stamps don't lie, Darling, he's put a *number* of years into his investigation of my father. But I can't quite put my finger on *why*. Can you shed some light?"

What the fuck was he talking about? Cass had been investigating Chase's father? Why?

"I'd offer to ask him for you," I replied in a cool voice, "but I don't think fate would save *two* bastards from my bullets. Some secrets really do go to the grave."

Chase's lips thinned like he wanted to accuse me of lying. Like he suspected I knew exactly why Cass was researching Channing Lockhart and just wasn't letting on. Unfortunately for him, and me, I really had no clue.

"Fine," he hissed eventually. He waved his hand in the air, and a moment later a very stressed-looking waiter came hurrying out of the kitchen with two steaming bowls of soup. His hands shook as he set them down in front of us, and then he all but ran back to the kitchen, where he must have been hiding.

"Eat your fucking food, Darling," Chase snapped, picking up his spoon. "You're too skinny."

When I made no move to even touch my soup spoon, his temper snapped and he slammed his fist down on the table. Soup sloshed, and my champagne fell over, spilling wine all over the tablecloth and onto the floor.

"I said *eat*," he snarled. "Or pretty little Stephanie loses a finger."

I stiffened, my heartbeat thrashing in my ears as panic flooded my system. Chase didn't have his phone in sight, but I didn't doubt he could make that call in a snap.

Swallowing hard, I picked up my spoon and dipped it into the creamy green soup. Even if it was spiked, I'd survive. I always did.

The soup tasted like ash on my tongue, but Chase didn't let up with the murderous glare until I'd swallowed that first mouthful. Then his whole demeanor shifted like he'd unzipped a skinsuit, and suddenly we were back to charming dinner-date Chase.

"I'm so sorry about what happened to your apartment building," he commented as casually as if we were discussing the weather. "That must have been such a blow, losing all your pretty cars like that."

I resisted the urge to gag as I took another tiny spoonful of soup. "The loss of innocent lives somewhat eclipsed my love for those cars, Chase. I understand that you severely lack in empathy and basic human emotions, but you're not stupid. Stop acting like you are."

His eye narrowed at me, flashing with anger. Then he tossed his head back in laughter—full-belly laughter like I'd just told him the funniest joke on earth.

"I missed that smart mouth of yours," he commented when his

laughter died down, then his expression quickly shifted to something darker, more dangerous. "I can think of so many things I'd like to do to that mouth. Five years has given me so very much time to think about our reunion."

Bile curdled in my stomach. "No, thank you. Zed's been more than keeping my mouth busy at home." I knew better than to provoke Chase, but I couldn't fucking help myself.

Chase stood up abruptly, knocking his chair over in the process, and stepped around the table to snatch a brutal handful of my hair. Enraged, he hauled me out of my seat with my scalp screaming and slammed his mouth into mine so hard it made my mouth fill with the sharp tang of blood.

Horrified and repulsed, I clamped my teeth together hard, not giving an inch as he mauled my face. When I remained stiff as a board, he shoved me back with aggression and frustration, making me stumble.

"I seriously suggest you defrost, my sweetness," Chase snarled at me, a streak of my blood marring his lips, "and defrost *fast*. Or Stephanie will pay the price for your noncompliance."

And there it was, the whole point of the ridiculous dinner-date facade. Chase wanted to fuck me, but he wanted to break me by making me a willing participant.

The screen of my phone lit up on the table, and I glanced down to read the message I'd been waiting on all goddamn day, a message that sent a wave of relief so intense I almost collapsed.

GC: Package secure.

Letting a small smile play across my lips, I picked up my phone and slid it into the back pocket of my pants. Then I tucked my Ducati key into my palm, curling my fingers around it as I straightened up.

"Now that I think about it, Chase, I'm not in the mood for

dinner after all." I started to brush past him to leave, but his hand snapped out and grabbed me by the hair again, dragging me back to him.

"Where the *fuck*—"

His inane question never got finished as I lashed out with my fist, slamming my knuckles right into his mouth. The key gripped in my hand only strengthened my punch, and he staggered backward into the table.

Movement in the shadows made me glance up, but Chase's guard seemed to have no inclination to intervene. Instead, he just watched as I leaned over and slammed my fist into Chase's temple, knocking him out cold with his cheek in a bowl of soup.

Clearing my throat, I wiped my knuckles off on a napkin, then left the restaurant with my head held high.

Seph was safe.

CHAPTER 29

Adrenaline coursed through my veins the whole way home, doubled by the reckless way I drove the Ducati, and when I pulled into Zed's driveway, my heart was pounding hard.

Zed was pacing a line across the garage floor and barely even waited for my engine to shut off before he hauled me off the bike. He yanked my helmet off, then took a sharp breath when he saw my bloody lip.

"I'll fucking kill him," he growled, his whole expression pure venom as his thumb touched my puffy split lower lip.

I gave him a grim smile back. "No, I will. Eventually." Peeling myself out of his strong grip, I headed inside the house. I needed to take my clothes off and burn them, then gargle some hand sanitizer to get the taste of Chase out of my mouth.

Zed followed tight on my heels as I made my way up the stairs, and Lucas popped out of his bedroom as we got to the top.

"Hayden, thank fuck!" he exclaimed, rushing to sweep me up in a tight hug. "He hurt you." It was an accusation mixed with resignation. He'd known I wouldn't walk away totally unscathed, but I for one was calling this a win. A split lip was fucking *nothing*.

"I need to shower," I told him with a soft smile, shifting out of his grip. "Then we can debrief."

Lucas didn't need any further explanations, stepping out of my way so I could get to the bathroom down the hall. I left the door open as I stripped out of my clothes and kicked them into a ball under the vanity. Then I cranked the shower to scalding and stepped in with a long sigh.

"Cass wants to know what his orders are," Zed announced as I let the scorching water sluice over my skin. Cracking my eyes open, I found him perched with his ass on the side of the vanity, his eyes locked on me through the glass shower screen like he thought I might magically disappear if he looked away.

Lucas leaned his shoulder against the doorframe, his arms folded and his brow set with a faint line of concern.

"Tell him to come home," I replied to Zed, leaning back under the water to wet my hair. "Bring Seph with him. I need her here for a bit, and there's no one else I trust to keep her safe outside of Shadow Grove. Not anymore."

I was severely disappointed in not just Archer, Kody, and Steele, but also in Demi. She knew what Seph was like. She should have been watching her more carefully.

Scrubbing my hands over my face, I muttered some quiet curses because, as angry as I was, I also knew it wasn't *actually* any of their faults. It was Seph's for being a stupid fucking self-involved bitch. It was *mine* for sheltering her so damn hard that she had no freaking clue how much danger she was really in.

Zed had looked away as he'd conveyed my orders to Cass on his phone, but he soon looked back up. His gaze almost seemed to burn through my skin as I used body wash and a loofah to scrub the poisonous taint of Chase Lockhart off my body.

Lucas's gaze was equally heavy, and only the steam and condensation clouding the shower screen prevented both of them from getting an eyeful of my naked body. Not that they hadn't seen all

228

of me before…but I'd never been naked in front of both of them at the same time. It had me remembering various things I'd seen at Meow Lounge the other night.

Crap. That thought had my nipples turning to diamonds, despite the burning-hot water I was showering under. I needed to get the hell out and put some clothes on before I turned into a full-blown succubus. As it was, my pussy had barely recovered from my Zed fuck-fest; I needed a bit more downtime.

I hurried through the shampoo and conditioner process, feeling the sting in my scalp where Chase had ripped some strands out, while Zed and Lucas just lurked there in the bathroom, making me more and more conscious of my nudity with every passing second.

I turned the water down to ice cold to rinse out my conditioner, and by the time I turned the taps off and squeezed out my hair, I was shivering lightly.

"Pass me that towel," I said to Zed, nodding to the one hanging over the rail right by where he sat.

He picked it up, then held it out directly in front of him and out of my reach. Funny bastard. He really thought I wouldn't call his bluff?

With a shrug, I pushed the shower door open and took the two steps it required to reach Zed and the towel he held. He grabbed on to me as I snatched the towel, though, cupping the back of my neck tenderly as he leaned in to kiss my aching lips. It hurt, but goddamn, I needed it.

I didn't fight him, sighing into his kiss and letting him shift a small measure of tension off my mind with each stroke of his tongue. I stubbornly ignored the sting from my cut and the taste of copper on his kiss. Then, as I pulled away to wrap my towel around my body, I caught Lucas's eyes in the mirror.

"Gumdrop," Zed growled, "fuck off for a minute, would you? Or an hour. Or more." There was no mistaking his intentions as his hands caressed my body through the towel, but I shook my head at Lucas in the mirror.

"Not how it works, Zed," I chastised him, prying myself out of his grip and grabbing another towel for my wet hair. With a sharp warning look, I left him sitting there and padded back to my bedroom to hunt down some clothing. I needed the physical barrier on my flesh if I was to keep my wits about me.

"What's *that* supposed to mean?" Zed called after me, and I just knew he was going to push me into a corner on this. I'd thought our honeymoon period might last longer, but…oh well.

Simmering with annoyance, I spun around in the middle of my room to glare at Zed, only a few paces behind me. "You know exactly what it means. You don't get to bitch me out all fucking day about doing the *only* thing that could be done to ensure Seph's safety, then throw a hissy fit when I leave, *then* dismiss Lucas like a naughty puppy because you want to get your dick wet."

"I might…leave you guys to have this out," Lucas said from my doorway, looking way too fucking entertained about Zed being in trouble.

"Good," Zed snapped, and I glared death at him.

"Stay," I barked, contradicting Zed. "Zed needs a reality slap."

My second gaped at me like he was actually offended by that statement. Like he didn't know full fucking well he had it coming. "I need a reality slap?" he repeated in disbelief. "For fucking what?"

"For this," I replied, poking him in the chest, which was most definitely puffed out. Fuck me, what had I been *thinking*, getting involved with multiple men? Worse yet, multiple men who all suffered a severe case of overconfidence and didn't play well with others. Who said women didn't think with their dicks? Because that was the only logical explanation here.

"This isn't going to work between us, Zed," I told him in a marginally calmer voice. "This…thing we have. It's too much. It's all-encompassing, and I can't give you what you want."

Pain flashed across his face, and his brow dipped in a frown. In the corner of my eye, I caught the flash of movement as Lucas disappeared, no doubt trying to give us privacy to work through our shit.

"Don't," Zed uttered with dread. "Don't fucking do this now. Not now. You said that you love me."

I swallowed back the scream in my throat. "I do. But I also love Lucas. And Cass. And you're *not* okay with that, I can see it all over your face. The last thing I ever want to do is force you into a situation you're not comfortable with. But..."

The frown on Zed's face dipped lower. "But you won't choose me over them. So you're pushing me away now, thinking it won't completely rip my soul to shreds because...what? Because we only fucked a dozen times?"

Shit. I hadn't thought this through *at all*. Of course I couldn't do that to him or to me.

Spinning away, I raked my hands through my wet hair, grabbing onto the strands with frustration. "I don't fucking know what to do here, Zed," I admitted. "How is this meant to work? You can't honestly say you're okay with me being with Lucas and Cass now that we're together. Lucas has already told me how insanely jealous he gets when I'm... And then there's Cass, and he's..." My thoughts were all tripping over each other, so my voice trailed off in a small, exasperated scream.

Zed's arms came around me from behind, hugging me to his chest as he kissed my shoulder, soothing the raging storm of emotions erupting within me.

"Dare, baby," he murmured. "Just take a breath. I know this isn't ideal, but I fucking *swear* to you I'm okay with this. I'm okay with them. They make you happy like I've never seen you before. I wasn't able to do that for you. It wasn't until Gumdrop came along that the light went back on in your eyes, and I couldn't be more grateful to him for that."

My heart thumped hard against my chest, aching, but his words calmed me. I sighed, leaning my head back against his chest. "You're okay with it?" I repeated, skeptical as hell.

Zed huffed a small laugh. "Maybe that's an exaggeration. But if sharing you with them means I get *you*...then that's a sacrifice I'm willing to make. I can work through my jealousy shit. Sounds like Lucas might need to as well."

My lips curled into a wry smile as he kissed my neck again, his lips hot against my damp skin. "I want *so* badly to believe you, Zed," I whispered, my voice hoarse. Of the three of them, he was the one I could least see accepting the polyamorous lifestyle. He was too controlled. Cass had the growly alpha-male shit going, but he was a hell of a lot more relaxed when it came to sex.

"Let me prove it to you," Zed murmured back. "Please. Let me show you that I can play nice, given the right motivation."

Turning around in his embrace, I placed a hand on his cheek and gave him a soft smile. "Zed..." I already felt like the worst kind of asshole for blowing up on this topic so soon after we'd crossed the line into *relationship* territory. I'd just hit the gas and sent us from zero to a hundred in three seconds flat.

"Please," he whispered again, kissing my palm. "At least let me try."

Shit. How could I say no? Especially when that was what I so desperately wanted. Needed. If Zed was willing to try, who was I to push back?

Licking my broken, throbbing lower lip, I drew a deep inhale through my nose, nervousness making me feel lightheaded and stupid. Indicating for him to follow, I left my room and padded softly down the carpeted corridor to Lucas's room.

His door was open, but he was lying on his bed with headphones and his eyes shut. As I drew closer, I could hear the steady beat of music from his headphones, and I smiled. He'd been so determined to give us privacy that he was drowning out our voices...also probably not wanting to hear it if things turned sexual.

I paused right next to the bed, and his thick lashes fluttered open. For a second, he looked confused, then he tugged his head-phones off and sat up.

"Hey, is everything okay?" he asked, concern rippling through his expression as he looked from me—still in my towel—to Zed, who loomed in the doorway like a storm cloud.

I bit my lip, already losing my nerve, then instantly regretted that movement because it *hurt*. "Yeah. Yes. I just…" I cringed, screwing up my nose and hating how awkward this was making me feel. "Zed wants to prove a point."

Lucas took a moment, then understanding dawned and a grin tugged at his lips. "Shit. This is going to end up with me getting punched, isn't it?"

I groaned. "I really hope not."

Leaning back on his hands, he gave a short laugh. His gaze flicked over Zed, then returned to me filled with mischief. "I'm game."

My breath hissed from between my teeth, and I winced. "This is such a bad idea." But I still leaned down and brought my lips to Lucas's in a tentative kiss. My back prickled with the knowledge of Zed standing there watching. I'd kissed Lucas and Cass plenty of times in front of him, but this was *different*. So freaking different.

Lucas kissed me back skillfully, but kept his hands braced against the mattress behind him, allowing me to take control and set the pace.

After a few moments, paranoia made me pull away and glance over at Zed for a reaction. His expression was shuttered, his jaw tight as he folded his arms and leaned his shoulder into the door-frame. When I met his eyes, he just cocked a brow as if to say *See? Totally fine.*

Lucas must have seen it, too, because he snorted a laugh and the next thing I knew, his hands were under my towel as he pulled me to straddle his lap. I gave a small gasp as his lips captured mine once more, the sting of my injury still hot and fresh, then moaned into his kiss as he devoured my mouth. His strong hands held me tight against him, grinding me down on his hard dick and making me quiver in response.

I knew what he was doing. He was putting on a show to really push Zed's control. I didn't think either of us really expected Zed to let us get far, but Lucas sure as shit wasn't backing down from the challenge. With a quick tug, my towel dropped away, and I caught the sound of Zed's sharp inhale.

Any minute now, he would snap and rip me away from Lucas, I was sure. Not that I wanted him to; it was just inevitable. Right?

Lucas's kisses moved down my neck as his hands moved to my breasts, his fingers tweaking my nipples. I arched my back, pushing into his hands with a gasp, and he gave a soft chuckle against my neck as he bit me gently. I got the distinct impression he was laughing at Zed, not at me, but I had officially tossed caution to the wind.

"Lucas," I breathed when he mouthed one of my breasts, his teeth pulling at my nipple in a way that sent wave upon wave of ecstasy straight to my cunt.

"How ya doing over there, Zeddy Bear?" Lucas asked, looking up at me with pure wickedness written all over his face.

"Shut the fuck up, Gumdrop," Zed snarled back, shocking the hell out of me, "or are you getting stage fright?"

My brows hitched, but my back was to Zed, so he didn't see my surprise. Lucas just grinned wickedly as he traced his tongue around my swollen nipple.

"Babe, I feel like Zed just challenged me." He murmured it quietly but clearly didn't give a shit if Zed heard him.

I bit back a slightly delirious laugh and shook my head. "Sure sounded like it to me."

With that permission, Lucas wrapped his arms around me and flipped our positions, slamming my back into his pillows while he hooked my legs over his strong shoulders. I only got a split second to panic that I was now on full display to Zed before Lucas's tongue found my clit and my eyes rolled back.

Fucking hell, he was a quick study. My fingers threaded into his hair, my back arching as he tongued my cunt and my breath coming in heavy gasps. My lids cracked open, and I immediately locked eyes with Zed, which sent such a violent wave of arousal through me I almost came.

He'd moved from the doorway to the armchair at the foot of the bed and sat forward with his elbows braced on his knees and his eyes blazing hot with ardor. The tight lines of his jaw and bunched shoulders told me he was still warring with himself, but fuck me, he looked equally turned on.

Lucas pushed a finger into me, making me gasp and pulling my attention away from Zed once more. My fingers tightened in Lucas's hair, holding him to me and silently begging him for more. He complied, adding a second finger and making me thrash with the way his tongue played my clit.

"Shit," I gulped as the intense sensation between my thighs built higher. "Lucas, fuck, you're gonna make me come."

"Do it," Zed ordered, his voice rough and his gaze scorching. "Come on his face, baby. We all know you're capable of more than one."

My only response was a low groan because he was so right. But also hearing him tell me to come on Lucas's face ramped everything up a whole extra level.

Lucas pushed a third finger into my pussy, and I shattered. My thighs gripped his face so tight I worried he might suffocate, but I was totally helpless to let him go. He just had to ride it out with me as my back arched and my toes curled with my climax.

When my convulsions slowed and my contracted muscles started to relax, Lucas sat back on his haunches with a huge smile on his face. He threw a quick glance over his shoulder at Zed, then pulled his shirt off in a smooth, one-handed stripper move. Then as I watched with bated breath, he tugged his sweatpants down and fisted his huge erection. His back was to Zed, but I had a prime view and couldn't help licking my lips eagerly.

Lucas smirked, in his damn element, and reached out a hand to me.

"Come here, babe. Zed wants a show, I reckon that's what we can give him." He pulled me up to sitting, then swiveled around to sit on the end of the bed himself, patting his lap in invitation.

Zed hissed a breath through his teeth, shaking his head with a silent laugh, and it took me a second to realize he'd just gotten an eyeful of Lucas's secret weapon.

"I'm not even fucking surprised," he growled, shooting Lucas an accusing glare. "Of course the fucking teenage stripper has been smuggling a goddamn anaconda in his sequin G-string."

I tried not to laugh as Lucas guided me to the position he wanted me in, on my knees across his lap, but facing Zed. From this position, I would be staring straight at him as Lucas fucked me, and I had no doubt that was precisely what Lucas had intended.

"Ah, don't be jealous, Zeddy Bear," Lucas teased as he coaxed me to lift up on my knees so he could get his huge cock lined up. "It's not about the size of the boat, it's the motion of the ocean." His tip engaged with my pussy, and he returned his hands to my waist, pulling me down onto his length while my brain short-circuited and my whole body quaked. The sounds that escaped me were borderline embarrassing, but I was past the point of controlling that shit.

Lucas guided me up and down a couple of times, penetrating deeper into my cunt with each stroke, and Zed's eyes remained glued to that point of entry like someone had just hit his pause button.

When Lucas eventually got his whole dick inside me, I was panting and whimpering, my fingernails clutching his abs behind my ass, and he gave a throaty laugh.

236

"Then again, maybe boat size helps too," he added, and Zed's scowl darkened. He didn't say anything back, though, just shifted his position in the armchair as Lucas gripped my waist and encouraged me to ride him.

So I did. Flexing my thighs, I pushed up and down, bouncing on his huge cock and locking eyes with Zed every two seconds. It was insane and such an incredible turn-on. I wanted Zed to join us. I wanted his hands on me and his cock in my—

"Shit," Zed muttered with a pained groan, sitting back in the chair and letting his knees fall to the sides. His pants were so tight the fabric looked like it wanted to tear, and I couldn't help but stare. Then I licked my puffy lips, and Zed cursed again under his breath.

"Just get it out, Zeddy Bear," Lucas taunted. "Show Hayden how bad you want her. Unless you have stage fright?"

Zed glared daggers past me at Lucas, but I nodded my encouragement, totally lost in the heady euphoria of really great dick.

At my nod, though, Zed's glare shifted back to my cunt and the way Lucas's dick slid in and out of me unapologetically. He swiped a hand over his face, then loosened his pants and freed his straining erection.

He palmed it, and I let out a moan of appreciation, my pace faltering in Lucas's lap. To give me a break, Lucas stilled with his dick deep inside me and reached around with his long fingers to play with my clit.

I shuddered with new waves of arousal but didn't take my eyes from Zed's proud cock for even a second. He stroked it up and down with long movements, his own eyes locked on my pussy. On the way Lucas was working me over.

"Zed," I panted when it was all becoming too damn much. "Zed, come here."

His gaze snapped back up to my eyes, his brows raised and his hand still on his dick. "Dare..."

"Please," I gasped, writhing on Lucas's lap. "Please, I need to taste you."

Those were the magic words. Zed jerked to his feet, closing the short gap to where Lucas and I were performing on the end of the bed. His hand stroked over my hair, gently, lovingly, and I reached out to wrap my fingers around his shaft.

At that first touch of my hand, he inhaled sharply, but when I leaned forward and ran my tongue around his tip, he leaned into me.

Lucas grunted and lay back onto the mattress, spreading his legs to push mine wider until I was balanced on my knees with my hands gripping Zed's waist. My aching lips closed around Zed's crown, sucking and tasting the salty sweetness of his precum as he groaned.

A moment later, Zed's fingers threaded into my hair, holding me gently as I took him deeper into my throat. Lucas started moving beneath me, fucking me from below, and it was pushing me into a frenzy. I needed more...but I was in such a precariously balanced position I didn't know how to get it.

Lucas always seemed to read my damn mind, though.

"Harder," he snapped at Zed as his own fingers gripped my ass tight enough to bruise.

"What?" Zed snarled back.

Lucas gave a low chuckle. "She wants it harder," he elaborated. "I can tell. Get rough."

Zed's grip on my hair immediately released, but I gripped his hips tighter, pulling him closer and peering up with wide eyes.

"Fuck," he hissed, looking down at me. "Seriously?"

Lucas slammed up into me, making me jolt in the best way. "Seriously, bro. Fuck her throat and pull her damn hair."

I shuddered with an intense wave of preclimax. Lucas knew me so well already. Zed arched a brow, but when I dug my nails into his skin, he groaned and tightened his fingers in my hair.

"Yes, Boss," he muttered, holding my gaze as he said it, then did as he was told.

It was all I could do to just hold on for the damn ride as Lucas fucked me hard from underneath and Zed pummeled my throat, his grip on my hair holding my head in just the right position, then occasionally forcing me to take him so deep I thought I couldn't breathe.

When I came, it was the kind of orgasm the poets would have written masterpieces about. Filthy, dirty masterpieces. Zed finished himself into my throat with some rough thrusts, filling my whole damn mouth with his cock as a trickle of blood ran down my chin from my broken lip.

Lucas only lasted a fraction of a second longer, like he was trying to prove something himself, then exploded inside me with gasping moans.

Boneless and aching, I collapsed off Lucas and swiped a hand over my sweaty forehead as I blinked up at Zed, who was tucking his dick back into his pants.

"All right. You win." My statement was a hoarse croak, but Zed heard me, nonetheless. His smirk was pure victory as he leaned down to kiss me soundly.

"Did you expect anything less?"

CHAPTER 30

Breakfast the next morning was a surreal sort of experience. The guys let me sleep in, and when I dragged my aching body down to the kitchen, I found Zed plating up smashed avocado on seeded toast with a perfectly poached egg on top.

Lucas was at the island with his textbooks spread out in front of him and was reading out a question that my brain was far too foggy to even comprehend. Zed understood, though, shooting back an answer as casually as if they'd been doing this all morning.

"What are you guys doing?" I asked with a yawn, tucking my arms around myself. My split lip was throbbing, but hopefully that was just it healing itself up. I'd dabbed it with antiseptic cream and knew from experience that lip cuts healed crazy fast anyway.

"Gumdrop has exams coming up," Zed replied, leaning down to kiss me softly before continuing with his task.

Lucas gave me a grin. "Zed was helping me study, but I feel pretty confident with this one." He closed the textbook he'd been reading from and moved it to the pile at his side.

I swung my gaze between the two of them, feeling like I'd just woken up in some weird kind of reverse Stepford Wives situation. They were way too freaking comfortable. Was this what happened to dudes after they shared a girl in bed, like some kind of magical bro bond?

I peered at the thick spines of the books Lucas had been using and gave him a curious look. "Those seem like advanced subjects for high school."

Zed snorted a laugh, and Lucas shrugged. "I took a couple of extra online courses," he admitted, and I vaguely remembered him mentioning something about it to me before.

"Gumdrop is studying emergency medicine, Boss," Zed told me with an arched brow and something strangely close to respect in his eyes when he nodded to Lucas. "Tell her why."

Lucas gave me a sheepish look. "I need a practical skill to become a more *useful* member of Team Hades, and, uh, no offense but you guys all kind of suck at first aid. Which, given how often you all get hurt? Is a bit worrying."

My lips parted in surprise. He wasn't totally wrong, but… "I do not *suck* at first aid," I protested. "I patch Zed up all the time."

Lucas bit back a smile. "Well…anyway, it seems like a skill gap in our crew, and I thought I could fill it. I was studying for my normal school classes anyway." He gave a shrug like it made no difference to add an online EMT program to his existing coursework.

Zed placed a plate of food down in front of Lucas, then pushed one across to me and nodded to the empty seat I was standing near. I slid my butt onto the stool and accepted the cutlery Zed passed across.

"Did you know Gumdrop wants to go to medical school?" Zed asked casually as he set about making coffees.

I swiveled in my seat to peer at Lucas curiously. "No, I didn't. Since when? And when did you two become such good friends?"

Lucas arched a smile at me as he took a bite of his breakfast. "Um, it was a recent idea. You were the one who actually got me thinking about it when you suggested becoming a psychologist.

241

But I think I want to do more practical medicine, at least to start off. Zed got Dallas to forge me a GED so I could enroll in the EMT program early."

"Also, we're not suddenly *friends*," Zed corrected, passing a coffee to me. "But I decided to ask some questions and get to know the Gumdrop."

Lucas rolled his eyes. "He interrogated me, Hayden. It was brutal."

Zed gave an easy smile as he leaned his elbows on the counter opposite us. "You're not bleeding, so it wasn't an interrogation. Besides, I wanted to clear the suspicion that Lucas was older than he seems."

I lowered one brow. "I didn't realize you were serious about that."

"When it comes to your safety? Always. But with Lucas's cooperation I found enough of a paper and photo trail to verify his story." Zed met my eyes, unapologetic.

Lucas placed his hand on my knee, giving me a reassuring squeeze. "It's fine, he wasn't a total dick about it. And I was curious, too. At least now we know *that* wasn't something my mom lied about."

I was still frowning, though. "Yeah, but how freaking early did you wake up?"

Lucas laughed, and Zed grinned.

"You do sleep like the dead, Boss," Zed teased. "Anyway, eat up. I've organized for Alexi and Bulldog to meet us over at the Anarchy training room. It's about time we ramp up Gumdrop's training and make him less of a target for Chase."

I couldn't argue with that fact. Luckily, Lucas's prior athletic training had him progressing with leaps and bounds under Zed's guidance. I was proud of him, but I still cringed to think how the day might turn out. If Zed had called Alexi and Bulldog for help, he was moving Lucas into more realistic attack situations.

"I'm excited," Lucas confessed with a small grin.

The gate buzzer sounded through the kitchen, and I jerked my face up toward Zed. "Cass and Seph aren't due to arrive until tonight."

He arched a brow, inclining his head. "Their flight should only just be leaving now." Because Cass was a dead man, he couldn't fly commercial. They'd needed to wait for a less *legal* means of travel in order to avoid detection.

Zed headed over to the security panel, which would give him a video feed of the front gate, and pressed the intercom. "Yes?"

"Delivery for Hayden Darling Timber," the woman at the gate announced. "I'm from Grove Gardens."

I recognized the business name as a florist in town but not why they were delivering anything to me.

Zed seemed to ponder for a moment, then pressed the gate release button to allow the florist in. "Wait here," he told me, and I arched a smile at him.

"Wasn't planning on moving," I replied, picking up my coffee.

Zed huffed a laugh and pulled a gun from one of his hiding places before going to answer the front door. One never could be too careful with unexpected deliveries, after all.

He was gone for a couple of minutes, within which Lucas and I ate our breakfast. Zed was seriously ruining me for the day I had to move back into my own place and survive off takeout again.

The door closed once more, and Zed strode back into the kitchen carrying an enormous bouquet of black roses. Immediately the food in my stomach soured, and I snatched the card before he'd even set the vase down on the counter.

"He never fucking lets up," I muttered as I ripped into the envelope and flipped the card open. "'Dinner was sensational, Darling. I already feel so much closer to you.'"

"What does that mean?" Lucas asked, screwing his nose up at the morbid bunch of flowers.

Zed and I exchanged a long look, and I shrugged, tossing the card on the counter. "With Chase? Who fucking knows." Sliding off my chair, I grabbed the whole bouquet and carried them over to the trash. "I'll get changed, and we can go."

After the night I'd just had and the new connections forged with Lucas and Zed—most importantly with Zed—I refused to let Chase ruin that. He was trying to get into my head, constantly trying to stay in the front of my mind. I wouldn't let him. Not today.

I showered and dressed for work, making sure my carefully crafted mask was firmly in place. The bruising on my lip was still slightly puffy, but extra makeup covered it well enough that it wasn't noticeable.

Lucas and Zed were waiting for me by the car when I got back downstairs, and both of them watched me approach with the kind of predatory hunger that instantly made me reconsider the need for work today.

"Keep looking at me like that," I muttered as I reached for the passenger-side door handle, "and we're not leaving the house."

"Fine by me," Lucas replied with a grin.

Zed gave a frustrated sigh. "Wrong answer, Gumdrop. You wanna gain everyone's respect and be treated like an equal? You need to upskill enough not to need bodyguards. Get in the damn car."

Lucas pouted in playful disappointment but did as he was told, sliding into the back seat of Zed's Mustang. I couldn't help smiling at Zed as we took our own seats, and he shot me back a heated look.

"If you manage not to get your ass kicked too badly today," Zed continued, glancing at Lucas in the mirror, "I'm sure Dare will be open to rewarding hard work."

I gave a short laugh. "You pimping me out, Zeddy Bear?"

He turned on the ignition as the garage door rolled open, then

leaned over to kiss my neck. "I told you, Boss. I like to watch…
and be watched." His voice was low and husky, sending a palpable
wave of desire rushing through me from head to toe. Fucking hell,
working with Zed was going to be a whole new experience with
these new developments.

I didn't reply but leaned into his touch when his hand found
my knee.

"Well, shit," Lucas drawled from the back seat. "I'm on board
with that plan. Grumpy Cat probably won't be, though."

Zed and I exchanged a knowing look, remembering the
way Cass had encouraged Zed to watch when he ate me out by
the fire.

"I think you'd be surprised," Zed commented with a chuckle
as we slowed down to wait for the front gates to open.

"That's weird," Lucas murmured, sitting forward and pointing
through the windscreen. Across the road from Zed's main gates,
another property had an ornate entrance, and it was opening as a
car idled on the other side. That same property had been vacant
for almost six months, the owner's children being locked in an
inheritance dispute.

"Huh," Zed huffed. "I didn't know anyone had moved in."

"Why does this give me a bad feeling?" I groaned, shaking my
head. Zed glanced at me with concern but turned the car out of
the driveway a fraction of a second slower than his new neighbor.
The other car turned toward us, slowing as we started to pass, and
the driver's window rolled down.

Zed immediately hit the brakes. My breath caught in my chest
as the sick feeling peaked.

"What the *fuck*?" he snarled. Shooting me a pained look, he
rolled his own window down.

"Good morning, neighbor!" Chase called out with a broad,
smug-as-fuck grin on his bruised face. "Lovely morning, don't
you think?"

"You can't be fucking serious," Zed snapped, his jaw twitching with fury.

Chase scoffed a laugh. "I never joke about a nice day, old friend." His one-eyed gaze shifted past Zed to me, and it sparked with excitement. "I trust you got my flowers, Darling? I'd love to stay and chat, but you know how it goes. Business waits for no man. See you 'round." With a cheery wave, he hit the gas and accelerated down the street.

Both Zed and I just sat there a moment, speechless. Then Lucas sat back with a long string of curses.

"I couldn't have said it better myself," Zed murmured, hitting the gas once more.

I had no words, though. Fucking Chase was still four steps ahead.

CHAPTER 31

The groan of pain that escaped Lucas as he rolled back to his feet made me flinch internally, but I did nothing to intervene. Instead, I just nodded to Alexi, who'd grabbed a towel to wipe his sweaty brow.

"Go again," Lucas grunted.

Alexi sighed, then shrugged and tossed his towel aside. "You're tough, kid," he commented with an edge of respect. "Try to keep your left guard up a bit tighter."

"Boss," Bulldog spoke up, his voice strained, "mind if I sit this round out?" He was still hunched over in the corner with an ice pack to his groin. Lucas had caught him with a sly knee after I offered him some advice on fighting dirty.

I gave a sharp nod, then left them to it. Alexi and Bulldog had been kicking Lucas's ass up and down the training gym for almost two hours, but I felt like Lucas was learning a lot. So I'd let him make his own calls on whether he was okay to continue, and so far he wasn't giving up.

"I think I'm starting to like that stubborn little shit," Zed muttered, falling into step with me as I strode across the Anarchy grounds toward the offices.

I scoffed a laugh. "Starting to? You're so full of shit."

Zed didn't disagree, just arched a lopsided smile as he caught my hand in his. After a quick look around us, he tugged me into his embrace. Two steps and he had me against the wall, his lips on mine as he kissed me.

"Zed," I whispered against his lips as his hands found my waist. "We're at work."

"I don't care," he replied. "I can't keep my hands off you." Or his lips, apparently, as he kissed me again softly. His tongue traced the seam of my lips, lightly stroking over the aching split and making me arch my body into his. Tossing professionalism aside, I kissed him back eagerly.

"Hey, Zed." Hannah's familiar voice jolted through the bubble we'd just constructed. "Have you seen—" She cut off as I jerked out of Zed's grip and cleared my throat. "Oh. Boss. Uh... Shit, this is awkward now." Her wide-eyed gaze darted between Zed and me.

I pressed the back of my hand to my lips, trying to chase away the lingering burn of Zed's kiss so I might be able to focus. "You're fine, Hannah," I replied, sweeping that same hand through my hair. "You were looking for me?"

Her big brown eyes darted between Zed and me again, then she squared her shoulders and refocused. "Yes, sir. I need to discuss a few things, if you have some time?"

I nodded, stepping away from Zed. "Absolutely. Zed, go back and make sure Lucas is still alive."

He gave me a sidelong glance, then scrubbed a hand over his short hair. "Sure can, Boss. I'll see you later, then?"

Not answering him, because it was a stupid fucking question, I led the way into the admin building with Hannah tight on my heels. Not that I had a proper office at Anarchy, but we had a security office and it wasn't currently in use, as the venue wouldn't be open until much later in the day.

"Okay, what's new?" I asked my new assistant as I sat down

and indicated she take the other swivel chair beside me. The various security screens showed all different angles of Anarchy, and I deliberately tried not to look for Zed on them—or for the feed that would show the inside of the training room where Lucas was getting his ass kicked.

Hannah perched on the edge of her chair, the picture of professionalism. "First of all, sir, I hope you're feeling better today. Zed mentioned you were quite unwell the other day."

I needed to bite the inside of my cheek in an attempt to stop my face from coloring as I remembered how Zed had called us in sick so we could fuck all day.

"Much better," I replied with zero inflection to hint at anything untoward. "What's happened while I've been out?"

Hannah bobbed a nod. "So, someone has been getting in the ear of print media," she informed me, cutting straight to the chase. So to speak. "A journalist for the *Shadow Grove Gazette* called looking for an interview yesterday, and this morning I had calls from both *Cloudcroft Daily* and *Rainybanks Post*."

I arched a brow in interest. "What do they want an interview about? The explosions?"

She shook her head. "No, sir. They want to talk about how the Timberwolves are still a functioning crime syndicate who've been operating in the shadows for the past five years. They asked to interview Hayden Timber, *not* Daria Wolff."

Anger flashed through me, but I quickly got a handle on it. "Chase," I muttered with a small sigh.

"Um, what?" Hannah tilted her head in confusion.

I grimaced. "My ex. Chase Lockhart. He's using the alias Wenton Dibbs and making my life fucking *painful* right now. This has his name all over it."

Hannah's eyes widened, and she nodded slowly. "Let me guess, a violent abuser who can't take no for an answer, no matter how long it's been?" She wrinkled her nose. "That is something I can understand. Don't worry, sir, I handled the journalists. I just thought you should be aware."

I offered her a smile. "I appreciate it. You're fast becoming invaluable, Hannah. If Johnny Rock is still being a problem—"

"I've got it handled," she assured me. "But thank you. It means a lot. You know, it's funny... People are so scared of you, but you're one of the nicest people I know."

My brows shot up. "I think you're confused. I've got a hair-trigger temper and more blood on my hands than a serial killer."

Hannah shrugged and smiled. "Yeah, but I stand by my statement. Anyway, the other thing I need to discuss is the missing 7th Circle staff." She pulled a tablet out of her purse and powered on the screen. With a few swipes she brought up a few employee-intake photographs. "These three have been unreachable since a few days after the building burned down. We've tried contacting them multiple times about new shifts at other clubs but got nothing back. Zelda in the head office said to give up, that they probably just found work elsewhere, but..." She trailed off with a shrug.

Curious, I leaned forward and took a closer look at the three employees she was concerned about. They were all back of house—sex workers—so it wasn't out of the question that they'd taken work elsewhere.

"Your gut tells you otherwise?" I asked, handing the tablet back.

She inclined her head. "Yes, sir. I just have a bad feeling. Would it be okay if I stopped by their listed residential addresses?"

"Go for it," I agreed. "Follow your gut. But take backup with you, just in case. Alexi can assign someone he trusts to shadow you."

Hannah gave a tight smile. "Absolutely, sir. Thank you."

Motion in one of the security cameras caught my eye, and I leaned in to get a better look at what was happening. When I recognized the guy climbing off one of the motorbikes that had just pulled up, I frowned.

"What the fuck does Roach think he's doing coming here uninvited?" I murmured, forgetting for a second that Hannah was still there with me.

"Um, that's the third thing I wanted to discuss," she offered with a cringe. "But I guess he decided to come and speak with you in person."

The security office was near the main entrance, so I pushed to my feet and headed outside to meet the new Reaper's leader myself.

"This is unexpected," I commented with an edge of reprimand when Roach approached. Two other tough-looking fuckers trailed a step behind him, obviously backup, which only made me more curious. Why did Roach feel the need for backup?

"Hades, sir," the young Reaper leader greeted me. Tension held his posture tight and his brow furrowed deeply as he seemed to be visibly forcing himself not to lose his cool. "I apologize for the intrusion, but this matter is urgent. A business in my territory was targeted in the early hours of this morning, front window smashed in and the entire interior vandalized. Not a single piece of furniture or equipment was left untouched."

I arched one brow. "Sounds like a gang dispute, Roach. How is this my problem?"

His eyes tightened further. "Because the business destroyed was Nadia's Cakes. Considering your recent *altercation* there, I can't help thinking this was your fucking fault." There was a bitterness to his voice that made my anger heat.

"Watch yourself, Roach," I responded, cool as ice despite the agonizing guilt running through me. "You'd be a very, *very* stupid man to come here and throw around accusations."

He met my gaze, his nostrils flaring, but he kept his mouth shut.

After a moment, I breathed out a calm breath. "Is Nadia okay? Was she hurt?" Because Cass would *kill* me if his grandmother got hurt in my war with Chase.

Roach shook his head. "She's fine. A couple of my guys have been camping out at her place this week, but the damage was just to her café."

A small sigh of relief ran through my chest, and I wet my lips. "Good. Make sure she stays protected. I'll send my team over to clean up her café and repair the damages. Please let her know she has my apologies for the inconvenience."

Roach gave me a puzzled look. "Th-that's it? Just...like that?"

"Did you expect less? Nadia's is a Shadow Grove institution, Roach. It's in everyone's best interest to get her back on her feet. Was there anything else?"

His lips moved, but no sound came out. Then he swiped a hand over his shaved head and gave me a tight nod. "Thank you, Hades. Nadia will appreciate it."

"You can leave now," I told him. "And next time you want to show up at one of my venues outside of business hours and start making accusations? Don't. You're fast running out of leniency with me, Roach. Cass's endorsement of you as a competent leader only goes so far."

Roach stiffened, and his face flashed with anger and regret. "Well, he's dead now, so I'll have to stand on my own two feet. I appreciate your support." He stalked away with his shoulders tight, and his backup followed silently like they couldn't get away fast enough.

It was kind of nice to see I hadn't lost my edge with the Reapers. I was starting to think my guys had softened me too much. Or that Chase was succeeding in making me look weak. I worried that I'd lost the hard-won fear and respect I held from the criminal component of Shadow Grove.

But the fearful glances one of Roach's guys flashed over his shoulder warmed my cold heart. I still had it...for now.

CHAPTER 32

Thanks to the development with Zed's new neighbor, we were forced to make some changes to Cass and Seph's arrival home. I couldn't take the risk that Chase would see them. Either of them. Even though I knew I couldn't keep Seph hidden forever, since she'd never accept that.

I kept myself busy patching up Lucas's scrapes and bruises, rubbing peppermint bruise balm into a solid three-quarters of his body. He tried to convince me to join him for a nap, but I was way too keyed up and anxious.

Sometime around midnight, Zed took pity on me and dragged my ass into the gym. Running me through training drills helped keep my mind off the worry of Seph and Cass making it back safe and gave my body something more useful to do than pace a hole in the floor.

When the gate buzzer *finally* sounded through the house, I was stunned to see two hours had passed.

I tried to run for the door, but Zed tripped me, the shithead, and I crashed to the training mat with a groan.

"What the fuck?" I demanded, glaring up at him.

He scowled back at me. "Slow the fuck down. We don't even

know if it's them." With a pointed look, he stalked toward the foyer and grabbed a gun from one of the many, *many* hiding places. He checked the video intercom, then smirked and pressed the gate release without even speaking.

"It's them," he confirmed, his grin spreading wide. He'd taken care of the new travel arrangements for Seph and Cass, coming up with a plan to have them arrive here undetected. Supposedly. I had no idea what that meant, and he hadn't let on.

Zed strode to the garage and hit the button to open the door so the vehicle crawling its way up the driveway could roll straight in. As they got closer, I squinted to read the flaking-off logo on the side of the ancient panel van.

"Betty and Bill's Best Plumbing," I read out loud, then arched a brow at Zed. "Friends of yours?"

He quirked a sly smile and pulled out his phone to show me Betty and Bill's webpage. Apparently they were a husband-and-wife plumbing team who'd been in business for over fifty years. Betty and Bill were also a severely unattractive couple, well into their seventies.

The van rumbled and clanked to a stop within the garage, and Zed closed the roller door, sealing us off from any curious neighbors with a telescope.

A second later, the van doors opened, and a small, skinny, gray-bearded man in saggy overalls stepped out of the passenger side. The brisk stride that Bill took toward us was a solid indication, though, that this was not Bill at all.

"Dare!" the little old man exclaimed in a seriously feminine voice, then launched himself at me with a sob. A girlie sob.

Grinning, I returned my little sister's hug. "Hey, brat," I greeted her. "Nice disguise. I take it you're Bill?"

She pulled back from my embrace and smirked, stroking her fake beard. "Wait until you see my lovely wife, Betty."

My eyes shot to Zed, and he looked like he was just barely

holding the laughter inside as the driver climbed out of the van. *Betty* looked remarkably like her picture, her coveralls straining over an enormous bosom and butt and her gray hair hanging in lank curls around her face. Her very manly, bearded face.

"Oh, come on." I chuckled. "This was the best disguise you could think up?"

Zed shrugged, looking way too proud of himself as *Betty* stopped in front of us with her hands on her hips. "Best? Nah. Most entertaining? One hundred times over, *yes*." Snickering, he raised his phone and snapped a picture of Cass in drag, then narrowly ducked a punch swung at his head.

"You're just begging to get your ass kicked, Zeddy Bear," Cass snarled, tugging his wig off and tossing it aside. He still wore Betty's jumpsuit, padded out in feminine curves, and the whole thing was just too absurd for words.

"What? It got you here undetected, didn't it?" Zed defended himself as the four of us made our way to the kitchen. "No one would look twice at an ugly-as-sin woman like you and wonder if you were really the recently deceased Cassiel Saint, would they? No. So quit your crying. I'll get you a drink."

Seph tugged her own wig and beard off as we reached the kitchen, and Zed pulled out a bottle of whiskey from his bar.

"Where's Lucas?" she asked, looking around the empty room with a small downturn in her lips.

I narrowed my eyes briefly, then shook off the spike of possessiveness. I was overtired and majorly stressed out—probably reading way too much into an innocent question. "He's asleep," I told her. "He spent all damn day training with the boys at Anarchy and had a few bumps to recover from."

Cass and Zed exchanged a quick look, and I resisted the urge to smack their heads together. I couldn't have anyway because Seph got in front of me to wrap her arms around Cass's huge, padded belly in a hug.

"Thank you for saving me, Saint Cass," she simpered, batting her lashes as she peered up at him.

Cass glanced over at me, then awkwardly patted her on the head. "Don't mention it, mini-Red."

"I'm kinda tired, Zed. Which room is mine?" She smiled over at my second like the sun shone out of his damn ass.

Zed's brows hitched. "Uh, loft space. I made the bed up for you earlier."

Seph pouted. "The loft? What about the guest room opposite yours?"

Zed's eyes met mine briefly before answering her. "We've got a bit of a full house right now, Seph. In case you hadn't noticed."

She rolled her eyes dramatically and sighed. "Fine. Loft is fine, I guess. Thanks, Zed, you're the best." She hopped over to him and kissed his cheek before dancing out of the kitchen, yelling over her shoulder, "Night!"

For a long moment, none of us spoke. I just stared after my little sister in stunned disbelief, waiting for her to turn around and acknowledge me for saving her freaking life. But nope, a moment later we heard the sound of her thumping up the stairs and then a slamming door.

"Wow," I murmured. "Not quite the reaction I'd expected."

Cass grimaced. "Trust me, it was worse being trapped on a cargo flight for fifteen hours with her bitching on and on about how we'd all *lied* to her."

I scowled. "Lied to her? About what?"

He arched a brow. "Uh, me being dead, for starters."

Zed snorted into his whiskey glass. "No shit, she's not exactly the best secret-keeper alive."

I nodded my agreement. "Precisely. Besides, it was none of her fucking business. I'd have thought after being kidnapped and held as leverage for two days she might have been just the tiniest

256

bit appreciative of everything I do for her, but apparently that's asking too much."

My mood officially foul, I snatched up one of the glasses of whiskey and knocked it back in one mouthful.

"I'm going to bed too," I commented. "I'm so fucking angry right now I either sleep or I'll find myself strangling Seph in her bed."

Zed caught my arm before I could pass by him to pull me in close and kiss me hard. "I'd say go to my room, but I feel like Cass might have dibs tonight."

I grinned and kissed him back. "You'd be right." I looked over my shoulder at Cass, still in half his drag outfit. "You coming, Betty?"

Cass glowered at Zed. "I'll be up in a minute, Red. I think Zeddy Bear and I need a quick chat first."

Why did that statement make me both apprehensive and aroused? Shaking my head, I left them to it and headed upstairs by myself. As I started up the stairs, the solid sound of a fist hitting flesh echoed up to me, followed by a slightly pained laugh from Zed.

Fucking alpha-male bullshit again. I was much better off letting them deal with it themselves. So long as they didn't kill each other, I didn't need to intervene.

I paused outside my bedroom door, looking down the hallway to the loft door at the end. The temptation to storm up there and give Seph a solid piece of my mind was strong. But the desire to reconnect with Cass was stronger, so I stepped into my room and closed the door behind me.

Not knowing how long Cass needed to *talk* with Zed, I started stripping off my sweaty gym clothes. Two hours of training drills with Zed had definitely left me less than fresh, so I tossed a silk robe on and headed down the hall to the bathroom for a quick rinse.

When I arrived back at my room, Cass was stretched out on my bed in nothing but a pair of boxer briefs and a sly smile.

"Thank fuck you ditched the Betty outfit," I murmured, pushing the door closed with my heel and heading over to the foot of the bed. "I love you, but those boobs weren't doing it for me."

He watched me with heavy-lidded eyes as I placed a knee on the end of the bed, then proceeded to crawl up his body until I straddled his waist and cupped his face in my hands. The scarring on his shoulder was red and angry but seemed to be healing well. Same with the scrape along the side of his head.

"It feels like forever since I had my hands on you," he rumbled, all deep and sexy. His fingers tugged the tie of my robe undone, and I shrugged the slippery fabric off my shoulders. "Fuck, you're gorgeous, Red."

Grinning, I leaned into his touch as he hauled me against his body and flipped us over. His mouth met mine in a crush of passion and intensity, stealing my breath away as he kissed me deeply. Overwhelmed with desire, I met his tongue stroke for stroke as my fingers dug into the flesh of his back, desperately holding him closer. I needed him so bad it hurt, so within seconds I was tugging his underwear down and rocking my hips in a wordless plea.

Cass chuckled against my kiss as he shucked his boxer briefs but didn't immediately fill my pussy with his cock like I wanted him to.

"Not so fast, Angel," he growled. "I have something to give you first."

I blinked a couple of times, attempting to force coherent thought back into the front of my mind. "You got me something? You weren't exactly on vacation, Cass."

His only response was a low, throaty laugh as he kissed his way down my body and mouthed my clit. As soon as his tongue found that tight cluster of nerves, all questions about what he wanted to give me flew from my brain. My thighs tightened around his face, and I moaned as he worked me over like he'd memorized a map of my vagina.

He pushed two fingers into me, fucking me with his hand as

well as his mouth. It made me come *way* too damn easily as I rode his face and groaned curses, which only seemed to amuse him further.

Cass waited until the waves of my orgasm subsided, then flipped me over onto my belly in one smooth motion. Nudging my legs apart, he leaned over to grab something out from under one of the pillows.

"What—" I started to turn and look, but he pushed my face back into the pillow with a firm yet joking movement. "Cass!"

"Shhh, Angel," he rumbled. "Humor me."

How could I argue with a simple request like that? Especially when he coaxed me up onto my knees and stroked his fingers back into my still throbbing cunt from behind. Shit, he knew just where to touch me to spark more arousal heating through my pussy too.

Then he was rubbing wet circles over my backdoor while I squirmed on the fingers of his other hand, and I got the flash of insight that he'd had lube stashed under my pillow.

"Cass…" I groaned his name as he pushed one finger inside.

"Shh, Angel," he breathed, his fingers still stroking in and out of my cunt with lazy movements, driving my attention away from the finger in my ass. I had nothing else to say, though, because I was fully on board with whatever the fuck he had in mind. Hell, he probably could have tied me up in shibari ropes and hung me from the ceiling and I'd have just asked for more. I was *that* addicted to Cassiel Saint.

He used his fingers to spread the lube, making my breathing sharpen and my heart race with every touch, and then I stiffened when his fingers were replaced by something larger.

Not his cock, not that large. But something definitely *not* his fingers.

"Relax, Angel," he urged, his own breathing rough. "Trust me."

Jesus fucking Christ, magic words. Letting my breath out with

259

a shaky exhale, I forced my body to relax and followed his husky instructions as he worked the toy into my ass. I wasn't an anal virgin by any means, but it'd been a while and it'd never been my favorite thing in the bedroom. Cass was all about flipping what I knew on its head, though, because by the time he was satisfied with the toy's placement, I was a writhing, squirming mess.

"Now what?" I moaned as he patted my ass cheek in satisfaction.

He gave a huff of laughter. "What do you want, Angel?"

My shoulders tightened, and I swallowed hard. "I want you to do whatever the fuck you want, Saint. You're calling the shots here, not me."

He didn't respond for a moment, his palm caressing my butt cheek tenderly. Then his hand cracked down across my flesh, making me yelp.

"Right answer," he growled, then slammed his thick cock into my already soaking core with one hard thrust, making me scream with pleasure. The combination of his cock in my pussy, the toy in my ass... I wasn't a fucking idiot. I knew damn well what he was preparing me for, and I was mentally going on the record to say I was one hundred and fifty percent keen on it.

Like Lucas had said, sometimes it just took good memories, good experiences to override the bad. Well...that and a shitload of therapy done via cold-blooded, violent murders. But I wasn't recommending my methods for anyone but me.

Cass leaned forward, gathering up a handful of my hair, and pulled my head to an awkward angle as he fucked me ferociously. Every thrust had his hips smacking into my ass, jolting the plug and making shock waves of sensation ripple through me. When I came again, it was intense enough that I blacked out slightly.

Then he flipped me over and drove back into me before my orgasm had even finished. My leg flexed like a gymnast's under his hands, my knee meeting my shoulder as he fucked me harder and deeper, pushing me into a violent third orgasm that made my throat raw from screaming and my toes curl like some kind of demonic possession.

Only when that third one passed did he let up. He shifted to stand beside the bed, then hauled my jellylike body up and pushed me to the carpet in front of him.

Panting and eager, I rose up on my knees, feeling the thickness of the toy still lodged inside me as I opened my mouth and took Cass's thick, hot length.

He gave me a feral grin as he gripped my hair, shoving his dick deeper into my mouth.

"Fuck, I missed you," he growled as he fucked my throat, making me gag with every second stroke. Then, right as his shaft started to swell, he clicked a button in his hand and the plug in my ass started vibrating violently.

I came again, moaning as Cass gripped my hair tightly and filled my throat with his cum. Then I collapsed in a trembling, delirious heap on the floor.

CHAPTER 33

Cass, it seemed, was determined to make up for lost time. He barely let me sleep all damn night, then around dawn I crashed like a ton of bricks. It was that sort of physically exhausted, totally satisfied sleep that gave me the best rest. No dreams, no nightmares, just sleep.

It was midafternoon by the time I dragged my ass out of bed and followed my grumbling stomach downstairs.

Lucas was at his favored study spot at the kitchen island, his books spread out around him, but this time he had company in the form of my bratty little sister. She had a faint shadow of a bruise on her cheekbone, but otherwise she seemed in great health for a two-day imprisonment.

Cass was at the coffee machine, yawning as he started pouring some liquid gold for both of us—I hoped. He had only gotten up ten minutes before me and looked wrecked.

"Good morning, gorgeous." Lucas grinned as he spotted me, holding out an arm to beckon me closer. I willingly stepped into his embrace and sighed into his kiss as he brought his lips to mine.

The fake gagging noise from my sister made me pull away a lot sooner than I'd have liked, though, and I gritted my teeth to keep from snapping at her.

"Morning, Seph," I greeted in a cool tone. "I take it you've fully recovered from your ordeal if you're back to your usual charming self?"

She rolled her eyes and shrugged. "Whatever. It wasn't even that bad. They were never going to actually hurt me."

Lucas's grip on my waist tightened, and Cass glanced up from the coffee machine to meet my eyes. They knew, like I did, that the only reason she hadn't been hurt was because I'd played Chase's fucked-up game. She'd been leverage, nothing more.

Still, I didn't tell her all of that. I just gave a tight smile and kissed Lucas's shoulder before heading over to Cass and the coffee.

"Fuck yes," I moaned as he handed me one of the mugs. I inhaled the rich aroma of freshly brewed beans, and my mouth watered.

Cass just watched me with those intense, dark eyes, then pressed a hand to my lower back to kiss me. When he withdrew to sip his own coffee, my sister drew my focus once again with a small scoff.

Drawing a deep breath, I prayed for sanity and patience as I turned back around to face her. "Do you have something to say, Seph?"

She wrinkled her nose, like she was debating backing down, but the break away from me must have given her a new sense of bravery. She pursed her lips and tilted her chin up defiantly.

"Uh, yeah," she sneered. "What, are you just, like, fucking multiple guys now? I thought you were in love with Lucas."

I resisted the urge to rub at the building headache between my eyes. "I am," I replied, and Lucas flashed me a grin. "But I'm also in love with Cass." I bumped the big, silent grump at my side, and he leaned back into me. "And Zed," I murmured after a small hesitation.

Seph's brows shot right up at that admission. "Zed too?"

I rolled my own eyes at her theatrics. "You just spent six weeks in Italy with your best friend and her *three* husbands. What is so

263

hard to wrap your brain around here, Seph? Love isn't a finite commodity, so get the fuck over it and shove all that self-righteous bullshit back where it came from. Last I checked, you weren't exactly qualified or experienced enough to give any kind of opinion on the matter."

My tone was a lot harsher than I intended, but fuck *me*. She had barely been back a day, and she was already on my last damn nerve. Maybe due to the fact that she had all but ignored my role in saving her stupid ass. Maybe because she hadn't apologized for being a judgmental prick when she thought I'd killed Cass. Or maybe it was her vaguely flirtatious glances at my guys that was setting me off. Regardless, she just stared at me with wide eyes for a moment.

Then those pale-blue eyes, a fucking carbon copy of my own, started welling up with tears.

My anger deflated in a rush of breath, and guilt washed over me. "Seph, I didn't—"

"No, you meant every word," she snapped, sliding off her stool and sniffing hard. "And you're right. I *don't* know what love is because you've never even let me go on an innocent fucking date, let alone have the kind of sex that *you* were having all damn night."

"Of course not," I barked back, "because your judgment fucking sucks! Look what happened with *Paulo* in Italy!"

Seph flinched at that, and I ground my teeth in frustration. I was usually so much calmer when dealing with her tantrums; I didn't know why I was losing my temper so badly now.

"Yeah, well," she replied, tears already running down her cheeks, "maybe if you hadn't controlled every damn aspect of my life I'd have been able to make better judgment calls. Dad never would have suffocated me like you do. He'd have let me make my own choices, just like he let you and Chase get engaged when you were fifteen. You're nothing but a controlling egomaniac, Dare, and I'm sick of it."

With that cutting barb, she tore out of the kitchen, brushing past Zed in the doorway, and stomped her way upstairs. The dramatic sound of her wails echoed as she retreated until eventually the loft door slammed and all was quiet once more.

"Save it," I snapped, my glare meeting Zed's as his lips parted. "I know perfectly well what you're going to say, and I'm not in the fucking mood."

Anger radiated through his features and his fist clenched at his side, but I knew he wasn't angry at me. Not directly. He was furious at Seph for throwing such a caustic insult at me *again*, and he was mad as hell that I still refused to let him tell her the truth.

"She's pushing it too far, Dare," he growled.

Cass huffed a sound beside me, his thick, tattoo-covered arm warm against mine. "Agreed. That was too far. She was nothing but fucking painful the whole way home, too."

I shook my head. "She's just being a normal eighteen-year-old drama queen." I swallowed hard and met Lucas's sympathetic gaze. "A normal, spoiled, sheltered eighteen-year-old. And *normal* is all I've ever wanted for her. Just let it go, they're only words."

Zed was still seething but nodded tightly nonetheless. "Yes, Boss."

Clearing my throat, I raised my coffee back to my lips with a slight tremble in my hand. "Did you just come from Anarchy? How are preparations looking for tonight's event?"

He held my gaze a moment longer, then scrubbed a hand over his face and continued into the room, taking the stool beside Lucas that Seph had just abandoned. "Yeah, all smooth. I just had a gap of time and thought I'd come home and check in with everyone. I'm guessing you haven't had time to debrief with Grumpy Cat yet?"

"Not yet," I replied, licking my lips. My stomach rumbled loudly, and Zed rolled his eyes.

"Sit down," he ordered. "I'll cook, Cass can talk. Lucas, keep cramming for your econ exam. If you fail that, we will all give you no end of grief."

Lucas smirked. "So bossy." But he still flipped the page in his textbook and picked up his highlighter.

Cass nudged me to take Zed's seat, then boosted his ass up on the counter near the fridge. He seemed so comfortable in Zed's house that I could almost forget he was the reason Zed was sporting a black eye today. Almost.

"I imagine you weren't done when we called you away on Operation Rescue Seph," I stated, and Cass inclined his head with confirmation. "Well, in that case we will need to work out how to get you back out there without Chase spotting you." I grimaced. Even though Zed lived on an eight-acre lot so there was no chance of neighbors peering through the windows, I was still paranoid as hell having Chase right there across the road. Exactly what he'd intended, no doubt.

Cass nodded. "I've got a few ideas. We also need to discuss how to handle the Reapers. At some stage, they're going to work out that I'm not dead. Then it'll be a matter of blood betrayal."

I shrugged. "Then I'll squash them, just like I did the Wraiths."

Cass shot me a tiny, indulgent smile. "I'd rather you didn't, Red. I'm sure we can think of something else."

With a nod, I watched what Zed was preparing for me to eat. It looked like he was making some variation on parmesan-and-garlic angel-hair pasta. Yum.

"Chase asked me something at dinner the other night," I said after a moment of silence. "About you." My gaze shifted from Zed's muscular back at the stove and across to Cass.

He arched a scarred brow. "What was it?"

"He said that he went snooping through your apartment while we were planning your funeral and that he found a hard drive full of information on Channing Lockhart." I left it as a statement, inviting him to fill in the blanks of the story himself.

Cass tipped his head back against the cabinets, looking up at the ceiling for a long moment. Then he scrubbed a hand over his

266

short beard and returned his steady gaze to mine. "That was an encrypted drive." Irritation was clear in his rough voice.

I shrugged. "Not well enough, apparently." I paused, biting the inside of my cheek as apprehension twisted my gut. "Why were you researching Lockhart Senior, Cass?"

Lucas carefully put his highlighter down and dropped his hand to my knee, squeezing gently in a sign of support, but I didn't take my eyes from Cass.

After a tense moment of silence, Cass exhaled and shook his head. "Because he took something of mine, and I want it back."

My brow furrowed with confusion. "Channing? How? He's been dead for five years."

Cass grimaced. "I'm aware. He took it a good twenty-three years ago. I started looking into where he might be keeping it right before you killed him."

"I don't get it," Lucas commented. "Why would he still have it? Or…where would it even be now? What happened to the estate when everyone was presumed dead?"

"The Lockhart estate was passed to the closest living relative, an elderly third cousin living in Alaska," Zed replied, clearly having already looked that fact up. I'd never even given a second thought to who would inherit the Lockhart coffers when they were all dead, but clearly, somehow, it'd all found its way back to Chase. How else could he be funding his war?

Cass gave a tight nod. "That's what I found, too. Except the old guy is totally out of his mind and nonmobile. My best guess is that he signed it all back over to Chase, under the Wenton identity."

I drummed my fingertips on the counter, thinking, and Zed placed a steaming, fragrant bowl of delicate pasta in front of me. "Okay, but that's a long time to hold onto something. You're sure it's still in the estate?"

Cass huffed a short laugh. "One of the original Fabergé

Imperial eggs? Yeah, I'd have heard if it sold. He still had it, the old goat. He was too self-important to have ever sold it."

My jaw dropped, and I wondered for a second if I'd heard him wrong. "What the hell were you doing with a Fabergé egg at age"—I quickly did the math—"eleven?"

Cass sighed, his shoulder slumping. "It's not *mine*, exactly. It's my grandmother's. I want to get it back for her."

Zed leaned against the counter, his arms folded and a crease of confusion in his brow. "Nadia's? Okay, what the hell was *Nadia* doing with a Russian Imperial heirloom worth millions of dollars? And how did Channing Lockhart get his greedy paws on it?"

A shadow of a smile passed over Cass's lips. "She was given it as a wedding present from the love of her life, a man named Kristoff Valenshek. He was a thief, and a damn good one too. He stole it from the Kremlin itself, simply to give to her on her wedding day to another man." His eyes flicked back to catch mine. "It was one of those tragic romances, you know?"

"Sounds like it," I murmured, my heart breaking for Nadia. Why'd she marry someone else if a man was willing to steal a Fabergé egg for her? "So she kept it, obviously."

Cass nodded. "She hid it from her shitty, abusive husband as they immigrated to America. He died when I was six, liver disease from a lifetime of excessive drinking. After his funeral, I found Nadia looking at the egg in the fancy, velvet-lined case she kept it in. She told me not to tell my mom, but I was a kid and thought it was just a pretty egg." He heaved a sigh, rubbing his forehead.

I could guess where this story was going. "Your mom stole the egg from Nadia?"

He shrugged. "Sort of. Times were tough, and my mom… Well. She was no gem. I never knew my dad because he was just one of her many clients, but she did her best to raise me. Mostly let Nadia do it, though, while she was off on benders or…with men. When I was maybe eight or so, something changed."

Cass paused in his story to take a gulp of his coffee. It wasn't in his nature to speak so much, and I could tell it was grating on his nerves. It was important information, though. So I didn't offer any quick excuses to let him off.

"She showed up with some guy she claimed to be in love with," he continued, his jaw tight with old anger. "Started bringing him home, telling me he was going to marry her one day. Apparently, they were old *acquaintances*, which was just a nice way of saying he was a client. This prick had no intention of actually marrying her. He couldn't, seeing as he was already married with kids of his own."

Zed grimaced. "Lockhart."

Cass nodded. "The same. He just used my mom for sex and a convenient punching bag. I couldn't tell you how many times I had to call my grandmother 'cause I thought my mom was dead after one of his visits. Then one day, the stupid bitch thought she'd try to blackmail him, tried to force him to leave his wife by threatening to expose their affair."

"I bet that went down well," I whispered. I'd met Channing Lockhart—knew him far more intimately than I'd ever cared to—and there was no question in my mind that Chase was a product of his upbringing. Channing was as sick and twisted as they came.

"He killed her that night. I tried to stop him, but I was this... skinny, malnourished kid. *Weak*." He spat that word out like it was coated in poison. "One backhand and I was knocked out. I woke up just in time to see him put a bullet through her head. Then he took the egg that she'd stupidly fucking shown him and left."

For a moment, no one spoke. What the fuck should I even say to that? I'd had no clue Cass had any history with the Lockhart family. No wonder he'd backed off so hard when I'd mentioned having previously been engaged to Chase. Cass would, understandably, despise that family.

"Here." Zed held out a bottle of whiskey to Cass. "You need something harder than coffee."

Cass gave a lopsided smile, accepted the liquor, and took a long swallow straight from the bottle. "Fucking oath."

"So, you want to get the egg back for Nadia?" Lucas asked, propping his chin on his hand and watching Cass thoughtfully. "That's sweet."

Cass's gaze turned to daggers. "Fuck you, Gumdrop."

Lucas just rolled his eyes. "I wasn't being snide, I meant it. You obviously care a lot about your grandmother, and this was a piece of her past that meant a lot to *her*. It's admirable, you big grump. Take the fucking compliment."

"That's why you got into the Reapers?" I asked quietly, processing the information he'd just shared.

Cass slid off the counter and approached me, threading his fingers into my hair as I turned my face up to look at him. "Yeah," he replied. "Without my mom…I lost my way. Ended up in a bad crew and then got taken in by Damien D'Ath. He raised me like a son, so I felt like I owed it to Zane to stick by him when he took over."

It made sense. But…

"Why didn't you tell me any of this, Cass?" It *hurt* that he hadn't told me about such pivotal parts of his childhood. Did he not trust me? Or just think I didn't care?

His lips downturned, and he stroked a thumb across my brow. "Because of this expression," he rumbled, no louder than a whisper. "Because I didn't want to see this look of fear and uncertainty in your eyes, Red. Not without hard evidence."

I took a breath. "I'm not—"

Cass gave a huff of humorless laughter. "Don't even try telling me you're not thinking Chase and I could be related. I know it was the first thing I thought, too."

"You think Channing could have been your bio father," Zed commented, his tone neutral. "Easy enough to check, now that we have DNA samples from you and Chase both."

Cass nodded sharply, his focus still entirely on me. "I wanted to get your lab to run the test before bringing any of this up. I never wanted to be another weapon in Chase's psychological warfare against you, Angel."

Did I believe that?

My chest ached as I searched Cass's dark eyes for any sign of deception, but all I found there was sincerity. Love. He was telling the truth. I was sure of it.

Releasing my breath, I gave a shallow nod. "That's understandable," I murmured. "I'll call the lab and get them to compare your sample against Chase's."

Cass's shoulders relaxed as I said that, and his fingers applied pressure to the back of my neck, urging me to tilt my face back so he could kiss me long and hard. "Thank you," he murmured against my lips. "Thank you for trusting me."

I swallowed. Trusting anyone other than Zed was still *such* a daunting experience. For so long, he'd been the only person alive worthy of my trust, but now I was expanding my circle to include Cass and Lucas. To some extent, even Dallas and Hannah and Gen… They were all earning small pieces of trust. It felt good.

Maybe I'd been missing out all these years because Lucas and Cass had made me realize Zed wasn't the *only* one anymore. But he was still the first and the best.

Meeting my best friend's eye across the kitchen, I gave him a reassuring smile. "Okay, let me eat this pasta before I turn into a raging, hungry bitch, then Zed and I should head over to Anarchy."

"I need to get some training in, too," Lucas commented. "Maybe Cass can teach me a thing or two while you guys are gone."

Cass gave a light chuckle, his hand still buried in the back of my hair like he didn't want to let me go. Not just yet. "We'll see, Gumdrop. You look pretty rough already. I'd hate to mess up that pretty face."

The two of them started bantering like *friends*, and Zed gave me another pointed look. I knew what he was asking without him having to say a word, so I gave him a firm nod. Yes, I trusted Cass.

Zed gave a faint nod back and left it at that. But I knew we were on the same page.

CHAPTER 34

Our event that evening at Anarchy was a relatively big fight night set up by our marketing team as a trial run for the high-profile main event we had scheduled for two weeks away. Before we even left the house, though, Zed got a call from Rodney over at Club 22.

"Couple of drunk suits got handsy with Maxine," he told me when he ended the call.

I frowned at him in the mirror as I applied my makeup. "Maxine's capable enough to handle them, even without security."

He smirked. "She did. But now they're shouting about pressing assault charges against her. Rodney needs me to come in and have a chat with the idiots."

I couldn't help smiling back at that. "Go. Let Maxine know she's got our support. No one touches my staff and gets away with it."

"You got it, Boss. I'll meet you at Anarchy once I'm done." He dropped a kiss to the back of my neck that warmed me all the way through. "Maybe bring Gumdrop. It'd be good for the Wolves to see him with us."

I paused my eyeliner, giving him a surprised look, then nodded my agreement. "Good thinking. I'll see you soon. Don't have too much fun, though."

Zed's devilish grin told me he was already planning on a whole lot of fun with the handsy bastards over at Club 22. I expected nothing less.

I finished getting ready after he left, then made my way down to the gym in search of Lucas. Seph hadn't reemerged from her loft room, and the loud music that thumped through the floor indicated she had settled in, at least for the time being.

What I found when I pushed through the gym door shocked me speechless.

A few days ago I'd overheard Lucas talking to Zed—joking, I thought—about getting a pole installed in the gym to get him back into shape for shifts at Club 22. Apparently, Zed had taken him seriously and installed a fully bolted-in, brass spinning pole.

Except it wasn't Lucas hanging shirtless and upside down on the pole. It was Cass.

"What the fuck?" I muttered aloud, and Cass jerked. His grip loosened, and he crashed to the mat, just narrowly tucking his chin to protect his head.

Lucas started laughing, and Cass scowled absolute death at him from the floor where he'd landed.

"Gumdrop was talking smack," Cass grumbled. "I had to prove a point."

Lucas was laughing too hard to add any further information and had to scramble out of Cass's reach when he swiped at him in retaliation.

"All right, children," I drawled. "As much as I want to see a repeat of whatever just happened, we should get over to Anarchy. The first fight starts in half an hour so the venue will already be filling up."

"Who's fighting?" Cass asked, grabbing his T-shirt from the floor and tugging it over his head.

I scowled at him. "No one important, and no, you can't sneak out to watch. I need you here to keep an eye on Seph."

His shoulders slumped, and he hung his head in disappointment. "Babysitting. Again."

"Did you forget you're supposed to be dead?" I arched a brow and folded my arms.

Lucas, still snickering, clapped Cass on the shoulder as he passed him. "Tough break, old man. I'll take care of our girl tonight."

"Little shit," Cass muttered as Lucas disappeared out of the gym. His micro-smile was all amusement, though.

I tilted my head to the side, running my gaze up and down his body. "You wanna show me that move on the pole? I could offer some pointers, maybe sort you out with some tear-off pants and a sequined thong."

His glare flattened. "Funny, Red. Real funny. I was just proving a point to the kid." He clasped my waist with his hands and backed me into the wall beside the door. "And if you want me to take my clothes off, you just have to ask nicely."

Goddamn, that was a tempting offer—one I only hesitated on thanks to my phone ringing in my pocket. I groaned and pushed Cass back with a hand on his chest. "I need to check that," I told him regretfully. "Don't go anywhere."

His dark gaze heated, but he waited patiently as I fished the phone out of my tight denim pocket. The display told me it was Gen calling, and I instantly got a bad feeling.

"Gen, what's happened?" I asked, bringing the phone to my ear when it connected. "I take it you're not calling at this time on a Friday night because you want to grab drinks."

"I wish," she replied, sounding pained. "You'd better get over to Anarchy. The SGPD just executed a *random* drug raid with dogs and the whole fucking deal."

Irritation zapped through me. Of course they chose a fight night to pull that shit. I'd never appreciated how useful it was to have the local police in my pocket until they no longer were. "So they caught a couple of coked-up patrons, that's nothing too drastic," I replied. "Or am I missing something?"

"Yeah, it's worse than that," she replied. "In addition to the expected coke users, they've also picked up twenty-eight patrons in possession of PCP. Hades, the patrons are all singing like birds, claiming it was sold to them by *Timberwolves.*"

That fact made me stiffen and push Cass gently away. "They're saying *what*?" I hissed, fury rippling through my veins.

"I know," Gen replied. "First the reporters, now this. Someone really wants to out us. Just…how soon can you get here? I'm doing my best, but one of the cops asked for you specifically."

I grimaced. "Lieutenant Jeffries?"

"That's the one."

"I'll be there in twenty minutes. Zed might be quicker. I'll call him now." I ended the call and immediately dialed Zed as I strode out of the gym with Cass following me like a shadow.

The call went straight to his voicemail, so I hung up and tried again.

"No answer," I muttered, glancing up at Cass. "Go hurry Lucas up, we need to get to Anarchy ASAP."

He nodded in understanding and took the stairs three at a time while I tried calling Zed again. This time when it reached his voicemail, I left a terse message telling him to get his ass to Anarchy.

Lucas came running into the garage as I popped the Mustang's door open, but unfortunately, he had a petite redhead trailing after him.

"What's going on?" Seph asked, scowling at me in accusation like I'd deliberately orchestrated some drama to ruin *her* life.

"Just got some work to deal with," I snapped back, not remotely in the mood for more of her attitude. "Lucas, get in. Cass, you know what to do."

Cass nodded, his dark eyes serious as he placed a hand on Seph's arm and tugged her back into the house, out of view of when I opened the garage door, just in case.

Confident I was leaving Seph in capable hands, I didn't hesitate before speeding out into the night with Lucas by my side.

"Can you try calling Zed again?" I asked when we paused for the gate to open. "He isn't answering."

"That seems odd for him," Lucas murmured, pulling out his own phone. "What am I telling him if he picks up?"

I drew a deep breath, then gave Lucas a quick overview of what Gen had told me. His brows shot up, and he nodded quickly.

"Got it," he assured me, dialing Zed's number and putting the call on speaker. This time it actually rang, but still eventually went to voicemail. What the fuck was he doing? He never screened my calls.

Biting the inside of my cheek, I tried to push aside my personal fear that something had happened to him. This was Zayden De Rosa; he was basically indestructible. No, he was probably just busy beating the shit out of those suits and had turned his phone on silent or something.

"Call Alexi," I told Lucas instead. "He should be at Anarchy. I want to know why Gen called this in and not him."

Lucas nodded his understanding, swiping through his phone for Alexi's number. Again, he put the call on speaker so I could hear it myself when his call *also* went to voicemail.

"What the fuck is going on?" I exclaimed, beyond frustrated and driving like a bat out of hell to get us to Anarchy.

Lucas ruffled his fingers through his hair, clearly thinking, then turned back to his phone. "I'll try Hannah. Maybe she knows something."

It was a long shot, but it felt more productive than leaving voicemails for my second-in-charge and my head of security.

Hannah picked up on the second ring. "Lucas, hi. What's up?"

"Hey, Hannah," he replied. "We're on our way to Anarchy.

There's been a drug raid, and it sounds like a setup. Do you have any idea where Alexi is? Or why his phone is off?"

She made a thoughtful sound. "I don't, but I can find out. Give me ten minutes. I'll call you back." The line went dead before we could ask more questions, and I arched a questioning brow at Lucas.

"No idea," he replied, "but I'm curious. Are we far?"

"Five minutes or so," I replied, taking the next corner way too fast and almost losing traction on the back wheels. "Sorry."

"No apologies needed, babe. I love when you drive aggressively." His grin was bright with excitement, and I stifled an eye roll. Lucas was a bit of an adrenaline junkie, I was starting to find.

My phone then rang through the car's Bluetooth, and I hit answer on the steering wheel without waiting for the ID to generate on the screen.

"Zed?" I barked.

"Sorry, no," the woman on the other end replied. "Agent Hanson. I take it you're on your way to Anarchy right now?"

I slowed my breakneck speed slightly, wanting to focus on this call. "I am. I take it this has something to do with you?"

Agent Hanson scoffed a bitter laugh. "Not likely. Or…nothing to do with *me* anyway. It was a setup for sure. Nothing about that raid looked even remotely legal or sanctioned. Look, I'm just going to cut the bullshit and get to facts. I got fired today because I was digging further into your open case."

I frowned, exchanging a quick look with Lucas. "What open case?"

Dorothy Hanson clucked her tongue. "As if you don't know the FBI has been watching you for years. They've just never had enough evidence to arrest you on anything that would really stick."

"So you got fired for looking into my case? Why?" Something wasn't adding up. Something had my nerves tight with anxiety.

Agent Hanson snorted. "I wish I knew. To be honest, Ms.

Wolff, I think someone in the Bureau *thinks* I found something that I didn't actually find. It was all very suspicious, and that leads me to one logical conclusion."

Shit. I had a feeling I knew what she was about to say.

"Someone in your organization is working for the feds, Ms. Wolff, and has been for a long time. I think I got fired to protect the mole's identity." She sounded bitter and resigned.

I drew a sharp breath. "Why are you telling me this, Dorothy?"

"Because it reeks of corruption, and I hate that. You might be a criminal, Ms. Wolff, but so are the agents on your case. They're deliberately trying to set you up for something big. I can just—" Her sentence cut off with a shriek, and then the phone seemed to drop to a hard floor with a clatter.

I slammed my foot on the brake, pulling us over onto the shoulder and listening as Dorothy fought off an attacker. The car filled with the sounds of a struggle, grunts, and screams, then eventually a wet gurgle, followed by the heavy sound of a body dropping lifelessly to the floor. I'd heard that sound enough to know it unquestionably.

A second later, Agent Hanson's phone was picked up and a couple of gasping breaths sounded before the call cut off.

For a moment, Lucas and I just sat there, shocked into silence. Then I turned to him with wide eyes. "She just got killed for telling me that," I murmured.

Death was nothing new to me, and I held no real personal connection with Agent Hanson. So hearing her murder wasn't what held me stunned almost speechless. It was her accusation that someone in the Timberwolves was a fed. Not someone new, either. Someone who'd been with me for *years*, potentially. Someone I trusted.

And that person had likely just killed her to keep that secret.

CHAPTER 35

After our brief pause to audibly witness Agent Hanson's murder, Lucas and I got to Anarchy just as a handful of cop cars were leaving the parking lot, no doubt with their PCP-carrying patrons in the back seats. Most of the other patrons had already left, and understandably so with a rude interruption like that.

When I stepped out of the car, I found one of the SGPD peons putting a police-tape barrier across the main entrance.

"Fuck," I hissed to Lucas, "they've shut us down."

Seething, I stormed across to where Gen stood with Lieutenant Jeffries some distance away from the macabre clown face that framed the entrance to Anarchy.

"Ms. Wolff," Lieutenant Jeffries greeted me with a tight smile. "Good of you to join us."

I scowled. "Good of you to let me know you'd be stopping by."

"Just doing my job, ma'am," he replied, then gave a small shake of his head. "Er, I mean sir. Anyway, orders are orders, and tonight we found a lot of your patrons carrying illicit substances. That's an offense that can't be ignored."

Nodding, I kept my expression calm and my voice cool. "It's an offense to be taken up with the Shadow Grove City Council and the liquor-licensing board. I cannot be held accountable for my patrons' illegal activity, which you well know."

His eyes narrowed slightly in irritation. "Be that as it may, we can and have shut you down until the licensing board can review the conduct of your staff and ensure that your organization had nothing to do with the sale and distribution of drugs. As I'm sure you've already been informed, a whole lot of those patrons arrested have told us they bought their supply from Timberwolf gang members." He gave me a pointed look, but I didn't flinch.

"That's impossible, Jeffries," I replied with a small smile. "The Timberwolves are extinct. Are we done here, or did you want to chitchat some more?"

He looked like he wanted to say more, but my phone rang and I walked away to answer the call.

"Hannah," I said on picking it up, "what have you got for me?"

"I pinged the GPS data on Alexi's phone," she told me. "He should be there at Anarchy somewhere."

I was impressed. "That was smart thinking, Hannah. I don't suppose you can do the same to Zed's phone?"

Her response was a laugh. "No, sir. There are no trackers on your phones, just on normal Copper Wolf employee–issued devices. Is there anything else I can help with?"

Rubbing at the bridge of my nose, I mentally ran through the mountain of work the Anarchy shutdown would cause. "Nothing tonight, Hannah," I replied. "Come by Zed's place in the morning, though. We can get to work sorting out this mess at Anarchy."

"Understood, sir," she replied. I ended the call as I recognized a familiar car pulling into the parking lot.

"Alexi!" I snapped as my head of security climbed out of his car. My voice cracked through the evening air like a whip, and he flinched visibly.

My employee made his way over to me, and I shot Lieutenant Jeffries a sharp look. "You can go now, Jeffries. We're done here."

The middle-aged cop looked like he was ready to stand his ground on pure principle, but a few stern words from Gen made him send me a tight nod before stalking toward his squad car.

I waited while the other remaining cops packed up their shit and left my property before flicking my gaze back to Alexi.

"Where the fuck were you?" I demanded. "And why didn't you answer your phone?"

His lips tightened. "I was on break," he replied. "I didn't know *this* would happen. Fuck, I just took an hour to grab some dinner, and..."

I arched a brow. "And?"

He shrugged. "This is obviously a setup."

"Obviously," I replied tartly. "Why didn't you answer your phone?"

Embarrassment crept over his face. "I didn't know it was you calling, sir. I thought... I didn't think it was important."

A frown tugged at my face, then I quickly connected the dots. I hadn't called him from my phone. Lucas had. And Alexi must be struggling to accept Lucas as being in a position of power above him. Hell, Lucas had the place Alexi had been chasing for years—at my side and in my bed.

Grinding my teeth together, I drew a calming breath. "You're on thin fucking ice, Alexi. Go over to Club 22 and see if Zed needs help with the suits he was persuading not to press charges."

Alexi gave a tight nod. "Understood, sir." He swiped a hand over his brow as he turned away to head back to his car, and I noted blood staining the cuff of his shirt. Not exactly uncommon in his line of work, but it stuck in my mind, nonetheless.

When he was gone, I turned back to Gen and Lucas with a frown. "Anyone heard from Zed yet?"

Gen shook her head, checking her phone, and Lucas ran his hand through his hair with a grimace.

"I'm sure he's just—" Whatever Lucas was about to say

cut off when my phone rang again, and I held my hand up to silence him.

"Zed," I barked, bringing my phone to my ear. "Where the fuck have you been?"

His casual laugh on the other end of the line set my nerves on edge. "You miss me, baby? I'm on my way to Anarchy now. Those pricks took more convincing than expected."

I bit the edge of my lip, analyzing his tone for any hint of deception. But why the fuck would he lie to me about being at Club 22 when there were plenty of staff there who could verify his whereabouts if I asked. I was just being paranoid. That was Chase's whole fucking game, and I didn't think for even a second anyone *but* Chase Lockhart was behind this mess.

"Dare?" Zed prompted. "You still there?"

I let my breath out in a rush, squeezing my eyes shut. "Yeah, I'm here. Don't bother coming to Anarchy. Cops have shut us down indefinitely. Just head home, and I'll fill you in when we get back."

Tucking my phone back into my pocket, I offered Lucas a weak smile. "Sorry, I was stressing over nothing. Zed didn't even know what happened here."

"I should head out," Gen commented, grabbing her car keys out of her purse. "This is going to be a hell of a lot of paperwork, and I'd rather get onto it sooner than later. I'll check in with you in the morning, Boss."

She gave Lucas a smile, then headed back to her own car. A few of the Anarchy staff were still making their way out, ducking under the police tape, but they didn't need me to stick around. Lucas and I made our way home mostly in silence, but his hand on my knee as we drove was a constant reminder that I wasn't alone. I no longer had to internalize everything because I had a team around me.

When we arrived back on Zed's street, our new neighbor was

conveniently out checking his mailbox and gave us a sarcastic wave when we passed by.

A shudder of dread rolled through me, and Lucas grimaced. "He's completely unhinged," he muttered. "Cass needs to be so fucking careful not to be seen."

I sighed because I agreed. The safest thing to do would be to send Cass back out on the job he'd been doing prior to saving Seph. But selfishly, I wanted to keep him close. Just for a little while longer.

Morning provided a little perspective in the sense that the Anarchy shutdown was simply an inconvenience. Money, mostly. Depending on how long they planned to keep us closed, we might have to postpone the main-event fight night. It'd sting and piss off some sponsors, but…fuck it. There were always more fighters and more fight nights.

The troubling parts to take away from the whole mess were the obvious attempt to start publicizing the Timberwolves again—directly contradicting my whole business model when it came to running my criminal empire—and the accusation Agent Hanson had made before getting her throat cut. Or that's what the method of murder had sounded like, anyway.

"I need to talk with you," Seph announced, busting through my bedroom door without so much as knocking once. "Dare, get up. I need to talk to you about—" She cut herself off, clearly having just noticed Cass beside me in bed, face down and sleeping but barely covered by my sheet.

With a silent growl of frustration, I slid out of bed and tugged Cass's T-shirt on before shoving my sister out of the room. I closed the door softly behind me, but I knew Cass would have woken up the moment I got out of bed anyway.

"Seriously, Seph?" I hissed at her, storming down the hallway as I pulled my tangled hair up in a ponytail. "You couldn't have spared three seconds to knock before barging in? You're fucking lucky you didn't walk in on anything more explicit."

I flicked a glance at her over my shoulder. Her cheeks were burning with embarrassment, and I rolled my eyes. Fuck, she was clueless sometimes.

"What did you so urgently need to talk about?" I demanded, heading downstairs with her tight on my heels.

"Uh, I wanted to tell you I'm going back to school on Monday." She announced it with a slight quaver in her voice, like she'd intended it to come out as a strong demand but had lost her nerve halfway.

I continued into the kitchen, where I found Lucas at his usual spot with his textbooks all around and an empty coffee mug in front of him.

"Hey, you," I greeted, dropping a kiss on his shoulder as I leaned in to pick up his mug. "Want another?"

He shot me a tired smile and nodded. "Thanks, babe."

"Dare," Seph snapped, posing with her hands on her hips. "Did you hear what I said?"

Ignoring my sister and her drama, I yawned and headed for the coffee machine to sort out mugs for both Lucas and me. Then, after a moment's indecision, I grabbed one for Seph, too.

"I heard you," I replied after an uncomfortably long pause, within which I could see her temper boiling hotter.

Her brows tightened together in a scowl as I continued making coffee. "And?"

I handed her coffee over to her, then delivered one to Lucas, which he accepted with a grateful kiss on my lips. A kiss that could have easily escalated if Seph hadn't made an irritated sound and started tapping her foot on the tile.

"Just give me a fucking second to wake up, Seph," I groaned. "I need a vacation so bad it hurts." Cupping my own coffee between my hands, I perched my butt on the stool beside Lucas and shivered when the cool seat met my bare ass. Seph hadn't exactly given me time to hunt out underwear.

"Look, this wasn't a discussion." Seph pushed, popping a hip out with so much attitude it made my teeth hurt. "I was just informing you so you could do…you know…whatever you do." She flapped her hand, clearly referring to my security measures. The fact that she thought it could be summed up with a hand flap said just how little she understood.

Cass slouched into the kitchen a moment later dressed in low-slung sweatpants and missing his shirt. Oh yeah, it was on me. He *could* have gone back to his own room opposite Lucas's to grab a new one, but I was more than okay with the shirtless look.

So was Seph, apparently, as her eyes just about bugged out of her head.

"What's going on?" he rumbled, heading for the fridge.

"Seph wants to go back to school," Lucas told him, sipping his coffee. A smudge of pink highlighter decorated the side of his nose, and I had to resist the urge to rub it off for him. Too damn cute.

Cass leveled a curious look at Seph, then gave a vague grunt and buried his head in the fridge without offering an opinion on the matter.

"Why?" I asked my sister as she continued standing there growing more and more agitated by the second.

She scowled. "Why what?"

It took everything I had to keep my patience. "Why do you want to go back to school? Haven't you been doing the online learning courses that Lucas is enrolled in?"

She folded her arms tightly across her body. "I have," she bit back. Then her gaze ducked away. "Sort of. I find it really hard to focus online. Besides, I'm bored as hell already and want to socialize with my peers. You know, be a *normal* teenager. Isn't that what you always go on and on about? Normal girls don't hide out in their sister's boyfriend's fortress and attend online classes under the guise of some long-term illness."

I clucked my tongue, feeling Cass's heavy gaze on me as he popped out of the fridge with a raw steak in hand. "Guess you've got me there, Seph."

She knew I was mocking her, and it wasn't amusing her in the least. Her glare just darkened, and her lips pursed with anger.

"I'll think about it," I told her with absolutely no intention of doing anything of the sort.

Frustration flashed over her pretty, doll-like face. She drew a breath to argue, but Lucas beat her to it.

"Actually, come to think of it," he commented quietly, "I would really benefit from going back for at least a couple of my subjects. We're so close to exams now, and it'd only really be a few weeks of classes. I could play bodyguard to Seph and make sure Chase doesn't snatch her again."

I swiveled my head to peer at him. "You could ask me for help with assignments."

He smiled. "I could. But I wouldn't actually be learning anything."

For a moment, I turned the idea over in my brain, then looked over at Cass to see what his thoughts were. He just gave me a miniscule shrug as he tossed his steak into a frying pan. Not amazingly useful, but also he was clearly not opposed to the idea.

"Fine," I acquiesced. "I'll set up a meeting with the school today and sort out their security. I'll have to move your schedules around to get you both in the same classes too."

Lucas smiled, leaning in to kiss my cheek. "Thanks, babe. You're the best."

Seph was just scowling even harder, though. "Oh, I see. So when I ask, it's all *I'll think about it*, which we both know means flat-out no. Then Lucas asks and you're okay with it? You're such a selfish bitch, Dare." She stormed out of the kitchen in her bratty rage, and I rubbed at my temples in my endless search for sanity.

"Is it just me," Cass rumbled from where he prodded at his cooking steak, "or would Seph really benefit from Phillip D'Ath's camp?"

I choked on my coffee as a laugh took me by surprise. Cass peered over at me, all fucking innocent, and I swiped a hand over my mouth.

"If only it was still running," I chuckled, shaking my head. But I wasn't serious. Even if that camp had still been active, I wouldn't send Seph there. She was annoying as hell, but I wouldn't kill her spirit like that.

Zed entered the kitchen with a confused look on his face, glancing back the way he came. "Uh, anyone know why Seph just told me we were all ruining her life before bursting out crying and slamming her door?"

I couldn't help myself; I started laughing. It was that or cry when it came to my little sister.

CHAPTER 36

Seph gave me the cold shoulder all weekend, even slamming her door in my face when I delivered her new Shadow Prep uniform on Sunday evening. But by the time she and Lucas got home on Monday after their first day back, all seemed forgiven.

She hugged me tight on getting back to the house, then sweetly asked if I wanted to have a Netflix date with her that night, just like we used to.

I missed my sister enough that I agreed and didn't call her on all the shitty attitude over the last few days. It earned me a few dark glares from Zed, but I just flipped him off behind her back. Then made it up to him later. Repeatedly.

So all things considered, I was in a good mood by the time Zed and I headed to Club 22 on Tuesday afternoon for my rehearsal with Maxine. I'd postponed my actual performance so many times it was starting to feel like I was just attending a class rather than preparing for a show.

Still, I wasn't prepared to give Zed even a hint of a preview, so I made him drop me off and come back when I was finished in a couple of hours.

Training with Maxine was refreshingly enjoyable. She'd long

since stopped treating me with the careful, fearful respect that my Hades face demanded and had started treating me like a real person. Like a friend. I liked it way more than I could ever admit, but it was part of the reason I kept stalling on following through with the bet. After I did the show, I had no reason to hang out with Maxine. She'd go back to being an employee.

Obviously, I knew that wasn't how things worked in the real world. But that wasn't the world I lived in. I couldn't afford to have *friends*. Hell, just having lovers was dangerous enough. Anyone I cared about was a liability, and I definitely didn't need to add to that list.

Zed arrived back *right* on time, to the minute, and it made me suspicious that he'd just lurked in the parking lot for the entire time, which was ridiculous because he had a shit ton of work to do. But the thought crossed my mind.

"Hey, I meant to say earlier," Maxine said to me as we both sat on the stage floor to take our shoes off, "I should have mentioned about me and Zed. I realized last session that you didn't know, and then I got all freaked out that you were going to... I dunno..." Her voice trailed off as Zed sauntered his sexy ass closer, clearly listening in. Prick.

I gave her a soft smile, letting her off the hook. "You thought I would flip my killer switch and come at you in a jealous rage? Maybe break into your house and bludgeon you with a stripper shoe?" Her eyes widened and her smile slipped, and I cringed. "Sorry, my people skills need work," I muttered. "No, we're cool. If I was going to kill every girl Zed had ever slept with, there would be a hell of a lot of blood on my hands." *More than there already was, anyway.*

Maxine's breath rushed out in relief. "Okay. Cool. 'Cause this"—she indicated between her and Zed—"is totally ancient history. Way, way in the past."

Zed gave her a tight smile back but added nothing more.

Not that I needed to know, but color me curious. "Why did you guys break up, anyway?" I asked, stretching out my leg and reaching for my toes. My hamstrings were screaming at me after today's session.

Zed's eyes widened, and Maxine made a small noise of surprise. "Oh, um, I figured you knew. We broke up because…" She let her voice trail off, looking at Zed in panic.

He gave her a reassuring smile, then answered me directly. "We broke up because Max accused me of being in love with you, and I couldn't deny it. Because it's true."

Oh.

"You know what? I'm gonna…go shower," Maxine mumbled, scrambling to her feet and grabbing her bag. "I'll see you later, H." She hurried toward the backstage area where our staff had a full locker room complete with showers, and Zed arched a brow at me.

"H?" he repeated.

I shrugged. "I like her."

His smile was smug and knowing. "I can tell. I don't think I've ever seen you with a friend before. It's cute as hell."

"Shut up, it is not," I muttered, pushing off the stage and heading over to the bar to fill up my water bottle. Because I was a lazy asshole, I boosted my butt up onto the bar top to reach over and grab the soda gun, and Zed leaned his elbow on the bar beside me. "Besides, *you're* my friend."

"I meant a *girl* friend. And before you say it, Hannah doesn't count. You like her, but as an employee, not a friend. And you just barely tolerate Gen because she's good at her job." He watched me with an amused smile as I gulped my water.

Putting my bottle back down, I flipped the conversation on him. "Okay, well, how long ago did you guys date? It must have been recent if you broke up because of me."

Zed huffed a short laugh. "It was three years ago, Dare. She was my last real relationship, and when she called me on loving *you*, I gave up trying. The rest were just…fun ways to pass time. Something to temporarily fill the empty void in my life that *you* belonged in."

My lips parted as I held his gaze. "That…is surprisingly romantic, Zed. In a really slutty manwhore kind of way." Then an unpleasant thought slammed into my mind, killing the fizzy affection that had been building. "Uh, speaking of your long, *long* list of previous conquests, have you—"

"I got tested before we slept together the first time." He cut me off, already knowing exactly what I was asking. "Like…weeks before that time. Just in case. I didn't want to risk anything on the chance things with us did work out."

I let my breath out in a long exhale. "Good. That's good." I gave a shaky laugh. "Probably something we should have discussed sooner, huh?"

Zed gave an easy shrug. "A lot of why we work so well, why we've always worked so well, is mutual trust. What about Cass and Lucas?"

I parted my lips, not really wanting to divulge Lucas's sexual history—or lack thereof—and internally cringing that I'd never talked STDs with Cass. He was such a control freak, though, there was no way he hadn't been getting regular tests.

"Do you really want to discuss Cass's and Lucas's dicks?" I peered down at him with a teasing grin. "But I know you've seen them both now. Any thoughts you want to share with the class?"

Zed scoffed a laugh, his palm warm on my thigh. I was still in a sports bra and hot pants so short they were basically underpants, so his touch made my skin shiver with delight. "If you're asking whether I have any bisexual tendencies, Boss…" He paused there. So *fucking* dramatic. "The answer is no." Oh, good. Or…damn. I wasn't totally sure whether I was pleased or disappointed by that statement.

"Or at least I have no secret desire to suck dick," he continued.

"Am I so straight that I would balk at the idea of another man seeing my dick buried in your pussy or in your mouth? Nah. I love an audience." His wink was pure sex, and it made my breath catch in my chest. Goddamn, this hadn't been my intention *at all,* but suddenly I was seriously considering fucking Zed on the bar top. We only had about fifteen minutes before Rodney would arrive for his shift, though...

Zed was apparently thinking the same thing because his hand crept higher and his fingertips hooked the elastic waistband of my pants. "You know what I've always wanted to do?" He shifted to stand directly in front of me, between my dangling legs. "Ever since we opened this club?"

"Hmm?" I replied, obediently lifting my hips as he peeled my hot pants off and abandoned them on the floor. "I think I can guess, but go ahead and tell me anyway."

Zed gave a dark chuckle, lifting each of my bare feet and placing them on bar stools to either side of where he stood, exposing my bare pussy to him. "I've *always* wanted to christen this bar the way it was meant to be done."

He bent down, kissing me in the most intimate way and making my toes curl. Drawing a deep breath, my eyes flicked to the clock, even as my hips tilted to give him better access to my pussy.

"Just this bar?" I murmured, gasping as he licked my clit and already quivering with need for more.

He laughed against my core, sending soft vibrations through my sensitive flesh. I squirmed under his touch, and he nipped my thigh with his teeth.

"Not just this one," he admitted, straightening up. "All of them. But this would be a great start, don't you think?" He licked his lips, and I groaned.

"Shit," I whispered. "I can't say no to you. Hurry the fuck up, though. Rodney—"

"Starts in ten, I know. Lie back." He swiveled me on the bar, then climbed up to join me, already loosening his belt. "And you'd better be quiet. Maxine is still in the shower."

I cringed. I'd totally forgotten about Maxine. But there was no changing my mind as Zed positioned himself on his knees, then lifted my hips and drove his dick deep into my throbbing core. "Ah *fuck*," I cried out, then immediately clapped my hand over my mouth.

Zed laughed as he shifted our position again, then used his grip on my hips and ass to hold me in just the right spot while he went to work. His thrusts were hard and deep, making soft grunts and gasps escape my throat with every push.

My back kept sliding down the polished bar top, though. Eventually Zed reached out and pulled me up to sitting. Then lifted me to straddle him as he hung his legs off the bar, and I sank back onto his cock fully.

"Oh yeah," he breathed as I found my seat. "Yeah, that's it. Fuck me hard, Boss. We've only got a couple of minutes left."

"Shit," I breathed, settling my weight and resting my forearms around his neck. I quickly found my groove, bouncing up and down on Zed's dick like an equestrian. He tugged my sports bra up to expose my tits, right in his face, and grabbed one of my nipples between his teeth just as I started to come.

My startled yelp fast turned into a moan as my pussy contracted around his dick, and he bit down harder.

"Fuck, Zed!" I screamed out as my lady bits imploded, blowing my damn mind all over the freaking bar. Zed grabbed my waist, holding me still as he thrust up into me a couple of times, finishing himself off as well.

For a moment, time stood still, and I just rested my forehead on his shoulder, panting and waiting for my cunt to relax. But then the unmistakable sound of the front door opening shocked us both out of our post-orgasm bliss.

Not wanting Rodney to catch me with my pants

down—literally—I made a snap decision and dove off Zed and behind the bar.

The sound of my best friend's laughter followed me, and a second later my hot pants flew over the bar top as Zed called out a greeting to Rodney.

CHAPTER 37

Zed and I had to work our asses off for the next few days trying to sort through the mess that Chase had generated for us with Anarchy. Not only had the reporters redoubled their efforts in trying to get the "Timberwolf story," thanks to the bullshit accusations of our drug-using patrons, we also had the city council to deal with.

Luckily, Chase hadn't managed to break *all* our alliances. Some of them had taken a long time to cultivate, and they weren't shifting allegiances easily.

Zed was leveraging one of those important contacts while I drove us home from the Copper Wolf office in his Ferrari. We'd worked late, again, and it was well past dinnertime, so my stomach was growling as I turned into the driveway. We had intended to order takeout while we worked but ended up fucking on my desk instead. Whoops.

"Understood," Zed murmured into his phone as I parked in the garage. He badly hadn't wanted to let me drive his baby, but I'd reminded him of that scratch on my McLaren. He'd given the keys up with a grumble. "Thank you, Gerald. I appreciate your assistance on this matter." He paused, glancing over at me with a smile on his lips. "You're right, we are overdue for a round of golf. How does Sunday sound? Rainybanks Country Club? Perfect. See you then, Gerald."

That was the main reason I had Zed on the call rather than me. He walked the walk and talked the talk. He could schmooze the politicians like no one else. He had a way of delivering the same threats and blackmail that I would but making them sound so very casual. It was scary as hell and equally impressive.

"Well?" I prompted after he ended the call.

His grin spread wide. "All sorted. Two-week closure, then we can reopen without any fines and no black marks on our record."

Climbing out of the car, I gave a small groan. "Two-week closure? Why?"

Zed rolled his eyes. "Seriously? We were facing a massive fine and potential loss of our liquor license. All Gerald asked was that we stay closed for appearances."

I pouted, but he was right. We were getting off easy. It was just shitty timing for our events. "I don't know how you do that shit," I commented, shaking my head. "Charming the pants off those old politicians."

Zed laughed, draping his arm around me as we headed inside the house. "I know. That's why I handle that part. It's what makes us a good team, Gorgeous. I subtly threaten them with the ax. You're the ax."

I couldn't help grinning at that description. He wasn't wrong.

"Uh, why does it smell like burning in here?" I wrinkled my nose and glanced up at Zed, who looked severely unimpressed.

"Fuck's sake," he groaned, "I told them to order in for dinner."

We made our way through to the kitchen, and sure enough, there was a flustered, red-faced Seph flapping a dish towel at the smoke billowing out of the oven.

"Seph, what the hell is going on?" he demanded, storming over and snatching the cloth from her, then kicking the oven door shut. "Why are you trying to burn my house down?"

"I wasn't!" she whined back. "I was *trying* to cook dinner for everyone. Your stupid oven is broken or something!"

Laughter bubbled up in my chest, and I bit the inside of my cheek in a weak attempt not to grin. Seph definitely wouldn't appreciate the funny side right now. Neither would Zed, seeing as he took his kitchen appliances *very* seriously.

"Right, Seph," he snapped, the sarcasm thick in his voice, "you're right. My eight-thousand-dollar Smeg oven must be broken. No user error involved." He shot a glare at me, like he knew I was about to lose it. "Seph... Don't you have homework to do or something?"

My sister glared at me as well, as though her failed meal was somehow my fault, then let out a frustrated scream and stormed out of the kitchen.

"Don't fucking start, Dare," Zed growled, pointing an accusing finger at me. "Go order pizzas. I'll clean this mess up."

Offering him a mocking salute, I pulled out my phone to call in a pizza order while heading upstairs to change into sweats. After spending all day in a pencil skirt, stockings, and high heels, the softness of my sweatpants was better than anything.

Cracking the loft door, I yelled up to Seph that pizza would be half an hour. The only response I got was a bratty "Whatever," so I left her to go in search of Cass and Lucas.

I found Cass first, in the middle of a shower with sweaty gym clothes on the floor. As tempting as it was to join him, I mustered up the strength of will to overrule my greedy cunt and instead just let him know about the pizza ETA.

Lucas was in his room but was fast asleep on top of a pile of his textbooks. He'd been pulling crazy late nights preparing for exams and juggling his EMT coursework; it was no surprise he'd crashed.

As gently as I could, I tidied up all the books, wiggling them out from under him and stacking them neatly on his bedside table. Then I grabbed a blanket from the closet and draped it over him before flicking off the lights and leaving him to sleep.

Back downstairs, Zed had managed to get rid of the smoke in the oven, but the smell clung to the air and a piece of charcoal-black meat—I think—sat in a roasting dish on the counter.

"Well, I guess it was nice she tried?" I suggested, coming over to peer at the dish.

Zed gave me a sidelong glance. "She was making beef Wellington."

I screwed my nose up and made a gagging sound. I despised mushrooms, and Seph fucking well knew it. It *was* Zed's favorite, though, so no points for guessing who my sister had been trying to impress tonight.

"Want a drink?" Zed offered, heading for the liquor cabinet. "I'll make you a cocktail."

Eagerly accepting, I perched on a barstool to watch as he mixed up my drink. Cass came in to join us a couple of minutes later, bending to kiss me, then giving Zed a bro nod.

"Suppose you want me to make you one too," Zed commented, pouring my velvety, delicious espresso martini into a frosted glass.

Cass grunted. "Nope. Whiskey will do for me."

"Easy to please." Zed grabbed out a bottle of whiskey and tossed a couple of ice cubes into a glass for Cass, then nodded toward the courtyard. "Let's sit outside where we don't have to smell this crap."

Cass eyed the remains of Seph's dinner and smirked. "Looks delicious," he muttered, standing back to let me outside ahead of him. Such a gentleman.

I loved Zed's courtyard. It was outdoors but totally private in the center of his fortress house. Unless Chase was flying drones, there was no way he could spy on us, nor could anyone else.

"Where's Lucas?" Zed asked as we got comfy on the couch.

"Sleeping," I replied with a smile. "He'd crashed out in the middle of his books."

Zed nodded like that was unsurprising. "He's been working hard lately. I'm impressed."

Cass grunted a sound of agreement. "He told me he wants to start doing practical labs as soon as his high school exams are done. Kid doesn't wanna waste any time."

"I hope he's not doing it because he feels like we *need* him to upskill," I commented thoughtfully. "I hope he isn't feeling pressured to do this just to be more valuable or something."

Both Cass and Zed stared at me for a moment, then Zed grinned.

"Seriously?" he asked. "Fuck, you're cute when you're clueless."

Confusion rippled over me as I sipped my drink. "Huh?"

Cass leaned back in his seat, pulling his weed pouch out to roll a joint. "That's exactly why he's doing it, Red. He wants to impress you. Doesn't make it a bad thing, though. Gave him a goal to strive toward."

The doorbell rang, interrupting whatever I might have said back to that, and I frowned. "That's too fast for pizza. They said they were slammed right now."

"I've got it," Zed murmured, pulling his gun as he moved inside the house.

I turned my attention to Cass, ready to argue the fact that Lucas wasn't doing all his EMT training just to *impress* me, but Cass met my gaze with a knowing smirk.

He got up from his seat and came to settle beside me as he lit the joint. He took a drag, then passed it to me as he draped his arm around me.

"Lucas is one hundred percent trying to impress you, Red," he rumbled, "but there's nothing wrong with that. He seems to enjoy the course material, so who cares what his motivation is?"

"I guess," I mumbled, drawing a deep lungful of smoke.

Zed returned then with no pizza in his hands but a manila folder instead and a curious look on his face. "That was Dallas," he announced. "I didn't invite him in because, well"—he waved a hand at Cass—"but he left this. Said it's the info on Lucas's genetic match."

I sat up straighter, passing the joint back to Cass, and held my hand out for the folder.

Zed handed it over, then sat back down. "Should we wake him up?"

I hesitated a moment, my finger under the envelope flap. Then I licked my lips and shook my head. "We can show him in the morning, it's not time-sensitive."

And yet I wasn't exactly putting it down. Zed arched a brow at me accusingly but didn't stop me when I tugged the paper out of the envelope.

"Oh shit," I breathed, my eyes scanning the first page before handing it to Zed. The second page was a photo of the man who was *not* Lucas's sibling…but his father. Or that certainly seemed to be what the results suggested.

"Captain Brant Wilson," Zed read aloud from the paper. "Date of birth and genetic matches suggest he would be Lucas's biological father. Says he was enlisted in the U.S. military until around ten years ago when he made the switch to working for… Ah, fuck." Zed had spotted the part that'd made me curse.

"The suspense is killing me, guys," Cass drawled, sounding anything but tense.

"Ten years ago Brant Wilson took a position within the FBI. All records past that date have been redacted beyond Dallas's capabilities." Zed held the paper out to Cass to read for himself and gave me a grimace. "That can't be a coincidence. Right?"

I snagged my drink from the table and downed the whole thing in one gulp. "Nope," I croaked, handing Zed the photograph of Brant Wilson that I'd been looking at. "Recognize him?"

Zed frowned at the picture a moment; then his eyes widened and flicked back up to meet mine. "Is this—?"

"Yup," I replied, feeling sick.

"Fill me in," Cass rumbled.

My mouth felt dry again, so I swiped his whiskey for a sip. "That"—I tapped the photograph that Zed handed him—"is someone who was caught snooping around the Cloudcroft docks a few months ago. He was caught taking pictures of incoming shipments, and when questioned, he claimed to be a spy for the Diamondbacks."

Cass blew out a breath, grimacing. "You killed him."

I nodded, dying inside. "I killed Lucas's dad."

CHAPTER 38

Seph and the pizza interrupted any more discussions we could have about Lucas's bio father and the fact that I'd put a bullet through his head just four months ago. Only one decision was made, and that was not to tell Lucas about my part in Brant Wilson's disappearance. We would give him the packet of information Dallas had delivered and leave it at that. For now.

It had me all twisted up with guilt and anxiety, though, so I'd gone to bed alone for the night. Besides, my poor, worn-out vagina needed a night to herself for recovery. I wasn't used to having such an active sex life, not that I was complaining, but every now and then I felt the overwhelming need to sleep alone. Be alone.

A desire I found myself regretting some hours later when I woke up to the cold bite of metal circling my wrist. It was the click of the cuff closing that'd woken me, and despite knowing I'd just been handcuffed, I still tried to jerk out of bed on instinct.

"Ah-ah," the shadow-shrouded figure above me scolded, stepping back so he was just out of reach. He'd only cuffed one of my hands to the headboard, but it was enough to trap me. "You look so pretty when you sleep, Darling."

A deep shudder ran through me as I wondered how long he'd been in my room watching me sleep. Fuck, I was never sleeping alone again.

"What the fuck are you doing here, Chase?" I snarled, yanking on the handcuff and testing how tight he'd done it. The whole idea of dislocating my thumb to slip off the cuff was pure fiction, and I wasn't stupid enough to attempt it...again. So I just had to hope he'd rushed and not done the cuff tight enough.

My ex chuckled softly, flicking my bedside lamp on so I could see his sick smile as he peered down at me. "Just paying you a little visit, my sweet. You never stop to chat when we pass in the street, and it hurts my feelings."

I tugged on the cuff again, furious that he'd caught me vulnerable and terrified at the idea he'd been able to break into Zed's house undetected. How many times had he broken in without us knowing?

"Your days are numbered, Chase," I growled, pulling my hand harder against the metal. It wouldn't be the first time I'd slipped a handcuff. It hurt to get over the joint at the base of my thumb but wasn't impossible. "You must know I'm coming for you soon. Not even you are deluded enough to think you're getting away with all of this."

His grin spread wider. "I look forward to it," he replied with total sincerity. "I can't wait to see you fight back. It's going to be so delicious." He pulled something from his pocket and stroked his cheek with it, like a lucky rabbit's foot or something. "So very delicious."

I jerked on my cuffed hand again and hissed as the metal ripped my skin open. A little blood would just lubricate it, though. "What did you come here for, Chase? Just to prove you could?"

He shrugged, that smile unshakable. "That, and I wanted to pick up a souvenir." He turned his hand around, showing me what he'd been rubbing on his cheek so affectionately. It wasn't anything so innocent as an animal's foot. It was a thick lock of copper-red hair.

I drew a sharp breath, my eyes automatically shifting to the spill of my hair across my pillow, but Chase's malicious chuckle made my blood run cold.

"Don't worry, Darling," he purred, "I wouldn't touch a single hair on *your* head. They're far too pretty right where they are."

A surge of adrenaline shot through me, and I wrenched my hand through the cuff with a blaze of pain. Chase darted out of reach as I threw myself toward the bedside table to grab my gun. Except...

"Looking for this?" he taunted, spinning my Desert Eagle around his finger, then kissing the barrel like an old lover. He was backing slowly toward the open window of my bedroom, and I knew I had a choice to make.

"You're a walking dead man, Chase Lockhart," I snarled. "I'm going to enjoy killing you again. This time I'll make sure it's painful."

He cackled with glee. "Not if I get you first, Darling. An eye for an eye and all that biblical shit."

With a quiet, frustrated scream, I did nothing to stop him as he disappeared out the window and into the night. I didn't have time, and he would live to die another day. I raced out of my room and down the hall to Seph's loft bedroom.

The door was open, and my whole body went weak with fear as I took the stairs three at a time to get into the loft space that Zed had set up for my sister. I burst through into her bedroom with my heart thundering so hard I could barely hear anything else, expecting to see the worst.

But there she was, still fast asleep and snoring like a lumber-jack. She hadn't even stirred with all the noise I'd made, which explained how Chase had cut her hair without her even noticing. Fucking hell.

For a long moment I stood there staring at her, my chest heaving and my fists clenched at my sides while I tried to get a handle on my rage and fear and *frustration*.

A movement on the stairs made me flinch hard, and then I let out a long, slow breath when I saw it was Zed. He gave me a puzzled, concerned look, and I laid a finger over my lips to tell him to be quiet.

He nodded his understanding and waited as I pulled Seph's blanket up over her shoulders. Then I checked the small gable window to ensure it was locked from the inside—even though I knew how Chase had come in. When I returned to Zed, I was only a fraction calmer than when I'd come running in to save my sister.

"What's going on?" Zed whispered as we tiptoed back down the loft stairs and quietly closed the door at the bottom behind us. "Did something happen?"

A small, slightly hysterical laugh bubbled up in my chest, and I raked my fingers through my hair. But Zed caught my forearm before I could complete the gesture and jerked me closer in alarm.

"You're bleeding. What the fuck happened, Dare?"

I peered at the hand in question and grimaced at the mess I'd made of the skin. It was nothing life-threatening, but now that he'd reminded me, it was stinging like a motherfucker.

Instead of standing there in the hallway and giving him the whole stupid story, I nodded in the direction of his bedroom. He took the hint and strode along the hallway with his fingers still tight around my forearm like he could somehow heal my scrape with the power of his mind. How useful *that* skill would be in my world made me wish I believed in magic.

Once we were safely in his room with the door shut, Zed pushed me over to his bed and glared down at me. "Stay here. Don't move." He grabbed a gun from his bedside table and disappeared out of the room again, no doubt going to do a sweep of the house and ensure Chase wasn't still lurking behind a potted plant or something. Not that he knew who he was looking for, but he knew a sweep was warranted.

When he got back, he didn't look any calmer. Hell, if anything, he looked *more* stressed out. "Dare, start fucking talking before I have an aneurysm."

"Chase," I muttered, looking up at him with regret. I knew he was about to blast me for not calling out for help. "He broke in. Cuffed me to the bed."

Zed's whole body went rigid, and the air crackled with violence. "What—"

"I'm fine." I cut him off before his imagination could run wild. "He just wanted to prove he could. And he took my fucking gun." That was probably more distressing than him breaking into my room in the first place.

Zed's brows hiked. "He took the Desert Eagle?"

I gave a sour nod. "He's been obsessed with it since he's been back. I kept catching him eyeing it when we met in person. I knew he'd try for it at some stage, but…I wasn't expecting this."

Zed blew out a long breath and sat down on the edge of the bed beside me. "Why didn't you call out for help? Any one of us could have come to—"

"Come to my rescue?" I snickered, trying to soften the mocking in my voice. "I wasn't in any danger. Not really. And at first I was worried that if I screamed, Seph would come to investigate and get hurt."

Zed scowled, taking my injured hand into his lap to examine further. "And then?"

I hissed when his fingertip pressed a sore part of my wrist. "And then he made it clear he'd already visited Seph, so I made the decision to let him go and make sure she was unharmed. Which, as you saw, she is. Just missing a chunk of hair."

Zed gave me a disgusted look, and I agreed with a hollow laugh.

"Want me to wake Lucas up to clean this up?" Zed offered, arching a brow in question. "He needs practical medical experience."

I bit my lip, another worry running through my head. "Zed... what if Chase found Cass while he was looking for Seph's room?"

He shook his head, unconcerned. "Cass isn't here. He got a lead on one of his projects and headed out disguised as me again."

I wrinkled my nose. "Maybe that's why Chase decided to break in tonight. He thought you were gone, and...*shit*." I jerked up from the bed. "What if he hurt Lucas?" I was already out of the door before finishing that question. Rushing over to Lucas's bedroom, I shoved the door open.

Yeah, I wasn't a big one for polite knocking when I was worried about my loved ones' safety.

"Hayden?" Lucas mumbled, raising his sleepy head to squint at me in the darkness. "What's going on? Is everything okay? No, what? That's such a dumb question, of course it's not or you wouldn't be—"

"Lucas, shut up," Zed cut him off as he rambled in half-asleep panic. "Wake up and come to my room. Dare needs some first aid and a fucking hug, but it's not urgent."

With a firm hand on my back, Zed turned me around and steered me back into his room, giving Lucas a minute to scrub the sleep haze from his eyes.

"He's fine," Zed murmured, confirming what I'd just seen. "You're all kinds of twitchy, though. Understandable, but unnecessary. Everyone is okay. I'm guessing Chase was already nervous about being caught. Knowing his time was limited, he'd have gone straight to Seph and back to you,."

I nodded, knowing he was probably right but still anxious as fuck. It could have ended so much worse. He could have hurt Seph or Lucas. He could have found Cass still alive. He could have...

"Shit," I breathed, dropping back onto the edge of Zed's

bed with a heavy sigh. "Zed, he's messing with my head, and it's *working*."

Zed smiled sadly, nudging me further onto the bed. "I know, baby," he whispered, "but we'll win the war. You know we will."

I clenched my teeth hard but forced myself to nod. I didn't always believe it, though. Some days I really did wonder if Chase would win…and what that would look like.

"I'm here," Lucas announced, entering Zed's room as he tugged a T-shirt over his bare chest. "First aid kit?"

"Under my bathroom sink," Zed told him, nodding that way. "It's just a skin abrasion, should only need antiseptic cream and a bandage."

Lucas nodded, following Zed's directions to grab everything he needed along with a warm, wet washcloth to clean up the blood.

Before he started, though, he placed everything down on the bedside table and leaned down to wrap me in a soul-warming hug that I never wanted to end. The kind of hug that instantly eased my tension.

"What's that for?" I muttered when he pulled away again.

Lucas shrugged. "Dunno. Zeddy Bear said you needed a hug, so I provided. Now show me what the damage is."

I obediently held out my hand to him, shooting an amused look at Zed. "I wonder what else you'll do if Zed tells you." As soon as the words left my lips, I bit my cheek. That had been *supposed* to stay inside my head, but…oh well.

Zed's gaze flared hot; he was completely on the same page as me.

Lucas flicked a glance up from my wrist, a playful grin on his full lips. "Be a good patient, and you can find out."

Lust and anticipation swept through me, dissolving the fear Chase had left behind. There really was no better therapy. And besides, there was no way in hell I was going back to sleep alone tonight.

"Done deal," I murmured, grinning wickedly at Zed, who simply rolled his eyes and closed his bedroom door. Then locked it. We definitely didn't need Seph interrupting.

CHAPTER 39

Seph gave an exaggerated yawn as she made her way into the kitchen for breakfast, her school uniform perfect but her hair a mess. "Dare," she groaned, "can you braid my hair for me? I can't seem to make it sit right this morning."

I exchanged a quick look with Zed over my coffee mug, then gave Seph a warm smile. "Sure thing, brat. Come sit." I hopped off my barstool and patted it.

She gave me a frown. "What happened to your hand?"

"Um…" I glanced down at my bandaged hand and wrist. The scrape over my thumb joint had been deep, so Lucas had needed to apply a gauze dressing, then secure it all with an elastic bandage around my hand and wrist. "Picked up my curling iron at the wrong end," I lied.

From the corner of my eye, I caught Zed giving an irritated shake of his head, but too damn bad. There was no need to panic Seph by telling her what'd happened last night. We'd tighten up security today, and it'd never happen again.

Seph shrugged, accepting my lie as she sat down and handed me her hairbrush. "Thanks, big sis," she said sweetly as I started dragging the bristles through her mane. I used to braid her hair all the time for school, taking over after our mom had died, so it was an oddly nostalgic task.

I worked carefully, making sure the short strands were well disguised within a tight French braid while Seph helped herself to my coffee—a fact I only noticed when I finished tying off the tail of her braid and picked up my empty mug.

"I'll get you another," Zed murmured, kissing my temple as he scooped up my mug.

"Me too?" Seph asked, fluttering her lashes.

Zed just snorted and laughed and shook his head, but he did grab an extra mug, nonetheless. "You know you snore, Seph?"

Her mouth dropped open in outrage. "I do not!"

"Do too," he teased. "We could hear you all the way from my room."

I snorted a laugh, and she shot a glare at me.

"Oh really, Zed-man? I wouldn't have thought you could hear anything over the sound of my sister moaning. You know I had to turn my music up just so I could shower in peace this morning?" She cocked her head at us, all fucking attitude, but I was way too full of endorphins to give a fuck.

So instead I just grinned. "Oh, we know."

Lucas came into the kitchen then, looking half-asleep with his uniform barely even on his body. His belt was still unbuckled and his shirt hanging open with the Shadow Prep tie slung around his neck. Scrubbing a hand over his sleepy face, he made a beeline straight to me and kissed me breathless before even saying good morning.

"*Ahem*," Seph fake-coughed loudly. "You have an audience, Lucas."

He took his time pulling away from my lips, kissing me softly a couple more times before smirking at Seph. "Audience never bothered me before. Isn't that right, Zeddy Bear?"

Seph screwed up her face in confusion for a second, then gasped dramatically. "Oh my *god!* Ugh. You guys… Zed, I'm gonna take my coffee to go, thanks. Lucas, hurry up, or we'll be late for school."

Zed obediently poured her a travel mug of coffee, which she took with a quick thanks and sashayed out of the kitchen again, presumably heading to the garage to wait for Lucas to drive them both to school.

Lucas yawned as he buttoned his shirt slowly, then tucked it into his pants before doing up his belt. "Guys, I'm gonna fall asleep on my desk in the middle of algebra, and it'll be all your fault."

Zed gave a wicked laugh. "We'll leave you to sleep next time."

Lucas jerked like he'd been slapped. "Hell no. Best fucking reason to skip sleep *ever.*" Then he swooped back in to kiss me again until I was all but trying to climb him.

"Get to school, Gumdrop," Zed ordered in a rough voice. "We'll sort out the security breach while you're babysitting Persephone."

Lucas gave a pained groan but kissed me again quickly before turning to leave. Zed barked his name again, making him pause in the doorway. Then he rushed back to grab the travel mug of coffee Zed held out for him.

"Thanks, big bro, you're the best." Lucas grinned and took off toward the garage.

Alone again, I turned to face Zed with a wide smile on my face. "You're such a soft touch, Zayden."

Zed snorted a laugh, coming back over to the island where I sat. "He earned it." He slipped a hand into the back of my hair, tilting my head back to kiss me softly. "I love how much you smile these days. It wasn't so long ago I was wondering if I'd ever see this smile again." He dragged his thumb over my lips, and I nipped it playfully with my teeth.

"I could say the same about you," I replied, gazing up at him with way too much dopamine drugging my stupid, girlie brain.

He didn't seem to mind, though. He just kissed me again, slowly and carefully, as his strong fingers rubbed the base of my skull where I often carried stress headaches. "Dare," he murmured on a sigh as he ended our kiss, "you know how much I fucking love you? You're my whole damn world."

My heart fluttered, and I couldn't stop the stupid smile curving my lips again. Zed looked like he had something else he wanted to say. Something important. But heavy footsteps in the foyer had him stepping away with a hard exhale.

"Morning, Red," Cass rumbled, slouching into the room still decked out in Zed's bike leathers. He placed a hand on my lower back, leaning down to kiss me, then gave Zed one of those dude nods. "What happened last night? Got your message earlier this morning, Zed."

I shot Zed a grateful smile because I'd been too busy riding dick all damn night to message Cass myself and fill him in with Chase's visit.

"Dare had a late-night visit from our neighbor," Zed explained, keeping it brief.

Cass stiffened, and fury and violence rolled off him in palpable waves. "Fucking *what*?"

Zed clucked his tongue, heading for the fridge. "You hungry, Grumpy Cat? I've probably got some canned food in here somewhere."

The sound that rumbled from Cass was anything but amusement, and I laid a hand on his arm to try to calm the situation down. Of course, I'd forgotten about the bandage on my hand, and Cass's eyes only widened further when he saw it.

"I'm fine," I assured him in a low, soothing voice. "I promise. He was just being a fucking creep. But it does raise the serious question of how to secure this place against any further intrusions. It was just fucking lucky you weren't here."

"Me?" Cass barked. "Who fucking cares if he saw *me*? It's you who—"

"I care," I snapped, cutting off his alpha-male, big-dick

rant. "So settle the fuck down and help us work out what to do next."

Cass glared at me hard, like he could hardly believe what he was hearing. Then after a moment, his eyes softened and his shoulders sagged. "Fine. What are we working with?" His question was aimed at Zed, but his arm tightened around my waist, pulling me against his side as he stood beside my stool like some kind of personal bodyguard. A conjoined bodyguard.

Zed grinned as he laid out a baking tray with portobello mushrooms and dressed each one with a dab of butter and a squeeze of crushed garlic. I despised mushrooms like they were made of pure shit, but Cass ate those big flat bastards like they were made of Wagyu steak.

"I've placed a work request with my security firm this morning," Zed told us as he seasoned the mushrooms, then slid them into the preheated oven to roast. "And I'm confident with their help we can get this place impenetrable."

"How can we be sure Chase doesn't have a mole in that company?" Cass rumbled. "He could have preempted this and is waiting for us to hand him all the access codes on a platter."

Zed tossed his tea towel aside and braced his hands on the counter opposite us. "We don't. Not really. But none of us have the knowledge or skill to install high-tech security devices throughout this entire house within the next eight hours, so where does that leave us?"

I drummed my fingertips on the side of my fresh coffee, thinking. "No, we don't. But...Dallas probably has the technical knowledge to do it."

Zed nodded. "I thought of him, but he doesn't have the equipment or the manpower. We're talking about installing motion-detector alarms on *every* window, door, fucking air vent of this entire house. It's not a one-man job."

"I could get him the equipment," Cass said thoughtfully, "if you have reliable manpower."

315

Zed gave him an exasperated stare. "How, Cass? You're dead, remember? You can't just call up your buddy for a favor."

Cass lowered one brow. "I have my ways. Do you have the manpower to make it work or not?"

Zed shifted his gaze to me, silently asking if we did. I pondered it a moment, running through all the options in my brain and discarding each and every one. Agent Hanson's dying advice that someone in my trusted level of Timberwolves was a traitor had been lingering in the back of my mind and was now vetoing all the usual wolves I'd call for a job like this.

But there was one option. Someone who owed me a few favors and wasn't affiliated with any gangs. Except I'd been very carefully, very deliberately keeping Seph well away from him since we'd moved to Shadow Grove.

"Rex," I murmured. "He's got the manpower in his shop."

Cass gave a grunt of surprise. "He does... Why would he do it, though?"

I tilted my head back to give him a smile. "I have my ways. Actually...as much as I hate to suggest this, Rex might also solve one of our other security issues."

"What's that?" Cass replied, his lips set in that grumpy line that was his resting Cass face.

Zed gave a huff of laughter, nodding his understanding. "Bratty little Persephone. She needs a new watcher."

Cass stepped away a pace and stripped off Zed's leather jacket, which he'd been wearing. "We can just call Archer back in," he suggested. "He's the best choice."

I scoffed. "He got her abducted because he was too busy arguing with Demi about his wife's boo-boo. No, I won't be calling him back in."

Zed gave a small shrug like he agreed with me, and Cass made an exasperated sound. He was too smart to keep pushing that issue, though. I didn't give two shits if Archer D'Ath was declared a saint next week, he'd fucked up. And when it came to Seph's safety, I wasn't the forgiving type.

"Look, I don't know what your connection is with Rex," Cass rumbled, "but he's bad fucking news."

I shot him a tight smile. "I know. But he'd also rather slit his own throat than betray me to Chase. As much as I dislike the guy, he's the best option we have. We *can't* keep Seph safe and go up against Chase. It's stretching us too thin already and endangering her. Chase still knows she's my biggest weak point, so that's where our reinforcements need to go."

Cass scrubbed a hand over his tattooed scalp. The designs on the left side were distorted now by the pink line of scarring, thanks to my bullet. But it just made him look sexier, if that was even possible.

"I thought Gumdrop was playing bodyguard to her," he muttered. "What happened to that?"

I grimaced. "He still is. At school. But he can't watch her around the clock. There will be plenty more times when he needs to be with us—with me—and he *will* ditch Seph if he thinks I need him more."

Zed nodded his agreement. "As we all would." His shrug was unapologetic. "I think you're right about Rex. Dallas can draw up the security plans. If Cass can somehow magically make the equipment appear, then Rex's boys can install it all—hopefully get it done before Seph and Lucas make it home from school."

"I think that sounds like a better option than relying on a potentially compromised security firm, don't you?" I tilted my head, meeting Cass's eyes. As much as I was used to simply making these decisions with Zed alone, I *wanted* Cass to be in agreement with us. We were a team, after all. In it together and all that crap.

He held my gaze for a long moment, then nodded once. "Agreed. Let's sort it out."

Flashing him a smile, I hopped off my chair and rose up on

317

my tiptoes to kiss him. "I love when you see things my way, Saint. Makes me all turned on and shit." With a wink, I headed upstairs to get ready for the day. I already had a full schedule as it was, and I'd just added to it.

First things first, I needed to suck up the strength and patience to call Rex Darenburg. I could safely say I'd *never* expected to be asking that murdering prick for help, but here we were. Never say never.

CHAPTER 40

My call to Rex didn't take long. He knew I wasn't really giving him an option to decline, so he gruffly announced his boys would meet Dallas at Zed's house around noon to install the equipment. The call to Dallas was just as quick; he advised that he'd send me a list of everything he needed within half an hour. How Cass planned to get it all, I had no clue. But I was also willing to trust him.

I was dressed for work and had applied my makeup with my calls on speaker. Cass appeared in the bathroom doorway as I finished curling my hair and just stood there watching me as I completed my well-practiced hairstyle, spraying it with a light hold, then gently combing the curls through so they sat in a vintage-Hollywood glam way. My wrist wasn't looking too bad, so I'd swapped out the bandage for a couple of adhesive dressings. Much better for my range of motion.

"Did you need something?" I asked after several minutes of silence. He'd changed out of Zed's bike leathers and was back in his own clothes, black jeans and a dark-gray T-shirt. In answer to my question, he stepped into the bathroom and closed the door with his heel before prowling closer.

"I always need something from you, Red," he confessed in a

rough whisper. "Have I told you how painfully beautiful you are today?" His hands bracketed my hips, his body warm against my back and his eyes dark in the mirror.

I held his gaze, leaning back into his touch. "You haven't. I thought you hated when I wore my Hades skin."

Cass's answering chuckle was hot against my skin as he swept my hair forward so he could kiss my neck. "Hate it? Fuck no. Not even close." He pulled my ass back against him, proving that point with the thickness of his erection. "I know you need to go to work. But I want to play a game."

Surprise widened my eyes. "What game?"

His lips curved in a wicked smile against my neck, his eyes darker still in the mirror. "Do you want to play, Red? Yes or no."

I gave a soft groan, rubbing my butt against him like a goddamn cat in heat—as if I hadn't had enough fucking attention from Lucas and Zed last night. "Yeah, I'll play."

Cass flashed a grin at me. "Perfect." He gripped each of my wrists—being gentle with my injured one—and placed my hands flat on the vanity, toward the mirror. Then he slowly tugged my tight skirt up, giving me plenty of opportunity to change my mind. Not that I fucking would; I was all kinds of hot and bothered already just at the mischief in his eyes.

Licking his lips, he hooked his fingers under the elastic of my panties and dragged them down my thighs but left them above my knees. Then he pulled a bottle of lube and the magical vibrating butt plug from his pocket and placed them down on the vanity beside me.

"Cass…" I wet my lips and glanced from the toy to him as he squeezed a liberal amount of lube onto his fingers. "I have meetings today. Important ones."

Rumbling a sound of amusement, he spread the cold lube over my backdoor, making me gasp. "I know," he replied. "That's the point." He teased the lube all around my ass, then pushed a finger inside. "Well, one of the points."

My protests evaporated as he fingered my ass, stretching my tight muscles out and ensuring there was plenty of lube spread around. Then he confidently worked the toy into place as I panted and trembled with my hands braced on the vanity. My face was just inches from the mirror, leaving me nowhere to hide from how flushed my cheeks were or how hungry Cass's gaze was when he admired his handiwork.

Then he simply pulled my panties back up and rolled my skirt back into place, smoothing his hands over the fabric to erase some creases from where it'd been bunched over my hips.

"Cass!" I exclaimed when he coaxed me to stand back up straight. "You're not serious."

He spun me around to face him, dipping his head to kiss me deeply. "I'm dead serious, Angel." He gave my ass a slap, making me yelp as my muscles tightened around the plug. "Keep that in while you work. Don't *fucking* remove it. Understood? Only I get to take it out." He kissed me again, harsh and demanding, *claiming*. It made me quake with need. I wasn't even going to make it to the office at this rate.

"Saint, you're not playing fair," I groaned, bending my body against his as my arms tightened around his neck. "I'm already so keyed up I could come just from walking down the stairs."

"Good," he growled. "You can come all you like, Angel. Just don't touch that plug. It's mine."

He kissed me again, then exited the bathroom with a smug-as-fuck grin on his face. Talk about the cat who got the cream.

"Shit," I whispered, clenching my butt and letting out a small moan at the foreign object I'd be taking with me to my meetings. Cass was trying to kill me, no question about it. This must be pay-back for shooting him.

"Dare!" Zed shouted from downstairs. "You ready to go? We're late!"

With a string of silent curses, I grabbed my shoes and

purse and made my awkward-as-hell way downstairs to meet up with him.

"You okay?" he asked when I hurried into the garage. "You look a little flushed."

My smile was tight, and I could feel the heat still sitting in my face. "Yup, totally fine. Let's go."

He squinted at me a moment longer, then shrugged and climbed into the driver's seat of his Ferrari. As I took my own seat, I needed to hold my breath to keep from moaning out loud. Then it seemed like every damn corner, every fucking traffic light was designed to torture me.

By the time we reached Copper Wolf offices, I was sweating. Fucking Cass was going to get a nut-punch for this stupid game. And yet I was too stubborn to just end it.

"Are you sure you're okay?" Zed asked as we rode the elevator up to our company floor. "You seem really...on edge." Then his brows rose, and he grinned. "Oh shit, Saint edged you, huh? What a prick." He hit the emergency stop button, and the elevator ground to a halt.

"What are you doing?" I asked, peering up at him as he backed me into the corner.

Zed just smiled, his hands caressing my waist. "Offering my assistance, Boss. Want me to lend a hand? You've got three guys to pick from. You don't have to let him leave you hanging."

With a short laugh, I tilted my head back and kissed him longingly. "You have no idea how bad I want to take you up on that," I whispered. "But we really are late, and this is a meeting we can't skip."

He gave a groan of frustration, then kissed me back. "Fine. Rain check until lunchtime?"

I nodded firmly as he backed off and restarted the elevator. "Hell yes," I agreed. "Count on it."

The morning's meetings were to sort out the mess Chase had created with our approaching opening for Timber. He'd screwed with our liquor and gaming licenses *and* filed all kinds of irritating complaints that'd caused us to waste a crapload of time organizing additional inspections, pest control, environmental impact statements, and noise pollution reports. It was a headache and a half, and there weren't enough bureaucrats in the Cloudcroft council to simply make it all disappear.

Thankfully, that's what our meetings were set to handle. It was safe to say the distraction of Cass's toy in my ass the entire time was less than ideal for my concentration. Yet by the time we all walked out of the boardroom, we'd reached a satisfactory result.

Timber *would* open per our original schedule, and it would be done with the full support of the Cloudcroft mayor.

"So," Zed murmured as the mayor and her aids disappeared into the elevators, "about that lunch date."

I gave a soft laugh. "I'm actually starved."

Zed's gaze was *pure* filth. "Same."

"I've got you sorted, Boss," Hannah offered, standing up from behind her desk and giving me a wide smile. "When your meeting ran so late, I called in an order with Zampati's down the road. They should be delivering your lunch in a couple of minutes. I got you the honey mustard chicken breast with wild rice, and, Zed, I ordered you the shrimp linguine. I hope that's okay?"

Zed looked irritated as hell, but my stomach was rumbling, so I gave Hannah a grateful smile. "That sounds perfect, thank you." I made my way back to my office with Zed following along. So was Hannah.

"Sir, I wanted to talk to you about those 7th Circle staff members that I was looking into?" She waited until I was seated— carefully—then sat down in one of my visitor chairs opposite.

Zed shot me a meaningful glare, silently begging me to get rid of Hannah so he could fuck me stupid before lunch arrived. But it was just entertaining me, so I ignored him. Besides, the butt plug was kind of comfortable now that I was used to it.

"Yes, I remember," I replied to Hannah. "What about them? I'm guessing they got poached by another venue."

Hannah frowned, her perfect black brows tight. "Not...that I can tell. One of them, yes, that was Jack Hugeman. He thought we had no shifts for him and needed to pay bills, so he took a job at Swinging Dick's." She cringed at that, and so did I. "I hope I didn't overstep, but I told him he would need a full health work-up if he wanted to return to Copper Wolf venues."

"Agreed." I nodded. "What about the other two?"

Hannah puffed out a breath. "They've been reported missing by their families. No one has seen or heard from them in weeks."

I stiffened, my lips pursed. "Remind me of their names?"

"Monica Carrie and Kelsey Gregson. They worked under the aliases Michela and Katherine. Both have been, er, sex workers for 7th Circle pretty much since you opened. Always punctual, popular with repeat clients, good employees." She gave a small shrug, the concern clear on her face. "There are open missing-persons cases for both of them."

Giving her a small nod of understanding, I drew a deep breath as I processed that information. First Maryanne got murdered, then these two girls went missing? It had to be Chase.

"Thanks for letting me know, Hannah. Keep me posted for any developments." I shifted my gaze to Zed, who looked like he'd just been hit with a stun gun. "Anything you want to ask, Zed?"

He gave a tight shake of his head, and Hannah politely excused herself, saying she'd bring our lunch in when it arrived.

After she closed the door softly, I narrowed my gaze at Zed. "What?"

He glanced at the door, then exhaled heavily as he came over to sit in the chair Hannah had just vacated. "Monica and Kelsey...

They were both…" He waved his hand and winced. I didn't really need any more of an explanation as my mood soured.

"You were fucking them both. Right." My words were clipped and angry, and Zed groaned.

"Not recently, but yeah, in the past I spent some time with both of them. They're pretty girls and…" He scrubbed a hand over his face in frustration. "Chase is deliberately targeting women I've slept with."

"No shit," I muttered. I grabbed a pen and notebook out of my drawer and pushed it across the desk to him. "I suggest you make a list of every girl you've been with. They're all in danger."

Zed looked way too uncomfortable with that suggestion, but his protest was cut off by a knock at my office door.

"Come in," I snapped, expecting Hannah to have returned with our lunch. It was our lunch, but it was Gen who brought it in with a bright smile. "Oh, hey, Gen. I didn't expect you today."

She placed the bags of food on my desk, then dragged a chair over to sit beside Zed. "I know. I didn't mean to drop by unannounced. I was at Zampati's getting my own lunch order and saw yours waiting for the courier. Figured I'd bring it up myself and check how the meeting with Leah went."

Leah Harris was the mayor of Cloudcroft and a personal connection of Gen's. It was thanks to her that we'd been able to iron out the mess with Timber, so I really did owe her thanks for that. I was just in a shitty mood about Zed's promiscuity coming back to bite us all in the ass, and the coy glances Gen seemed to be shooting him constantly set my nerves on edge.

"Thanks, Gen," Zed started to say, clearly about to dismiss her. "We were just—"

"Finishing up," I cut him off, giving Gen a smile. "You're welcome to stay for lunch. We can discuss strategy for the Copper Wolf vodka distillery expansion." Zed shot me a hard glare, but I just nodded to the notepad. "You have a list to write, Zayden. Get to work. I don't want to be here late tonight."

He scowled but reluctantly picked up the notebook as Gen started unpacking our food. Hannah had also ordered a range of sides and desserts to go with our mains, so there was enough food to keep us fed all afternoon. Much to Zed's annoyance, Gen and I found plenty of things to discuss, so she ended up not leaving until we were all ready to head home at the end of the day.

CHAPTER 41

As badly as Zed wanted to clear the air between us, fate was working against him. Both our phones were going nuts before we even got into his car, and we spent most of the drive home fielding calls about a million-and-one work-related matters. Then, just as we parked in the garage, he got a call from our foreman at Timber to say there had been an electrical fire in the new kitchen area.

"Go check it out," I told him with a sigh. "I'll get up to speed on the new security system."

Before I could head inside, Zed grabbed me around the waist and pinned me to the side of his car, kissing me hard. "I know you're pissed at me," he whispered, sounding pained.

"I'm not pissed," I retorted, giving a slight shrug.

Zed sighed in exasperation. "Fine, then you're *irritated* at me. But I can't change my past, Dare. And all those girls? They're in the past. I've only ever loved one woman, and that's you. Never forget that."

My heart softened at the sincerity in his eyes, and I tilted my head to kiss him softly. "I know. Go sort out Timber, and we can hit that rain check when you're back."

"Count on it," he replied, kissing me once more, then getting back into his car.

As he reversed back out of the garage, I made my way inside and found Dallas standing in the foyer with a laptop balanced on his arm. He was tapping the keyboard one-handed, his eyes on a wall panel where he was doing...something, but he looked up when I got closer.

"Boss, hi," he said with a tight smile. "Almost done. Sorry, we ran overtime."

I checked the clock on the wall and noticed it was a solid hour later than I'd told him to be finished by. Not that it really mattered, but I hadn't wanted Seph to notice the increased security.

"Don't worry about it," I told him. "Have Rex's guys gone?"

Dallas nodded. "Yeah, they left before Seph and Lucas got home. I figured you wouldn't want them hanging around your sister."

I flashed him an appreciative smile. "You figured right."

His eyes returned to what he was doing. "I told Seph we were just running routine maintenance checks. She seemed none the wiser."

"Sounds like her. Thanks, Dallas."

He nodded again, then tapped a few more keys on his laptop until the wall unit beeped five times and flashed green. "All done," he announced with a triumphant grin. "Want me to run you through it all?"

I accepted, and Dallas followed me to the kitchen so I could drop my bag and remove my weapons. He spent about fifteen minutes talking me through the new security system: motion detectors, cameras, spotlights, even heat sensors and gas particle detection units. I'd thought Zed's home was a fortress before? Not even close. *Now* it was a fortress. Seph would be lucky to sneeze without an alarm going off somewhere.

When Dallas was done, I showed him out, then armed our

new alarm system as he'd shown me. I just needed to remember to disarm it before Zed got back, seeing as he didn't have the code.

"We all secure?" Lucas asked as I returned to the den, where he'd been studying on the couch. He'd listened to bits of what Dallas had been telling me, but I could tell his head was in his books. That was perfectly fine by me; it was nothing I couldn't show him when he needed to know.

I nodded, moving some of his textbooks to the coffee table so I could sit beside him. Then I squirmed as the plug shifted in my ass.

"Yup, all done," I replied, wetting my lips. "Where's the brat?"

Grinning, Lucas capped the pen he'd been using and set his work aside. "In her room," he replied, snaking an arm around my waist.

"Hmm," I hummed, glancing up to the ceiling like my X-ray vision could tell me if she was likely to come down anytime soon. "And Cass?"

Lucas shrugged. "No clue. Haven't seen him since I got home. Either he's gone out—sneaky cat—or he's hiding somewhere to avoid Dallas seeing him alive." He pulled me into his lap, making me squirm again. "So for now, it's just us."

"Just us, huh?" I repeated, draping my arms around his neck. He was still in his Shadow Prep uniform, the tie tugged loose and his top button open. "I can't decide if I'm turned on by this uniform or totally creeped out," I admitted, pulling the tie undone and tossing it aside.

Lucas nodded in understanding. "I should take it off, just to be safe."

Giving him a soft laugh, I unbuttoned his SP-monogrammed shirt and pushed it off his gorgeous shoulders. "Oh, much better," I murmured teasingly. "Wait. I'm interrupting, and you have exams coming up." I scrambled out of his lap in an attempt to be responsible, but Lucas caught me with his hands on my hips before I could make it far.

"I think I can take a study break, Hayden," he told me with a small laugh. He was still seated, and he tipped his head right back to hold my gaze. "Promise. It'll actually make me study *better* because I won't be distracted by my raging hard-on."

I pursed my lips, trying not to smile at his charming bullshit. Damn it, I couldn't say no to Lucas. Fucking Lucas. "What kind of mood was Seph in when she went to her room?" I asked.

He took that as the permission it was, his long fingers skating around to the back of my pencil skirt to drag the zipper down. "Terrible one," he replied, wrinkling his nose. "She got in some argument with a girl at school, and I wasn't super sympathetic about it on the way home. She slammed the door pretty hard." My skirt dropped to the carpet at my feet, and my blouse joined it a moment later.

A small part of my mind told me I needed to go and talk to my sister, find out what had upset her at school. But a bigger part rubbed its hands together in glee because if she was in a shitty mood, she was unlikely to come down until dinnertime. So I made no move to stop Lucas as he stripped my bra and panties away, leaving me standing totally naked in front of him.

"You're so damn beautiful, Hayden," he whispered, his voice hoarse as he ran his hands over my skin. His huge hands cupped my breasts, his fingers tugging at my nipples and making my back arch in response. He wet his lips at that, his eyes hungry as he continued touching my skin. When he reached my ass, he grabbed a firm handful of my butt cheeks, and I jerked.

His gaze shot back to my face, curious, and I just grinned. I wasn't going to tell him; he could just find out for himself. Which he did a moment later when he stroked his fingers down the length of my pussy and brushed the hard base of the butt plug.

"Babe, what…" He tilted his head to the side, curious, as his fingers explored.

I huffed a short laugh. "Cass," I said by way of explanation.

Lucas gave an understanding nod, then an impish grin. "Am I going to get in trouble here?"

I got the feeling he didn't give a shit if he *did* get in trouble. He definitely wasn't planning on stopping, at any rate.

"No." I shrugged and rocked my hips as he left the plug alone and sank two fingers into my pussy instead. "Or I don't think so. He just said not to take it out, not that I couldn't fuck you with it in."

Lucas dragged his lower lip through his teeth, his gaze thoughtful as he slowly teased me with his hand, making me shudder and rock against his palm. "Well," he murmured after a long pause. "Color me intrigued."

I grinned, fucking loving how Lucas had gone from virgin to one hundred in no time at all. He was all about new experiences, and I loved that about him.

"Well good," I replied. "But you have to let me do something first."

Reluctantly, I pushed his hand away before he could make me come too damn quick and sank to my knees in front of the couch where he sat. My eyes locked on his, I unbuckled his belt and trousers and freed his monster erection. My hand wrapped around it as he hissed a breath and leaned back to give me better access. He knew damn well what I wanted and was more than willing to facilitate.

Leaning in, I teased the tip of my tongue around his crown, still holding his gaze as I did and quietly getting off on the way his expression shifted. I stroked his shaft firmly, my fingertips not even meeting around his girth, then I closed my lips around his velvet-smooth head, sucking gently.

"Oh shit," Lucas cursed on a hard exhale as I took him deeper. "Hayden...babe..." He groaned as my hand moved in time with my mouth, making up for the distance I couldn't fit down my throat. I was getting better, though. Practice makes perfect and all that.

Lucas's hands went to my hair, his fingers pressing the back of my head as his hips jerked, forcing his dick deeper and lighting me up with intense arousal. There was just something about feeling like I was totally choking on cock that made my pussy flood.

After a couple of minutes, though, he pulled me up and gave me a desperate stare. "Babe, I need to feel that sweet pussy," he confessed, his voice rough.

Smirking my satisfaction and driving him wild, I climbed into his lap, balancing myself with my hands on his shoulders as he fisted his cock and lined up with my opening. Just as he started to sink into my warmth, the toy in my ass started vibrating, and I jolted like I'd just been electrocuted.

"What the fuck?" Lucas exclaimed as I stiffened and gasped.

"Cass!" I shouted, both enraged and goddamn tipping close to the edge of orgasm.

His dark chuckle echoed through the room, and I craned my neck to find him lurking in the shadows near the kitchen, the little toy remote in his hand. Lucas groaned a curse and gently bit my breast that was temptingly close to his mouth already.

"What'd I tell you about our game, Red?" Cass asked, sauntering closer with a smug tilt to his lips.

I rolled my eyes. "I told Lucas he couldn't take it out. What'd I do wrong?"

Cass shrugged. "Nothing. Just checking you remembered."

Seething at the interruption, I narrowed my eyes at him. "Well then, in that case…" I reached down to reposition Lucas's cock and sank onto him an inch. "Lucas and I were in the middle of something."

Cass's expression was so often unreadable, but not then. Nope, that one was all surprise as I held his gaze defiantly while spreading my knees wider and taking Lucas deeper into my cunt.

"Oh wow," Lucas murmured with a short chuckle, his hands tight on my waist. He could clearly feel the difference with the plug in my ass, just like I could. It was a tight fit, but not uncomfortable. Just…tight. Lucas lost his control a second later and held my hips firm as he bucked his own, slamming the rest of his cock into me and making me cry out.

For a brief moment, I totally forgot Cass was still standing there, then I felt a second pair of hands on my body, cupping my breasts as Lucas held my hips. A second mouth on my skin, kissing my shoulder as Lucas sucked my nipple. Fuck, yes.

Then I felt pressure on my ass as Cass tugged on the toy, and I leaned into Lucas harder. "Cass," I moaned as he played with the fucking thing, pulling it halfway out, then pushing it back in. Fucking me with it, even as Lucas's hips moved beneath me, his thrusts shallow.

"Hush, Red," Cass grunted, pulling the toy out completely, then squeezing more lube in its place. "I'd say it's a damn good thing you're letting me claim this ass first." His thick, hot tip pressed against my hole, and Lucas stilled beneath me.

"Oh yeah?" I shot back, breathless as fuck while he ever so slowly pushed inside. His dick was so much bigger than the plug I'd been wearing all day, but I knew how to take it. "Why's that?"

Cass gave a rough laugh, pushing in further and making me gasp. "By the looks of things, Gumdrop would have put you in the fucking hospital."

A burst of laughter escaped me at that, and Cass took the opportunity to push home.

"Holy fuck," I breathed, feeling both of them fully seated within me. It wasn't my first time…but it was for damn sure the first time I'd enjoyed having two dicks inside me at once. And make no mistake, I was *thoroughly* enjoying it. "Yes…shit, Saint…"

He hummed a contented sound, his hands skating up my body until he reached my face. With a strong hand on my jaw, he turned my face until he could kiss me roughly, then released me with a wink. "I've got you, Angel. You good down there, Gumdrop?"

"Fucking excellent," Lucas breathed, his hands finding my breasts once more and his teeth teasing my aching nipple.

Cass dropped his hand from my jaw to my throat, then kept it there as he started to move. He went slow at first, and Lucas followed suit. But gradually, carefully, they both picked up the pace. The harder Cass fucked my ass, the more his grip on my throat tightened. I was only just holding off on my orgasm, determined to drag this session out, but Cass wasn't letting me call the shots.

His other hand gripped a fistful of my hair, jerking my head back and lifting my whole body almost flush to his chest.

"Lucas," Cass growled, his breathing harsh in my ear. "Make our girl come. She's being stubborn."

A delirious smile curved my lips, but I didn't argue. Cass held me tight, his broad hand still lightly choking me as Lucas's talented finger found my clit. I was powerless to hold it off anymore, and I detonated like a nuclear bomb. Little splattered pieces of my consciousness hit every surface of the room while the guys continued to fuck me, their rhythms synced up scarily well.

Lucas was next to come, his thrusts getting deeper and more forceful, and a long groan tore from his chest as he jerked and exploded within me. Then Cass picked me up with one arm around my waist, plucking me off Lucas and shoving me face-first into the couch. The intensity that he fucked my ass with made me see stars, and as he started to come, Lucas snaked a hand under me and pinched my clit again.

Fucking hell. I died. *La petite mort.* Now I finally understood that phrase.

CHAPTER 42

Despite how thoroughly exhausted I was after the three-way with Cass and Lucas, I struggled to get to sleep that night. I'd sent Lucas back to his room to study after dinner because I could tell how stressed he was about exams, and Cass had disappeared like a magician around the same time.

Seph had come down and been less of a shithead than usual, so I extended the olive branch and turned *Hart of Dixie* on the TV for her to watch with me. She hadn't wanted to talk about school, and I hadn't pushed the issue.

It wasn't until Zed got home—I'd called him with the security code earlier when he was held up at Timber—that I realized why I was so on edge. I'd been tossing and turning in my bed for ages, and when I heard his footsteps in the hallway, I sat up with a jerk.

Just as I was about to get out of bed and go to him, my door cracked open and he slipped inside silently. Then froze when he saw me awake.

"Hey," he murmured, sounding slightly guilty at being caught. "I thought you'd be asleep by now." He unclipped his gun holster and placed it down on my dresser, along with his phone and wallet.

I grinned, lying back down into my pillows. "So you thought you'd sneak in? What if I was with Cass or Lucas?"

Zed approached the bed, unbuttoning his shirt as he moved. "Then I'd have very quietly told them to fuck off. Or picked you up like Sleeping Beauty and taken you to my room." He carefully laid his shirt over a chair near my dresser, then undid his pants. "I'd have worked it out."

"Mmm," I hummed, enjoying the view of his shadowed form stripping down. "I bet." After a pause, within which Zed laid his pants over the shirt and slipped under my covers in nothing but his boxer briefs, I added, "You checked Lucas's room first, huh?"

Zed just chuckled and leaned in to kiss me. "A magician never reveals his tricks, Dare." His hands found my waist beneath the T-shirt I was wearing, pulling me close, and I shivered.

"Your hands are freezing," I complained, but didn't pull away. Quite the opposite, I molded my body against his so I could warm him up with my own heat.

Zed didn't need any further invitation; he fused his mouth to mine and kissed me with an edge of desperation. I knew he'd been just as tense as I'd been, feeling uneasy after the way we'd left things this afternoon. But he'd been telling the absolute truth when he'd said those girls were his past. I'd known about them all at the time, and no, he couldn't go back in time. I had no right to be shitty about it now.

All that mattered now was that he was mine.

Just as our kisses turned heated, Zed's phone vibrated on my dresser. We both froze, but Zed gave a tiny shake of his head. "Ignore it," he murmured against my lips. "This is more important."

But then it was my phone vibrating on the nightstand, and I grinned against Zed's lips. "Sounds important." As I said that, his phone vibrated again, and he groaned.

With a laugh, I rolled over and snagged my phone to see what was urgent enough to message both of us at midnight. The message was from Alexi, but when I clicked into it, my blood ran cold.

"Get dressed," I snapped to Zed, leaping out of bed. "We need to get to Anarchy."

He didn't need telling, already halfway into his pants and checking his own messages as he muttered curses. "I'll get the car, you tell Gumdrop."

I nodded sharply, buttoning up my jeans, then pulling a tank top over my head. Fuck wearing a bra; there was no time for that shit. I hurried down to Lucas's bedroom while still buckling my shoulder holster—with my new gun to replace the Desert Eagle.

Lucas roused as I entered his room, blinking at me like an owl when I crouched beside his bed.

"Hey, babe," he mumbled, his lids barely open a crack.

"Zed and I have to go take care of something at Anarchy," I told him in an urgent whisper. "Seph's asleep, but Cass is still gone."

He understood perfectly, nodding as he pushed himself to sitting. "Guard duty. Got it. Stay safe, okay?"

I flashed him a grateful smile and leaned in for a quick kiss. "Always. We'll be back soon." Confident he would keep Seph safe, I raced back downstairs to meet Zed, only pausing momentarily to grab a pair of shoes.

Zed's Ferrari was already in front of the house, and he took off before I'd even fully closed my door. But I sure as shit wasn't chastising him for it. The faster we got to Anarchy, the better. I could smell another setup, and this time I wanted to beat those douchebags at SGPD to it.

"How long ago did Alexi find the break-in?" Zed asked as he navigated the streets between his place and Anarchy with ease.

I pulled my phone back out, rereading the message Alexi had sent informing us that he'd found a busted lock on the door to the Anarchy underground storerooms—the same area where Chase had held and tortured Lucas not so long ago. Most of the tunnels

337

had been permanently sealed up, but some were still accessible as they were useful storerooms.

The fact that Anarchy had been vacant, thanks to the police shutdown, meant we had no clue when the break-in had happened.

"He texted us the minute he found it," I replied. "I've told him to hold off on investigating in case it's a trap. I wouldn't put it past Chase to have rigged the fucking tunnels with explosives or some shit."

Zed flicked a sharp look at me. "Then why the fuck would *we* go down there?"

I snorted. "Because Chase doesn't want me dead. So I'm the best insurance policy against him blowing shit up."

Zed huffed in disagreement. "Tell that to your apartment building. Or 7th Circle, for that matter."

I wrinkled my nose. "The apartment building was deliberate. He waited until I was within sight but not in danger. As for 7th…I actually think he fucked up on that one. I wasn't supposed to be there at that time, and I definitely wasn't supposed to have tissues stuffed up my nose to block the smell of the gas."

Zed scowled. "Even so, I'd rather not experience any more fuckups. I just got my hands on you, Dare. I'm not losing you now. Not for anything or anyone. Clear?"

A heady rush of love shuddered through me, and I clamped my lips shut before I started simpering like an idiot over how infatuated with him I was. Instead, I turned my attention to the window and smiled when Zed's hand found my knee.

The twenty-minute drive to Anarchy was over in ten, and when we skidded to a stop beside Alexi's car, there wasn't a single other vehicle in sight. That was a good sign, at least. The main lights for the park were off, seeing as the venue was closed, but we knew where we were going and hurried to meet up with Alexi using nothing but the light of the moon.

"Bosses," he called out as we drew close, stepping out of the shadows near the door in question. "You got here quick."

"It seemed time-sensitive," I replied, grim. "Have you gone in?"

Alexi shook his head. "No, sir. As advised, I haven't moved from this spot."

"How'd you find it?" Zed asked, his eyes narrowed at our head of security. Alexi had been with us since before I massacred two-thirds of the former Timberwolves. We'd known him a long time, and I was confident in his loyalty to us. Or...I had been until Agent Hanson had gotten into my head with her suspicions.

"Bulldog drove past here earlier," he told us, his expression serious. "Said he saw people with flashlights inside the park. He figured it was just dumb teens or some shit, but I came to check it out and found that." He nodded to the broken lock on the door that led to our underground storerooms. It wasn't just broken; it had been obliterated, like someone had shot the whole thing out with a large-caliber weapon.

"Anything else we need to know?" I asked, my tone sharp as I drew my gun. It wasn't the same as my Desert Eagle. Lighter. I was going to have to get that gun back from Chase, sooner rather than later.

Alexi frowned. "Yeah. I thought I heard someone crying a couple of minutes ago. But...I dunno. Maybe it was a fox or something." He jerked his head toward the forest that butted up against one side of the old amusement park and shrugged.

My insides twisted with apprehension, though. Somehow, I didn't think it was a fox. "Let's check this out. If it's another setup, then we can expect another visit from SGPD at any minute."

"Hopefully, we got here in enough time," Zed murmured. "Chase wouldn't have expected anyone to come check on things at this time of night, and the venue is closed for another week and a half. He might not be in any hurry."

I grimaced. "We can hope, but I don't think I'll rely on luck here. Stay alert."

Taking the lead, I stepped cautiously down into the darkness while Alexi shined his flashlight ahead to light the steps for me. We didn't turn the main lights on, not wanting to announce our presence to anyone who might be lurking, but I sniffed the air continuously to check for gas.

When we reached the bottom of the stairs, Zed took the flashlight from Alexi and swept the beam of light over every inch of the wall, floor, and ceiling in the tunnel ahead checking for explosives, now that I'd put the idea in his head.

After he decided it was clear, we started down the corridor cautiously but quickly. I felt the clock ticking in my head, making me more anxious by the second, but I was determined to beat Chase this time.

"There," Alexi hissed, making us all freeze. "Did you hear that?"

I stayed dead still, tilting my head to the side and listening. A moment later, I heard what he was talking about, and a deep chill ran down my spine. "That's not a fucking fox."

Panic clawing at my stomach, I took off running, totally ignoring Zed's shout to wait. I followed the sound of the crying all the way to one of the locked vault rooms. It was a room we kept for interrogations, and a heavy iron bar across the door prevented anyone inside from escaping.

Zed reached past me, lifting the bar before I could get my hands on it. The sound of crying was louder now, and he met my eyes with concern as we shoved the heavy door open.

Inside, my fears were confirmed. The small, dirty, bloodstained room should have been empty, but instead it contained over half a dozen people. Dead or sleeping, it was hard to tell, so I knelt next to the closest body and searched for a pulse. It was a woman, her skin still warm, and there was a steady pulse, which made me release a long breath of relief. Not dead, then.

In the corner, one of the mystery occupants was awake and tucked up in a ball, sobbing. She looked young, from what I could tell. Too fucking young.

"Shit," I breathed, looking back down at the woman whose pulse I'd taken. I rolled her over gently and groaned. She wasn't a *woman* at all. She was just a child. Horror rolled through me, and my skin broke out in a cold sweat. But I had to push aside all pity and personal feelings. There simply wasn't the time.

"Alexi, get me some transport here *immediately*. I need all of these girls moved to a safe house." The rest of that statement didn't need to be said. But they needed to be moved *before* SGPD showed up and charged me with human trafficking and sex slavery. Hopefully they were all alive. Since I was an owner of brothels, trafficking wouldn't be a difficult charge to make stick, either. Chase had really stepped it up on this one. As the icing on the cake, I couldn't stop thinking how close Seph had come to being one of these girls. They were just *kids*.

Alexi was already on his phone in the hallway, barking orders to one of his team about getting a van here, brought to the south entrance. Smart call; the last thing we needed to do was drive right past the cops on their arrival.

"Dare," Zed said softly, his hand on my arm like I'd just zoned out. "What do you want me to do?"

I swallowed hard, blinking a couple of times to find my focus. Then I locked eyes with the terrified girl in the corner.

"Call Nadia," I croaked. "Have her meet us at the safe house, the one on Wattle Lane. These girls aren't going to want a bunch of scary, tattoo-covered men around, and that's all I have who I can trust in the Timberwolves right now."

Zed gave a tight nod, retreating into the hall with Alexi to make his call, and I cautiously approached the crying girl. She was the only one awake, but I had to hope that the other girls would all regain consciousness soon.

"Hey," I breathed as I paused near her. I tried for my most soothing, nonthreatening voice, but I doubted I was fooling her. Everything about me screamed *dangerous*, and I knew it. "We're not here to hurt you. My friends are arranging somewhere safe for you to go, okay? We'll get you home to your family soon."

She flinched hard when I said the word *family*, and my heart sank. These girls—or this one in particular—likely hadn't been stolen. They'd been sold.

"You know what?" I dropped the soothing bullshit and gave her a dry tone instead. "Fuck family, they're usually a bunch of assholes. We'll get you somewhere safe and just work it out from there, okay?"

The girl's head lifted slightly at that, her crying slowing to silent tears, and I knew I'd struck the right chord. But now that I could see more of her face, I could see *just* how young she was. Maybe seven or eight at best.

Swallowing down all the horror at what might have happened to her, I mustered up my very best nonthreatening smile and held out my hand to her. "Will you come with me? I want to take you somewhere safe."

She hesitated, and I didn't fucking blame her. But the ticking in my head was getting more urgent with every passing second. The unconscious girls would be easy to move, but I didn't want this one screaming and fighting if we forcibly moved her. Not only would the sound attract attention, but it'd also scare the crap out of her, and I suspected she'd been through enough already.

"Look, I'll be real with you. The people who brought you here? They might be coming back, and I don't know when. I want to get you out before they do. Will you trust me?" It was a huge ask—I knew that better than most. But sometimes you just needed to take a chance and hope for the best.

The girl's brow creased, and her eyes shifted to the unconscious girls. "What about—"

"Them too," I promised with another encouraging smile. "I want to get you all out safely. Please…"

After another hesitation, she sniffed heavily and reached out to take my hand. The relief that rushed over me was enough to make my knees weak, but I just pulled her out of the corner as gently as I could and hurried her into the corridor where Alexi and Zed were both on their phones.

Seeing them, the girl gave a scream and cowered behind me. I instantly cursed at myself for not seeing that coming, but I crouched down to wrap my arms around her on instinct.

"It's okay. These two are my friends," I told her, trying to be soothing as she clung to my neck. "No one is going to hurt you anymore. I promise. No one."

How the fuck I was going to follow through on that promise, I had no fucking clue. I could protect this child while she was in my territory but what then? More to the point, why was I making it so damn personal? I should have just called in my Wolves to handle it all, and yet here I was hugging a dirty, tearstained child.

"Boss," Alexi softly called out. "Transport is incoming. ETA two minutes to the south gate."

I gave him a nod of understanding, my stomach a mass of anxiety as I thought about what would happen if these girls were taken in by the dirty SGPD. They'd never make it to any kind of child protection agency. They'd be handed straight back to Chase's slimy associates to be sold on the flesh markets.

"What's your name, sweetheart?" I asked the girl softly, feeling the tug of her fingers twisting my hair. She was locked around my neck now and didn't seem willing to let go.

"Diana," she whispered back, her little face tucked into my neck. "But my sister calls me Deedee."

Cute. Diana was the Roman version of Artemis, goddess of the hunt. I wonder if Deedee knew that.

"I don't like it though," she added in a small, angry voice. "My sister is mean."

A smile curved my lips, and I sighed. "I'm taking Diana down to meet the cars," I told Zed and Alexi. "Get those girls in there moved *as fast as possible*. We can*not* be caught off guard again. Anything less than flawless on this job will be your last strike, Alexi."

It was unfair of me; he was racing the clock just like I was. But fuck fair. People worked harder when they were properly motivated, and Alexi badly needed to impress me right now.

He jerked an understanding nod, and I scooped Diana up in my arms as I stood. She was light as a feather, and I'd be able to get us out a crapload quicker if I wasn't waiting for her to keep up.

"Dare..." Zed started to follow, but I put out a hand to stop him.

"Stay here and help. There are eight more girls in there who need saving. Save them." My tone was hard, but Diana just clung tighter. Crap, I was scaring the kid.

Zed nodded tightly, and I hurried back toward the stairs we'd entered through. As we got to the top, I whispered to Diana to stay silent.

Somehow, I managed to wiggle my gun free, and holding the child with one arm I swept the area, ensuring we were alone before I raced across the complex. I sent a silent thanks to fate for making me pick up sneakers instead of heels when we left the house, because it made the run a hell of a lot easier with a passenger around my neck.

Three dark vans were pulling into the south gate as I approached, and I recognized the plates as being from Timberwolf garages. Two huge men climbed out of each van, and I jerked my head in acknowledgment at Bulldog. Without his tip, we never would have known those girls had been stashed.

"Interrogation room," I told them. "Be *quick* and silent. I want everyone gone before cops even get their fucking anonymous tip."

The men all murmured their understanding and took off in the direction I'd come from. Only Bulldog remained behind, silently offering to take Diana from me. I tried to hand her over to him, but the instant she tensed up and tangled her hands in my hair, I knew it wasn't going to work. Poor kid was scared shitless and had latched onto me as her savior.

"It's fine," I murmured. "I'll stay. Go help the guys. I want you all back here in less than five minutes."

It was a made-up timeframe, but it got my point across. Bulldog grunted his understanding and loped off into the darkness, shockingly quiet for such a heavy dude.

Alone again, I shoved the side door on one of the vans open and sat on the step, Diana in my lap. "We're alone," I told her quietly. "My friends are going to get all the other girls out, then we'll take you somewhere safe."

The kid relaxed her hold on me slightly, raising her head just enough to look around cautiously. When she was sure I'd told the truth, she carefully climbed out of my lap and sat beside me instead. The tears were all gone now, replaced with a stubborn determination I could relate to.

"Then what?" she asked, blinking up at me. Her face was grubby and her hair greasy and tangled like she'd been denied a shower for way too fucking long. Fury boiled my blood, and I vividly pictured what I would do to the people responsible for her imprisonment—and to her fucking family if they had indeed sold her knowingly.

"Then..." I replied, still imagining violent, messy murders, "then we work out what to do. But I promise you, kid, no one will hurt you."

She stared up at me for a long time, then nodded. Just like that.

CHAPTER 43

As it turned out, my Wolves didn't need the full five minutes. They arrived back in three, each of them carrying an unconscious girl. Zed confirmed they'd swept the rest of the rooms and everything was clear, so I ordered the vans to move out—get the girls to our safe house on Wattle Lane where Nadia would meet them.

Diana shed some tears when I told her she needed to go with the other girls. But I reminded her of my promise, and she visibly pulled herself together. Tough little cookie.

Still, there was a sick feeling in my stomach as Zed, Alexi, and I watched the vans pull away with their cargo, like I should have gone with her if for no other reason than to keep her calm.

Shaking it off, I turned back to Alexi and Zed. "Let's do a sweep of all the buildings," I told them. "Turn lights on if you want, but let's double-check in case this is a decoy."

Alexi grimaced. "A distraction in the form of trafficked kids, while the real setup is right under our noses."

I shrugged. "I don't put anything past that psychopathic fuck. Best be sure. Alexi, call in some more teams and get all of our venues swept the same."

He nodded, and the three of us split up to check over the rest of

Anarchy. Having been transformed from an old amusement park, it had a *lot* of places to check. And yet by the time we were done over an hour later, still no cops had turned up on an *anonymous tip* to find the girls.

I dismissed Alexi, telling him to collect reports from all the other sweep teams and report back. Just as he was about to climb into his car, I called out again.

"Good work tonight, Alexi," I told him, my jaw tight. "This could have all ended a hell of a lot worse."

He seemed shocked by my praise but dipped his head in acknowledgment and drove off into the night. Zed met my gaze over the hood of his car, his eyes questioning, but I didn't have the answers. What the hell had happened here? Why stash those girls and *not* call the cops in to frame me? Was this all just a headfuck?

My phone vibrated in my back pocket, and I pulled it out. The caller ID was unknown, but I answered it anyway.

"Yes?"

"Can you tell me, Hades," Lieutenant Jeffries asked, "why I got woken up in the middle of the fucking night by a tipster who claimed you were smuggling human cargo through your fight club?"

My brows hitched. "I wish I could, Jeffries. This tipster seems to be very active lately."

He gave a grunt like he was deeply unamused. That made two of us. "What's stranger still was that not five minutes later I got another call to say it was a false alarm and not to investigate."

I wrinkled my nose as I leaned my back against Zed's car, looking out into the night. "Do you make a habit of doing whatever this prick tells you to do? I didn't pick you for a lazy cop, Jeffries." As much as that would've caused issues for me, I was disappointed he didn't investigate. What if that tip had been for real? Was this guy so concerned about his sleep that he wouldn't at least send a squad car?

"The second call came from my boss," he muttered back,

"which I thought odd. So I've been sitting here watching a security feed of your parking lot, and so far all I've seen is you, Mr. De Rosa, and your head of security. No suspicious shipments of captive women or drugs or weapons or anything. So I'm gonna ask you again, what the hell is going on?"

I snorted a laugh, looking around until I located the camera he'd been using to spy on us. It was on the opposite side of the street, on public land, but turned away from the traffic to point directly at Anarchy.

"I'd have thought that was obvious, Jeffries," I drawled, opening Zed's car door. "You're being used to harass me. I sure hope you're getting a tasty slice of the pie your boss must be getting to justify all this shitty policework."

Ending the call, I flipped off the camera across the road and slid into Zed's car. I slammed the door behind me and waited for Zed to pull out of the parking lot before filling him in on that conversation.

He didn't say anything for a few moments, his brow creased in thought. Then he glanced over at me. "So someone saw us arrive and realized we'd beaten them to it."

I huffed in frustration. "Sounds like it. They figured out that we had enough head start to make the tip irrelevant and called it off, opting for head games instead. No doubt Chase didn't expect Jeffries to *tell* me about the aborted tip, so I'd have been left puzzling over the point of it all."

Zed blew out a long breath, his hands tightening on the steering wheel as he drove. Then he perfectly summed up my feelings in just three words.

"What a cunt."

Blame the stress of the evening, but I started laughing. "That's an insult to actual cunts, Zed," I scolded him between bursts of laughter. "Chase could never compare to the real deal."

Zed snorted a laugh, flicking a glance at me, then down at

the body part in question. "Fair point. Speaking of your delicious cunt..."

Grinning, I shook my head. "Later. We need to get over to Wattle Lane and sort out the girls. Hopefully, Doc Greene was able to get there to check them all out. Fuck knows what they've been drugged with or why Diana was awake before the rest of them."

Zed grimaced. "Good question." He ran a hand over his short hair, looking tired, then dropped that hand to my knee.

We drove the rest of the way in near silence, both a bit lost in our thoughts. In my head I was trying to work out what in the hell we would do with nine girls if they didn't want to return to their parents...wherever the fuck they were. I had no clue where they'd been taken from. But I sure as shit wouldn't be sending them back to abusive families who would just sell them again the second we were gone.

"You were really good with that girl, Dare," Zed commented as we parked in front of the friendly suburban house that had long been a Timberwolf safe place. The neighbors on each side were nice, normal middle-class couples, but they were also heavily on our payroll.

I leaned into his touch when he wrapped an arm around my waist on the way up the path to the front door. "I'm not a total monster, Zed. I've raised Seph pretty much since she was three, remember?"

He flashed me a smile. "I remember."

Inside the house, Nadia had all the girls in the living room. Most of them were awake, but one girl was still unconscious in a makeshift bed on the floor. The others were all huddled together on the couches while Nadia handed out steaming mugs of hot chocolate. A huge platter of baked goods sat on the table in front of them, and Diana looked like an overgrown chipmunk with her cheeks full of cake.

When she saw me, she jumped up as if she wanted to hug me. Then her wide eyes shifted to Zed, and she stiffened.

I gave a small sigh, shooting Zed a sympathetic look when his shoulders tensed. "Maybe call Hannah? I'm thinking the girls aren't going to want big scary men around right now."

Nadia grunted, coming over to us with her empty tray in hand. "You can say that again. They won't even let Doc check them out. He's gone to wake his wife up, seeing as she's a nurse." She eyed me hard. "Do I even want to know where you found this lot?"

I gave her a warm smile, shaking my head. "Not really. Thank you for coming."

She huffed another grumpy sound, but her eyes were soft. "No thanks needed, sir. You're practically family." Her wink said it all; she knew *exactly* what Cass meant to me. And I to him.

Zed sighed, pulling out his phone. "I'll call Hannah and Gen, maybe Maxine too." He headed back out the front door to do that, putting himself well out of sight of the terrified girls.

When the door closed behind him, I turned back to Nadia. "I know you said Doc hasn't checked them out, but how do they seem? That one hasn't stirred?" I nodded to the unconscious girl.

Nadia shook her head. "I kept them all down here together so none of them woke up terrified and alone. That way I could keep an eye on them all as a group, since I'm only one woman."

I nodded vaguely, looking over to find Diana still staring at me with huge eyes. Her hot chocolate was clutched in her hands and crumbs covered her face, but the poor kid was still covered in grime.

"That was good thinking," I told Nadia. "Hopefully, Zed can get some trusted women to come in and help, maybe get them cleaned up while we figure out what in the hell we do with them."

Nadia indicated to Diana. "That one's been asking for you. Go sit with her a minute, and I'll get you a drink."

I did as I was told, making my way carefully over to where the girls sat. I gained more than a few suspicious looks—and I didn't blame them—but no one started screaming or crying. That was something, I supposed.

Diana gave me a tight smile as I sat down but otherwise didn't seem in the mood for conversation—which was fine by me. I was nowhere even close to qualified to talk these kids through what had happened and what needed to happen next. Better that we get some more maternal women here to help as soon as possible.

Nadia returned a couple of minutes later with a mug of the same hot chocolate for me, then crouched down to check the girl on the floor.

"Doc's wife, Maria, should be here any minute," she told me quietly. "She can see if this one needs more urgent medical care."

"She hit her head," Diana said in a small voice, making both Nadia and I turn to look at her.

Nadia raised a brow. "That's good to know, sweetheart. Thank you."

"What's going to happen to us?" one of the other girls asked, her confidence seeming to spark with Diana breaking the quiet. This girl seemed older, maybe thirteen or so, and had a French accent.

Nadia flicked a quick glance at me, then pursed her lips as she returned her gaze to the girl who'd spoken. "Well, we have a friend coming now to check that you're all recovering from the drugs. Then I think it might be nice to have some showers and clean up. What do you think?"

The girl gave a halting nod, her scared gaze flicking between Nadia and me. "But what then? Will we be sold again?"

Nadia blinked a couple of times, then shook her head. "No, child. I told you when you woke up that we're here to take care of you. You're safe."

"Told you," Diana muttered, glaring at the older girl. "They *saved* us. Idiot."

The other girl's expression darkened like she wanted to reach out and smack Diana for insulting her, but her response was interrupted by the polite chime of the doorbell.

"I'll get it," I muttered, placing my drink down and hurrying to the door.

It was Maria, our nurse, who gave me a quick greeting before bustling through to the living room with her huge medical supply bag tucked under her arm. Before I shut the door again, though, I spotted another car pull up.

Maxine and another girl from Club 22, Sabine, climbed out, both dressed in sweatpants and slippers like they'd rolled straight out of bed, but their faces were creased with worry as they hurried up the front steps to where I waited.

I stepped out onto the porch and gave them an abridged version of events to fill them in.

They both listened attentively; then when I was done, Maxine gave a firm nod. "Got it. Clean them up and get as much personal information as possible so we can get them home again."

"Or not, depending," Sabine added with a shrug. She'd fully understood the subtext when I'd glossed over the need to reunite the girls with their parents.

I nodded. "Exactly."

Maxine gave me a knowing look. My past was closely guarded, but all the current Timberwolves knew about the massacre. Maybe not what sparked it, but they knew that the majority of victims that night had their hands in the flesh trade. Every one of my Wolves knew how deeply I abhorred traffickers, so it really shouldn't have been a surprise that they were so ready and willing to help out.

"We've got this, H," she assured me with a small smile. "Sab and I are good with abused kids."

Sabine snorted. "Birds of a feather and all that shit."

The two of them headed inside, leaving me out on the porch alone. Having them there, along with Nadia and Maria, eased the tension across my shoulders. I fucking sucked with kids, no matter what I'd said to Zed. Hell, maybe if I'd been better, Seph wouldn't be such a spoiled princess now. I screwed up trying to raise her, and I would inevitably screw up trying to talk to those girls in there.

Better someone with a more approachable personality handled them. Maxine and Sabine were perfect.

So instead of heading back inside, I sat my ass down on the porch and waited for Hannah and Gen. A minute later Zed finished his call from where he'd been standing on the lawn, then came to sit on the step with me.

His arm wrapped around my shoulders, pulling me into his side, and his lips pressed to my hair.

"You want to go?" he asked softly after a couple of minutes. "There's not much more we can do tonight."

I nodded vaguely. "Soon."

He didn't question that response, just sat with me in silence until Hannah and Gen pulled up in separate cars just seconds apart.

Shivering, I pushed to my feet to meet them and give the same rundown I'd given Maxine, then told Hannah to use my credit card for anything the girls might need.

She gave me a confident smile in return. "Absolutely, sir. We've got it handled."

I nodded back. "I'll keep my phone on. Call if you need me."

Hannah agreed and continued up the steps to the house. Gen lingered a moment, though, a worried frown creasing her brow.

"This is dangerous," she murmured, unnecessarily. "If there are missing-person reports out and they're found here..."

I shrugged. "It's a risk we'll take. I'm not dropping them off at the dirty-as-fuck police station just to be tossed back into the skin market. Max and Sabine are going to try and get some names. Your job—"

"Run them through the database," Gen finished for me, her mouth tight. "Understood."

353

With a quick smile to Zed, she hurried up into the house. Only once she was safely inside did I nod to Zed that we could leave.

As we climbed into his car, I flicked my eyes around and checked off all the backup. All of Alexi's guys, the ones who'd transported the girls, were still present, just out of sight. Smart guys.

CHAPTER 44

Cass was already home by the time we got back to the house, sitting at the dining table and playing poker with Lucas. Neither of them was drinking, though, and both had their guns sitting within reach. High alert.

Exhaustion was making me lightheaded, but at the same time I was so keyed up I doubted I could have slept even if I tried. So I sat my ass down and summarized everything that had happened, while Zed made me a Baileys on ice.

After he placed the drink in front of me, he gathered my hair up and tied it in a loose knot. Then he proceeded to massage my shoulders while I talked, and I quickly retracted my mental statement about not being able to sleep.

"You reckon they were all sold by their families?" Cass rumbled when I was done. The anger in his voice was dark enough to make me shiver, and I didn't blame him.

"Probably not all," Zed answered for me, "but the little girl Dare spoke to seemed that way."

Lucas blew out a long breath, raking his fingers through his hair. "Fucking hell," he murmured. "Poor kids. Is there anything I can do?"

I shook my head, leaning into Zed's hands harder. "Not tonight. They're well looked after tonight."

Cass grunted a sound of agreement. "Nadia's there, they'll be fine. Everyone should go to bed."

Lucas snorted a laugh. "Okay, *Grandpa*."

In retaliation, Cass cuffed him around the head. "Watch your mouth, Gumdrop."

I gave a short laugh at their teasing and finished my drink with a large swallow. Then I pushed to my feet with a yawn.

"Any movement from Seph?" Zed asked as we all made our way upstairs.

"Nothing," Lucas replied. "I even checked in case she'd, like, somehow crept out of her alarmed window, but she was snoring with her mouth open and drool all over her pillow."

I smiled. It wasn't the *safest*, but I liked how deeply Seph slept. It meant she wasn't plagued by the nightmares and horrors that the rest of us were.

When we got close to Zed's bedroom door, he wrapped his hand around my wrist and tugged me inside with him while Lucas and Cass made sounds of protest behind us.

"Not cool, Zeddy Bear," Lucas called out when Zed slammed the door.

Zed just snorted a laugh. "Suck my dick, Gumdrop!"

"Careful," I murmured, grinning as he unbuckled my gun holster for me. "One of those two might take you up on that offer."

He wasn't even remotely worried, I could tell. "Not likely," he replied with a grin. "Come on, sleep with me. I need to feel you in my arms tonight."

His kisses as he stripped me out of my clothes were slow and loving, and then he tugged one of his own shirts over my head to sleep in. We were both too exhausted to fuck like rabbits, so we just snuggled until we fell asleep. It was almost like old times when we were nothing more than friends.

Until morning, of course. I woke up with Zed's sleep boner crushed against my ass and lacked the willpower to ignore it. Surely, there weren't many better ways to wake up than with some epic sleepy sex with a man you were totally in love with?

By the time we made it to the shower to get clean, then dirty again, then *finally* drag some clothes on, Lucas and Seph had already left for school.

"Morning, Red," Cass rumbled when I looped my arms around his waist from behind. He was at the stove cooking eggs that smelled…less than amazing.

Zed clearly thought so too because his face screwed up like he was being personally insulted. "The fuck did you do to those eggs, asshole?" He reached over and grabbed the frying pan straight off the gas burner.

"Hey," Cass protested, holding his spatula up. "What the hell?"

Zed just wrinkled his nose and dumped the entire contents of the pan into the trash before rinsing it out. "Gross," he muttered. "Make coffee or something. I'll sort out eggs."

Cass gave Zed a long-suffering glare, but when he turned to the coffee machine, I caught a smug grin on his lips.

"Sneaky cat," I whispered, tucking under his arm when he hugged me into his side.

He just winked down at me and set about making us all coffees.

"No calls through the night?" Cass rumbled, passing me the first mug and letting his fingers linger on mine.

I shook my head. "Nothing. I'm going to head over to Wattle Lane this morning, though. No doubt Nadia would have just dealt with shit herself rather than calling me."

Cass huffed in amusement. "Sounds right. I wish I could come with you."

Holding my coffee tight, I rose up on my toes to kiss him. "I know," I murmured. "But you're still dead. Besides, the whole tough-guy biker look isn't going down real well with these scared kids."

He grunted, but I knew he understood. The whole situation was making me insanely glad I had a handful of women I could semi-trust to help out. But it also highlighted how dick-heavy I'd let the Timberwolves get—something I'd wanted to avoid when I took over. I needed to work on that.

The three of us enjoyed a strangely cozy breakfast together, but I missed Lucas. We weren't complete without him. I really should have gotten up earlier to see him before he left for school, but I'd make up for it. If all things went to plan and Chase didn't start any more shit in the next thirty-six hours, then I'd be finally putting on my show at Club 22. I'd dragged my heels on fulfilling that bet long enough, and we couldn't make any new ones until I'd paid up.

Zed offered to drive me over to Wattle Lane, and as badly as I was itching to take my Ducati out for a drive, I accepted. For one thing, we would need to go to work after checking on the girls. And for another, I didn't want to be alone.

Chase had gotten under my skin, and now I was feeling eyes on me every time I left the safety of Zed's house.

Zed must have had a similar thought, because he walked me all the way to the front door of our safe house. It wasn't something we discussed out loud, but I appreciated the gesture, no matter how unnecessary.

"I'd better wait in the car," he said softly as I pressed the doorbell. "I'm here if you need me, though." His hand pressed into my lower back, bringing my body close as he bent down to kiss me.

The door swung open the moment our lips locked, though, and I reluctantly pulled away to greet Nadia. Except it wasn't Nadia staring up at us with a disgusted look on her cute little face.

"Ew," Diana announced, giving Zed a look like he smelled awful. Then her big, green-eyed gaze shifted to me, and her smile increased in brightness. "Hades! You're back! I knew you would be." She launched herself at me, her arms banding around my waist as her face buried in my stomach.

Startled, I just stood there for a moment as the kid hugged me and Zed struggled not to laugh. Behind Diana, he gave a very pointed look at the girl's now clean hair, then met my eyes with a wide grin.

"You're so fucked," he whispered, then smacked another quick kiss on my lips before retreating to his car. Laughing.

Glowering after him, I tried to peel Diana off my waist. "I'm not huge on the hugs, squirt," I muttered. "Let's get inside. What the fuck were you doing answering the door, anyway?"

No sooner were the words out of my mouth than Nadia swatted me around the ears with a tea towel. "Language," she scolded, as if on instinct. Then her eyes widened, and she drew a deep breath through her nose, like she wasn't sure how I'd react to that.

But I just chuckled and nodded. "Yeah, fair enough." I pushed Diana gently in the direction of the living room where I could hear feminine chatter and cartoons playing on the TV. "Go. I need to talk to Nadia."

Diana gave an exaggerated huff but did as she was told, leaving me to peer at Nadia.

"Is it just me," I said, quietly enough that we couldn't be overheard, "or does that fucking kid look like she could be related to me?"

Nadia scoffed, glancing in Diana's direction. The kid's shiny copper hair was unmissable among the other girls. "Not all redheads are related, Hades. Goodness me, did you fail high school science?"

Rolling my eyes, I followed her to the kitchen, where Maxine was washing up the dishes with Hannah. They were talking and laughing together like old friends, and the whole room—the whole *house*—had a drastically different energy than when I'd left in the early hours of the morning.

"So, what did I miss?" I asked, taking a seat at the island when Nadia pointed to it.

Gen popped her head up from the dining table where she had

her laptop set up. Her hair was messy and her eyes looked tired, but she seemed content. Pleased.

"Boss, you're back." She smiled.

"First things first." Nadia took over. "The poor little girl who wasn't waking up from the drugs—Maria took her in to Shadow Grove Memorial. She was worried that it was more the head knock than the drugs keeping her under. Far as I know, they're still treating her this morning."

My brows hitched slightly, but I'd trusted them to make the right calls. "Okay. What else?"

Nadia folded her arms under her breasts. "Most of the girls have been easy to identify. Once they understood we were genuinely trying to help them, they became chatty, even the two who don't speak a lick of English."

"Five of the nine were reported missing by their families and genuinely seem to want to go home. Of course, we will investigate a little further, but it *seems* like they were kidnapped, not sold," Gen offered, capping her pen and closing the notebook she'd been writing in beside her computer.

Surprise rippled through me, and I tilted my head. "Well, shit, that's better than I expected. The girls want to go home?" Nadia nodded. "Well then, let's sort it out sooner rather than later. What about the other four?"

"One is the girl in hospital." Nadia ticked off on her fingers. "Then there're the two who don't speak English. One speaks Spanish, which luckily Maxine is fluent in, and we were able to learn she comes from Colombia. She was crying for her family, but..." Nadia grimaced, indicating to Gen.

My lawyer screwed up her nose, looking angry. "I investigated the family and did some digging. I'm at least ninety percent sure she was sold by her parents to clear a bad debt."

Anger filled my veins, and my fist clenched at my side. "How the fuck can any parent do that?" I growled, furious.

Gen shrugged. "Happens more than people realize. Anyway, it looks like the father is mixed up in some shady shit. If we sent her back, they'd likely just sell her again."

I let my breath out on a long exhale. It sucked, but it was sort of what I'd expected. If my father had succeeded in selling Seph off in the auction house then she'd returned a month later, he wouldn't have blinked twice before collecting a second paycheck.

"The other girl is Russian," Nadia continued, looking more pissed off than I'd ever seen her. "Sounds like she's been held the longest of all of them."

A flash of understanding hit me. "You speak Russian," I commented.

Nadia gave a short nod. "*Da*. Her family are all dead. She has no one to return to."

Sympathy for that child rolled through me, and I stubbornly refused to let my mind wander over all the horrific things that could have happened to her while being held for transport. She hadn't been sold to her final owner yet, but that didn't mean her captors would have treated her with any kind of respect.

"Fuck. All right. And the last one?" Because they'd only told me about eight of the nine so far.

Hannah gave a short chuckle, sharing a glance with Maxine, and I gave them a suspicious look.

Nadia clicked her tongue at them both before turning back to me. "Diana," she said, and somehow I wasn't even slightly surprised. "She won't tell us her surname, where she came from, how long she was captive…anything."

I frowned in confusion. "I don't get it. She speaks just fine and seems confident as hell today. What's the problem?"

This time Nadia herself seemed to be trying to hide a smile. "She said there's no point in telling us who her family are because…" Nadia cleared her throat before continuing as if in a direct quote from Diana: "'Because fuck family, they're a bunch of assholes.'"

My lips parted, but no sound came out. Consider me speechless. And judging by the way Nadia glared at me and Hannah grinned behind her hand, I was willing to bet Diana had told them I'd been the one to say that originally.

"Well," I said after a painfully long pause, "she's probably not wrong."

Nadia threw her hands in the air, and Hannah seemed to shake with silent laughter until Maxine elbowed her.

"Where's Sabine?" I asked, changing the subject away from my appalling influence on impressionable young children.

Maxine pointed toward the living room. "In there, braiding hair. She's having an amazing time."

"Cute," I murmured, then shifted my attention back to Gen. "Let's sort out those five who want to go home. If Maria is happy with their physical health, then we should reunite them as soon as possible."

Gen nodded. "Yes, sir."

"What about the other three?" Nadia asked.

I bit the edge of my thumbnail, thinking, then gave a small sigh. "Nothing, for now. I'll talk it over with Zed and see what we can do for them. Obviously the Russian girl—"

"Zoya," Nadia offered.

I amended myself. "Obviously Zoya can't be sent back to Russia with no family and, I'm assuming, no money. And I don't feel comfortable sending…"

"Angelina," Maxine supplied.

"Sending Angelina home to a family who knowingly sold her." I gave a small groan, rubbing my eyes. "How old are these girls? Old enough to make their own choices?"

Nadia shrugged. "Depends on the choice."

"Fair point," I muttered. "Let me think on it. I'll come up with some options, but in the meantime…" Shit, I couldn't just ask these women to babysit indefinitely.

Nadia reached out and patted my forearm where I leaned on the counter, giving me an understanding smile. "I'll look after them. After all, I have some free time on my hands right now." She gave me a pointed look, and I cringed.

"I'm sorry about your café," I told her sheepishly.

She shrugged. "I'm not. You should see the beautiful renovation you're paying for." Her grin was all Cass, and I couldn't help smiling back.

"Yeah, I deserve that. It'd better be awesome. Anyway, is there anything I can do here before I go in to work?" I glanced around at everyone with that question, and they all looked equally confused.

Nadia answered first, though. "We've got this handled, Hades. You get on in to work, but be sure to tell Diana you're leaving. That little girl thinks you walk on bloody water, she does."

I gave a short laugh as I slid off my stool. "Hero worship. She'll get over it when she realizes what a cold bastard I really am."

Hannah chuckled from where she was drying dishes. "Okay, Boss." Then she checked the time and hissed a curse. "Shit, sorry, I should be at work too."

"Go, we've got this," Maxine told her, tugging the towel from her hands.

Nadia nodded. "I'll send you a grocery list to pick up on your way back, Hannah." Then she nudged me through to the living room to say goodbye to Diana.

Luckily for me and my aversion to hugs from people I wasn't sleeping with, Diana was getting her hair braided by Sabine when I got in there. So instead of clinging to me like a spider monkey again, she just pouted and asked if I'd be back later.

Fucking kid was too good at puppy-dog eyes for her own good—or mine—and I found myself agreeing to swing past after work.

Nadia followed me out and waved to Hannah, who was already getting into her car. But then she paused me with a hand on my arm.

"Hades," she murmured, "how's my boy?"

She kept her face neutral, but there was no hiding the deep concern filling her eyes or the slight tremble in her voice.

Guilt flooded through me, hating that we'd made Cass's grandmother think he was dead for even a minute. "He's good," I whispered back. "Made a full recovery already and itching to be resurrected."

She gave a sad smile. "Well, tell him to be patient. Not everyone will be pleased to see him breathing."

With that ominous warning, she stepped back inside the house and closed the door. A moment later, the lock clicked home. Good. Nadia wasn't taking chances.

CHAPTER 45

That afternoon I found myself leaving work early just so I could swing past the safe house and visit the girls like I'd promised. Not that I had any intention of joining in on the hair braiding and shit, but I didn't like to break my word.

Zed once again waited in the car, but Diana peered at him through the window, then asked if he was my *boyfriend*. Ugh, kids were the fucking worst.

We arrived home just a couple of minutes ahead of Lucas and Seph. I'd barely even stripped out of my weapons when I heard the Mustang pull into the garage.

"Dare!" Seph's shout echoed through the house, alarming me. "Dare! Come here! Zed, are you home?"

I raced back through to the garage to where she hovered nervously in the doorway while the garage door rolled back down.

"Seph, what's going on?" I demanded, striding over to the Mustang, where Lucas was climbing out slowly. He winced as he pushed the driver's door shut and held his ribs like he was in pain. "What the fuck happened?"

A more critical glance at Seph told me she wasn't nervous after all. She was...excited?

Lucas gave me a pained smile. "I'm fine, babe." Even though he was definitely *not* fine. "I handled it." He sidestepped me and circled to the trunk of the Mustang, then popped it open.

Inside, I found the absolute last thing I'd ever expected Lucas and Seph to bring home from school: a bound and gagged man all squished into the tight trunk space, blood coating half his face as he thrashed and twisted.

"Is that... Did you restrain him with your tie?" I asked in disbelief, unsure whether I should be amused or horrified.

"Dare," Seph interrupted, bouncing on her toes with excitement, a huge smile on her face. "Dare, oh my god, you should have seen it! This guy just jumped out of fucking *nowhere* and, like, tried to strangle Lucas with this rope thing and—"

I stopped listening to her high-speed babble, grabbing Lucas's arm and spinning him to face me. Sure enough, there was an angry red line around his throat, and he winced as I touched a gentle finger to the welt. This *dead man* had tried to garrote my Gumdrop.

"Then Lucas tied him up and chucked him in the trunk, and we drove back here *super* fast." Seph was still gushing, her smile so wide it had to be hurting her face and her eyes sparkling. "Dare, you should have seen him! Like, *bam* and *pow* and *pop*! Lucas is legit such a badass, like, wow."

"Where was your backup?" I asked him quietly, ignoring Seph.

"Huh?" My sister shrugged. "What backup? We don't have any. Besides, we don't *need* any because Lucas is a total weapon."

Lucas gave a faint smile. "He was across the road," he replied to me. "It was quicker to deal with it myself, and seeing as we were right by my car..." He shrugged, but I understood. Better to stash the bleeding, bound man out of sight before someone went calling the cops.

"Careful," I muttered, smoothing a finger over his bruised cheek. "Don't let Zed hear you call it your car."

Lucas snorted as Zed and Cass came into the garage to investigate Seph's yelling.

"Well, that's unexpected," Zed commented, peering into the trunk with us. Then he glanced over at Seph, still grinning from ear to ear. "Seph, head inside."

Her smile disappeared in a flash, replaced by a scowl. "Fuck you, Zed."

"Get inside, Seph," I ordered, my voice sharp with anger. "Or would you actually like to watch me cut this guy's fingers off one by one until he tells us who sent him to kill Lucas today?"

My sister paled, but her eyes flashed with stubborn defiance like she was actually going to call my bluff. Except I wasn't bluffing. Nor was I offering her a choice in the matter. I wasn't going to torture a man in front of my innocent eighteen-year-old sister.

"Come on, Seph," Lucas said gently, placing a hand on her arm. "I'll show you how to check for broken ribs."

Outrage was clear on her face, and I knew she wanted to stand her ground. But Lucas gently pulled her away from the car, and she sighed as she followed him. Zed, Cass, and I waited in silence until they were back inside the house, closing the door to seal us off.

"He shouldn't have brought this guy here," Cass rumbled, peering down at the man. "Gonna have to kill him now."

The bound man's eyes widened, and he made muffled sounds of protest as Zed reached in and hauled him out of the trunk.

"Fucking hell," Zed muttered. "Lucas is cleaning that blood up. Little shit should have put some plastic down first."

I scoffed at both of them. "All right, geez. We all made mistakes with our first time, too. He's learning. Seph said he took this guy on without help from the backup I'd assigned."

"As he damn well should," Zed commented, dragging the bloodied man away from his cars to the workshop area of the garage. "I haven't busted my ass training him to have him garroted on the school playground."

367

"Parking lot," I corrected, going to the workbench to pull out a thick wad of plastic sheeting from a drawer. Shaking it out, Cass and I laid it down on the concrete floor before Zed marched his captive over to the middle and shoved him to his knees.

It was a routine Zed and I had been through countless times, and I imagined so had Cass in his own way. So it was nothing new or exciting for us to interrogate the guy. In fact, with Cass's input, we got the answers we sought with ease. Only when we were satisfied that the guy had divulged everything he knew did I put a bullet between his eyes. And two in the chest, for good measure. One never could be too cautious these days.

"What do you want to do with the body?" Cass asked as Zed washed his bloody hands in the small sink. "Benny's? Or shark food?"

I flashed him a grin. We were way too similar. "Nah, I've got a better idea. Roll him up."

Cass grunted and went to work packaging up the messy remains of Lucas's attacker, rolling the plastic like a giant rice paper roll. Or joint. When he was done, I grabbed a thick black marker pen from one of the tool drawers, and in clear block letters, I wrote on the plastic *RETURN TO SENDER*.

"Drop him on Chase's doorstep," I told the guys. "Let him deal with the mess."

Zed laugh sharply, shaking his head. "Done. Help me load him up."

Cass grabbed one end of the package, lifting with Zed to heave the body into the trunk of a car. Then Zed climbed into the driver's seat with a feral grin to go deliver our package to the neighbor.

We watched him back out of the garage, then Cass banded his arm around my waist and boosted me up onto the workbench to kiss the ever-loving crap out of me.

"What was that for?" I asked when he eventually let me breathe.

His beard scraped my face as he dipped in to kiss me again. "I need a reason?" he growled after a few moments. "I've never been so fucking horny during an interrogation in my life. Fuck, you're beautiful. Like an angel of death."

Laughing, I pushed him back slightly and shook my head. "You're too damn charming, Saint. Come on, we need to go deal with Seph. She was probably in shock or something before."

Cass huffed a short laugh. "She didn't seem in shock. Too busy fawning over Lucas like he'd just outed himself as the newest Avenger."

I rolled my eyes, but he was right. She hadn't seemed scared or stressed out. Her hero worship for Lucas was all-encompassing.

They weren't in the kitchen, but I took my sweet-ass time pouring a glass of wine anyway. Zed was only taking the body next door; he'd be back any minute, and maybe he could deal with Seph for me. Such a cop-out, but whatever.

Cass could hardly keep his hands off me as I moved around the kitchen and had me giggling like a teenager when he pinned me to the counter with his hips—and his rock-hard dick—while he cleaned blood splatters from my face with the kitchen sponge. So hygienic.

Zed came in before things could get too heated in the kitchen and gave us both an accusing glare. "You"—he pointed a finger at Cass—"are a sick kitty, getting turned on by that mess."

Cass just shrugged and gave my neck a teasing bite as he kissed me there.

"And you"—Zed pointed at me—"need to go talk to Seph. Now. Move it."

I gave him an exaggerated pout back. "Do I really have to? Lucas seems to be handling her just fine." Zed's glare flattened, and I huffed. "Fine. Hold this thought, Saint." I gripped his dick through his jeans so he knew exactly what thought I was talking about. As if there could be any confusion.

No doubt Seph was going to want to know what we'd done

369

with that guy, and I really wasn't ready to explain to her how we'd maimed him in excruciatingly painful ways to make him talk, then shot him before we dumped him on Chase's doorstep. So I very reluctantly dragged my feet upstairs to find my sister.

I took my wine with me, though. Dutch courage.

Voices came from Lucas's room, so I headed in that direction but paused just outside when I heard my name. It wasn't the most mature decision of my life, but I was curious to hear what they were talking about without my presence influencing Seph's attitude.

Zed and Cass had followed because of course they weren't missing out on the entertainment, and I held up a hand for them to wait while I tilted my head to listen.

"Look, Seph," Lucas was saying in a kind but firm voice, like he was repeating himself. "I understand where you're coming from, but I'm not comfortable having this conversation. You need to speak with your sister directly."

Seph gave a frustrated sound that I was all too familiar with, and I rolled my eyes. I raised my hand to push open the door that was already cracked, then stilled when I heard what she said next.

"I don't *get it*!" she exclaimed. "Why are you so freaking obsessed with Dare? She's, like, *old*, for starters. You know she's probably getting wrinkles and gray hair soon."

My jaw dropped in outrage, and my eyes flicked to Zed, who was grinning like a shithead. I glowered at him, and he just shrugged.

"She's twenty-three, Seph," Lucas replied with a laugh, "not fucking fifty."

"Yeah, well, even so, you deserve better than her, Lucas. I know she *says* she loves you, but do you seriously think she even knows what that word means? She's like the dictionary definition of coldhearted. All she ever does is ruin the people who love her, too. First Chase, then my dad. And look what she's done to Cass! He's literally given up everything to play her little sex slave. Don't tell me you're *okay* being another one of her toys to be used and thrown away when she breaks you too hard."

Wow. That one hurt. I shot Cass a guilty look, but he shook his head firmly, disagreeing with Seph's statement.

"Seph," Lucas replied with a long exhale, "I'm trying to be nice here. I'm trying to be your friend. But for *fuck's sake*, I just got my ass beat by a guy trying to *kill* me, and you're in here bad-mouthing the woman I happen to be *in love* with? Nah, sorry. I'm done. Go do your homework or something. I've had enough."

Zed gave a soft grunt of surprise, shooting me a grin as we listened. "Smart kid," he whispered.

"Excuse me?" Seph damn near shrieked. "You can't be serious!"

"I'm dead serious," Lucas snapped back. "If anyone deserves *better*, it's Hayden. She deserves better than this shit from her little sister for whom she has sacrificed so goddamn much. She loves you harder than you can clearly understand, so wake the fuck up. And stop flirting. With me, with Zed, fucking hell, even with Cass. It's insulting, and one of these days Hayden's going to slap the shit out of you for it."

Biting my lip to hold back a smile, I decided we'd eavesdropped enough, so I pushed the door open fully and met my sister's startled gaze unflinchingly.

When I said nothing, she threw up her hands in a rage. "Oh, I suppose you heard all of that, then? What are you, twelve? Who listens at doors?"

Choosing to take the high road, no matter how badly it grated on my nerves, I bit my tongue to hold back my cutting replies. Instead, I just crossed over to where Lucas sat on the armchair at the end of his bed, holding an ice pack to his ribs over his T-shirt.

"Are you okay?" I asked him softly, tilting his chin up to check the mark around his neck. I was beyond impressed that he'd managed to break free from what looked to have been a *tight* garrote hold. Zed really had trained him well. I could hardly wait to see what Cass could do to hone his skills once he had more time at home with us.

Lucas's answering smile was pure adoration, and he kissed my wrist. "I'm fine. Alexi roughed me up worse than this last week."

"You're not going to ask how *I* am?" Seph demanded, her hands on her hips. "I could have been traumatized from that attack, and you don't even care! You never have. I'm not even a real person to you, am I, Dare? Oh, sorry, I mean *Hades*." The scathing sarcasm in her voice made my shoulders tighten and my teeth clench.

Drawing a calming breath, I turned back to face my sister. "I think from what we overheard, you're just fine."

Her face turned blotchy with embarrassment, knowing full well what I'd heard her say, but true to Seph style, she just popped a hip and tilted her chin up stubbornly. "So what? Now you're punishing me because I told Lucas the *truth*? That he should be running as far and as fast away from you as possible because you're nothing but a walking death trap? You're *Hades* through and through, killing everyone who ever tries to get in your way or tell you no. Dad would be ashamed to call you his daughter if he could see you now. At least he ran the Timberwolves with integrity and respect, not just fear and *death*."

As hard as I was trying not to snap at her over hitting on Lucas *again*, I was unprepared for that insult. I flinched, and Zed saw it. He met my eyes for the briefest second, and I knew Seph had finally pushed it too far. Nothing I could say now was going to stop him.

"Sit down, Persephone," Zed said in a glacial voice, stepping into Lucas's room. Cass lounged against the doorframe like some kind of security guard backing Zed up and preventing Seph from escaping.

Seph clearly didn't identify the danger, though, screwing up her face as she spun around to spew more of her venom in his direction. "Screw you, Zed," she sneered back. "You're so fucking pussy-whipped by her you can't even—"

"Sit *down!*" Zed barked, fury coating his voice.

It was enough to shock Seph into doing as she was told, and she meekly perched on the edge of Lucas's bed with big eyes. "Happy?"

Zed glowered. "Not even *close*. It's high fucking time you had a dose of truth, Seph." He looked over at me, the apology clear on his face. "I'm sorry, Dare. She needs to know."

I shook my head, feeling numb because I knew I wasn't talking him out of it this time. We'd gone way past the point where I could just threaten to shoot him for disobeying me.

"I need to know *what?*" Seph demanded, folding her arms over her chest.

Zed held my gaze, resigned, then gave a small nod toward the door. "Go," he told me. I understood him perfectly, and as much as I desperately wished it hadn't come to this, it was also the only way the truth could ever come out. She would never hear it from me. *Never.* But her ignorance was going to get her killed one of these days.

"Wait, why the hell does *she* get to leave?" Seph protested, glaring pure venom my way. "This is about her, isn't it?"

Zed snapped his gaze back to my sister and shut her up with the force of his anger. "Yes, it is. And it's about *you*. But Dare gets to leave because *she* doesn't need to hear all this dredged up out of the past. She lived it, and I'd do anything to save her from having to *re*live it. Clear?"

"As mud," Seph sulked. Until that point, I thought I'd tough it out and stay while Zed filled her in on what had *really* gone down with our father, whom she idolized. But the salty look on her face made me want to scream or slap her or...something. No, Zed was right. I *didn't* need to hear it.

Silently, I just nodded to Zed and left the damn room. I trusted him to give her the whole story, but no way did I need those memories plaguing my brain. Not now, while I was barely clinging to sanity with Chase back in my life.

As soon as I was out of the room, I started running. I flew down the stairs and into the garage. I couldn't just sit down in the hallway while Zed laid out the darkest, most disgusting parts of my life for my sister…for *Lucas* to hear. Nope, I needed to go far and fast. I was well overdue a run on my Ducati anyway.

I snatched one of Zed's spare guns, tucking it into the back of my pants before climbing onto my bike. I didn't bother grabbing a jacket, but I wasn't stupid enough to go out unarmed again. Nor was I dumb enough to forego my helmet.

A minute later, I was tearing out onto the cold, dark streets of outer Shadow Grove. Totally alone. Only when I was miles away from Zed's house did I let the tight hold on my emotions slip. Silent tears flowed from my eyes as I drove, clouding my vision enough that I eventually needed to pull over. It was either that or risk a crash. Like I said, I wasn't dumb.

I reduced my speed and pulled into a scenic overlook somewhere in the hills above Shadow Grove, then climbed off my bike and tugged my helmet off to shake my hair out. The night air turned my wet cheeks cold, and I swiped my hand over them in a pathetic attempt to dry my face.

It was pointless, though. So I just sat my ass down in the grass and curled my arms around my knees, crying soundlessly.

I should have known better, though. I wasn't alone. Not anymore, not *ever* again. I'd barely sat my ass down there in the damp grass before another motorcycle roared up the hill and parked beside mine. Then a moment later, I was being hauled into Cass's lap as his strong, leather-coated arms wrapped around me in a hug that made me feel like I could disappear.

We sat like that for ages, him rubbing my back as my eyes leaked endlessly against his warm chest. But it simply wasn't in my nature to wallow in self-pity for long. It served no good purpose. So after a while, I consciously started to calm myself. I controlled my breathing, relaxed my muscles, and forced the dark, panicked thoughts from my mind. I was strong. I was resilient. I was Hades.

All those things Zed was telling Seph… They were my past, but they'd helped shape me into the woman I was today. I refused to be ashamed of that.

"There she is," Cass whispered when I sat up and met his sad eyes.

I leaned in and kissed him softly, conveying all my thanks in that gesture. Then I climbed out of his lap and rolled my shoulders, shaking off the weakness.

"How'd you find me?" I asked as we headed back to our bikes.

Cass shot me a sly wink. "I have my ways, Angel."

He trapped me with his hands on my waist before I could get back on my bike, leaning in to kiss me again, then just *holding* me until I was so damn calm I could have happily fallen asleep right there in his arms.

"It's better that she knows," he rumbled as he released me.

I nodded. "I know. I should have told her a long time ago, but…" I'd always claimed I wouldn't tell her because I didn't want to hurt *her*. I didn't want to ruin *her* memories of a loving father or taint *her* view of the world.

But that wasn't the real reason. I was just too scared, too ashamed to admit my own part in the myriad mistakes I'd made as a teenager. I didn't want to see her judgment or, worse than anything, I didn't want to see her pity.

"Come on," Cass rumbled. "Zed and Lucas will be having kittens by now, worrying about you."

I snickered quietly at that imagery, then pulled my helmet on. Cass did the same, wearing Zed's helmet once again, and I nodded to him. "Race you home?"

Cass's muffled laugh warmed me. "Deal. Winner gets his dick sucked." Then he took off without waiting for me to be ready. Dirty cheater.

He knew exactly how to cheer me up, though, because by the time we got back to the house, I was grinning under my helmet and my whole body felt lighter.

We pulled into the garage and waited for the door to roll closed before taking our helmets off. That's when I spotted Seph, sitting on the step between the garage and the house and looking like her puppy had just died. Her eyes were red and puffy and her nose shiny, but she was dry-eyed. For now.

"I'll give you a minute," Cass rumbled, kissing the side of my head before passing Seph to head inside.

My sister stood up, her glassy eyes locked on me as she stepped forward. "Dare," she croaked, "I'm *so* sorry. I didn't—"

I cut her off with a shake of my head. "Doesn't matter, Seph. The past is the past." And I didn't want to fucking talk about it. Then, now, or ever.

"But—" She tried again, reaching out like she wanted to hug me. Then she changed her mind, and her arms dropped to her sides.

For some reason, that one incomplete gesture hurt more than anything else. It solidified that everything she'd said about me before, she still believed now. That I was a cold, heartless bitch.

Maybe she was right.

"Forget it," I told her, my voice hard. "It changes nothing." I moved past her, heading inside. Then I paused and drew a deep breath before spinning around to face her. "Today's attack on Lucas made me realize I need better protection on you. I've spoken with an acquaintance to help out. He'll be here tomorrow when you get home from school."

Seph squeaked a sound of outrage. "You're sending me away? Again? Why? Because I said some shitty things about you?"

I bit my cheek in a reminder to myself not to lose my cool. "Seph, you can say all the shitty things about me that you want. You can *think* all the worst thoughts about me. It won't change how

I protect you, and right now I can't do it alone. So I'm calling in help. It's as simple as that."

Rage darkened her face, and her hurt glare turned accusing. "Because I'm *such* an inconvenience, huh? I'm just this…liability to you."

Jesus fucking Christ. "Did you listen to a word Zed told you, Seph?" I exclaimed, officially losing my fucking cool. "*You* were the one person on this whole fucking planet I loved enough to do the things I did. Chase knows it, too. So you're not a liability, you're a *target*. He's going to try and hurt you to hurt me. Do you understand that? Do you understand that this is all one huge, twisted game to him? *I can't keep you safe alone!* For once in your life, *listen* to what I'm telling you."

Her eyes had turned as wide as saucers as I yelled at her, and when I was done, they started leaking. Fucking hell, I'd made my sister cry.

But instead of bursting into dramatic sobs like she did when things didn't go her way, she just gave a small nod.

"I understand," she whispered, her voice choked with emotion. Then she carefully walked past me and up the stairs to her loft bedroom. A minute later, I heard her door slam.

Sick anxiety filled my whole body like poison, making my limbs tremble as I headed through to the kitchen. Lights were on in the courtyard, and when I stepped out, I found all three of my guys sprawled out on the lounge, sharing a joint.

When they saw me standing there, Lucas held out a hand, and Zed held out the joint. Their silent message was clear and totally accurate. What was done was done, and it was done for the *better*. She needed to know, no matter how shitty it felt now.

CHAPTER 46

A shiver ran through me as I twisted in the mirror to inspect my ass. It was barely even covered by the tiny, fringed skirt I wore. And that was the *over*-costume. Underneath it, all I had on was a micro-thong made of dental floss and diamantes. As for the top half…

"This is…" I let my voice trail off, failing to find expressive words that wouldn't offend Maxine. After all, it was a red and black replica of the costume she herself wore every Friday night for her feature show at Club 22.

She flashed me a knowing grin. "Spare me the false modesty, H. You know you've got a banging body. You can more than pull this off." She flicked some of the fringe hanging from my bra top and winked. "Those boys are going to be dead in their seats before you even take the top layer off."

I gave a small groan. "It's not them that I'm worried about. It's the mess I'll need to clean up if any of the patrons make comments within earshot."

Maxine laughed, the kind of easy laugh I envied. "I wouldn't worry about that, Boss. Besides, the way the lights are set up here, you can't see anyone past that front row. It'll be like you're all alone, just putting on a show for your men."

I went to run a hand through my hair, but Maxine slapped it away. Fair call, seeing as she'd just barely finished styling my hair and makeup.

"You'll be sensational," she assured me, then grabbed a shot glass from the tray that a waitress had delivered some time ago. "But here, drink this just in case."

I tossed the shot back and then snatched hers out of her hand before she could drink it.

"Hey!" she protested.

"Too slow," I teased, knocking hers back, too, and letting the liquor warm me from the inside.

Maxine rolled her eyes, then jerked her head toward the stage. "All right, you're up. Go rip the Band-Aid off, and next time, make sure you don't lose the bet."

Grinning, I took a couple of steps toward the curtain that led to the stage. Then I paused and turned back to Maxine, feeling all kinds of awkward. "Hey, uh, this is weird, but…are you doing anything on Tuesday?"

Her brows rose. "During the time slot that I usually whip your skinny butt around a stripper pole? Nope, not anymore. Why, you wanna get coffee or something?"

I shrugged. "Yeah."

A bright smile lit up her face, and she nodded. "I'd love to. Now go, or you'll miss the start of the song." She smacked me on the ass, and I grinned as I slipped through the curtain and out onto the darkened stage.

Lights were dancing around the room and music boomed through the club, but the main stage—my stage—was in total darkness to allow me a moment to get into position.

My heels clicked on the hard stage floor and my breathing seemed way too fucking loud, but I didn't waste time on nerves. I just repeated exactly what Maxine had taught me over and over in rehearsal. When the lights flared bright on my stage, I was in my starting pose, ready.

Maxine had been telling the truth about being blinded to the rest of the club, but right there in the front row, within touching distance of the stage, were my guys. Or…two of them, at least. Cass, sadly, was still a dead man and couldn't really attend a busy Friday night at Club 22.

So as I began to move with the music, following Maxine's routine as perfectly as I could, I locked eyes with Lucas and let his wide, playful grin fill me with joy as I possibly made him cringe with my subpar pole work. Then it was Zed's steady, awestruck gaze that moved me through the next section, making the rest of the world melt away. The intensity of his stare made me feel like we were totally alone, like I was dancing just for him.

Then, as I twisted up into an inverted spin on the pole, all of a sudden there was Cass, right there in the front row, looking like a goddamn spicy snack in his leather jacket and distressed jeans. He shot me a smirk as I dismounted upside down, then rolled back to my feet.

What *the fuck* was he doing here? Anyone could see him. That was too damn dangerous. The whole routine was only three minutes long, but my worry for Cass's safety had me rush the ending, then when the song faded away and the stage lights dimmed, I climbed straight off the front of the stage to where they sat.

"Cass, what the fuck are you doing?" I hissed, trying to be stern and threatening while only wearing a string thong and sequined nipple pasties. It really ruined the whole vibe.

Cass must have thought so, too, because he didn't seem even slightly panicked that his secret would get out. In fact, he just smirked and leaned forward to run his hands up my near-naked body.

"Look around, Red," he told me with mischief in his eyes.

I frowned down at him, then squinted around the room. Now that I didn't have the stage lights blinding me, it was easier to make out the other tables. All the *empty* tables. Confused, I swiveled my head to look all around the totally vacant club. Not a single other person was in sight, staff included.

"What…" I blinked down at Zed. "Where is everyone?"

He arched a brow and shook his head. "You didn't seriously think we'd be cool with a packed house of leering guys seeing you do all of *that*, did you? Hell no. It's bad enough I have to share you with these bastards, but no way am I putting you up on display for anyone else."

I gave a surprised laugh, looking between the three of them. "Aw, you guys are so cute when you're all possessive. What about the staff?"

"Gave them the night off." Zed shrugged. "They left just before your song came on. The lights and sound are all set to computer timers."

Cass's hands were still caressing my skin, and when I made no move to pull away, he lifted me into his lap. "Besides," he rumbled, "no way in hell was I missing this show." He tilted his head back, claiming my lips in a rough kiss that made my whole body heat. His hips rocked against me, and I got a clear picture of just how much he'd enjoyed my strip show.

"I'm glad you were here," I told him in a husky whisper when our kiss ended. From the corner of my eye, I caught Zed and Lucas watching with anticipation, and a wicked idea crossed my mind. After all, we had the club all to ourselves, and I was almost naked already…

Peeling myself out of Cass's lap, I climbed onto Zed's. But instead of kissing him, I leaned over to kiss Lucas, who was sitting beside him.

Zed gave a low chuckle, his palms skating up the sides of my rib cage to rest on my breasts. While I locked lips with Lucas, letting his tongue explore my mouth and his fingers tangle in my hair, Zed thumbed the sequin pasties covering my nipples, secured with nothing more than a bit of adhesive tape.

A long, drawn-out moment later, Lucas released my lips, and I shot Zed a sly grin. "Did you lock up after Rodney?"

"Of course," he replied with a nod. "Place is fully secure. Maxine left through the staff exit, and it'd lock behind her."

"Good," I murmured. "So there's no risk of anyone catching us all naked."

Zed's brows rose, and he cast a quick look to either side of him at Lucas and Cass. "Dare..." He chuckled. "You really wanna do that here?"

I shrugged. "Why not?"

"Good enough for me," Lucas commented, tugging his shirt over his head and tossing it aside. Then he shimmied out of his jeans and boxers all in one and kicked back on the lounge with his huge dick proudly in hand. The bruises on his throat and ribs were dark under the low lights, but they didn't seem to impact his desire to fuck, so I wasn't going to comment.

Zed and Cass exchanged a long look, and Cass gave a disapproving shake of his head. "You just know he's been waiting to show that beast off," he grumbled.

Sliding out of Zed's lap, I gave the two of them a shrug. "Join in or just watch, your choice." Then I sank to my knees on the carpet between Lucas's legs and took him into my mouth.

He was already so damn hard; all three of them had clearly enjoyed my dance routine. I ran my tongue around his tip, smiling when he twitched under my touch, then closed my lips around him to suck.

Lucas pulled a sharp breath as I wrapped my fingers around his shaft and stroked him slowly. His desire to tease the other guys was totally forgotten as his hands went to my hair and his hips rocked in encouragement.

Then Zed was muttering some curses under his breath as he yanked his own clothes off and sat back down with his dick on display. I couldn't comment—my mouth was a bit full—but I showed my appreciation by taking him in my hand as I sucked Lucas's thick cock deeper into my throat.

Zed let out a small moan as I pumped my hand down his cock, giving me a warm tingle of satisfaction. I turned my face as far as I could with a whole mouthful of dick and glanced across to Cass. He met my gaze right back, his dark eyes gleaming with desire, but he'd only removed his jacket so far.

I withdrew from Lucas's cock, letting him fall past my lips with an audible pop, then tilted my head at Cass. "Come on, Grumpy Cat," I teased. "I'll let you fuck my ass again."

Zed's hips jerked, and he gave me a wide-eyed look of surprise, then glared at Cass. "When the fuck did I miss out on that?"

Cass gave a sly grin. "I dunno how. I made her wear a plug all day at work with you. Figured you'd have found it for sure in one of those *late meetings* you'd been taking."

Zed gave a sound of dismay as Lucas chuckled like a demon, and I shifted across to Zed. I kept Lucas in my hand, but soothed Zed's hurt feelings by swallowing his cock. Apparently it worked, too, because in a flash he had his hands on my head, urging me to take him deeper.

Cass shifted off the couch, coming to kneel on the carpet with me, and cupped my breasts from behind as I sucked Zed and pumped Lucas with my hand.

"Don't worry, Angel," Cass purred in my ear, his teeth nipping my lobe as his fingers peeled the pasties from my nipples. "I came prepared for any situation." I was willing to bet he didn't mean with weapons.

Then again, maybe he did mean weapons because he pulled a dagger from somewhere and sliced the waistband of my thong with it. Necessary? Not even close. Sexy? Oh my god, yes. So much yes. Just that cool touch of metal against my skin when he made those two cuts caused a deep shudder of arousal to run through me, and I leaned back into his body with desperation.

Cass gave a low laugh, knowing damn well what he'd just done. "Kinky bitch," he teased, biting my neck as he kissed me. His hand skated down my belly and dipped between my legs as I continued with my task at hand...and mouth.

But when Cass's long fingers pushed into my pussy, I gasped and sat back. Not that Zed and Lucas seemed to mind. They happily took over themselves, watching with hungry eyes as I leaned back into Cass and rode his hand until I was panting and needy.

"Fuck, Angel," Cass murmured as I writhed on his hand. "You're too damn perfect. This tight pussy...shit." He kept his fingers at work but used his free hand to unbuckle his pants, and a moment later I felt the hot, hard crush of his erection against my ass. "Bend forward," he ordered, pushing me back into Zed's lap and hitching my hips higher before sinking his dick straight into my pussy.

I cried out at that first thrust, then all further sounds became muffled as my mouth returned to Zed's dick.

Cass thrust into me a couple of times, making me rock back against him as I reached for Lucas. For some time, we stayed like that, Cass fucking me from behind, Zed in my throat, and Lucas in my hand. Then Zed pulled me up and nudged me over to Lucas. I licked my lips, then stretched them over Lucas's girth while Zed guided my hand to his dick, all wet and slippery with my saliva.

Behind me, Cass slowed his thrusts, picking a lazy rhythm as he drizzled lube over my asshole. Yep, he really had come prepared. Smart man. I definitely appreciated the forethought.

He took his time rubbing the lube around, then when he pushed the first finger inside, I found myself shuddering with the first strains of an orgasm. Crap, too damn soon.

"Relax, Red," Cass growled, pushing his finger in deeper. "We've got all night."

He fucked me a minute longer, then abruptly pulled out and

smacked my ass hard. "Gumdrop's turn," he announced, getting up to sit beside Zed on the couch.

Lucas grinned at me as he got up and let me pick a position on my knees where he'd been sitting. One that let me lean across Zed to take Cass in my mouth as Lucas pushed into my pussy from behind.

I moaned long and low as he made his way inside, needing a couple of thrusts to get all the way in. But then he hit home, and we were fucking golden.

Zed fondled my tits as I took Cass in my mouth, tasting myself on his inked cock, but Cass had other ideas. He handed Zed the little travel size bottle of lube, and I tilted my face up just in time to see Cass's pointed look.

Any comments from me were impossible as Cass pushed my head down into his lap, jamming his dick down my throat and making me gag a little. Damn if my pussy didn't tighten up around Lucas's dick with that move.

"Oh," Lucas said as Zed reached over and rubbed a teasing, lube- wet circle around my ass. "Yeah, okay."

Cass gave a huff of laughter at Lucas's clear inexperience with group activities, but I was past the point of casual banter. I was already trembling and flushed with heat. Lucas always made me come hard when he fucked me from behind. His huge dick just hit me in the right place.

Then, with Zed's fingers in my ass, stretching and spreading my muscles, and Cass fucking my face, I was a total lost cause. I came with muffled screams, bucking back onto Lucas's cock and Zed's fingers, soaking up every last drop of that orgasm as though it was my last.

It wasn't though. No freaking way. When my shudders subsided and my tight muscles relaxed, Lucas pulled out and Zed lifted me to straddle his lap.

"Hey, baby," he panted, kissing me as he pulled me down onto his throbbing cock. I moaned into his kiss, my cunt adjusting to the new size seamlessly. My orgasm had barely even finished, and I was still tense enough that it was a tight fit for him, but within a couple of thrusts we were back in business. Wave on wave of sensual bliss crashed over me as I rode Zed's dick, increasing in speed as another orgasm started building.

Cass and Lucas had their hands on my body, kneading my flesh, toying with my nipples, kissing me, biting me, leaving their marks. It was a goddamn dream. Then Cass was at my back, his fingers pushing back into my ass again and making me cry out with encouragement.

"Lean into me, baby," Zed coaxed, his voice rough as he pulled me closer as he slouched down the couch. He stilled in my pussy as Cass lined himself up, and I licked my lips when I met Lucas's eye.

Cass took his time working his way into my ass, so by the time he got his whole dick inside, I was a trembling, whimpering mess. Then Lucas's dick was back in my mouth, and the guys started fucking me together. I shattered. My orgasm smacked me around harder than a fight at Anarchy, but the guys didn't stop. They fucked me senseless, filling me up in the most perfect way and making me come again only seconds later.

Lucas gripped my hair, fucking my mouth how he knew I liked it, seriously choking me with his thick cock. Then he came, too, his hot load shooting straight down my throat as I swallowed greedily. When he pulled back, we were both gasping for air, but Zed and Cass weren't done yet.

Zed's hands gripped my hips, holding me with a bruising grip while Cass's hands claimed my breasts. The two of them worked together, grunting and panting as they fucked me into another screaming orgasm, then Cass filled my ass with his own climax.

Not Zed, though. He grabbed my lips with his again for a harsh kiss, then lifted me up when Cass withdrew. "Turn around," Zed ordered me.

I knew what he wanted without needing any further instruction, so sat back in his lap with my back to him, letting him reach down between us and push his cock into my ass.

A low groan rolled from his chest as he pushed inside, and I let my shoulders rest on his sweaty chest as I took him deep.

"Babe," Lucas said in a rough voice, pulling my attention. He was kicked back on the sofa again, his cock back in his hand, and looked raring to go. "Mind if I..." He raised his brows, and I nodded eagerly.

As he shifted off the couch, coming around in front of me, Cass let out a scoff of laughter. "Shit, Gumdrop," he exclaimed, "didn't you *just* come?"

Lucas smirked, pushing his cock into my pussy and making me moan. "Yeah," he replied to Cass, filling me up and making Zed whisper a curse beneath me. "But I'm nineteen, bro. And what better incentive is there than this?"

Lucas cupped a hand around the back of my neck, kissing me as he and Zed fucked me together. The next time I came, they both did too.

CHAPTER 47

After our team-bonding activities at Club 22, we were reluctant to head home. Seph was still there under Rex's watchful eye, and I knew we would have to be way too quiet if we wanted an encore performance. So we lingered at the club a while longer and eventually headed home fully satiated and worn out.

Somehow I convinced all three of them to crash with me in my bed in a big old snuggle, and I slept one of the best sleeps of my entire life. How could I not? I finally saw a future for the four of us. Together. I hadn't realized just how anxious I'd grown about what our future might look like until that piece clicked together. Now it genuinely felt like we were a team, no matter how unlikely the players.

Zed was first to stir, kissing a line down my bare back until he reached my butt, which he bit playfully, making me swat at him sleepily.

"I'm going to get breakfast started," he told me in a husky whisper, kissing my cheek before climbing out of the pile of limbs.

The movement roused Lucas slightly, and he rolled over to tuck his arm around me, drawing me in tight against his body before drifting back to sleep. I cuddled into his warmth, letting my eyelids drift closed once again, but just dozing.

So when Cass stirred on the other side of me, I opened my lids to meet his sleepy gaze.

"That's a view I'd happily wake up to every morning," he mumbled, his cheek smooshed into the pillow just inches away.

Lucas made a sleepy sound of annoyance, burying his face in my hair like he was still desperately clinging to sleep. Except his body had other ideas, as his hand shifted to my breast and his erection pressed into my back.

"What's that?" I teased Cass in a whisper. "Your girl being groped by another man?"

Cass gave a huff of a laugh, then reached up to gently stroke some hair from my face. "My girl," he clarified.

Before our wake-up could turn heated, Zed came rushing back into the room with his phone to his ear and a stricken look on his face. He went straight to the wall-mounted TV facing the bed and flicked it on while Cass and I watched him with curiosity.

"Zed, what—" I started to ask, but he shushed me with a gesture, flicking through the channels until he reached a news report.

"Yep, I found it," he said in a grim voice to whoever he was speaking to. "Hades is here too. Give us a second." Shooting me a pained glance, he turned his attention back to the TV and to the news report playing out on the screen about a break-in at an apartment in West Shadow Grove in the early hours of the morning.

As the story developed, I sat up in shock, jostling Lucas awake in the process. The pretty brunette reporter was detailing the crime, describing how the female resident had been asleep at the time of the break-in. She was thought to have surprised the intruder, who then beat the girl so badly the first responders had called the coroner before realizing she was still breathing.

"Zed," I breathed, dread clawing at my chest. "Please don't tell me this is another of your exes..."

389

The look in his eyes was pure guilt when he turned to look at me. "It's Maxine. She's been taken to Shadow Grove Memorial, but they don't think she'll make it. Her parents are there now, talking about taking her off life support."

On the TV they were interviewing the neighbor who'd called the police after hearing screams. "Never seen anything like it," the haunted man was saying. "There was so much blood, all over the place. She was dead. I was *sure* of it. No one can survive that..."

"Turn it off," I barked, clambering out of bed and grabbing clothes from my dresser, not really paying attention to what I grabbed. "Shadow Grove Memorial?"

Zed nodded, his eyes sad.

"Fine. I'll be ready in five. We need to get over there." I started out of the bedroom, heading for the shower so I wasn't turning up to the ICU covered in dried semen.

"There's nothing we can do for her now," Zed called after me, making my shoulder blades tighten.

I paused a moment, my teeth grinding together, before spinning around once more. All three of them watched me with cautious expressions bordering on pitying.

"Maxine wasn't hurt because she's your ex, Zed," I told him in a hollow voice. "She was hurt because she's my friend. I have to go and see her...even just to... I don't know."

"I get it," Lucas offered. "I'll go with you." He hopped up and grabbed his pants, heading for his own bedroom to get dressed.

I hurried through a shower, scrubbing my skin red and mentally cursing myself for spending the night getting my brains screwed right out of my head while Maxine was being beaten to death. There was no question in my mind Chase was responsible. Again.

When I got downstairs, I found Zed and Lucas already waiting beside the car for me, and Cass decked out in his nondescript black bike leathers.

"What's the plan?" I asked with a small frown. I was racked

with guilt about Maxine, but I didn't need to risk Cass just to hold my hand.

He crossed over to me in three long strides and cupped a hand around the back of my head as he kissed me. "I got the tip I was waiting for. I'm not sure when I'll be back."

My stomach dropped and a cold shiver ran down my spine, but I nodded my understanding. Before he could turn away, I grabbed the front of his jacket and yanked him back to me for another searing-hot kiss.

"Stay safe," I whispered, my voice rough with emotion. "Come back to me."

"Always," he responded. He kissed me again, then released me and headed for Zed's motorcycle that he'd claimed. "You two fuck-ups better keep my girl safe, or I'll gut you both with my hunting knife. Clear?"

"*Our* girl," Lucas corrected in a drawl as Cass tugged his helmet over his head. Not a single inch of skin showed to reveal his identity, but his attitude was still there as he flipped Lucas off with a gloved hand.

He tore out of the driveway at high speed, and I slid into the passenger seat of Zed's car. Just as soon as my butt hit the seat, I groaned and ran my hand through my hair.

"I need to talk to Rex," I muttered, looking reluctantly back to the house. "He's moving Seph into his place today so his boys can guard her around the clock."

"Uh, is that a good idea?" Lucas asked from the back seat. "Not about trusting Rex. If you say he's loyal, then I believe you. But Seph...doesn't have amazing judgment or life experience."

I blew out a long breath, agreeing with him. "What other options do we have? None good. I need her protected twenty-four seven, and we can't do that ourselves. I don't trust other gangs. I don't trust the Guild anymore."

Zed drummed his fingers on the steering wheel. "She'll be

fine. Rex knows he's already on thin ice, so he's the best guy for the job. Worst thing that happens, Seph develops a couple of innocent school-girl crushes."

I scoffed. "Or gets pregnant." Then I cringed at my own statement. "Fuck, I'm glad she already has an IUD."

"I'll drop you at the hospital, then call Rex to sort everything out," Zed decided. "You don't need to see him personally. Better, even, for me to handle it. Can't have him thinking you want a relationship with the old bear."

I wrinkled my nose but buckled my seat belt. "Good point. Let's go."

Zed pulled us out of the garage and headed down the driveway as I glanced back at Lucas.

"Aren't you supposed to visit with your mom today?" I asked, noticing how tired he looked. Not that it was surprising; we were all wrecked today after all the group activities that had happened last night. Who knew there were so many different ways one woman could fuck three men?

"Yeah," he replied with a shrug, "but she won't notice. I texted her nurse and let her know I'd stop by later."

We slowed to wait for the gate, then Zed let out a soft curse when we exited the driveway. Standing right out in the middle of the road, flagging us down, was my eye-patch-wearing, sociopathic nemesis.

"What the fuck do you want, asshole?" Zed snarled, rolling his window down.

Chase grinned wide, coming around to his side to peer into the car.

"Good morning, neighbors," he leered, giving me one hell of an eye-fucking before switching his attention to Zed. "You know what's odd? I could have sworn I just saw you leave a couple of minutes ago on your motorcycle."

Shit on a pancake. Seriously?

392

"But here you are," Chase continued, licking his lower lip like he could *taste* a secret. "And there's pretty little Lucas in the back and my gorgeous, delectable Darling too. So who was on the bike, hmm?"

Zed gave a brittle smile in response. "Eat shit, Chasey." He gunned the engine and ripped away from our creepy fucking neighbor without entertaining his crap any longer. It was a smart choice, but goddamn if I wasn't mentally kicking myself for letting my paranoia slip. Of course he was watching—he was *always* watching. I just had to hope he assumed it was Alexi or someone else. Anyone but Cass.

"It'll be okay," Lucas reassured from the back seat. I flicked him a grateful look and reached my hand back to tangle with his fingers. Just touching him sometimes could calm the wild storm of my emotions.

This wasn't one of those times. But I still liked to touch him anyway. Zed said nothing, but his hand found my knee while he drove. None of us really spoke again for the rest of the drive to the hospital.

When we arrived, the attending nurse wasn't all too happy about letting us in to see Maxine. Apparently, my friend had been in surgery since she was brought in at three in the morning, but the doctors had done all they could. She'd been brought out for her parents to say their goodbyes before switching off life-support.

It was only when a more senior nurse recognized Zed and me that we were given access but warned sternly to turn our phones off and respect Maxine's understandably distraught family.

I paused outside the room they had Maxine in. Her parents were both in there, along with a younger girl who looked so much like Maxine she had to be her sister. They were utterly devastated, gathered around the hospital bed that Maxine lay totally lifeless in. A breathing tube covered her lower face, and her neck and forehead were strapped into a type of brace that indicated spinal damage.

393

What little could be seen of her face and arms was so covered in bruises and lacerations that she didn't even look human.

"Hayden," Lucas said softly, his hand gentle on the small of my back. "Do you want to go in?"

Swallowing hard, I shook my head. "No." Because I'd seen enough. I didn't need to intrude on her family's goodbyes. That wasn't my place, nor was it my right. It was only guilt that had brought me to the hospital, but I wasn't selfish enough to push it any further.

Zed looked through the window, his face creased with pain, but he nodded his agreement. "You're right. Let's go."

He wrapped his arm around my shoulders and walked with me back to the nurses' station, where I paused to speak to the nurse who'd let us in to see Maxine.

"Do you know when they plan to switch her off?" I asked, forcing my voice to be level and calm once more.

The nurse gave a sympathetic smile and shrugged. "When they're ready. Could be now, could be tomorrow, could be never. Every family deals with loss differently."

"Got it," I replied, then let Zed and Lucas lead me back outside. When we passed through the hospital doors, I switched my phone back on. I needed to get my head back into work mode. My hardest shell was always in place when I was dealing with business. No one cracked Hades.

I trailed slightly behind Lucas and Zed as I checked my messages, noticing a voicemail from Alexi. I tapped the button to listen and brought the phone to my ear, pausing to wait for an ambulance to pass while Alexi's voice started.

"Boss," he said in a hushed whisper, "I need to speak with you, urgently. Some shit has gone down... I'd feel better speaking with you in person." There was an awkward pause, then he sighed. "Preferably alone. I'll be at Club 22."

That was the end of the message, and I frowned at my phone as I hurried to catch up with Zed and Lucas.

"What's up?" Zed asked when I reached the car.

I climbed into my seat and relayed Alexi's message, adding that he had sounded strange.

"Sounds like a setup," Lucas offered, meeting my eyes in the rearview mirror. "You're not going to 22 alone, right?"

I gave him a smile. "Of course not. But Alexi wouldn't set me up. It's probably just—"

"Him shooting his shot at joining Team Hades?" Zed suggested, giving me a knowing smirk. "He's probably decided to go all in and declare his undying love or some crap, like he's totally forgotten how many times you've subtly rejected his attention over the years."

Lucas snickered. "Well, it worked for you."

"Dare never rejected me," Zed replied. "She just didn't notice I was flirting in the first place."

I gave a small, embarrassed groan and raked my fingers through my hair. "Whatever. Just…let's go to 22 and see what he wants. Then we can deal with Rex and Seph."

"Yes, sir," Zed teased, starting his car.

As we drove away from the hospital, I let my gaze drift out the window. Silently, I told Maxine how sorry I was and how badly I would make Chase pay for her brutally painful death. Because he would. Sooner or later.

CHAPTER 48

Alexi wasn't at Club 22 when we got there, and the cleaning crew said they hadn't seen him either. Rodney and the rest of the staff wouldn't start until later in the day, so Zed called Rex and sorted out the details for Seph's move while I drove Lucas over to his mom's house.

"Do you want to come in?" he asked when I pulled into the driveway.

I shook my head. "Nah, not today. I've got some shit to do. I'll come back and pick you up in a couple of hours. Or if you want to stay, we can get you on our way back from Timber tonight." Zed and I had some meetings on-site at Timber to look over the finished bar and check off with our inspector, and it was one of those meetings we couldn't miss—especially given the trouble we'd landed in with Anarchy.

"I'll come to Timber with you," Lucas replied with a smile. "I'm dying to see it all." He opened his door but leaned over to kiss me soundly before he got out. "Don't worry, babe. I've got my gun, and I won't open the door to strangers. Besides, I just spotted Big Sal inside chatting up Claudette."

I rolled my eyes. Big Sal—short for Salamander, of all fucking things—had taken quite a shine to Sandra's live-in nurse and was actively requesting to be assigned guard duty here.

Lucas headed up the steps to the house and turned to wave before disappearing safely inside. Even so, I waited another minute in the driveway, just to be sure. Then I swung back past Club 22 to pick up Zed before reluctantly heading over to my Copper Wolf office.

Hannah was at her desk when I arrived, greeting me with a tearstained face. No doubt she'd heard about Maxine.

"Hannah, I'm trying to track down Alexi," I told her, making it clear I didn't want to discuss feelings. "Can you get him on the phone for me?"

She dabbed her eyes, then gave me a tight smile. "Yes, sir. On it."

Zed brought his laptop into my office, and for a few hours we worked in relative silence across the desk from each other. Hannah popped in at some point to let me know Alexi wasn't answering his phone but that she'd left a message for him to call back. When he hadn't called back by the time Zed and I needed to leave, I asked Hannah to check his phone's GPS location.

It simply wasn't like Alexi to drop off the radar like that. Especially after leaving me that cryptic voicemail.

"Got him," Hannah announced, looking up from her computer. "He's at Timber."

Zed and I exchanged a quick look, but I thanked Hannah and told her to take the afternoon off. She worked too damn hard, anyway, and I knew she was keen to go and check on Nadia and the girls before the first of them started the journey home.

"Why would Alexi be at Timber?" Zed mused aloud as we rode the elevator down to his car. "The build finished yesterday, and if there were any issues, they'd have called me."

I had no damn clue. "I guess we're about to find out," I commented. "But I did tell Lucas we would pick him up now, so Alexi can wait."

Zed huffed a laugh. "Damn, there goes my plan to nail you against the bar at Timber. You *did* promise we could christen it properly."

I smirked back at him. "Why would Lucas stop you from doing that?"

He gave a quiet groan, his gaze heating as we stepped out into the parking lot. "Fine, but he has to sit and watch. First fuck in our venues has to be just us, Dare. You and me." He paused when we reached his car, pinning me to the door with his hips and his hard-on. "Deal?"

My pulse raced as he dipped his face to kiss me softly. "Deal," I breathed against his lips. "But can we do it on the VIP poker table?"

Zed hummed a thoughtful sound, grinding against me and making me gasp with desire. "I think we can make that work." He kissed me again, more deeply this time, then released me to open the car door.

I heaved a frustrated sigh as I got in, waiting for him to take his seat before I pouted at him. "Now I'm going to be doing this building inspection with wet panties. Thanks a lot."

Zed barked a laugh. "Better than doing it with an aching boner." He shot me a quick look as he drove us out of the parking lot and into the road. "Just take them off."

My lips parted in surprise. "So I can talk to our building inspector with damp thighs instead? How does that solve the problem?"

Zed's smile was pure evil. "Just trust me, it would." Then he shrugged. "Or maybe it wouldn't, but goddamn, it'd be hot knowing you weren't wearing anything under your skirt."

With logic like that, who was I to disagree? So I hitched my skirt up a bit and wiggled my panties down until I could take them off completely. Zed gaped at me like he hadn't actually expected me to do it, then when I dangled my underwear from a finger, he snatched it to stuff in his pocket.

"No takebacks," he told me with a triumphant grin. "You're committed now."

"You're such a fucking child," I replied with an eye roll.

A couple of minutes into our drive, it became all too clear what his plan had been. His hand had been resting on my knee, like it often did, but after a while he started shifting it higher. Inch by inch.

"Zed," I warned as his fingers stroked over my pussy, "you're driving."

"I'm a good multitasker, Dare." A fact he demonstrated by sinking his fingers inside me while overtaking a truck on the freeway.

The danger of it had me all kinds of turned on, so instead of pushing his hand away and demanding my panties back, I grabbed his wrist and pulled him closer. He sucked in a sharp breath of surprise but didn't hesitate to give me what I was asking for.

For the rest of the drive to Lucas's mom's house, Zed navigated the roads and my pussy with skillful mastery, making me writhe in the passenger seat as I came on his hand right before we turned onto Lucas's street.

After we stopped in the driveway, I needed a moment to catch my breath before tugging my skirt back into place and glaring at Zed. "Can I have my panties back now?"

He scoffed, then sucked his fingers in an overly sexual way. "Hell no," he purred. "Go get your Gumdrop. I want this meeting at Timber over with as fast as possible."

Lucas was already jogging down the front steps, though, and climbed into the back seat with a grin that quickly morphed into a suspicious scowl.

"You guys, it totally smells like sex in here." His eyes flicked between Zed and me accusingly, and Zed snickered.

"Don't look at me," he replied, innocent as a damn nun. "I was driving the whole time."

I whacked him with the back of my hand as he laughed. "Shut

up and get us over to Timber. We're going to be late at this stage, and I still want to know what the hell Alexi is doing there."

"Alexi's at Timber?" Lucas asked. "Why?"

Zed gave him a droll look in the mirror as he backed out into the street once more. "That's what we want to know."

Changing the subject, I shifted in my seat to look at Lucas as I asked how his mom was doing. He took the hint, spending the drive over to Timber filling us in on Sandra's health and how badly her mind was slipping. He'd apparently discussed it with Claudette at length today, and the nurse agreed that it didn't *seem* like that was from Sandra's MS. All the tests at Sunshine Estate had come back inconclusive, but maybe it was worth running them again through our own pathology lab.

We parked directly in front of the main entrance to Timber and headed up the steps. My phone buzzed in my hand, and I took the call as Zed unlocked the door.

"Hades, it's Nadia," Cass's grandmother said unnecessarily. "I want to let you know that the little girl from the Anarchy basement passed away this morning in hospital. Feds were there, and someone heard your name mentioned. Figured you should know."

My stomach dropped, and I sighed. "Thanks, Nadia. I'll keep my eyes open."

Yet more bullshit setups. I'd bet Chase was somehow salvaging his sex- trafficking frame-up to pin me for that little girl's death. I just needed to stay alert and ahead of him.

"Door was already unlocked," Zed told me as I joined him.

I grimaced. "The building crew are probably madly trying to finish everything in time for this meeting."

We headed inside, but instead of our building crew, I spotted a blond woman standing in the middle of the room speaking with a salt-and-pepper-haired man. Something about her seemed so familiar, even though her back was to me. It wasn't until she turned around that it clicked.

"Jeanette?" I asked, coming closer. She'd been one of my down-stairs neighbors in the building that blew up, the woman with the dog that peed a lot. "This is unexpected." I arched a brow at her and glanced at the man she was with. He didn't strike any notes of familiarity, so I shifted my attention back to my former neighbor.

Her smile was cold as I approached. "I'm aware," she replied. "That's usually how these things go."

Seemingly from nowhere, the room suddenly filled with armed officers, all of them with their guns pointed straight at me. This had been a setup. But by whom? Alexi? Or Hannah when she told us Alexi was here?

"You're going to want those hands in the air, *Hades*," my sweet, cheery neighbor Jeanette sneered. "You have no idea how long I've looked forward to this moment."

"What moment is that, Jeanette?" I asked, keeping my tone calm as I eyed her. Now that I was paying attention, her whole demeanor had shifted slightly. Mother*fucker*. Jeanette had been undercover FBI the whole time she lived downstairs from me.

Her eyes flashed with anger. "Put your *fucking* hands in the air," she barked. Slowly, because we were surrounded by a solid fifteen to twenty armed officers, I did as I was told.

Jeanette nodded to the man beside her, and he quickly dis-armed me. I could only imagine they were doing the same to Zed and Lucas behind me, but I wasn't turning to look. My eyes were locked on Jeanette.

Her smile was wide and slightly feral as she pulled a pair of handcuffs from the pocket of her ugly pants. That should have been my first giveaway. The Jeanette I knew wouldn't have been caught dead in boxy man-pants and flat shoes.

"Hayden Darling Timber," she recited, practically dancing over to me with her handcuffs ready, "you are under arrest for *so, so* many things. Let's start with the murders, shall we?" She started listing names that she'd clearly memorized. Some of them I recognized and was guilty for, some I wasn't sure about, and some were definitely not me. Like Maryanne Green—Zed's ex.

"Brant Wilson?" Lucas repeated, interrupting Jeanette as she grabbed my wrists and hooked them together behind my back with the cuffs. "Did you just say Brant Wilson?"

Jeanette paused, looking over at Lucas, who was *not* handcuffed but did have his hands up nonetheless. "Yeah, former FBI director Brant Wilson was tortured and killed by your sugar mama."

Lucas's stricken gaze met mine, and I died inside.

"Tell me that's a setup," he croaked.

My heart screaming in pain, I couldn't lie to him. Not like this. Not when he was asking whether I was responsible for killing his bio dad before he'd even met him. Not even my Hades armor, dented, cracked, and slow to form, could bear it. So I took the coward's route and just closed my eyes against the agony in his glare.

Jeanette snickered a nasty laugh, then continued her list of crimes I was supposedly responsible for. Only one made me jerk in shock.

"You're under arrest for the attempted murder of Maxine Hazelford—"

"Wait, what?" I blurted, outraged. "I never hurt Maxine." There were a great many deaths I was responsible for, but Maxine's wasn't one of them.

Jeanette smirked. "No? So you didn't threaten to bludgeon her to death with a stripper shoe? The exact same weapon used to put her in the hospital last night?"

My heart stopped dead in my chest, and my eyes flew to Zed. I'd been joking with Maxine when I said that...and he'd been the only other person present.

His expression was tight and shuttered, betraying *nothing*, and that struck me as deep as a knife through the chest. Only then did I realize that he wasn't being arrested with me. Nor did he have any guns pointed at him.

"That was really useful evidence that Agent De Rosa collected for us, I gotta say," Jeanette continued, her voice threaded with malice. "Without that little soundbite, I doubt we'd have been able to make this all stick."

Agent De Rosa.

He wouldn't even look at me. His cold gaze just fixed on a point past my shoulder as Jeanette marched me out of Timber with my hands cuffed behind me. Outside, official cars were clustered around where Zed had parked.

Jeanette confidently pushed me toward a black sedan that must have been her own but paused briefly to open the door. Then she spotted someone coming down the street and gave a grunt of surprise.

"Huh, look at that. The new FBI director is here to witness this monumental arrest. I bet I get a juicy promotion for this." She gave a sneering grin, and I looked in the direction she'd been facing.

Just when I thought things couldn't get worse, Chase mother-fucking Lockhart dressed in a sharp suit strode along the sidewalk and gave me a sarcastic little finger wave.

"You've got to be kidding me," I whispered as Jeanette shoved me into the back seat of her car and slammed the door. I was help-less to do anything but stare in horror, my heart and soul shrivel-ing up to die as Chase walked up to Zed and clapped him on the shoulder.

My lip-reading wasn't as good as Lucas's, but even I could make out those four words spoken from Chase to Zed. Those four damning words that burned like acid across my mind.

Good work, old friend.

AUTHOR'S NOTE

Daaaaaamn…that one stung a little bit, huh? Naughty Zeddy Bear. There's always two (or more) sides to a story, though, and to find out what's behind this nasty little betrayal you'll need to hold out for *Timber*! I know, I know, I'm an asshole. But you know it makes my shriveled black heart happy when you curse my name.

Club 22 put me through the wringer a bit. I'm not even going to lie. It's sex-heavy, no question about it, but it's for a damn good reason. But aside from all the fucking, Hades made me dig deep to get into her head. She was in a dark place, needing to face her own damage, having the monsters in her closet claw their way out… It was a tough one. And as much as we authors like to pretend we're "just telling a story," that's total bullshit. These characters are real people, simply living inside our head worlds. When we spend all day every day sharing a brain space with a character who is experiencing trauma, facing her demons, acknowledging her shortfalls, it bleeds over. The lines get a bit blurred.

And it's only going to get worse before it gets better. I feel now, more than any book I've written to date, that I need to warn you, the reader, to proceed with caution into *Timber*. Shit's getting dark. I think by this point of the story you know what I mean, and I hate giving spoilers. So please consider this a possible trigger warning for *Timber*!

Despite how exhausting and personally challenging this series is turning out to be, it's also the most rewarding series I've ever worked on. I'm loving every (painful) moment that I'm spending with Hades and her boys, and it's a bit surreal to think it's almost over.

Just one book to go. How wild is that?

Don't worry, though, there will be plenty more from the Shadow Grove world still to come! You've already met two of the main characters from my next connected series. Can you guess who? Post your guess somewhere on social media—Facebook, Instagram, Pinterest, TikTok, whatever—and tag me! I love to see speculation and theories.

On that note, be sure to join the discussion over at my readers group, The Fox Hole.

Thank you for reading. Thank you for trusting me. Thank you for reviewing (wink wink, nudge nudge) and thank you from the bottom of my heart for supporting me on this wild ride that is Hades.

xxx Tate

ABOUT THE AUTHOR

Tate James is a *USA Today* bestselling author of contemporary romance and romantic suspense, with occasional forays into fantasy, paranormal romance, and urban fantasy. She was born and raised in Aotearoa (New Zealand) but now lives in Australia with her husband and their adorable crotchfruit.

She is a lover of books, booze, cats, and coffee, and is most definitely not a morning person. Tate is a bit too sarcastic, swears far too much for polite society, and definitely tells too many dirty jokes.

Website: tatejamesauthor.com
Facebook: tatejamesauthor
Instagram: @tatejamesauthor
TikTok: @tatejamesauthor
Pinterest: @tatejamesauthor
Mailing list: eepurl.com/dfFR5v